Dean's presentation, like his demeanour, was that of a lecturer concisely establishing with facts and assessments and analyses a problem that phrases and words like 'potentially catastrophic' and 'cataclysmic' and 'nightmare' did not exaggerate. He also referred to 'political sensitivity' and 'extreme caution' and 'essential cooperation' and Charlie knew they weren't exaggerations either. Dean concluded, 'So that's your brief, to liaise with the Russians and with the already appointed Americans to do everything you can to stem the flow of nuclear material to the West . . .'

'And don't suffer the slightest doubt at our seriousness,' endorsed the deputy Director. 'There *are* changes to our function. This is one of them: *you're* one of them. So you've got to change, like everything else about the business we're now in. There's no place for anyone disobeying orders. That clear enough?'

'Completely,' Charlie said, caught by just one part of the threat.

ALSO BY BRIAN FREEMANTLE

Fiction

The November Man
Charlie Muffin
Goodbye To An Old Friend
Clap Hands, Here Comes Charlie
The Man Who Wanted Tomorrow
The Inscrutable Charlie Muffin
Deaken's War
Face Me When You Walk Away
Charlie Muffin's Uncle Sam
Madrigal For Charlie Muffin
Charlie Muffin San
Kremlin Kiss
Rules Of Engagement
Charlie Muffin and Russian Rose
The Runaround
Comrade Charlie
Charlie's Apprentice
The Factory
The Bear Pit
Little Grey Mice
The Button Man
No Time for Heroes

Non Fiction

KGB
The Steal
The Fix
CIA
The Octopus

BRIAN FREEMANTLE

charlie's chance

An Orion paperback
First published in Great Britain by Orion in 1996
This paperback edition published in 1997 by Orion Books Ltd,
Orion House, 5 Upper St Martin's Lane, London WC2H 9EA

A CIP catalogue record for this book is available
from the British Library.

ISBN 0 75281 119 3

Typeset by Deltatype Limited, Birkenhead, Merseyside
Printed in Great Britain by Clays Ltd, St Ives plc

For Tom Mori,
superb agent of the East.
And my friend.

prologue

The purpose was to provide as forceful a warning as possible to any other Russian or supposed middleman who thought it was easy to cheat, so the man who'd tried this time had been horrendously tortured throughout the night.

First they had cut out his tongue, to quieten his screams. His testicles formed the gag, completed by his lips being sewn together. The body, naked to show the mutilations, was cast adrift in a skiff on Berlin's Wannsee Lake. It was mid-afternoon before a curious rower came close enough to discover it. And went insanely hysterical.

chapter 1

Stanislav Georgevich Silin had prided himself – become complacent – that he'd done it all, knew it all. Which he had. And did. Except for this. Which was a dangerous mistake. Fatal, even. Except that he'd been warned in time. Still, something he shouldn't have allowed to happen. Hadn't he, when he'd made his bid, *used* complacency, like his was being used against him now? Trying to be used against him now. But wouldn't be, because now he knew. He smiled across the room at Petr Markov, who'd guarded him for so long and given him the warning on the way here this morning. Misunderstanding, Markov crossed the room enquiringly towards him. Silin hadn't wanted the man for anything – except to show his gratitude, which he would do, later – but then he thought of Marina and changed his mind. She was never alone – since becoming boss of bosses Silin had always ensured she had her own bodyguards – but he didn't want to take any chances now. Certainly not with Marina: she could never be endangered. He whispered his instructions before sitting back in his chair at the table around which the rest of the Commission were assembling, still annoyed with himself. He should never have forgotten how he'd used complacency as the weapon to get where he was now, at the pinnacle.

Silin, a silver-haired, determinedly courtly man, savoured the word, enjoying it. The pinnacle: the absolute peak. Where he'd been for so long. And intended to stay. Complacent again, he thought: *wanted* to stay. And would, at any cost. But not to himself. To others.

Through thick-lensed glasses Silin gazed steadily around

the assembled group, decided who those others were going to be, separating friend from enemy. Wrong again, like complacency. No friends. Never had been. Theirs wasn't a business of friends. Theirs was a business of stronger or weaker, winner or loser, living or dying. Who then, until it suited them to change, was loyal; which of these six, each the head of a Family in his own right, was prepared to go on supporting him as boss of bosses of the Dolgoprudnaya?

Impossible to assess, Silin decided. Making everything so uncertain. He should have moved on his earliest suspicions of an overthrow, not waited for Markov to confirm it. He'd given Sobelov time to get organized, to trickle his poison and make his promises and establish the rival allegiances. Too late now to cut out the cancer by the obvious incision. By now the bastard most probably had his informants within the Dolgoprudnaya itself – Silin's own Family – so Silin knew he couldn't risk a hit being turned back upon himself.

He had to do it another way and knew he could. He simply had to be cleverer than Sergei Petrovich, prove himself and his worth to the Commission, and let them make the choice. Which he was sure they would when he declared his own intended coup. And in his favour. Because he had the way – a better way than a bullet or a bomb – although none of them knew it yet. All he had to do was let Sergei Petrovich Sobelov over-expose himself and his inadequacies for the rest of them to realize how close they'd come to disaster by doubting him. That would be the time physically to dispose of Sobelov. He'd make it as bad as he could, as painful as he could, as an example to any other upstart. And not just Sobelov. Those of the six – and as many traitors as he could find lower down – who'd already pledged themselves to his rival, too. The Militia were never a problem and certainly wouldn't be now, after he'd set everything up, so the bloodier and more obscene the killings the better, as a warning to all who deserved to be given one.

It wasn't complacent to think he could virtually stop worrying about Sobelov and concentrate on the snares for those others he hadn't, at the moment, identified. As the thought came to Silin his rival rose from the table around which they were grouped and went to where the drinks were. Visible disdain for the benefit of the rest of the Commission, Silin recognized. In the past, just a few months ago, there would have been a gesture, not for permission but some sign of deference. But not that morning. Sobelov simply stood, without even looking at him. And didn't appear immediately interested in the drinks display, either. Instead, briefly, the towering, deep-chested man stood splay-legged, his hands on his hips, regarding central Moscow beyond Ulitza Kuybysheva as Silin supposed would-be invaders of the past would have stood triumphantly on the battlements of the just visible Kremlin. Silin enjoyed his analogy. Would-be invaders of the past hadn't succeeded in conquering the city and neither would Sergei Petrovich Sobelov.

The posturing complete, Sobelov turned back into the room although still not to Silin but instead to the two men, Oleg Bobin and Vladic Frolov, who'd seated themselves either side of him. Both nodded acceptance and Sobelov poured vodka for all of them. Such a little thing, Silin decided. But so significant. They weren't accepting vokda with those nods: they were accepting their death penalty. He'd have them tortured, of course. Just as badly as Sobelov, so it would be fully reported in the newspapers. Maybe have them tied together and thrown into the river, to float on public display through the centre of the city, like that idiot who had been cast adrift on the Berlin lake by whoever he'd tried to cheat and whose death was in all the newspapers that morning.

The reflection took Silin's mind to Berlin. No cause to doubt his people there. Proper family: blood relatives. And all very important to him, vital to him, in defeating Sobelov. He'd have to arrange a quiet recall, when most of the other things were finalized. It might be interesting, in passing, to find out what the lake business had been about: whether his people knew the would-be purchaser who'd demonstrated his anger so obviously.

Silin straightened in his chair, a thin, fastidiously dressed man. Wanting the censure, as well as a warning to the uncommitted, to be understood, he said, 'Does anyone else want a drink . . . ?' And after the various head-shaking refusals finished, 'So let's begin, shall we?'

'Why don't we do just that?' said Sobelov, at once. The voice fitted the man's size, loud and deep.

'You've got a point to make?'

'The same that I've made at two previous meetings,' said Sobelov. 'The Chechen are encroaching on our territory. We should hit them.'

'You want a war?' invited Silin. It was important to draw the man as much as possible, for the others in the Commission to judge between them.

'I'm not afraid of one,' rumbled Sobelov, predictably.

'None of us are *afraid* of one,' said Silin, hoping the others would appreciate how much Sobelov remained part of a past where everything was settled by a gun or a grenade. 'Do we need the distraction of one?'

'It's my particular territory they're coming into: they've taken over six of my vodka outlets in the last month.' Bobin was a small man so fat he seemed almost round and the protest squeaked out, like a toy squeaks when it is pressed.

'Doing nothing will be seen as weakness,' supported Frolov. He was another man who considered a gun his third hand; before breaking away to form his own Family, just before the collapse of communism, he'd been Sobelov's chief enforcer.

'I don't think it's a good idea at the moment to draw too much attention to ourselves,' said Silin.

'From whom?' sneered the exasperated Sobelov. 'The Militia! More policemen work for us than for the Interior Ministry!' He answered the smiles of the others at his sarcasm with a grimace of his own. Emboldened, he said, 'And what the hell's timing got to do with it?'

'Everything,' said Silin. 'I want to concentrate on the biggest single nuclear robbery there's ever been.' And by so doing, he thought, prove to everyone that things should stay just the way they were, apart from the changes he had in mind.

Fifteen hundred miles away, in London, the problem of things staying just the way they were was occupying the mind of Charlie Muffin. It had been, for weeks, but at that moment an internal messenger had just handed him the summons and said, 'Tough shit, Charlie. Looks like you're next.'

chapter 2

The last time Charlie Muffin had felt like he did at that moment he'd been standing in front of a red-robed judge about to be sentenced. And had been, to the maximum of fourteen years, unaware what the buggers were really up to.

There wasn't anything to work out today. The Cold War had melted into a puddle of different political bed partners and different priorities and the worst change of all affected poor bastards like him. So it was all over, lock, stock, barrel and boot. There'd already been the two seminars, addressed personally by the Director-General with all the deputies and division chiefs nodding in solemn-faced agreement to all the bullshit about fresh roles for a streamlined service. And immediately after the second conference there'd been the appointment of a relocation officer, with promises of alternative employment in other government ministries or advice on commuting pensions.

And finally this, the official memorandum that Charlie was fingering in his pocket on his way to the seventh floor. 'The Director-General will see you at 14.00. Subject: Relocation.' Ten words, if he included the numerals (and the worst of them all, 'relocation') ending the career of Charles Edward Muffin in the British intelligence community.

The only thing he couldn't understand was being called before the Director-General himself. There were at least six deputies or division chiefs who could have performed the function, which in Charlie Muffin's case roughly equated with shooting an old warhorse that had outlived its usefulness and needed putting out of its misery. Or someone in Personnel. It could even have been done by the newly appointed relocations officer, who might have been able to throw in the offer of a lavatory cleaner's position or a school caretaker's job.

Charlie's feet began positively to ache the moment he emerged from the elevator on to the seventh floor of the new Thames-side building. Charlie Muffin's feet invariably ached. Afflicted as they were by dropped arches and hammer toes, they were literally his Achilles heel, the weak point at which every bodily feeling or ill ultimately manifested itself. Sometimes they hurt because he walked too far or too long, a problem he'd largely overcome by rarely walking anywhere if there were alternative transport. Sometimes the discomfort came from his being generally tired. Sometimes, although again rarely, the problem was new shoes, a difficulty he handled by treating the comfortably beaten-into-submission Hush Puppies with the tweezer-tipped care Italian clerics show the Turin Shroud. And sometimes they twinged at moments of stress or tension or even suspected physical danger, the bodily focal point again for the inherent, self-defensive antenna which Charlie Muffin had tuned over the years to the sensitivity of a Star Wars early warning system. And of which Charlie *always* took careful heed.

Today's discomfort was, momentarily, such that Charlie paused to flex his bunched-up toes to ease the cramp. He hadn't expected it all to be as abrupt as this, as bad as this. But why not? Always before, when the shit's-about-to-hit-the-fan pain had come like this, it had been in an operational situation and what he was about to face was going to be far more traumatic than anything he'd ever confronted in the field.

He was going to be dumped from the service – from which he'd briefly dumped himself when he'd run with the CIA's half million and regretted every single waking and sleeping moment until they'd caught him, a regret quite separate from the scourging, always-present agony of losing Edith in the vengeance pursuit – and there was nothing he could do to prevent it.

Although there couldn't be the slightest doubt about the

forthcoming confrontation, a lot of Charlie's uncertainty came from his not having been able to prepare himself. Charlie had never liked going into anything totally cold. Without any conceit – because the last thing from which Charlie Muffin suffered was conceit – he knew he was a cerebral Fred Astaire when it came to responding on his feet to unexpected situations, even though he couldn't physically match that mental agility. Despite which he'd always tried to get as much advantage as he could, in advance. Maybe he should have gone first to see the relocations officer. Charlie had spent his life talking people into admissions and revelations they'd sworn on oath never to disclose. So extracting from a form-filling, form-regimented government bureaucrat every last little detail of what they intended doing to him would have been a walk in the park, unfitting though the analogy was for someone with Charlie's feet. The belated awareness of an overlooked opportunity further disturbed Charlie. It had been a bad mistake not to have done it and he'd lived this long relatively unscathed by not making mistakes and most certainly not bad ones, as this was. Another indication, to add to the foot pangs, of how disorientated he'd been by the single line command from on high.

The Director-General's suite, which Charlie had never entered, was a contrast to that of the service's old headquarters in Westminster Bridge Road, to which he had quite regularly been admitted, usually at the very beginning or the very end of a disciplinary enquiry.

The outer custodian was male – another difference from the past – a sharp-featured, flop-haired man who didn't stop writing at Charlie's arrival, to remain distanced from ordinary mortals. The determination didn't quite work, because Charlie caught the quick eye-flicker of identification at his entry. Henry Bates, read the nameplate proudly displayed on the desk. Charlie stood, accustomed to waiting for acknowledgement: it often took supermarket check-out operators several minutes to realize he was standing in front of them. The attention, when it finally came, was expressionless. 'They're waiting.'

'They.' So he was meeting more than just the Director-General. And they, whoever 'they' were, had already assembled, even though he was still ten minutes early. Insufficient straw from which to make a single brick. But, adjusting the metaphor, enough for a drowning man to clutch, before going under for the last time.

There were five men in a half circle around the conference table, but apart from Rupert Dean, the Director-General whose identity had been publicly disclosed upon his appointment, Charlie could identify only one other by name.

Gerald Williams was the department's chief accountant who had transferred from the old headquarters and in front of whom Charlie had appeared more times than he could remember to explain particularly high reimbursement claims. Which Charlie had incontestably defended on every single occasion until it had become a challenge between the two of them, in Williams' case amounting to a personal vendetta.

Williams, who was a fat but extremely neat man, was at the far end of the half circle. His neighbour was as contrastingly thin as Williams was fat, a stick-figured man with a beak-nosed face chiselled like the prow of an Arctic ice-breaker, bisected by heavy-framed spectacles. At the opposite end, seemingly more interested in the river traffic than in Charlie's tentative entry, lounged a bow-tied, alopecia-domed man who compensated for his baldness by cultivating a droop-ending bush of a moustache. The man next to him was utterly nondescript, dark-haired and dark-suited and with the white, civil service regulated shirt, except for blood-pressured apple-red cheeks so bright he could have been wearing clown's make-up.

Rupert Dean sat in the middle of the group. His appointment had, more than any other, marked the change in the role of British intelligence. For the first time in over a decade a Director-General had not entered the service either through its ranks or along diplomatic or Foreign Office routes. Until three years earlier, he had been the Professor of

Modern and Political History at Oxford's Balliol College from which, through numerous newspaper and magazine articles and three internationally acclaimed books, he had become acknowledged as the foremost sociopolitical authority in Europe.

Dean was a small man whose hair retreated in an upright wall from his forehead, as if in alarm. He, too, had glasses but he wasn't wearing them. Instead, he was shifting the arms through his fingers, like prayer beads. At both seminars he'd appeared conservatively and unremarkably dressed – the same grey suit and unrecognized tie on both occasions – but now Charlie decided the man had been trying for an expected appearance, like Charlie would have tried if he'd had longer warning about this interview by getting the stain off his lapel and wearing an unmarked tie and fresh shirt.

The only other Director-General Charlie had known uncaringly wear the sort of bagged and pockets-full sports jacket like the one Dean was wearing had been Sir Archibald Willoughby, Charlie's first boss, protector and mentor, and Charlie's immediate impression was that, given the chance, he could have found a lot of fondly remembered similarities between the two men. Without needing to see, Charlie knew the trousers hidden below the conference table would lack any proper crease except for the ridges of constant wear and would more than likely be stained as well. And the shoes would be comfortable old friends, although not as ancient or as wearer-friendly as the Hush Puppies he wore.

'Muffin, isn't it?'

'Yes, sir.' Charlie always had the greatest difficulty showing deference to people in authority – and certainly towards anyone whose professionalism or ability he doubted – yet he had felt not the slightest hesitation in instinctively according it to the new service head. The last controller who had automatically instilled such an attitude had again been Sir Archibald.

'Quite so, quite so. Come in, man. Sit down.' Dean spoke quickly but with extraordinarily clear diction. There was a thick file in front of the man which Charlie guessed, nervously, to be his personal records. Dean shuffled through the topmost sheets but then abandoned whatever he was searching for, pushing the dossier away more disarranged than when he started. 'Much to discuss,' he announced, hurried-voiced, extending both arms sideways figuratively to embrace the men sitting on either side of him. Gerald Williams, expressionless once more, allowed no response to the introduction. The thin man immediately to Dean's right managed a single head nod of his own at being identified as Peter Johnson, Dean's deputy. A lot of the surprise at Dean's appointment had been fuelled by the open secret even before the transfer from Westminster Bridge Road that Johnson, for ten years the department's Foreign Office link, resented being passed over for the very top job in favour of a schoolmasterly outsider. The bald-headed man broke away at last from his fascination with the river to produce a brief, functional smile when Dean listed Jeremy Simpson as the department's legal advisor. The red-faced man emerged last, as political officer Patrick Pacey.

Charlie's mind was way beyond the Director-General's staccato delivery. Whatever this meeting was about, it certainly had nothing to do with his dismissal or enforced early retirement. What then?

The Director-General made another ineffective foray into the pushed aside file, abandoning the search as quickly as he had begun it to rotate his spectacles. Closer, Charlie saw one of the earpieces was padded with surgical tape for comfort. Tapping them against the discarded dossier, Dean said, 'We're in times of change.'

'Yes, sir.'

'You think you can change?'

'Yes, sir.' Into a pumpkin if I have to, Charlie thought.

'How would you feel about living permanently abroad?'

'Where, exactly?'

'Moscow.'

Natalia Nikandrova Fedova rarely thought about him any more. When she'd finally accepted he was going to go on failing her it had been a positive effort to keep him out of her mind but it had become easier as the months passed. But it was unavoidable today. Natalia smiled, the sadness of the past dimming her all-absorbing love of the present, as she watched Sasha whoop and scream with the excitement of opening each new birthday gift. Maybe he didn't know about Sasha. Natalia had convinced herself she'd found the way to tell him; made up her mind he would understand because he was so very good at the business they were both in – the best she'd ever known, far better than she could have ever been – and hated him for not suddenly arriving, unannounced, as she had sometimes fantasized he would. It shouldn't have needed a child to bring him back if he'd loved her.

The KGB had still existed, although uncertainly, when she'd tried to reach him: if she hadn't headed its First Chief Directorate it would have been impossible for her to have tried at all. It didn't exist any more: not, at least, by name or with the omnipotence with which it had once operated. But his service did and there would still be regulations against his coming to Moscow. But knowing him as well as she believed she did, Natalia knew regulations would not have stopped him. So if she had reached him there was only one conclusion: he didn't want to see her again. Ever. And wasn't interested in his child. She'd made a mistake, like she'd made a mistake with the first man to let her down, which she'd compounded by marrying him. Not a good comparison, she told herself, as she had on many previous memory trips. Her second trusting attempt had for all the obvious impossible barriers stopped short of marriage, although that had once been another fantasy, and had most certainly not been the disaster of the first. She had Sasha around whom her life revolved and with whom she was complete, without the need for anyone or anything else.

Or was she?

As if on cue, Aleksai Popov came into the Leninskaya apartment, the brightly wrapped package high above his head for the game Sasha recognized at once, leaping and jumping around his legs in the futile attempt to reach it before he knelt, solemnly to offer it to her.

It was a battery-operated cat that waddled and emitted a purring growl and got the biggest scream so far from Sasha who, unprompted, threw her arms around the man for the thank-you kiss.

Popov disentangled himself to come up to Natalia, kissing her lightly on the cheek: they were still very careful in front of the child.

'That was far too expensive,' she said. It would have come from one of the Western-goods shops.

'I love her. Think of her as mine.'

Natalia was unsure whether or not to be glad of the remark. Sasha hadn't asked any questions yet but it wouldn't be much longer. 'You still shouldn't have done it.'

Popov shrugged the protest aside. Able, from the way he was standing, to conceal the heavy seriousness between them from other parents in the room he said, simply, 'Hello.'

'Hello,' said Natalia, just as serious. Should she, *could* she, take another chance?

Stanislav Silin knew he had them rattled, Sobelov most of all. It was a good feeling, like it had been a good feeling watching the bombast leak from the man when Sobelov realized how easily the size of the robbery would re-establish things in their proper order.

Silin had guessed, of course, about the money involved but he didn't think it was an exaggeration to value 250 kilos of weapons-graded material, which was what he'd been promised, at $75,000,000 at least. They'd been dumbstruck by that, as he'd known they would be because he had been when the size had been put to him. Sobelov had tried to recover, questioning both the amount and the profit, but the others hadn't doubted him. They hadn't just believed him, they'd backed him, not even Bobin or Frolov supporting the demand that there should be a change in the system to involve all of them in the negotiations instead of leaving it to him alone, which was his agreed right as the boss of bosses.

Silin had been worried at that insistence, unsure how much ground he'd lost: the fact that everyone apart from Sobelov was prepared to leave the brokering to him, like it had always been in the past, had to be the best indicator he could have wished that he could defeat Sobelov's challenge.

But he still couldn't afford to relax.

He'd always protected his sources but this time the secret had to be absolute, not just for their benefit but to prevent Sobelov trying to take over, which the man might attempt in his desperation. Just as secretly as he had to set things up in Berlin and for the same reasons.

And when he'd put everything in motion he could start planning how Sobelov was going to die. He was going to enjoy that.

Silin looked to the side of the room at Markov's re-entry, for the nod of assurance that Marina's guards had been properly briefed.

Everything was working out perfectly.

chapter 3

Questions crowded in upon him but Charlie Muffin was too experienced to interrupt. It wasn't just what Rupert Dean was saying. Or the awareness that he had been professionally reprieved. There was the overwhelming personal implication. But which couldn't be allowed to *become* overwhelming. Anything personal had to be blocked off, later more calmly to be assessed. For the moment the posting was the only thing he could afford to let into his mind.

So Natalia had to be forgotten.

Dean's presentation, like his demeanour, was that of a lecturer concisely establishing with facts and assessments and analyses a problem that phrases and words like 'potentially catastrophic' and 'cataclysmic' and 'nightmare' did not exaggerate. He also referred to 'political sensitivity' and 'extreme caution' and 'essential cooperation' and Charlie knew they weren't exaggerations either. Dean concluded, 'So that's your brief, to liaise with the Russians and with the already appointed Americans to do everything you can to stem the flow of nuclear material to the West.'

Charlie wondered if the telephone boxes in Moscow would be large enough for him to change into his Superman outfit. 'There are officers from this department already attached to the British embassy in Moscow. Others from SIS, too.'

'Engaged in their normal functions, which remain quite separate from what you are being appointed to achieve,' said Dean. 'Our role was extended years ago to combat the terrorism in Northern Ireland. Now it's being widened even further. And what's coming out of Russia and its former satellites provides the potential for the worst terrorism imaginable.'

'To whom will I be responsible? The station chief? Or direct to London?' Charlie had rarely engaged in an operation where jealously guarded territory did not have to be respected. Diplomatic niceties were always a pain in the ass.

'London. But through the embassy,' ordered the sharply featured Peter Johnson.

'What's my officially described position to be?'

It was Patrick Pacey who responded. 'An attaché. Don't for a moment forget the genuine political importance of what you're doing . . .' He made a hand movement over the conference table and Charlie became aware that each of the group had his personal dossiers before them. 'There won't be any of the nonsense of the past,' continued the department's political advisor. 'Just one example of what you've always explained away – *and* got away with – as necessary operational independence and you're on the first plane back to London. And in this building only long enough to be formally dismissed from the service once and for all.'

'And don't suffer the slightest doubt at our seriousness,' endorsed the deputy Director. 'There *are* changes to our function. This is one of them: *you're* one of them. So you've got to change, like everything else about the business we're now in. There's no place for anyone disobeying orders. That clear enough?'

'Completely,' Charlie said, caught by just one part of the threat. 'This isn't seen as a temporary assignment: one specific operation?'

'The Americans got agreement a long time ago to appoint an FBI office in Moscow specifically to monitor nuclear smuggling,' reminded the deputy Director. 'You're our equivalent.'

'To *liaise*,' instructed Simpson, the moustache hedge seemingly moving slightly out of time with the man's upper lip. 'That's your sole function . . .' He gestured sideways to Pacey. 'You've got to do more than simply think what the politics are. Whatever it is, it will be inextricably tied up with legality. The Russians are the law, not us. We have – you'll have – no legal jurisdiction. All the nuclear stuff haemorrhaging across Europe is coming overland through Poland and Hungary and Germany and the two countries that made up Czechoslovakia and what was Yugoslavia.'

Minefield was too much of an appalling pun, thought Charlie. 'It'll be a waste of time even bothering,' he declared. 'Before we've even begun working our way through the officials we'd need to consult, every terrorist group, despot or dictator will have atom bombs up to their knees.'

'Let's be more specific,' said the distinctively voiced Director-General. 'We decide here in London who should be consulted and who shouldn't. The important thing for you to understand, *totally* and at *all* times, is that you must never, ever, act without consulting us.'

He'd made the protest to maintain his credibility, which was all that mattered. There were other, more essential parameters to be established: one more important than all others. 'I don't think I can operate effectively – as I will *have* to operate – living in the embassy compound.'

'Why not?' demanded Williams, sensing a danger.

Because it would severely limit the enormous expenses benefits, thought Charlie. 'According to what you say, the nuclear trade is handled by gangsters: an acknowledged Mafia.' He briefly hesitated, wondering if Natalia had transferred to the Interior Ministry, just as quickly thrusting the intrusion aside. 'Would the Foreign Office like the idea of my meeting a questionable informant on embassy property . . . ?' He turned his attention to Simpson, warming to his argument. 'Wouldn't there even be a legal difficulty . . . ?' And then to Pacey. '. . . As well as a political one . . . ?'

'I still think. . . ' began Williams, anxious to continue his objection, but Dean cut the man off. 'There are obvious advantages to your living separate from the embassy.'

Push it as far as you can when you're on a roll, Charlie

told himself. 'Crime makes Moscow astronomically expensive. My cost of living allowance will need to be proportionately substantial. Considerably more than might normally be accepted, even in the high-cost diplomatic postings like Tokyo or Washington. And the justifiable out-of-pocket expenses will undoubtedly be larger as well. I'm going to have to go where the Mafias go . . . clubs . . . restaurants . . .' Charlie was close to enjoying himself: certainly he was enjoying Gerald Williams' obvious anguish.

'I don't think all this needs to be discussed today,' attempted the accountant, blinking nervously at the prospects for gain Charlie was working to establish.

'I think it's important to discuss and agree *everything* here today that might affect the success of what I have to do,' said Charlie, equally anxious.

Charlie was aware of the Director-General momentarily regarding him with what could have been a bemused smile. Then the man turned to Williams and said, 'I think things should be put on the highest scale. This is a new role that has to succeed, to stop the political sniping that the country doesn't need intelligence services any more. So I don't want anything endangered by penny-pinching.'

'I am to liaise with the Russians *and* whatever the FBI arrangement is there?' Charlie hurried on.

'Yes.' Dean resumed charge of the conversation.

'They know we're sending someone over specifically for the purpose?'

'Yes.'

'Just someone? Or has my name been put forward, for approval?'

'To the Russians, yes: more formal and official arrangements obviously had to be made with Moscow. With the Americans everything was left open, until today's meeting.' The Director-General paused. 'Is there a problem?'

If Natalia had transferred at the rank she'd occupied in the former KGB it was possible she'd even know he was coming! Nodding yet again towards his dossier, Charlie said,

'There will be an extensive file on me, both in Washington and Moscow.'

'The KGB is defunct. And their records, too. There obviously hasn't been the slightest association with what you once were and what you once did.'

'I don't think I'm particularly popular in America, either.'

'What you did, you did to the CIA, not the FBI. Each hates the other. The Bureau would probably approve, not criticize: find it amusing, even. And it's very ancient history, anyway,' dismissed the Director-General, showing how extensively he, and therefore everyone else in the room, had studied Charlie's file.

'Your sole primary concern is not making mistakes,' warned Johnson.

'I won't,' promised Charlie, carelessly.

'No more than once,' said Pacey. 'I've already told you that.'

'I like him,' judged the Director-General. It was a remark addressed more to his deputy than anyone else: Charlie Muffin had been Peter Johnson's recommendation.

'He's a liar and a thief,' insisted the financial controller, seething at Charlie's easy success with allowances and accommodation.

'Isn't that why he's being sent: poacher turned gamekeeper?' reminded the cadaverous deputy.

'There are others who could have gone, without the uncertainties that always surround this man,' argued Williams.

'Costing as much as possible is all part of the budgetary exercises,' said Johnson, defending his choice. 'We've not only to establish a new role for ourselves. We've got to establish a financial ceiling. The more we spend in expansion, the more important and necessary we'll appear.'

'That's cynical reasoning,' reproached Williams.

'Practical reasoning,' corrected Johnson, equally insistent. 'I want to build a new empire, not destroy one.'

I want, isolated Dean. He didn't want to confront the other man so soon but he had the worrying impression that Johnson's annoyance at not getting the directorship might become a problem. Maybe it hadn't been as wise as he'd thought to accept Johnson's suggestion about the Moscow posting: it could have made Johnson imagine an unnecessary reliance. '*We* want to build a new empire.'

'Muffin's not the man to do it,' insisted Williams.

'We're not relying on him doing it alone,' reminded the Director-General.

'I'll tell Fenby: he was very helpful,' said Johnson. John Fenby was the FBI Director. It had been Johnson's idea, too, to seek the political support of the Americans through government-to-government pressure for a specific British posting to Moscow to match their own.

'Is it really necessary to tell Fenby?' asked the Director-General.

'We're becoming more like the FBI: we'll need a close working relationship,' Johnson pointed out.

'You will keep me informed at every stage, won't you?'

'I don't *think* I need to be reminded to do that.'

This was becoming petulant, decided Dean. Which was ridiculous. Ending it by looking away from his deputy to include everyone else, he said, 'We've made an important decision today. Let's do all we can from this end to make sure it works.'

Peter Johnson's first act upon returning to his own office was to call Washington.

Stanislav Silin wasn't any longer accustomed to doing things for himself. He'd forgotten how to, like he'd forgotten his own stepping stones to power. When Stanislav Silin wanted something done, *anything* done, he told someone to do it and if the task wasn't performed to his total satisfaction then those who failed were punished. But not this time or this way. For this meeting and for this meeting place he couldn't trust anyone inside the Dolgoprudnaya, not even Petr Markov, and most certainly not outside. Apart, that is, from Marina. No man had been as lucky as he had with a wife like her. The hatred boiled up at the threat Sobelov had created. Soon, he told himself, soon he'd make the man sorry. But there were other things first. He'd had to find this very special apartment himself and arrange the lease himself and for the first time in almost fifteen years he hadn't been able to intimidate the landlord with the inference of who he was for fear the man might sell him out or be under threat from a higher or initially more feared bidder. Which was an irony Silin could appreciate, inconvenient though it had been: he'd even been amused when the landlord had tried to intimidate him with warnings of the consequences of his being a bad tenant.

Silin had specifically chosen the Ulitza Razina, in the oldest Kitay-Gorod district, because all the pre-revolutionary buildings, some actually minor palaces, had under communism been turned into apartment rabbit warrens with a warren's benefit of many different entrances, several from two streets quite separate from the Razina courtyard. Its most important advantage was the personal protection it gave him from Sobelov but it equally protected the people he was meeting that afternoon and upon whom not just his survival but an unimaginable business future depended. Like he could – and would – they could also arrive separately and leave separately and never use the same door or courtyard twice, making discovery or identification totally impossible.

The apartment was bare-board basic, of course, which he regretted. His two city mansions and the dacha in the outer hills were designer-decorated, the marble shipped from Italy, the wall and upholstery silk specially woven before being flown in from Hong Kong: the opulence awed people, giving him an advantage. For this operation, anonymity and secrecy were the only advantages he sought. His single addition was the bottles and glasses set out on the matchwood sideboard: he hadn't even bothered to cover the bed in the adjoining room.

They were coming to him and Silin solicitously arrived well ahead of the arranged time. Not that he intended to be subservient – that would have been quite wrong as well as difficult for him – any more than he expected them to be subservient towards him. They were going to meet and conduct their business as equals. His being there early was simply the politeness of a host.

The two men arrived together, which surprised him, and precisely on time, which didn't. The handshakes were perfunctory, without names: the namelessness had been their insistence from the beginning, after the initial confirmation of their identities, and Silin thought it theatrical but was quite prepared to go along with the pointless affectation. Both declined Silin's hospitality, making it another pointless gesture.

The seats made protesting noises when they sat and Silin's skin itched at once at the thought of who had sat on the lounge chair before him: he didn't lean back, wanting to minimize his contact with the upholstery as much as possible. The leader of the two, neither of whom appeared discomfited, briefly looked around the functional meeting place and said, 'This is well chosen.'

'I don't want what we're discussing going beyond this room,' said Silin. 'Or beyond us three.'

'Neither do we.'

'Everything you promised me is possible?'

'Guaranteed,' assured the spokesman.

'As much as 250 kilos?'

'Absolutely.'

'When?'

'Four months, maximum. We want to achieve more than just a robbery.'

Silin listened without interruption to the proposal, nodding at the awareness of how much it would, incredibly, benefit him. 'That would not be difficult to achieve between us.'

'So you could help?'

'Easily.

'That's how it will be done then. Opening up everything to us.'

'How much money are we talking about?' came in the second man.

'For the full 250 kilos, exactly what I guaranteed you in the first place: a total, for you, of $25,000,000 on completion of the sale.'

'With an initial deposit in Switzerland?' stressed the first man.

'You'll be handed the certified deposit books the day after I get the 250 kilos,' promised Silin. 'There'll be formalities before that: signatory authority forms, passport identification, that sort of thing.' His promise to them was $8,000,000 and he'd insist upon ten per cent in advance from the purchasers Berlin set up, so there was no financial risk whatsoever. He wished the Commission could have been here, to see how their business should really be conducted, *as* a business in a sophisticated, calm-voiced way, not screaming around the city in imported stolen cars with machine pistols on the seats beside them and posturing in nightclubs trying to outspend each other.

'It all seems very satisfactory,' said the leader of the two.

'And this will only be the beginning?' pressed Silin, anxious to get everything properly established.

'You can think of this as a trial run,' nodded the man. 'The way we prove our good faith to each other. What can follow is virtually unlimited.'

He would be unassailable, Silin thought: totally and absolutely unassailable. He'd watch what was done to Sobelov, inflict some of the pain himself perhaps. Laugh at the man when he begged for mercy and hurt him all the more.

'Are you sure you're all right?' Marina asked him that night.

'Of course.'

'I'm worried.'

'You're safe. So am I, now I know where the threat is.'

He cupped her face between both his hands, bringing her forward to kiss him. He was glad she didn't try to tint the greyness showing through in her hair: he thought she was the most beautiful woman he'd ever known, although he hadn't tried to know any other for the twenty years they had been married.

'Sobelov is an animal,' she warned.

'Which is how I'm going to treat him, when it suits me,' promised Silin.

chapter 4

Only during the subsequent briefings from Johnson did Charlie try fully to dismiss Natalia from his mind. Otherwise, in those first few following days, his mind ran the entire gamut of his totally misconceived (on his part), totally mishandled (on his part) and totally misunderstood (on his part) relationship with Natalia Nikandrova Fedova.

There was no guilt about deceiving her during their initial encounters. She'd been officially debriefing him after his supposed prison escape – defection for which he had been set up by that Old Bailey court sentence of fourteen years. His deceiving her then had been professional. She'd even accepted it – a professional herself – when the love affair had developed, after his Soviet acceptance. A further deception, Charlie acknowledged, forcing the honesty. Love hadn't been part of the affair, in the beginning. He'd been lonely and thought there might be an advantage in sleeping with a KGB officer and the 'sleeping with' had been good and sometimes better than good. He hadn't been able to concede love – definitely not allow it to overcome his professionalism – when he'd double-defected back to London. The job required he return and the job came first, before everything and everybody. Nor had he been able to recognize what had happened between them the first time she'd risked personal disaster accompanying an official Russian delegation to London to seek him out, not able to accept it wasn't a retribution trap for the damage he'd caused his misled KGB champion by leaving Moscow. Her second contact attempt, when she'd traced him with the photograph of their London-conceived baby, had finally proved to him how wrong he'd been. He'd tried, too late and too ineffectually, finally to go to her by returning to Moscow after Gorbachev and then Yeltsin, to keep her suggested rendezvous: by every day and at every hour going to the spot he believed she had identified by the photograph, until he decided he'd misinterpreted that like he'd misinterpreted so much else and that the photograph was her sad and bitter attempt to show how absolutely he had betrayed and abandoned her.

She had every reason to be sad and bitter, to despise and hate him. Having thought so much and for so long about what a fool he'd been, Charlie found it very easy to understand what he regarded as ingrained professionalism would by Natalia be seen as disinterested cowardice.

As the preparation days passed, bringing Moscow nearer, Charlie's initial euphoria gave way to realism and from realism to depression. Why should he have thought that Natalia would ever want to see him again? It was preposterous conceit to imagine that after five empty years and every rejection she'd even want him to be in the same city or the same country as her! Or to acknowledge or accept him as the father of the daughter he'd never seen and hadn't known about until the photograph with the four word inscription: *Her name is Sasha.*

He'd failed Natalia like he'd failed Edith, although the circumstances were entirely different. When he'd fled Moscow he'd fixed for Natalia to be the one to expose his initial defection as the phoney KGB discrediting exercise it had always been. When he'd humiliated, by brief Russian detention, the British and American Directors willing literally to sacrifice him – and run with their $500,000 to add to their shame – he'd thought only of his own retribution, not theirs to follow. It had been Edith who took the assassination bullet intended for him.

In his self-admission of failing them, Charlie wasn't thinking of physical neglect or abandonment. His failure, to both, was never being able properly to say 'I love you.' He'd uttered the words, of course, but automatically and emptily. He'd never told either of them spontaneously. His entire life had been spent living lies and telling lies and being someone he wasn't until the truth was so rare he didn't know how to express it or how to show it or, more often than not, even what it was.

He told lies even to himself, that ludicrous bloody defence – professionalism – always there to excuse or explain away what he didn't truly want or like to admit. Which *was* cowardice. He might be – *had* been, he corrected – a truly professional intelligence officer. But as a man he'd been inadequate.

Charlie fully accepted the intended permanence of his new role when Johnson confirmed there was no reason for him any longer to maintain his London flat. Charlie had only ever used it as a place to sleep and keep the rain off, so apart from the several photographs of Edith and only the one of Natalia and of Sasha and some books, there were no memories or fondness for the place. In the end there were only three cardboard wine boxes to be shipped care of the Moscow embassy. To empty his apartment Charlie employed one of those firms that strip properties after their occupants die and the men plainly thought that was what had happened to a relative of Charlie's. The foreman said most of the stuff was crap and it was surprising how some people lived, wasn't it? Charlie agreed it was. The man hoped Charlie wasn't expecting a lot for it and Charlie said he wasn't and he didn't get it. The furniture and contents of two bedrooms, a living room and a kitchen went for £450; the inside of the washing machine fell out of its case and smashed as the men were getting it from the kitchen and the television was sold as scrap to a dealer in old sets to be cannibalized for its parts. As Charlie watched the van and most of his lifetime's possessions disappear down the Vauxhall Bridge Road the warning echoed in his head that if he didn't adjust and conform he'd be withdrawn from Moscow just long enough to be fired: if it happened he wouldn't have anywhere or anything to come back *to*.

The disposal of the flat meant Charlie had briefly to move into an hotel, which he did ahead of consulting Gerald

Williams, which when the bills came in formed the basis of the inevitable dispute over which the deputy Director had to arbitrate. That the decision was in Charlie's favour worsened the already bad feeling between them. Charlie fought for, and got, the most expensive of the three apartments the Moscow embassy housing officer suggested, a sprawling conversion in a pre-revolutionary mansion on Lesnaya with bathrooms attached to both bedrooms and a dining room separate from the main living area. Charlie negotiated an extra £20 a day cost-of-living allowance, on top of the highest rate allocated in Washington and Tokyo, and had the longest and most heated argument of all to operate not on a system of fixed expenses but on fixed exchange rates. And to be allowed to submit claims for whatever he spent in the currency in which he spent it. As dollars were an even more common currency than roubles in Moscow it meant Charlie gained the Washington diplomatic dollars-to-sterling equal parity conversion to compensate for the official rate fluctuation. The ruling gave him as much as a fifty per cent profit on every dollar claimed.

Through the Washington embassy Charlie discovered the FBI agent specifically tasked with nuclear smuggling was James Kestler, although there was no file upon him. Neither was there any Records listing for the man in London archives, but a man named Barry Lyneham showed up as the Bureau's station chief. Charlie also studied all the traffic between London and Moscow about his posting, eager for the one Russian name that would have meant something to him. Natalia did not appear anywhere. Neither was she listed among Interior Ministry executives supplied by Moscow station. Maybe, Charlie thought, Natalia had left instead of being transferred. Or perhaps been moved to another ministry like so many former British intelligence officers had switched to other, peripherally connected departments.

From his Moscow enquiries Charlie learned the department's existing intelligence chief was Thomas Bowyer, whom he had not previously known but who sent a personal welcome. The interchange provided Charlie with a further advantage, although at that stage he wasn't sure how to utilize it: within an hour of the cable exchange between himself and Bowyer, Charlie was lectured by the deputy Director how Bowyer's seniority had at all times to be respected, convincing Charlie of a back-channel link between London and Moscow upon which his performance and activities would be constantly monitored. Forewarned was forearmed, he reminded himself.

One of Charlie's final acts, with the overseas disruption grant Gerald Williams predictably opposed but which Charlie quoted precedence to obtain, was to buy two new suits and a sports jacket and shirts and underwear, which was the largest expenditure on clothes he could ever remember making, another positive change in a changed life. The very last purchase was a new pair of Hush Puppies he had no intention of trying to wear in the immediate future but which he considered a worthwhile investment against the uncertainty of Russian footwear. At the same time he bought a set of shoe-trees two sizes larger upon which hopefully to stretch them until the tentative day he put them on.

Charlie never seriously considered a farewell party because he didn't have enough acquaintances to invite so he gatecrashed someone else's. Billy Baker had been chief of the Hong Kong station, which was being closed down entirely in advance of the colony's 1997 return to China and Baker arrived back in London the week before Charlie's departure with enough made-in-three-days, £20 Hong Kong suits to last a lifetime, a container load of Japanese electronic equipment, a Chinese mistress described as a housekeeper and a small, expenses-purchased William and Mary mansion in Devon from which, in his retirement, he intended to lord it over the manor like he'd lorded it over Hong Kong: a lot of the suits were tweed, for him to dress the part.

The whole affair was a parade – or maybe a parody – into the past. Baker staged it in the upstairs room of The Pheasant, the pub they'd all used when they were based at Westminster Bridge Road and when Charlie got there intentionally late, to cover his uninvited arrival, there were so many people he had difficulty getting into the room and even more difficulty getting a drink. The room was beginning to cloud with cigarette smoke and the ice had already run out. In the first five minutes, after which he gave up counting, Charlie identified twenty operational and London-based officers whom he had known and sometimes worked with, as well as a lot of Special Branch policemen who had been the legally arresting arm of the service. Everyone seemed to have a frenzied determination to follow the host's example and get fall-down drunk as quickly as possible. Billy Baker held court at the bar, the Chinese girl, who had to be thirty years his junior, bewildered by his side but doubtlessly happy at the escape from Beijing rule. When he saw Charlie, Baker embraced him wetly, thanked him for coming, and said wasn't it all a bloody mistake and a bloody disgrace. Charlie said yes, to both. It was the persistent, in fact the only, theme in every group he joined and just as quickly left, not having anything to contribute and not interested enough to invent a lie about what he was going to do in the future to make them all believe he'd been dumped, like they had. The constant movement took him frequently to the bar. He was there when the voice behind him said, 'Pretty depressing, isn't it?'

Charlie wished he could remember if her name was Juliet or June, which he should have been able to do because she was one of the Director-General's secretaries whose bed he had almost, although not quite, shared pursuing his pillow talk self-preservation policy. 'Very. Drink?'

'Gin. Large.'

'You OK?'

'Saw it coming, so I moved over to the Department of Health a year ago, before it turned into a St Valentine's Day massacre. Secretarial supervisor in the minister's office. Boring as hell but it's rent.'

She was still very attractive in a carefully preserved, carefully coiffeured sort of way, although the hair was beginning to stray in the heat and the crush. 'Wise girl.'

'Lucky,' she said, looking around the room. 'There's got to be at least forty people here who've been told to go or moved elsewhere.' She came back to Charlie. 'How about you?'

'Moving on,' said Charlie, which wasn't, after all, a lie.

'Sorry, Charlie.'

Would he be? wondered Charlie. 'It'll work out.'

'Charlie the Survivor,' she declared, gin spoiling the coquettish smile. 'That's what they always said about you, Charlie. Even the Director-General.'

Now she decides to tell me! thought Charlie. How much more would he have learned if she had admitted him to her bed? Too late to be of any use now: the Director-General she was talking about had died at least six years ago. 'Is that what they all said?'

She nodded. 'That. And a lot more. How are things otherwise?'

'Otherwise?' said Charlie, playing the game. It wasn't much but it was better than sobbing into their drinks like everyone else.

'You happy?'

'Happy enough.'

'With anyone?'

'On and off.'

'Nothing permanent then?'

'Nothing permanent.'

'Me neither.'

Why couldn't it have been like this when he'd tried to know her better? 'That won't last, someone as pretty as you,' he said, gallantly. She didn't try to refasten the top button of her shirt that suddenly gave way under the strain.

'Do you want to stay here much longer?' she invited.

'I wasn't going to, anyway,' said Charlie. 'Got something fixed up.' It had been a depressing mistake to come at all.

'Oh,' she said, crushed.

'I'm sorry,' apologized Charlie, still gallant. 'I didn't know you'd be here. Can't cancel it now.'

'Some other time maybe,' she suggested, without offering a telephone number.

'Sure,' agreed Charlie, without asking for one.

There was another wet embrace and the insistence they keep in touch from Billy Baker and a shrill giggle from the Chinese girl and a lot of damp handshakes as he made his way out of the room and down the tilting stairs into Westminster Bridge Road. The death of the dinosaurs, he thought, breathing deeply in the darkness: or rather, their funeral. He looked sideways towards the old headquarters building, expecting it to be in darkness, but it wasn't. It was bright with the permanent office lights of whatever ministerial department had taken it over. Gerald Williams would shit himself at the thought of the electricity bill, thought Charlie.

'Seems you've covered all that's necessary,' encouraged the Director-General.

'There's a scientific and military mission in Moscow at the moment. I've asked them to give him the technical briefing before they leave.'

'That's a good idea.'

'Williams is complaining we've made too many financial concessions.'

'He's memoed me direct, covering his back against any Treasury enquiry.' Dean was unaccustomed to bureaucratic politics. He'd started out finding it amusing, but not any more. If half his students had behaved in the back-biting, self-serving way of virtually all the people he worked with now, he'd have suspended them from their courses until they grew up. He wished he felt more comfortable with Johnson.

The deputy Director smiled. 'Muffin's certainly pushed it to the very edge.'

Dean made a vague gesture over his desk, somewhere in the disorder of which Johnson presumed Charlie Muffin's file was buried. 'He's always pushed everything to the edge.'

'I can monitor that closely enough.'

'It seems to have been difficult in the past.'

'I wasn't the person controlling him in the past.'

'Are you now? I thought the committee had been established to do that?' The other man's arrogance was irritating.

Johnson bristled. 'I meant on a day-to-day basis.'

'There's been a Director to Director note, from Fenby: he's making a personal visit to London to meet me,' disclosed Dean.

'You'll like him,' predicted Johnson, who already knew of the visit but wanted to remind the other man of his longer experience of the department. 'He sees the grand picture: the sort of man who knows that politics is the art of the possible.'

At the beginning of their relationship Dean had suspected Johnson's frequent invocation of Bismarck aphorisms to be a mockery of his previous academic career but he'd learned since that the German genuinely was Johnson's hero, which was perhaps understandable in view of Johnson's Foreign Office association. Dean twirled his spectacles prayer-bead fashion and said, 'I hope Muffin really understands just how much politics is involved.'

'I can monitor that, too,' insisted Johnson.

John Fenby thought being the Director of FBI was like being the maker of the best Swiss clock whose wheels and cogs meshed together without ever going wrong by a single second. It seemed to Fenby that virtually every FBI Director since Hoover quit or retired complaining at the impossibility of working with the President or the Congress or the Attorney General or of being the victim of staff incompetence, their only ambition from their moment of appointment to get away from Pennsylvania Avenue as fast as possible.

John Fenby didn't want to get away from Pennsylvania Avenue. If he had his way – which he was determined always to do – Fenby was going to have to be dragged kicking and screaming from Hoover's original seventh-floor suite from which, under two successive Presidents, he had moulded the Bureau into a personal fiefdom unmatched since the Bureau's creator.

Fenby, who was a small, rotund man not unlike Hoover in both looks and stature, coveted the Director's role for exactly the same reasons as its founder. He adored the Bureau jet.

And the chauffeured stretch limousine. And being part of an inner circle at the White House and up on the Hill. And of personally controlling an empire of thousands spread around the globe, anxious to respond to every command he uttered. Had Fenby not been, primarily for public awareness rather than religious conviction, a twice-on-Sunday churchgoer he would have believed himself God. He contented himself with Boss, which was a Hoover word. It was, in fact, a secret regret that he couldn't go out on arrests and be photographed with a Tommy Gun cradled in his arms, like Hoover had been. But that had been in another age. He couldn't have everything. What he had was good enough. And what he had most of all was an awareness of how things operated in the capital of the world.

Like today.

The corner table at the Four Seasons was reserved permanently for him, whether he used it or not, the other tables moved out of hearing. Although he was the favour-purveyor, Fenby was also today's host and therefore solicitously early, already seated when the Speaker arrived. Fenby enjoyed being included in the *frisson* of recognition that went through the restaurant as Milton Fitzjohn strode across the room, the political glad-hand outstretched. The required my-you're-looking-fine-and-so-are-you recital concluded with Fitzjohn ordering bourbon. The abstemious Fenby, who never risked alcohol during working hours, already had his mineral water.

'So how's my boy doing, sir?' Fitzjohn, whose iron-fist control and manipulation of Congress exceeded even that of Lyndon Johnson, occupied an original colonial mansion in South Carolina and assiduously cultivated a Southern gentleman mien to go with it. He didn't consider anyone, certainly not any White House incumbent from whom he was only two heartbeats away, his superior, but 'sir' was one of several insincere courtesies.

'A rising star,' assured the FBI Director. 'Someone of whom you can be rightfully proud.'

'I am, sir, I am. Mrs Fitzjohn will be particularly gratified to hear it.' Referring to his wife in the third person and never in public by her christian name was another affectation. 'Natural that she should be worried, though.'

'Quite natural,' agreed Fenby. He'd had reservations posting Kestler to somewhere like Moscow and certainly with the specific nuclear brief, but Fitzjohn had insisted his wife's nephew get a high-profile assignment.

Fitzjohn demanded a T-bone bleeding from exposure. Fenby ordered his customary salad and a second bottle of water.

'Mrs Fitzjohn is a little worried, I have to say, about some of the things she's hearing about Moscow. Lot of crime there: people getting killed.'

Only someone with Fenby's committed dedication to remaining in power could have greeted that statement with a straight face. 'I think you can tell Mrs Fitzjohn that I am taking every precaution to ensure James's safety. Not only that: to ensure his career in the Bureau, too.' The British approach had been very fortuitous, although Fenby knew very few directors, perhaps only Hoover himself, would have realized every advantage as quickly as he had.

'I'm extremely grateful to hear that, sir. Extremely grateful.'

Which is what Fenby wanted everyone in positions of power or influence in Washington to be, extremely grateful to him. Like the CIA would be grateful to him if he had to sacrifice the Englishman who had caused them so much embarrassment, all those years ago.

That afternoon he memoed the Bureau's Scientific Division at Quantico to ensure they had a sufficiently qualified nuclear physicist, if the need for one arose. He didn't expect there to be, but John Fenby left nothing to chance. Which was why he called Peter Johnson, in London, too.

'How were lessons?'

'All right.'

'What did you learn?'

'Numbers.'

'How many?'

'Can't remember.'

'You're supposed to remember.'

'Why?'

'You go to school to make you clever.'

'Are you clever?'

'Sometimes.'

'Why not all the time?'

'People make mistakes.'

'Do you make mistakes?'

'I try not to.'

'Why?'

'Because it's important not to make mistakes.'

'Do people get angry?'

'If I make bad mistakes, yes.'

'Why?'

'Because it upsets them.'

'Do you get angry if people make mistakes?'

'Sometimes.'

'I'll try not to make mistakes.'

'So will I,' said Natalia, a promise to herself as much as to Sasha.

chapter 5

The nuclear weaponry leakage from Russia and its former satellites worried Barry Lyneham far more than it worried most other people involved in its attempted prevention and for entirely different reasons.

Lyneham had had a good and fortunate career, virtually unblemished by any serious errors and certainly none he hadn't been able to disguise or dump on someone else, and he'd seen his Moscow appointment as the FBI section head as the smooth glide to contented, well-pensioned retirement for which the Florida condo with the boat slip at the back had already been bought, with the game-rigged cruiser ready for delivery when he gave the word.

He'd worked out way ahead of anyone else that Moscow was a snip, the best thing that could have happened to him. All right, it was a shitty, bad-weather, nothing-works place to live, somewhere he wouldn't have even settled his mother-in-law, but that wasn't the point. The point was that in the eyes and ears and opinion of Washington, Moscow was still the Cold War, high-profile posting that carried with it an automatic Grade 18 – with the fancy title of senior executive officer – with none of the Cold War embarrassment risks now there wasn't a Cold War any more.

Until the organized crime motherfuckers emerged from the woodwork, that is. And realized the profit trading nuclear shit to every Middle East towel-head with ambitions to replace Gary Cooper with a mushroom cloud in their remake of *High Noon*. Then it had become a whole new ball game altogether, top of the agenda, Director-to-President breakfast-table stuff and there wasn't anything higher profile than that.

James Kestler's appointment was another worry for Lyneham, which would have surprised a lot of people if he'd admitted it, which of course he didn't. On the face of it, the specific, named assignment removed the personal career danger to Lyneham from any foul-up.

Or would have done, if Kestler hadn't had the pull of being related to the wife of one of the most powerful men, maybe even *the* most powerful man, in Washington. Which was a bigger bastard than nuclear smuggling as far as Lyneham was concerned. There'd been the predictable crap from Fenby that Kestler was just another FBI agent, like everybody else, and shouldn't get any special favours. But Lyneham didn't believe that any more than he believed in virgin birth or that there was good in every man.

And Kestler was just the sort of prematurely promoted smart-assed son-of-a-bitch to screw up. He was only thirty years old, five years out of the academy, and rode so gung-ho into every situation it was inevitable he was going to shoot himself in not just one but both feet. And sooner rather than later, thought Lyneham, only half-listening to the younger man so full of pent-up energy he strode about the office when he talked. Lyneham would have thought the five miles the silly bastard jogged every morning, beside that part of the inner Moscow peripherique close to the US embassy, would have been enough.

'Sit down, for Christ's sake. My neck aches following you about.' Being the Speaker's relation didn't spare Kestler from being bawled out: Lyneham sometimes got relief from it.

Kestler sat, reluctantly. His left leg kept jigging up and down, as if he were keeping in time with something. 'So what do you think?'

'I think the Brits decided it was serious and important enough to appoint their own man, like we did.'

'But this guy!' exclaimed Kestler, who glowed with the health he strove so hard to achieve, pink-faced and hard-bodied. He kept his fair hair in a tight crew cut and wore jeans in the office, like he was doing now, which Lyneham allowed although he knew Edgar J. Hoover, in whose reign he'd joined the Bureau, would have gone apoplectic at the thought. But then Hoover had his own strange way of dressing out of office hours.

Lyneham glanced at the FBI file on Charlie Muffin faxed from Washington that morning. 'Quite a track record.'

'Track record! How the hell has he ever survived?'

That was a question that intrigued Lyneham far more than the litany of Charlie's misdemeanours, what he'd done to the CIA Director heading the list. Any guy who'd hung on – lived, even – through all that had to have a very special respect for his own ass and if he was going to work with Kestler he could be a very useful brake on the idiot's over-the-top-and-at-'em enthusiasm. Against which clashed the unarguable logic that the guy had to be one hell of an ornery bastard to have taken all the risks he had in the first place. On balance, Lyneham decided the arrival of Charlie Muffin was an additional cause for concern. 'I guess he's good.'

'How close am I going to have to work with him?'

Lyneham gestured to what had come from Washington. 'In the same sack is what they want.'

'How do you feel about that? You're chief here.'

Lyneham shifted uncomfortably at the reminder of ultimate responsibility. 'We're talking doomsday and Armageddon, son. If Washington want you joined at the hip, I'll do the stitching myself.'

'Who'll be in charge, if we're a team?'

It was a necessary operational question. And not one upon which he was going to commit himself, anxious to spread the accountability. 'I'll message Washington.'

Kestler thrust up, unable to remain still any longer, nodding to the other material on Lyneham's desk. 'Why don't we make him an arrival present of those?'

'Those' were the photographs of the mutilated man in the skiff on the Berlin lake. From his fingerprints the German Bundeskriminalamt had identified him as Gottfried Braun, a small-time hustler and con man upon whom their most recent intelligence was of his boasting close contacts with various Russian Mafia groups with available nuclear material.

'You know what they show?' demanded Lyneham.

'A guy with his balls in his mouth.'

Lyneham sighed, unamused. 'They show that no one in the nuclear business fucks about: that you've got to treat it all very seriously and not take any chances and think before you make any move. They don't take prisoners and they don't give a fuck about who or what the FBI is or about any other organization trying to stop them.'

'I do treat it seriously,' insisted the corrected Kestler, solemnly. Then he said, 'So shall I send the photographs to the British embassy? Show how keen we are to work together?'

'Why not?' agreed Lyneham.

Aleksai Semenovich Popov was the operational director against Russian nuclear smuggling, so it was to him that the advice of Charlie Muffin's politically agreed appointment was channelled from the Foreign Ministry. Popov brought to his position the forethought, planning and the minute attention to every detail that, had he not chosen an alternative career, would have gained him chess Grand Master ranking at international level. Such attention to detail made it automatic for him to check old KGB records and the discovery startled him. He read the file several times at the Interior Ministry building less than a mile away from where the two Americans had the same day had their discussion about Charlie Muffin. Finally he rose and went further along the corridor to the deputy Director's office.

'I think you should see this,' Popov said to Natalia. 'It seems you know this man.'

Charlie Muffin had not expected to be met at Sheremet'yevo by Thomas Bowyer and said so, when he thanked the man.

'Traditional courtesy to a newcomer,' said the station chief. The Scots accent was quite pronounced and Charlie supposed the suit could have been described as a Highland tweed. Bowyer was ruddy-cheeked and stray-haired and would, Charlie decided, have looked more at home on a moor than forcing his way through a crowd of taxi-touting Russians to the embassy Ford. As they got in Bowyer said, 'Been to Moscow before?'

So London had not sent his complete file. 'A long time ago.'

'Funny place. Didn't know it in the old days but people who did tell me it's changed a lot. Dangerous as hell now . . .' He nodded back towards the retreating airport. 'A lot of those taxi guys only take you halfway into town before mugging you, stealing your luggage and dumping you in the road.'

'I've heard.' The state of the roads didn't seem to have changed, thought Charlie, as the car thumped into a bone-jarring pothole.

Bowyer chanced a look across the car. 'What's it like, back home?'

Charlie understood the question and the gossip-eager reason for his being met in. 'Pretty bad. Blood all over the floor.'

'I'm damned glad I'm here, out of it.'

'It's the best place to be, out of it.'

'Can't say I envy you your job, though.'

Charlie hesitated, remembering the back-channel suspicion. 'It's going to take a while for me to learn what the job really is.'

'You're going to get some help on that,' offered Bowyer at once. 'There's been a scientific and military group here for the last fortnight: they're going home the day after tomorrow. London's fixed a briefing, before they leave.'

Charlie frowned, curious Johnson hadn't warned him in London. 'That'll be useful.'

'And anything else more generally you need, just ask.'

'I appreciate the offer,' said Charlie. More often than not in the past when he'd arrived in a city as an outsider he'd met resentment and even outright hostility from in-country embassy personnel. But he wasn't going to be an outsider this time, was he? Charlie still found the realization difficult and wondered how long it would take to adjust.

'You certainly seem to have some clout,' said Bowyer.

'To get what?'

'That sort of apartment on Lesnaya, for a start. The Head of Chancellery got turned down on cost grounds for one only half as grand as what you've got.'

Charlie hoped it wouldn't cause any jealousy: insular, bundled-together embassies were breeding grounds for all sorts of irrational attitudes and envies. Remembering again his belief that Bowyer was watching and listening for London's benefit, Charlie said, 'I didn't think it would have worked for me to be in the compound.'

'Everything still needs to go through the embassy,' said Bowyer, at once.

Heavily, Charlie said, 'You're the conduit to London. I know that.'

'We're not going to fall out over territory,' said Bowyer, reassuring in return. He looked across the car again and grinned. 'You're on your own, Charlie.'

Which was always how he'd wanted it to be, reflected Charlie, responsible for no one except himself. The self-accusation came at once. An attitude he'd let wash over into his private life and made him lose Natalia. Ahead, the Moscow high-rises were coming into view. Was he *really* going to live – think of it as home – in a place that all his working life had been the focus of everything he'd had to oppose and undermine? Hard-headed reality at once blew away the whimsy. Only as long as he didn't fuck up, he reminded himself.

Somewhere in this towered city, he thought, Natalia was living. With their baby.

By coincidence the Russian who headed the Dolgoprudnaya cell in Berlin arrived at Sheremet'yevo just an hour after Charlie Muffin. The man was met in, too, personally by Stanislav Silin, who had decided their meeting could be best, and most discreetly, conducted during a meandering car ride around Moscow. They'd worked that way before, several times, so the man wasn't suprised by what otherwise might have seemed inexplicable courtesy.

'What was that lake business all about?' asked Silin.

'The obvious. Some cunt thinking he could get away with a con.'

'Who did it?'

'The word is that it was The Turk.'

The traffic slowed, near the Skhodnaya turn-off, and Silin looked briefly across at the other man. 'I thought he was our buyer?'

'He's anybody's buyer. He's Iraq's main middleman and they want everything they can get.'

Silin smiled. 'Good. I've got a spectacular deal.'

'How much?'

'Two hundred and fifty kilos.'

'What? You've got to be joking!'

'Guaranteed.'

'We haven't been able to get hold of more than maybe three and a half, four and a half at the most, in the last three years!'

Silin picked up the outer ring road, going north. 'Nearer five. Like I said, this is spectacular.'

Silin was conscious of the other man shaking his head. 'It can't be genuine.'

'It is. Can you sell it?'

'Of course I can sell it. There's a queue.'

He'd have to trust this man more than he was trusting anyone else apart from Marina, accepted Silin. But he'd done that already, agreeing to the way their own Swiss account was established. 'I've promised the suppliers $25,000,000, with $8,000,000 up front. They want it in Switzerland.'

'What are they selling, uranium or plutonium?'

'I don't know, not yet.'

'It doesn't matter if it's authentic, weapons-graded stuff.'

'What could we expect to get ourselves?'

The man shrugged. 'I've never tried to broker this much. I doubt even The Turk would take it all. Nothing of any size has come from anywhere for a long time; just the shit that got the German killed. So like I said, there's a queue.'

The motorway began its gradual curve eastwards. 'Just an estimate?' invited Silin.

'Seventy-five million. Could go as high as $100,000,000 if it's uranium 235.' The man shook his head again. 'I just can't believe it! It's incredible!'

'And there's more,' promised Silin.

'What's the Commission say?'

Silin snatched another sideways glance. That was an impertinent question, even from someone with the special relationship they had. So he'd heard something. Maybe even been approached. 'Sobelov's making a bid,' he announced, bluntly.

There was a movement as the man turned towards him, but he didn't immediately speak. Then he said, '*Because* of this?'

Silin shook his head. 'It's my negotiation, my contacts, like it always is.'

To their left the signs to Dolgoprudnaya, where they'd both been born and from which the Family got its name, began to appear; Silin had intentionally gone northwards, as a psychological reminder to the other man of their long-standing loyalty to each other.

'He's a fool, like he's always been! No one's going to follow him.'

'I think Bobin and Frolov are with him.'

'Where's their edge?'

'They don't have one. Just muscle. They want a war with the Chechen.'

The man snorted a laugh. 'What are you going to do?'

'Nothing, immediately. I don't want anything to interfere with this. When it's all sorted out – when you've made the deliveries – I'll make some changes.' Silin briefly considered taking the Dolgoprudnaya road instead of going in the opposite direction into Moscow but decided against it.

'This will bring a hell of a lot of heat if it works,'

predicted the man. 'There's been nothing this big before. Ever. This is a lot of complete bombs.'

'That's for the physicists,' shrugged Silin. Bluntly again, he said, 'You had any contact from here, apart from me?'

'No,' denied the man at once.

'Would you tell me, if you had?'

'How can you ask me that?' demanded the man, outraged. 'Aren't we *real* family! Cousins.'

'I can ask when I'm confronting a challenge,' said Silin. He could have been wrong about the impertinence of the Commission question. They *were* cousins.

'If I had been approached, I would have told you,' said the man, positively. 'I haven't been.'

'It's good to have someone I can rely on.'

'You always have been able to. And always will be. You know that.'

chapter 6

Never before, not even when she'd faced the official enquiry into Charlie's return to London, had Natalia needed the diamond-hard control necessary when her current lover announced the Moscow arrival of her previous lover she'd never expected to see or hear of again. But she managed it. Just. And not rigid-faced, which would have betrayed the effort, or with any shake to her hand or quaver in her voice. She even succeeded with the required indignation at their not having been consulted ahead of the Foreign Ministry agreement and promised to make a formal protest – which she later did, both for the record and because there *should* have been some discussion – at the discourtesy.

Paradoxically – in a situation of utter paradox – Natalia was actually helped to cover her inner confusion by the stunning unexpectedness of the announcement. Few of her daydreams had been like this, in the early months and years when she'd had fantasies and daydreams, before she'd locked Charlie Muffin away for ever in her memories. She'd expected a letter or a telephone call, a warning of some sort so she could prepare herself and have ready all the words and feelings and even the recriminations.

All of which she supposed she could still do.

Only the fact of Charlie's assignment was a shock. It hadn't been a personal, abrupt confrontation. She didn't think – she *knew* – she couldn't have handled that: the self-control was strained to the limit as it was. But now she could prepare herself, take everything at her speed, do everything as and how and when she wanted.

Did she want to meet him again, let him back into her life again as if all the hurt and pain had never happened? It had always been part of the day-dreaming that she did: that he would reappear and finally commit himself and that everything would have a happy ending, like the bedtime stories she told Sasha. But now the daydream could become a reality Natalia wasn't sure any more. Charlie Muffin was in the past. She was with Aleksai Semenovich now. He was everything that her drunken husband and then Charlie hadn't been and couldn't be. Aleksai wanted to marry her but never pressured her, prepared to wait on her terms and for her decision. In the meantime he was a gentle and exciting lover who'd never failed her, either in or out of bed, and who genuinely did treat Sasha as if she were his own: it seemed quite natural, to him and to the child, that it was Aleksai who often read the bedtime story with the happy ending.

'You should refuse to accept him,' urged Popov.

Natalia hesitated, her mind divided by too many considerations. There was not the slightest risk of any personal involvement between herself and Charlie ever being discovered. One of Natalia's first actions after her elevation to chairmanship of the First Chief Directorate of the now long-defunct KGB – from which she had been transferred to become one of four, department-specializing deputy directors in the reformed Interior Ministry – had been to use her authority to retrieve and sanitize of every personal detail both her and Charlie's files. And she probably could successfully protest even at this late stage to Charlie's Moscow posting. Except that it *was* a very late stage: any objection now would have to be supported with the sort of reasons she didn't want to present and which, years ago, she'd even obliterated from the records.

There was, however, no reason why she ever had to meet him. Inconceivable though it would be, she could simply avoid ever coming face to face with him. Unless, of course, she chose otherwise. She had the power and the position to do what she liked. She was a department head, so much higher above Charlie in stature and rank that if she didn't want it to happen, they could remain in the same city for the rest of their lives without ever coming into contact.

Forcing herself at last to answer Popov's question she said, 'We need to think carefully about that.' Not an answer, she told herself, ahead of Popov's reply. She was letting him make the decision for her instead of deciding for herself. But how could she decide for herself? She needed time to *think*, like she'd always believed she would have had time to think.

'OK, let's do just that,' he pressed. It was another indication of their familiarity that Popov moved freely about the office and didn't sit or stand respectfully in front of her. He was at the window now, staring out over Ulitza Zhitnaya at the summer-defying grey day cloaking Moscow.

'Where's our advantage, in arguing against his coming here?'

'He's a spy! We could make sure his being sent back became public and cause an outcry about our Foreign Ministry accepting him.'

'It's obviously a political decision, taken at a high level. They could overrule our objections. And would, to avoid embarrassing themselves. All we would have done is alienate the Foreign Ministry.'

'Don't you think you should protest?'

'Not like that.'

'Our not being consulted wasn't an oversight,' erupted Popov angrily, turning away from the window to look directly at Natalia. 'First America, now Britain. The acceptance of foreign interference is a direct criticism of us – of me, more than you because I'm operationally in charge of nuclear smuggling.'

Gently, not wanting to antagonize him, Natalia said, 'The fact is, darling, we haven't been able to stop it.'

'That's not our fault! We didn't create the nuclear shambles of no one knowing how much of anything was made, where it was stored or who's in charge of it! All we got is the mess.'

'How the shambles came about, and who caused it, is in the past,' said Natalia, still gently. '*I* know it's so bad that proper ballistic or warhead counts were never kept, let alone any record of manufacturing materials. And I keep telling anyone who'll listen, at every meeting I go to. But until we establish where and how big *all* the stockpiles are, stuff is going to keep disappearing and we're going to be the butt of every criticism here and in the West.' Go! she thought. Please leave me alone, in peace, to think! At once she became angry with herself. Aleksai didn't deserve to be dismissed, even if the dismissal was only in her head.

'So do I do anything about this? The memorandum came to me.'

'Not immediately,' said Natalia, making a decision at last. 'It's as much of a political as a practical operational decision. I don't want to take a stance until I know if there's any secondary thinking behind it. My initial feeling is that there is probably more benefit for us to accept him, like we had to accept the American, than to make any objection. Let them learn from their own man the chaos we inherited and are having to try to sort out.'

'I expect he'll ask for a meeting. The American did.'

'You're the operational controller,' reminded Natalia, quickly. 'You handle it.'

'Personally?'

'It would be the right thing, politically. Show the proper level of concern. Which *is*, after all, our level of concern.'

'It's still a criticism!' complained Popov, again. 'Particularly sending someone like him. They're sneering at us.'

Natalia hesitated again, halted by a renewed awareness of the near absurdity of the conversation. It was the sort of situation Charlie would have probably found hysterical, she thought, and wished at once that she hadn't because what would or wouldn't have amused Charlie Muffin wasn't a concern of hers any more. Her first concern, her only concern, was Sasha. And then Aleksai Semenovich. 'All the offences happened in the old days. That's all over, like the KGB's all over.'

'You know him. What's he like?'

Had she known him? She'd thought she had but she'd never expected Charlie to abandon her, like he had. So perhaps she hadn't known him at all. But then he'd always been the chameleon: it had been his strength, to disappear into a background by adopting the colours of his surroundings. So what *was* he like? Dishevelled, although that had been part of the disguise, like a walking haystack, with hair to match. Invariably walking carefully, on feet that hurt. Very pale blue eyes that saw everything and a mind that missed nothing. And . . . Abruptly Natalia stopped the mental reverie, discomfited by it. Answering Popov's question, she said, 'Difficult for me to remember. He was just one of many and it was a long time ago. Quite small in build. Disarming, in that it was easy to underestimate him . . .'

'But you beat him!'

Oh no I didn't, reflected Natalia. Charlie Muffin had fooled her, totally, like he'd fooled a lot of much higher officials in the KGB. And brought them down with his redefection. At least he hadn't abandoned her there. She'd actually emerged from the deception with her reputation enhanced sufficiently for the transfer to her present position to have been virtually automatic. 'Yes. I beat him.'

'We could put him under surveillance,' offered Popov.

Charlie would detect it in a moment, Natalia knew. 'His being here is a Foreign Ministry decision, not ours. Any embarrassment will be theirs, not ours. Let's just see how it develops.'

'You sure you don't want to be involved in seeing him, to give him a very obvious reminder that we know who he is?'

'Absolutely positive.'

Popov appeared about to continue the discussion, but abruptly said instead, 'Shall I see you tonight?'

'Not tonight.' The rejection was too quick as well as being unfair to him again. Like the thought that followed was unfair although bizarrely fitting: instead of refusing to spend any time with him that night Natalia would have liked to have Aleksai with her, her closest friend and confidant, someone with whom she could have talked everything through and let him know – too late though it was ever now going to be for him to know – who or what Charlie Muffin really was, to her. Why, oh why, had the bloody man reappeared?

'I've got things to do for the next few nights,' he warned.

'The weekend, then.'

'If the weather's good we could take Sasha on a river trip?' suggested Popov.

'She'd like that.'

'Tell her I love her.'

'Tell her yourself at the weekend.'

The parting conversation unsettled Natalia even more, piling complication upon complication. She *was* with Aleksai Semenovich now, in every way and in every respect apart from their not being officially married or actually living together permanently. What had happened with Charlie Muffin had happened way in the past. Which was where it belonged: in the past. He had no *right* to come back like this, upsetting everything and everyone! Upsetting her, confusing her most of all. No right to . . . to what? To Sasha? she thought, her reflection ricocheting off at a wild tangent. Sasha was hers. Not Aleksai's or Charlie's or anybody else's. Just hers. Charlie wasn't even registered as the father: Natalia had used her past KGB influence and importance to pass off Sasha's father as her loutish, whoring, long-abandoning husband whose cirrhosis-induced death had only just conveniently covered the timing of the pregnancy and the baby's birth, which was the only useful act the man had ever done for her in their ten years of totally neglectful and sometimes brutalizing marriage. And even then he'd been unaware of doing it.

But it did mean Charlie Muffin had no legally provable right to Sasha: no right to anything. It was insane for him to imagine he could contrive an unannounced return like this, as he clearly had contrived it, and expect her still to be patiently waiting. As insane as it was for her to try to rationalize it, as she had been trying to do.

There *was* no reason or necessity why she should ever meet him; she'd already determined that. No reason or necessity, either, why she *shouldn't* meet him, if a confrontational situation arose. She was sure she could handle it. Publicly? she asked herself at once. She wasn't sure about publicly, in front of other people, an audience. Aleksai particularly. Privately, then? She wasn't sure about that, either. In a lot of ways she was more unsure about encountering him privately than publicly. Maybe it *was* best if she avoided him altogether. Why, Charlie? she thought, despairingly. Why the fuck did you have to come back and ruin everything?

It was Charlie who'd taught her to swear, like he'd taught her many other things, and she remembered every one of them.

The Lesnaya apartment was far grander than Charlie had imagined it would be. He actually came close to being overwhelmed by it in the first few minutes after following Thomas Bowyer into the airstrip-sized entrance lobby and accepted at once he'd upset a lot of people at the embassy even before he got there. The living room was more of a reception salon, dominated by a huge Venetian mirror over an ornately carved mantelpiece, the cavorting cherub motif continued in the bas-relief of the corniced and moulded ceiling. His entire Vauxhall flat could have fitted into the main bedroom, with room to spare for dancing girls to give the cherubs a rest. As it was the three cardboard boxes containing his pitifully meagre possessions sat at the bottom of the canopied bed like mouse droppings. Major error, conceded Charlie: a posh place to live and a victory over the parsimonious Gerald Williams, but where he really had to live and work from now on was the embassy and by getting this apartment he'd built a resentment barrier he hadn't needed to erect.

'Good enough?' demanded Bowyer, the eyebrow lift confirming Charlie's apprehension.

'More than good enough.' Deciding on the need to make friends even with someone who'd probably report back to London before the end of the day, Charlie dumped his suitcases unopened and held up invitingly the Heathrow duty-free scotch, Macallan. He hadn't been able to get his preferred Islay single malt at London airport.

'Wonderful,' accepted the Scots station chief.

Charlie didn't believe the tumblers he found in the kitchen were crystal but they certainly looked like cut glass. He served it neat, knowing to add water or to attempt to find ice would offend Bowyer.

'Death to the enemy, whoever they are,' toasted Charlie, looking directly at the other man.

'May they show themselves quickly,' accepted Bowyer.

'Would you like a cigarette?' offered Charlie, continuing his role of host. 'I don't smoke but I brought some Marlboro in because I guess I'll need them.'

Bowyer frowned. 'Why, if you don't smoke?'

Charlie felt a burn of embarrassment. 'When I was here before, to hold up a packet of Marlboro was the guaranteed way to get a taxi.'

Bowyer held back the smirk, but only just. 'I've heard about it. It's one of the legends. You *have* been away a long time, haven't you?'

Charlie decided that whatever Bowyer told London he'd include that, just to make him look a prick. Which he had been, trying too hard to show how smart he was. Not an auspicious beginning, he decided.

John Fenby frowned across his desk at the head of his Scientific Division. 'She's a woman!'

The scientific head, Wilbur Benning, ached to remind the Director that females usually were. Instead he said, 'Hillary Jamieson is one of the most outstanding young physicists I've ever encountered. Frankly I'm surprised she's with us: she could take any one of a dozen jobs paying four times as much as she's getting at her current grade.'

'So why isn't she?' demanded Fenby, an unshakeable believer in conspiracy theories.

'No one knows why Hillary Jamieson does anything,' said Benning. 'She's a free spirit, doing whatever she wants to do because she knows she's too damned clever ever to have to worry about anything.'

'But is she a threat?'

You prick, thought the scientist. 'To what?'

Fenby, whose fears were kept chilled by the Cold War, blinked. 'Any operation she might be involved in.'

Benning was enjoying himself, building up stories to tell in the bar later. The frown was exaggerated, further to unsettle the

Director. 'She's a headquarters-based scientist, not a field operative.'

Defeated, Fenby said lamely, 'But is she good?'

'There's no one better.'

The change of attitude was palpable. The deference was back from everyone except Sobelov and his demeanour was obvious, too. The man was scared, panicking, not thinking before he spoke and looking more and more foolish with every argument he attempted.

'They can't guarantee that much!' Sobelov protested.

'They can. And they are. And there's a revised value. It could be worth as much as $100,000,000, in total.'

'It's a trap,' persisted the challenger.

'Not for us it isn't. And the way I'm organizing it you get your war with the Chechen. Except we don't have to get involved or distracted by it. We just make the money while other Families destroy each other, making fresh opportunities for us.'

'It's brilliant!' said Oleg Bobin, publicly changing sides. 'Absolutely brilliant.'

Silin let the silence stretch for as long as he felt able. Then, heavily, he said, 'So I have everyone's confidence? And agreement to conclude the negotiations?'

The assent was unanimous and immediate, from everyone except Sobelov. Relentlessly, Silin prompted, 'Sergei Petrovich?'

'We should be involved in the negotiations,' persisted the man.

'It's always been this way in the past.'

The fool's worst mistake so far, isolated Silin. 'To suggest a change would frighten them off, risk the entire deal. Does anyone want it done differently?'

No one spoke.

'You seem to be alone, Sergei Petrovich.' Which was how the man was going to stay from now on, thought Silin.

'Negotiations, yes,' finally conceded the man. 'But what about the details of the robbery itself?'

That would leak anyway, from what he had already initiated, Silin decided. Patiently he set out how the robbery was planned but made it sound as if it had all been his idea, not that of the others.

'Brilliant!' enthused Bobin again, when Silin finished. 'Absolutely and totally brilliant!'

'It's too complicated!' protested Sobelov.

'No, it isn't,' refused Silin, sure of himself. 'Complicated for other people but not for us. Because we'll be orchestrating everything.'

'It only wants one person to break.'

'They won't,' said Silin. 'They'll die if they do. After watching their families die in front of them.'

chapter 7

Charlie genuinely tried the new Hush Puppies, wanting his renaissance to be complete, but they hadn't sufficiently spread and hurt like a bugger after a few practice steps around his mausoleum apartment, so he'd put them back on the stretching shoe-trees. The existing blancmange pair destroyed the attempt with the new blue striped suit and the just-unwrapped shirt and the pristine tie, but it would have been destroyed totally by his hobbling about like someone tortured by the medieval Iron Boot.

A solicitous Thomas Bowyer greeted Charlie with a much-endangered solemn-faced enquiry about difficulty getting a taxi and Charlie resigned himself to the nonsense with the Marlboros already in mocking circulation. He'd never particularly minded people taking the piss out of him: it always put them at the disadvantage of imagined superiority.

Bowyer said the scientific briefing was fixed for that afternoon, which gave them time to tour the embassy and make all the necessary introductions first. Very quickly Charlie realized there was no one he could remember from his earlier Moscow episode any longer stationed at the river-bordering Morisa Toreza, which was hardly surprising because Moscow was a strictly regulated, two-year term appointment.

The tour began, obviously, at the intelligence *rezidentura*, which Charlie remembered but nevertheless went through the new-to-everything charade of the appropriate noises, until he got to the room Bowyer declared to be personally his. It was definitely smaller than the hutch he'd so briefly occupied at the new Embankment building and automatically Charlie looked to the window, which was spared any pigeon assault. It was covered instead with layer upon layer of Moscow street grime so thick Charlie estimated any available light was filtered by half. The dimly obscured but familiar view was of a blank wall.

'Don't expect you'll want to occupy it for any length of time,' said Bowyer, in lukewarm apology. 'Somewhere to store your stuff, really.'

'It'll do fine,' accepted Charlie. Its only use was what Bowyer suggested, a storeroom. But one with a difference, a place he didn't mind inquisitive people prying into: somewhere, in fact, in which to leave lying about titbits of information he might very much *want* transmitted back to London.

It was a confrontation of icy formality with the Head of Chancellery, Nigel Saxon. Charlie listened with polite assertiveness to the familiar lecture against embarrassing the embassy and at its end he dutifully reassured the grey-haired, disdainful man he had been fully briefed in London. Saxon announced he would be attending that afternoon's scientific guidance and Charlie wondered who was going to be the greatest embassy burden, Bowyer or the Head of Chancellery: it would probably be a close-run contest.

Paul Smythe appeared not to want to talk about anything else but Lesnaya. As well as being the housing officer, Smythe was responsible for the diplomatic concessionary facilities for which the man went to great lengths to accredit Charlie, all the time trying to draw Charlie out on why he'd been allowed such accommodation privilege. Charlie realized Smythe believed his being allowed Lesnaya indicated power and influence beyond what was obvious from the stated purpose of his being there and decided the apartment could be less of an encumbrance after all. Intentionally feeding grist into the rumour mill, Charlie carefully remained vaguely ambiguous to Smythe's most direct questions, conveying just the right degree of over-familiarity with upper-echelon London names.

The last of the necessary moving-in meetings was with the embassy's financial officer, Peter Potter. Once more, Charlie cultivated the impression of unspecified London influence, which was even easier than it had been with Smythe because Potter had already received from Gerald Williams the scale of allowances Charlie was to be permitted and which clearly overawed the local accountant. He assured Charlie there would never be any difficulty in advancing expenses in any currency Charlie required, in addition to dollars.

Bowyer insisted on being luncheon host in the embassy dining room, where there were several further introductions and where Charlie was conscious of a lot of curiosity-at-a-distance attention from other people whom he didn't officially meet.

'Seems to be pretty much general knowledge what I'm here for,' said Charlie. He'd chosen steak and decided the food was better than he remembered from his other visits.

'It *is* generally known,' agreed Bowyer. 'There was no security restriction put out by London. The embassy was openly informed of your coming – and why – the same time as I was.'

'How have you handled this nuclear business up to now?'

Bowyer shrugged, toying with his wine glass. 'Accepting what we were told by the authorities. There's no other way. Until your coming here we didn't even *have* a remit to become involved; I'm not sure that we have even now. Everything I've seen so far talks of liaison.'

The excuse of an ineffectual man, thought Charlie.

'What's the relationship with the Americans?'

There was another shrug. 'Good enough. At least there's a designated agent who gets fed stuff from Europe and the Middle East, from other FBI stations. Which gives him some weight to pressure the Russians into cooperation.'

From whom or from where was he going to be fed material with which to negotiate? wondered Charlie. Something to be sorted out in one of his first exchanges with London. 'May be a good idea to make early contact with the Americans.'

'They sent some stuff across addressed to you last night.'

And he'd been in the embassy for more than three hours without being told, calculated Charlie. 'What is it?'

'I don't know.'

Bollocks, thought Charlie. 'Despite which, you decided it could wait until now, without even telling me!'

Bowyer looked sharply across the table. 'If it had been anything urgent they would have telephoned. That's the system.'

'I think we should establish one of our own,' said Charlie, even-voiced but slowly, a man anxious to avoid misunderstanding. 'We already seem to have agreed I won't be spending a great deal of time in the embassy. So I think it's important for me to be told when anyone tries to make contact with me as *soon* as they try, don't you?'

Bowyer continued to hold Charlie's gaze but didn't immediately reply. Charlie hadn't anticipated the first disagreement being quite so soon. He hoped it didn't have to be referred to London for adjudication, but operational working logic was in his favour.

'Then you'll have to maintain daily contact, won't you?' said Bowyer, at last.

Bowyer *was* the senior officer, to whom he had to defer, so he had to be the supplicant. Charlie always found that difficult. 'Of course. I expect to. But I hope our relationship will be good enough for you, or someone in the department, to make it a proper two-way exchange and not dependent upon the approach always being from me. Because that *wouldn't* be a working relationship, would it? That would almost amount to obstruction.'

Bowyer swallowed heavily, out-manoeuvred. 'That's an absurd remark! Of course it will be properly two-way.'

Let the man have his indignation, Charlie decided. He'd won the exchange so there was nothing to be gained exacerbating it any further.

Charlie worked at small talk, letting the other man's irritation ebb, striving just as hard to infer the impression of undisclosed connections in London as he had begun earlier with the housing officer. And was successful, intrigued at how quickly Bowyer fell into the gossip trap. The man was not, decided Charlie, a very adept intelligence operative. Charlie ended the lunch in no doubt that whatever he left in his embassy office would be disseminated not just to London but to anyone who'd listen within the embassy.

Bowyer produced the American package as soon as they returned to his room – at the front, overlooking the tended gardens – and courteously offered Charlie first the photographs and then the written German analysis of why Gottfried Braun had been tortured to death. 'Whatever he did wrong he won't do again, will he?' judged Charlie.

Observing pecking order protocol, Charlie asked for the FBI station chief, not the named nuclear officer, when he telephoned the American embassy and was instantly connected to Barry Lyneham. After thanking the man for the German package, Charlie said, 'I thought I might drop by sometime personally to say hello.'

'What's wrong with this afternoon?' asked Lyneham at once, anxious for a possible restraining influence as soon as possible upon James Kestler.

'Four,' suggested Charlie.

'Just right for Happy Hour,' agreed the American.

The room adjoined Saxon's office. The Head of Chancellery was already there, reinforcing his authority, and getting more obvious deference from the crumpled, vaguely distracted Andrew Burton, who smiled in strange apology at being described as a scientific expert, rather than as the second official. Paul Scott wore a crisp check suit, regimental tie and a haircut Charlie had only ever seen in films about American marines. Charlie thought a cast of two hardly qualified as a scientific and military mission: perhaps the others were still buying souvenirs.

'We've delayed our return to London for this,' announced Scott, at once, in the over-loud voice of a man accustomed to stiff-backed respect from those he addressed. He looked with frowned disbelief at Charlie's shoes.

'That's very good of you,' said Charlie. Don't forget diplomacy, he told himself. He was buggered if he'd stand to attention, though. Uninvited, he sat in what looked to be the most comfortable chair at the side of Saxon's desk, conscious of the tight-faced exchange between the Chancellery Head and Bowyer.

'What, precisely, is it you want to know?' demanded Scott.

'What, precisely, the risks are from nuclear material being smuggled out of Russia,' said Charlie. He hadn't intended to sound that mocking.

Scott hesitated. 'I would have thought that was obvious.'

Charlie felt a stir of impatience. 'If entire bombs are being sold to the highest bidder, the risk is obvious. If it's components that have to be assembled, it would be helpful to know what those components are and how much is needed and your impression of the extent of the trade, if any, you've come to believe exists as the result of your investigations.'

'Colonel Scott's report is restricted for the Cabinet,' intruded Saxon.

'I'm not asking for Colonel Scott's report,' sighed Charlie. 'I'm asking for his impressions. For which the mission's return to London was delayed *on* London's instructions, for me to be told.' If this was the way it was going to be, working in the embassy really was going to be impossible, thought Charlie, catching the second tight-faced understanding between Saxon and Bowyer.

'We were taken to several installations in and around Gorkiy,' recounted Scott, stiffly. 'In my opinion the security was excellent. The Russian officials who accompanied us admitted they suspected isolated thefts of small amounts of nuclear material in the past but stressed the majority had been from the republics that once made up the Soviet Union, not from Russia itself.'

So the Cabinet and whoever else was on the mailing list were going to get a load of crap, judged Charlie. Which didn't make this encounter at all a waste of time. He had his first report – a warning not to believe a word of Scott's official account – for the Director-General and he'd only been in Moscow a few hours. Turning hopefully to the second man, Charlie said, 'Let's talk about amounts and the danger they represent.'

The smile this time was gratitude, at being included. 'What

do you know about nuclear physics?' asked Burton, innocently.

'Actually, not a lot,' admitted Charlie.

'The explosive of a nuclear weapon is either uranium 235 or plutonium 239. Plutonium is actually created *from* uranium,' said the man, settling back in his chair. 'There's two ways it can be exploded. It's either surrounded by a tamper like beryllium oxide, which reflects neutrons and causes them to multiply when they're compressed into what's called a critical mass. Or two subcritical sections are driven together by what's called a gun-barrel arrangement. Either splits the atom, creating a chain reaction of more and more split atoms, which releases an incredible amount of nuclear energy.'

Scott, who'd obviously heard the lecture before, looked bored. Saxon sighed, equally unimpressed. Assholes, thought Charlie. 'What's the effect?' he coaxed. 'How many people can die?'

'There's only been two practical examples, Hiroshima and Nagasaki,' reminded Burton. 'Hiroshima used uranium, exploded by the gun-barrel method. 80,000 people died and 70,000 were injured. Nagasaki used plutonium, with a beryllium tamper. That killed 40,000 people and wounded 25,000.' The man hesitated. 'They were tests, you understand? To see which method was the more effective.'

No one was looking bored any more.

'How much uranium or plutonium is needed for bombs like that?'

'Technologies have greatly improved since 1945,' said the physicist. 'But below a certain amount there's neutron leakage which reduces the effectiveness. The generally accepted critical mass is around five kilos.'

'Five kilos of uranium can kill 80,000 and five kilos of plutonium can kill 40,000 people!' pressed Charlie, pedantically, determined totally to understand.

'At least,' confirmed the expert.

Charlie looked between the soldier and the scientist, momentarily – rarely – without words. One was a silly bugger who'd let himself be conned everything was safely under lock and key and the other existed in such a rarified atmosphere of pure physics that 80,000 and 40,000 were statistics, not death tolls, and who didn't realize the obscenity of describing the difference as tests of effectiveness.

'But the smuggling attempts – even what's actually been seized in transit in the West – aren't in kilos,' offered Burton, helpfully. 'The amounts have been far smaller.'

'What's to stop small amounts being stockpiled to make up an amount sufficient for a bomb if they're all bought by the same person or country?' demanded Charlie.

'Nothing at all,' admitted the man.

Scott cleared his throat, the prelude to a pronouncement, and said to Charlie; 'In view of what I understand your posting to be, you're probably already aware of discussions between countries within the European Union to create a Star Wars protection against some countries in the Middle East?'

Discerning the tone in the other man's voice, Charlie said, 'Which you don't think necessary, after your investigation here?'

'For God's sake man, it would cost £20 billion!'

As they walked to the entrance of the embassy, Bowyer said, 'I thought that was interesting, didn't you?'

Charlie looked quizzically at the station head. 'It frightened the shit out of me.'

Charlie felt instant empathy with Barry Lyneham, guessing at once he wouldn't have to go through any getting-to-know-you bullshit because he was sure he knew the man already. He put Lyneham around 55, although maybe a little older, because Lyneham had clearly stopped worrying about inflicting personal damage upon himself. His belly bulged over the lost waistband of his trousers, presumably supported by an equally lost belt and the shirt collar was loosened for comfort or even by necessity. Lyneham's face, particularly around his nose, was reddened from finishing too many bottles before too many evenings had ended and Charlie wasn't sure if the wheezing was caused by excess weight or asthma: probably a combination of both. The words, when they came, hinted the deep south birth and were never hurried anyway and Charlie was quite sure the pouched eyes saw everything, just like he was sure the man heard everything, even the words that *weren't* spoken, an operational trick instinctive to their craft. Barry Lyneham was an old timer who'd been there and done it and didn't need telling how to do it again. After the morning with Thomas Bowyer and the technical session that had followed it was refreshing to be with someone with whom he could relax but at the same time take seriously, confident he was on the same wavelength.

They went comfortably through the low foothill pleasantries of agreeing Russia was a bigger mess now than it had been under communism and would probably take years if not decades to get right and in the meantime it was causing a hell of a lot of people a hell of a lot of worry.

'Nuclear shit top of the list,' said Lyneham, starting the ascent to what mattered.

'I'd welcome whatever steer you can give to me.' He was in Lyneham's territory, where it was polite to appear at least to defer, but after what he'd already listened to he wanted some balancing, rational judgment. He was curious at the absence of James Kestler, but that, too, was Lyneham's decision.

'Total fucking disaster. Crime's king here, right? This is Capone country, reincarnated. You want anything, you get it from organized crime. The only way. It was always the way in the old days. Now nobody bothers to pretend any more. Yeltsin and all the others made all the right sounds and let the Bureau come here officially and now they've let you come and it doesn't add up to a row of beans. This country was so fucked up, lying about production norms and meeting quotas, that they don't even *know* what nuclear stuff they had in the first place so they sure as hell don't know what's gone or going missing.' Lyneham had to pause, to recover his breath after such a concerted diatribe. To cover his difficulty, he took a bottle of Jim Beam from a lower drawer and Charlie nodded acceptance although hardly expecting the tumbler to be half filled. 'Forgetting my manners by taking so long,' apologized the American.

More with which to doubt Scott's report, in his first account to London, Charlie recognized. 'How are we supposed to *operate*?' demanded Charlie.

'You find out, you let me know,' suggested Lyneham. 'You were warned in London about jurisdiction and protocol?'

'Endlessly,' confirmed Charlie. The whisky was very different from Islay or Macallan but was an interesting change.

'We *can't* operate, not properly. We've no effective investigatory facilities and no right to employ them even if we had. I've actually advised Washington how we're being suckered but it makes political sense for us to be officially recognized and based here so no one wants to hear it's all a heap of shit.' Lyneham's protest had been one of his first attempts at a defence against failure.

'Suckered?' queried Charlie.

'Liaison, right? Which in my book means a two-way trade. Not, apparently, in their dictionary. We get virtually *nothing* from the Russians. But they expect us to keep feeding them with everything we pick up in Europe and the Middle East. Which is the ass-about way of trying to do anything; by the time we pick up anything outside, that's where it is, outside and lost.'

'What about working backwards to prevent it happening again?'

Lyneham exploded into jeering laughter, adding to both their glasses. 'You're not listening, Charlie! The nuclear business is mafia business. And by mafia I *mean* Mafia: as organized and powerful as anything in Italy or what we've got in America. Bigger, maybe. We know – from Italy and from America, again not from here – they've even established working links, one between the other. And organized crime buys police and militia and anything else it wants to buy. Always has done. Always will.'

'The corruption can't be *that* complete!' Perhaps that was why there wasn't any trace of Natalia. She wouldn't have been bought.

'Not at the top, maybe,' conceded Lyneham, although doubtfully. 'But the top people don't go out kicking in doors and putting up road blocks around nuclear installations. It's the middle-ranking and operational people who do that, people like us, and in Russia those guys are as dirty as hell, believe me.'

Charlie did and was unsettled by it. Rupert Dean and the others who'd briefed him in London expected more than that, like he did himself. And if London weren't satisfied, they'd made it brutally clear he didn't have a job any more. With such an easily presented opportunity Charlie said, 'So why was Kestler specifically appointed: just part of the same empty politicking?'

Lyneham's within-seconds reaction was confusing and, having already decided upon the American's experience, Charlie wasn't completely sure whether it was genuine or feigned. 'Washington advised it was a *specific* appointment?' It wouldn't be right to talk about Kestler's favoured relationship back home in Washington: he didn't know the Englishman well enough yet.

'Yes.' Hardly the tell-me-more remark of the century, Charlie conceded to himself. But it would have to do.

'*That* was political.'

Charlie missed the point but didn't want to say or do anything to hint his disadvantage: hiding disadvantages was one of the most inviolable of all personal Charlie Muffin survival rules. 'So we're just going through the empty motions, like mentally screwing every girl with big tits we pass in the street?'

Lyneham smiled, lasciviously. 'I like that! Some day I'll use that as my own!'

Charlie was almost offended at the weak, avoidance-attempting flattery: he'd thought the other man better than that. 'So what's the answer?'

'Jamie's very keen. Superman role model, know what I mean?'

Charlie believed he did but he felt there was a message or a reason beyond the obvious. He tried to put himself into Lyneham's position, unsure if the tentative deduction was a flickering spark or a shining light at the end of the tunnel: close-to-weary old career man bothered by unpredictability of anything-but-weary young career man. Too early and too unsubstantiated to be considered seriously but something to be borne in mind. At this early stage there were other more important things that had priority. Charlie knew nothing was going to be easy – there was every eventual chance of this being the most difficult operation in a long and mostly difficult operational life – but he remained disoriented by the ease of things so far. Charlie decided that if he didn't more forcefully set the pace he risked Lyneham believing, figuratively at least, that he was as lightweight as Bowyer. 'Embarrassed by him?'

The remark brought the American forward over his whiskey glass, as Charlie hoped it would. 'What the hell does that mean?'

'Thought I would have met him at the same time as you,' said Charlie, accepting there were a hundred escapes for Lyneham to take. None of which the man did, which further intrigued Charlie.

'Wanted us to meet first,' said the Bureau chief, too simply.

For *what*, precisely, wondered Charlie. Aloud he said, 'I've appreciated that, too.'

'Keep in mind what I've said.'

'I will.'

James Kestler responded to his superior's summons as if he had been waiting on the other side of the door, entering the room as if there were some sort of spring device in his heels to enable him to move faster. Had he ever been as eager as this crop-haired, shiny-faced, bejeaned young man, wondered Charlie. He would have liked to think so but he doubted it. Charlie endured the pump-armed handshake and the repeated although slightly varied assurance they were going to be a good combination (a partnership Kestler appeared to believe already more definitely established than Charlie did, although there was still too much to be gained to dispute it) and the concluding demand to admit he saw himself at the very forefront against the most dangerous criminal activity currently being conducted by organized crime, not just in Russia but throughout the world. Kestler called it being at the cutting edge. Charlie said he supposed that's how he did see it, yes, not wanting to bruise the younger man's enthusiasm. Kestler stressed they had a lot to talk about and a lot to plan and a lot to accomplish and Charlie agreed with all of that, as well, because all of it was true. Throughout, Barry Lyneham sat overflowing his inadequate office chair, saying nothing and doing nothing but add occasionally to his and Charlie's bourbon glass. There'd been no offer to Kestler, from which Charlie guessed that Kestler didn't drink. The repeated gratitude at the German information, which had been officially delivered under Kestler's name, brought a renewed flurry of eager guidance from Kestler that there were as many con men in the nuclear business as there were traders with insider access. 'That's what Braun was, a punk.'

'I read the German file,' promised Charlie.

'It's the excuse the Russians use all the time,' intruded Lyneham. 'They say most of what we give them from outside turns out to be a set-up to con the guys with the big bucks in the Middle East or wherever.'

Charlie waited patiently until Kestler had virtually exhausted himself before asking for a contacts list at the Interior Ministry. The American file was far more extensive than that which Bowyer had produced, but Natalia's name still did not feature anywhere.

'I need to meet the right man,' said Charlie, unsuccessfully scanning the names for a second time and feeling he had to give a reason for the request in the first place.

'Aleksai Semenovich Popov,' identified Kestler at once, jabbing at the list. 'Operational head of the anti-nuclear smuggling division, with the official rank of colonel. Nice guy. Makes time *any* time.'

Which Popov did, agreeing to a meeting when, at Lyneham's suggestion, Charlie telephoned the Interior Ministry from the Bureau chief's office. Charlie's satisfaction was punctured at once when Lyneham said, 'Don't think everything's going to be as simple, Charlie. He's probably got nothing better to do.'

Nothing was going to be simple, Charlie accepted objectively in the taxi carrying him back to Lesnaya. He hadn't even started yet and if Lyneham was to be believed he was going to be bloody lucky if he was ever going *to* start properly. But it had been a good beginning, apart from the expectable embassy friction. And that was nothing he couldn't handle. The only disappointment so far, in fact, had been his inability to find Natalia. And if he was going to be sensibly objective, it had been ridiculous for him to expect to locate her so soon. If ever.

Back in the embassy, Lyneham said, 'Well?'

'Superfluous to requirements, put out to pasture,' assessed Kestler, in youthful instant judgment.

'Sure about that?' asked Lyneham, who wasn't sure himself but who hadn't been as impressed as he'd hoped to be. 'Don't forget that past record.'

'Trust me,' said Kestler.

I wouldn't trust your judgment if you had a beard and your name was Moses, thought Lyneham.

'When?' demanded Natalia.

'Tomorrow. He said he was calling from the American embassy. Obviously it's going virtually to be a joint operation,' judged Popov.

'It makes sense.'

'His Russian wasn't very good, but at least he tried. Which is more than the American did at first. We ended up with English, though.'

Charlie's Russian had been excellent, remembered Natalia, virtually fluent even in his use of colloquialisms. He'd obviously lost it through lack of use, like she'd probably lost a lot of her English, although she and Aleksai amused themselves sometimes, practising together. 'What did he say?'

'Just that he wanted to introduce himself.'

'Our not being told in advance of his arrival *was* a political criticism,' declared Natalia, positively, less distracted by personal intrusion than she had been before and therefore thinking more clearly. 'And there will be more, unless we manage something soon. Show him every consideration.

And make sure he knows he's getting it. I don't want any more complaints than we can avoid between here and London.'

'*Every* consideration?' queried the reluctant Popov.

'Give the impression of cooperating.' Natalia no longer wanted to be alone to think, as she had when she'd first learned of Charlie's arrival. The opposite, in fact. 'You said you were busy tonight?'

'Dinner with our regional commander, from the northeast. I don't think I should consider rearranging it; I'm not sure how long he's going to be here.'

'Of course you shouldn't rearrange it,' accepted Natalia.

'Maybe you should come?'

'Too late to arrange anything for Sasha.'

'What about the Englishman? Still sure you don't want to meet him?'

'No!' said Natalia, too loudly.

'What's the matter?' asked the man.

'Nothing.'

'There'll be a lot to talk about tomorrow.'

How much would there be of what she wanted to hear, wondered Natalia.

'A confirmed $100,000,000!' queried a staggered Frolov.

'Deposits already lodged, from every purchaser,' confirmed the Dolgoprudnaya boss of bosses.

'And there's no problem at the plant?'

'They're terrified. Doing exactly what they're told, when they're told, how they're told.'

There was a movement from Sobelov, the look for acquiescence before the man stood. Unasked, he poured drinks and put them before everyone and then raised his own glass. 'I think Stanislav Georgevich is to be congratulated,' toasted the man. 'I have questioned this because I doubted it could work. I no longer have any doubts. So I apologize and pledge my full support.'

Everyone drank and Silin briefly lowered his head in

appreciation. If the bastard thought that was going to save him he was an even bigger fool than he'd so far shown himself to be.

chapter 8

Charlie, who was not normally given to such impressions, thought Aleksai Popov was probably one of the most dramatic-looking men he'd ever met. The person who strode across the high-ceilinged baroque office of the Interior Ministry to meet him was tall, well over six feet, model-immaculate in a dove-grey suit accentuating the slope from broad shoulders to blade-thin waist. The height and the obvious athleticism and the autocratic way the man held himself would have been sufficient to make him outstanding in most surroundings, but it was his facial appearance that was most striking. Popov's deeply black hair ran into a very full but whisker-trim beard, fashioned into a definitive wedge, creating a startling similarity with all the photographs Charlie had ever seen of the last Tsar. The handshake was firm without being bone-crushing, the cologne subdued, and Charlie thought it was probably difficult for Popov to walk down a street without being tripped up by women eager to fall underneath him.

The simmering samovar was a nice traditional touch, although Charlie guessed the clear liquid in the close-by decanter to be alternative-choice vodka, and the chairs arranged without an intervening desk showed forethought, as well. Charlie was tempted, but he was enjoying the impression-making routine so he chose tea. Popov took vodka.

It was Popov who suggested they use English ('there will be many other meetings; we can alternate, each to practise upon the other') and they moved smoothly through the friends-and-colleagues preliminaries.

'The West is clearly becoming impatient,' suggested Popov, concentrating Charlie's full attention.

'Concerned,' qualified Charlie, diplomatically. 'The enormous problems you face aren't yours alone: they're international.'

'I'd like to think that was completely true,' said Popov. 'Our greatest problem is being judged by the efficiency and expertise of American and English law enforcement. And we don't have either.'

Charlie wasn't sure America or England had it, either. Or that misjudgment *was* Russia's greatest problem. 'Every reason, then, for us to cooperate as closely as possible.'

'The system has worked well with America. Your additional help will be appreciated.'

Charlie discerned the danger of the earlier cliché ping-pong. Despite Popov's indication of easy access, Charlie wasn't sure how easy it would really be to meet the Russian with any regularity and didn't intend wasting this or any other chance. '*Has* the system worked well?'

'Isn't it the opinion of London, and perhaps Washington as well, that it has? Or is doing?'

Jumpy, thought Charlie, recognizing yet again the sort of opening that had been falling at his feet ever since he'd stepped off the plane. 'I know from meeting the Americans here what their input is, from outside Russia. As I have already told you, mine will hopefully be on a similar scale, from what I receive from London . . .'

'. . . Which isn't matched in return by what we are providing from our side?' interrupted Popov, which was why Charlie had hesitated, hoping for just such a reaction.

I didn't say it, you did, thought Charlie. Which meant the Russians knew it already, were worried about it already, and that probably Popov, as the man in charge, realized his ass could be in a sling. And was therefore the most worried of all. 'A conclusive investigation, here in Russia, would reassure a lot of people.' Particularly certain people in London and keep me in a job. Charlie didn't understand the suggestion of a smile that briefly touched Popov's bearded face.

'Investigations *are* being carried out,' insisted the Russian. 'Several, in fact. Many in the past have proved to be *in*conclusive: criminals cheating other criminals.'

Charlie said, 'I'm aware of that side of the business. So are London. And Washington. But that's something quite different: it doesn't create the threat we're here to discuss. I can't, of course, speak for the Americans, but I believe my appointment is made with the expectation of even closer, mutual cooperation.'

Instead of responding at once Popov offered more tea but saw Charlie's eye on the vodka decanter and switched the invitation, which Charlie accepted. Charlie decided the drink-at-every-stop innovation was another example of how well his luck was holding. As he handed Charlie the glass, Popov said, 'Are you suggesting the *active* participation of yourself and the Americans?'

The tea-or-vodka delay had been intentional, for the man mentally to prepare the legally valid rejection, assessed Charlie. But it hadn't been prepared sufficiently. 'I'm very aware I have no legal jurisdiction here. So I don't see how we could actively participate throughout an entire investigation. It would be impractical as well as impossible from a manpower standpoint alone.'

Popov frowned, disappointed at being anticipated. 'What then?'

'You must understand this is a personal view,' said Charlie, in a voice carefully modulated to hint it went far beyond. 'But I wonder if it wouldn't be interpreted abroad, reassure a lot of people abroad, as just the sort of equally balanced cooperation if there was *invited* involvement towards the end of an investigation already established to be a genuine case of nuclear smuggling.' Charlie hoped his good fortune so far hadn't made him over-confident.

'It's a suggestion that hasn't been considered,' admitted the Russian.

'But perhaps one worth examining?' Lack of legal

jurisdiction could as easily have been invoked now as before and Charlie was intrigued the other man didn't use it. Maybe Popov hadn't intended rejection after all.

'I could discuss it,' offered Popov.

With whom? seized Charlie. His satisfaction at the apparent unqualified success he'd so far encountered was close to being outweighed by his disappointment at not finding any trace of Natalia. Which went against every sort of logic, reality and even the plain common sense by which Charlie normally operated. He'd hardly been in Moscow five minutes, done scarcely more than begin basically to establish himself, and here he was maintaining infantile delusions about a woman he'd earlier decided, with the hard-headed objectivity he seemed incapable of maintaining for very long, probably listed him as the shit of this or any other century. Pull yourself together! he thought, angrily. Buggering up by accident was all right, but buggering up when it could be avoided didn't make any sense. 'I appreciate your seeing me personally. And so quickly. With whom, and how, should I liaise in the future?'

Popov appeared surprised. 'With me, of course!'

Charlie *was* surprised. For him to have been received by the colonel in operational charge of the specific Interior Ministry division was an act of extreme courtesy; for the man to put himself forward as the day-to-day contact was the most positive proof of how concerned the Russians were about nuclear banditry. 'That would ensure the fastest possible reaction to what either has to tell the other.'

'Which is surely the first essential?' suggested Popov.

'Absolutely.' Would Kestler have reached the same understanding?

'This has been an extremely useful and fruitful first meeting.'

Back to verbal ping-pong, accepted Charlie. To attempt anything further would be trying too hard too soon. 'I hope so. Leading, I hope, to greater involvement.'

'It will be discussed,' promised Popov. 'We'll talk soon.'

Again, the earlier inexplicable smile wisped across the Russian's face.

'I'll call you,' suggested Charlie.

'No,' refused Popov. 'I'll call you.'

Working upon the well-established bureaucratic principle that bullshit baffled brains and that paperwork was the mile-high bullshit of bureaucracy, it took Charlie a long time setting out everything in his first report to London, reflecting as he did so that a lot of it wasn't even bullshit.

'I totally disagree with your interpretation of the meeting with Colonel Scott,' protested Bowyer, after it had all been transmitted.

'You're not in any way linked to the opinion,' Charlie pointed out. 'It's all down to me.'

'It reflects upon the embassy!'

Charlie guessed the station chief could hardly wait to scuttle along the corridor to Saxon. He'd have to devise some way of communicating with London without Bowyer having access to the traffic. 'I'm doing my job. It doesn't reflect upon the embassy at all.'

'Do you believe the Americans share what they get from outside?'

'They told me they did. That's why they're pissed off, getting nothing in return.'

There was a slight frown at what Bowyer considered an obscenity. 'You really think there's the slightest chance of your being included at the tail-end of a genuine investigation?'

'No,' admitted Charlie, honestly. 'But there wasn't any harm in trying, was there?'

'So it's not as good as it looks on paper . . . rather a lot of paper?'

Fuck you, thought Charlie. 'Why don't we wait and see?'

It was an empty response but Bowyer wouldn't know that. Would the sneaky bastard risk a direct intervention to London or leave it to Saxon?

Back at the Interior Ministry Aleksai Popov was coming to the end of his detailed account of his meeting with Charlie

Muffin. 'An unusual person. Certainly much cleverer than the American but then he's much older . . .' A man so obviously sartorially aware, Popov paused. '. . . Personally quite smart but with the strangest shoes.'

Natalia didn't need to be told what Charlie had looked like.

She'd watched unseen from the corridor recess no longer containing the Lenin bust just outside her office door as Charlie had been escorted to Popov's door. Although it was obviously Charlie, the crispness of the suit had surprised her, because he'd never dressed like that when she'd known him. But she'd recognized at once the puddled shoes and the eyes-missing-nothing head movement, actually jerking further into the recess in momentary fear he'd see her.

It hadn't been at all like she'd expected. There'd been the stomach lurch, the hollowness, and the slight tingling at the unreality of it all. But it hadn't been as bad as she'd feared. She hadn't been overwhelmed by any emotion, confused beyond being able to watch and think quite dispassionately. In fact 'dispassionate' perfectly summed up the way she'd felt, seeing again the father of her child and the man whom she'd once thought she loved. She no longer had any doubt about any difficulty in meeting him again, face to face. Not that she intended to. At that moment she was sure it didn't matter to her whether or not she ever met Charlie Muffin again. 'You don't have any doubt about the impatience, from both London and Washington?'

Popov smiled. 'I haven't told you yet about last night's meeting with our regional commander.'

The FBI Lear jet carried John Fenby to England and the fact that the Connaught was so close to the American embassy in Grosvenor Square was more than sufficient reason for his staying at what he justifiably considered the best hotel in London. He regarded the restaurant as the best, too, which was why he chose it for his lunch with Rupert Dean.

The British Director-General arrived politely ahead of time but Fenby, as always, was already waiting, the carefully chosen window table in the most discreet corner: he would have liked more distance between himself and the other tables but wasn't well enough known to get it, like he was at the Four Seasons. It was their first personal meeting, an assessment-for-the-future encounter.

Fenby had, of course, had a check run on Dean and knew the academic background and considered it unfitting for the position the man now occupied. But that was a British problem, not his. Rather, it was his advantage. He'd already decided how to use the British appointment in more than one way, which was why he'd so strongly supported it, and knew Dean was too naive ever to realize how he was being manipulated. There was, of course, no way that Peter Johnson could know, either, but Fenby knew the British deputy would understand. He and Johnson understood each other, like the professionals they were. If he invoked the insurance he had so carefully established, it was even possible Dean would be destroyed, in which case it was more than likely Johnson would get the appointment that should have been his in the first place. Fenby hoped it happened: Johnson was the sort of man he could work with.

Rupert Dean had had an identical check run on John Fenby and knew not just the legal history of the New York circuit judge but the rumoured determination to create another Bureau legend. Dean found it easy to imagine the pleasure the surprisingly small, blinking-eyed man would have attained jailing people for life and wondered if he didn't miss that particular power. He supposed Fenby had sufficient at the FBI to compensate.

Fenby was solicitous over the menu and suggested Dean order whatever wine he wanted, because he didn't drink, which was something else Dean knew and wasn't surprised about. Without consulting the wine list Dean asked the sommelier for a 1962 Margaux if it was available and when Fenby wondered if there'd be half bottles Dean said he wasn't thinking of a half bottle. There was a '62 and it was as good as Dean knew it would be. He savoured it even more than he savoured the American's disapproval of his excess.

‘Your man seems to have achieved a lot in a short time,’ opened the American.

‘He’s very experienced,’ said Dean, who as a bridge-building courtesy and at Johnson’s suggestion, had earlier that morning sent Charlie’s overnight reports to the Bureau office at the nearby embassy.

‘Unconventional,’ suggested Fenby. He’d already decided to have the possible operational concession achieved by the Englishman recorded on FBI files as James Kestler’s success. And to tell Fitzjohn as soon as he got back to Washington.

‘It’s an unconventional position.’ Dean had found the other man’s remark curious.

‘I’m keen for us to work as a team: I’ve told my people in Moscow.’ Because by having the Englishman associated at all times, it achieved the all-important function of keeping dirt off my doorstep, he thought, smugly. As well as protecting James Kestler from being shown as the run-at-anything operator he was worryingly turning out to be.

‘I think that’s probably a good arrangement.’ Dean decided he didn’t like the American. It had been necessary to work with him to achieve the department posting to Moscow but Dean had no intention of making a friend, or even an acquaintance, of the other Director.

They stopped talking while the meal was served. Dean had chosen confit of duck and accepted mashed potatoes, as well as sauce thickened with stock and wine. Fenby had cold meats and a plain green side salad, without dressing.

‘But we’re going to have to be very careful,’ condescended Fenby, actually preparing his ground. ‘That’s why your choice of operative surprised me.’

‘That’s his usefulness,’ said Dean. ‘He surprises people.’

chapter 9

'He's sure?'

'Of course he's not sure! How can he be?'

Natalia wished Aleksai hadn't been so brusque. 'Give me some idea!' she demanded, matching his impatience.

'He's sure it isn't a confidence trick,' allowed Popov. 'Oskin's had enough of those to recognize each and every sign. This time the approach has been made to the security head of a nuclear site about five kilometres outside Kirov: the nearest township of any size is Kirs. It's one of the installations we already know kept inaccurate records, to inflate their production norms.'

'What isn't he sure of?'

'Carrying out a proper investigation. There's still too much we don't know: too much that could go wrong.'

'Tell me about Oskin! How reliable is he?' Natalia's concentration had switched almost entirely from her deputy's meeting with Charlie, although he remained a peripheral part of what she and Popov were now discussing. On the surface, Russia's acceptance of yet another foreign investigator was the outward proof to the West of Moscow's enforcement commitment. Hidden beneath the surface from everyone except herself was what Natalia interpreted as a very clear and personal warning. If there was not soon some visible success to be trumpeted abroad, Natalia guessed the next political move – equally for foreign consumption – would be her very public replacement. Natalia's primary concern was not for herself. It would be impossible for her ever to get another privileged government job, probably any worthwhile job at all. Which endangered Sasha. Although she knew it was premature and unprofessional, Natalia felt the excitement surge through her at even the vaguest possibility of mounting an operation: of doing *something* at last! And it wasn't just excitement. There was a lot of relief mixed with it, which was equally premature and unprofessional.

'Nikolai Ivanovich Oskin is totally reliable,' assured Popov. 'He worked here at headquarters, as a regional supervisor before I appointed him the actual regional commander. And I did that because I was sure I could trust him.'

'You talked of false alarms before?'

'*Scams*, before,' qualified Popov. He got up from the chair in Natalia's office to move to his favourite spot, near the window overlooking the Ulitza Zhitnaya. Only half turned to Natalia, the man went on, 'Which goes even further to show his reliability. He waits, until he's sure. That's why he'd held back from alerting us to situations in the past that have turned out to have been deception, between crooks. He doesn't, he *won't*, cry wolf.'

Natalia felt a further stir of excitement. 'How much do we know about this new affair?'

'Oskin doubts the security in his office,' said Popov. 'So he moves around, making spot visits, a lot of them unannounced. He's established informants in the plants he's responsible for. At the Kirs site it's the head of security himself. He's a former Militia lieutenant: name's Lvov. Two weeks ago Oskin made one of his surprise visits. Lvov almost burst into tears with relief. He'd been approached by the Mafia. And told that if he doesn't cooperate, his wife and daughters will be killed. If he does what they want he gets $50,000 in cash . . .'

'Which Family?' demanded Natalia.

'No names, not yet,' said Popov. 'Lvov had been too nervous even to try to get a message through to Oskin: that's why he was so relieved when Oskin turned up. Lvov says his depot office is Mafia infiltrated and that any phone call or message would be intercepted. And his family would die . . .' Popov turned back in the office. '. . . That's why Oskin came down personally, rather than telephone or write to me. Lvov also told him our Kirov regional offices leak like sieves.'

'Does Oskin *really* believe that?' Natalia had no illusions about the extent of organized crime in Russia but she was genuinely shocked at the thought that the very departments formed to combat it might be so dominated.

'He's taking precautions. You saw those photographs, from Germany. Like all the others we've seen, from too many other places. He doesn't have any less doubt than Lvov that the people who've made this approach would kill the man's family. Probably in some obscene way like all the other killings.'

'If Lvov is this frightened, why did he tell Oskin? Why didn't he take the $50,000? That's surely what anybody would have done, frightened or otherwise!'

Popov smiled, but sadly. 'That was the first question Oskin asked him. Lvov said he would have done – *wanted* to – but he didn't believe he'd get the money: it's too much *to* believe, anyway. Like the amount they want is too much to believe.'

Natalia waited, irritated Popov didn't continue. Finally she said, 'I don't understand.'

'They've said they want two hundred and fifty kilos. The fact that they know there is at least that much convinced Lvov of the extent of their access inside the plant. He's also convinced they'll kill anyone peripherally involved who might talk under investigation. Which would mean him. The only way the poor bastard thinks he's got a chance is to run to us.'

Now it was Natalia's turn to get up, needing to move around. As she passed Popov she automatically trailed her hand along the back of his shoulders. 'Two hundred and fifty kilos of what?'

'I don't know, exactly. Enriched plutonium? Cassium? Uranium?'

'Sufficient for an *entire* bomb!' It was difficult for Natalia to contemplate.

'Probably several,' agreed Popov, far less awed. 'We'll need advice on that.'

Natalia was silent for several moments. 'That's incredible. Horrifying.' She was conscious of the inadequacy of the words. 'If it *is* being planned, and we don't stop it, we'll be the first victims, before anyone's killed by any bomb.'

From Popov's window Natalia gazed down at the traffic-clogged street, wondering how many of the status-symbol Mercedes and BMWs she could see were Mafia owned: most of them, she guessed. Now, finally, it looked as if she would be confronting them. She turned positively back into the room. 'When are you seeing Oskin again?'

Popov shook his head. 'He told me all there was to tell: there was no point in a further meeting.'

'*You* hadn't told *me*.'

Popov frowned at the rebuke. Then he smiled. 'To have abruptly changed his arrangements would have ruined the security.'

'I could as easily have met him outside the building, like you did!'

'Are you totally sure of the security within this building?' challenged Popov. 'I'm not, not totally. Neither is Oskin. But I'm sorry: I should have made an arrangement to speak to him again, after talking to you.'

It was probably the first time their personal intimacy had led to his taking her for granted, thought Natalia, uncomfortably. 'What arrangements *did* you make?'

'That I would go up to him, at once.'

Now Natalia frowned. 'Where's the security in that?'

'Not officially. And I'm certainly not going anywhere near the regional office. He certainly couldn't risk another trip to Moscow without arousing suspicion. I'll set myself up at an hotel, for as much contact as possible. Hopefully even go with him to Kirs . . .' The man smiled again. 'And I'll keep in daily touch with you.'

Natalia didn't smile back. 'I insist upon that. I want to know every development and every plan. I'll even come up there myself, if necessary.' She crossed hurriedly to Popov, reaching out to clutch at him, needing the physical security of his arms around her. Into his shoulder she said, 'For God's sake, be careful!'

'I won't say don't worry.'

'No, don't say it,' she implored.

The supervisor at the crèche thought Sasha's cough had worsened. Natalia had to wait only fifteen minutes for an appointment with the paediatrician who was reassuring it was a very minor infection easily treated with the mildest of antibiotic, which was dispensed at the adjoining pharmacy. The entire episode took less than an hour and as she left the Ministry clinic Natalia confronted the reality of her privileged existence. *In* office, at Natalia's rank, Sasha was totally protected; dismissed from office, without any rank, Sasha was totally unprotected. No mother without the influence that Natalia took as a matter of course would have even bothered to *try* to get a doctor to treat something as inconsequential as a minor chest ailment. So she couldn't lose office. Rather, she had to do everything not only to retain it but to strengthen it.

On their way back to Leninskaya, the normally chattering Sasha fell asleep and had to be carried drowsily into the apartment. She was irritable, pawing off Natalia's efforts to undress her, and Natalia decided not to bath her. Natalia sat in the bedroom chair, holding Sasha's hot hand as the child went at once into a heavy, breath-congested sleep. Had she been justified, feeling – and showing – the resentment against Popov for his not keeping Nikolai Oskin in Moscow for them to meet? She *was* the head of the division specifically entrusted to combat nuclear smuggling, so it was her right if not her duty to have met the man. But Aleksai *was* the operational director, the man officially appointed to mastermind investigations at street level. While the overall responsibililty was ultimately hers, it *was* overall, going beyond street and back alley practicalities. There would be time – she'd make time – to meet Oskin and Lvov, if necessary or feasible, and take part in every detail of every plan that was discussed. But in the meantime it was right the situation should be divided between them, Aleskai performing his function and she performing hers. Which, Natalia recognized, was political. Which in turn brought the reflection back to Charlie Muffin. But not, for the first time, to include any personal contemplation.

Natalia's sole consideration was the diplomatic reason and cause of his being in Moscow, as it was of the diplomatic reason and cause for James Kestler being accepted. Which made her job doubly or maybe trebly difficult, compared to what Aleksai Popov was setting off probably at this moment to achieve. He had successfully to stop a staggering nuclear theft. The full accountability for which, if he failed, became hers. But she additionally had to satisfy two Western governments that every step of the investigation was carried out, successfully or otherwise, in accordance with the agreements that had been reached with London and Washington. As well as keeping that investigation very firmly under Russian control, which completed the circle to bring the eventual responsibility back to her.

Natalia abruptly remembered there'd been discussion between Aleksai and Charlie of his, and by implication that of the American, participation in the concluding stages of any seemingly worthwhile investigation. Was that something seriously to examine? To allow it would certainly meet any Western criticism of either Moscow's commitment or intention to cooperate. But at the same time open the door to the interpretation that Russia was unable to police its own most serious crime, which was inherent anyway in the fact that the two men had been posted to Moscow in the first place. So she was damned, whichever choice she made.

Sasha stirred, snuffling half-coughs and pushing away the covers, flushed by her fever. Natalia separated the blankets, just pulling the light sheet higher around the child. Which course was personally the safer? Neither, totally. If whatever happened ended in disaster, as much blame as possible could be apportioned to foreign interference. But if it succeeded, there would still remain the inevitable impression that it could not have been achieved *without* foreign involvement.

Natalia's mind moved on, to what had shocked her almost as much as the size and potential capability of the nuclear theft. Was it really conceivable that Interior Ministry departments could be as corrupt as Aleksai had almost glibly declared? Natalia knew well enough it existed at street level: that very evening, driving home with Sasha fitfully asleep in her rear-mounted seat, Natalia had seen a foot patrol Militia man extracting a bribe from a motorist preferring to pay the man off than later to waste an entire day in a traffic violation court. And it was unquestioned common knowledge that an enormous number of displaced KGB personnel had moved into organized crime. But for a district command to feel operations in his own regional headquarters were so insecure he had to work by personally visiting trusted informers and disguise the true reason for a trip to Moscow was incredible. As incredible as the ease with which Aleksai had questioned the security of their very ministry in Moscow. The potential robbery from the Kirs depot was more than sufficient to occupy her for the moment. And would be, until whatever its conclusion. But Natalia made a mental note that after its conclusion she would have Aleksai conduct the most stringent internal security check in Moscow and then extend it throughout their district establishments.

Natalia was asleep when Popov telephoned, apologizing at once for awakening her. 'I thought you'd want to know where to reach me.'

'Of course,' accepted Natalia, fumbling for the light. It was just after one-thirty. 'Where are you?'

'The National. Room 334.'

'I'm glad you called'.

'How's Sasha?'

'She's got a chest infection.'

'How bad?' The concern was obvious in the man's voice.

'I've got medicine and it should be cleared up in a few days.'

'Take good care of her.'

Natalia smiled. 'Of course I will.'
'I love you,' he said.
'I love you too,' she said, meaning it.

chapter 10

Charlie went to the ochre-washed US embassy on the Ulitza Chaykovskovo the day after his encounter with Aleksai Popov to tell the Americans of the Russian's undertaking. And was stunned by the Bureau chief's immediate reaction.

'You've been here almost a whole goddamned year, fannying around and getting nowhere!' Lyneham erupted at Kestler, close to shouting. 'He's here five minutes and he's promised participation!'

'. . . I don't . . . I mean . . .' stumbled Kestler but Charlie hurried in, refusing to be the shuttlecock in any internal game he didn't want to play.

'Wait right there!' he said, bringing both Americans to him. 'There was no such *promise*! Popov said he would consider the idea, with others. That's as far as it goes. I made it quite clear that if they agreed then both of us – you as well as me – would be involved. We're not competing to get a good end-of-term report. No one's being cut out, from my side. If I thought otherwise I wouldn't have told you, would I? I'd have kept it all to myself.' The rebuttal was much stronger than perhaps the situation required but Charlie was determined against any operational animosity and the man with whom he expected to operate was Kestler, not Lyneham.

It was Lyneham who coloured now, although only very slightly. It was impossible from the look on Kestler's face for Charlie to decide if his correction had stopped any feeling growing between Kestler and himself. It was the younger

American who broke the strained silence. 'What do you think the chances are?'

'You've been here longer than me,' reminded Charlie welcoming the chance to strengthen any weakened bridge. 'What do you think?'

'Zilch!' declared Lyneham. 'He was going through the motions with a newcomer. He'll keep stalling and then say he'd like it to happen but people above him shat on the idea.'

Lyneham's response, a 180-degree about turn from the flare-up of minutes before, further confused Charlie. He was *sure* his initial impression of Lyneham as a hardened, no-overkill professional was right, but this encounter didn't fit. What *was* Lyneham so wrought up about? Charlie looked enquiringly at Kestler, for his contribution.

'It could go either way,' said the still-discomfited Kestler. 'I think you'll have to wait and see.'

'*We'll* have to wait and see,' said Charlie, wanting to give the younger man all the reassurance he could. 'I didn't quite expect the invitation always to deal with Popov himself. Arrival meeting maybe, for all the obvious reasons. But not on a day-to-day basis.'

'It's access to the top. Close to it, at least, which is where it counts,' said Lyneham. He was furious at himself, well aware he'd made himself look an asshole but worse, that it had obviously made the Englishman sympathetic to Kestler when he'd wanted Charlie apprehensive, deferring to his opinions. It wouldn't help if Kestler moaned privately to those who mattered back home, either. He'd really ballsed things up.

'How well does it work?' asked Charlie, talking directly to Kestler.

The young man shrugged. 'Usually all right. Sometimes it takes a while to link up but then everything in Russia takes time.'

'I'll give you any external lead I get from London, obviously,' promised Charlie. If the purpose of his getting information from London was to make it openly available to the Russians there was no reason why he shouldn't give it to the Americans in the hope of getting something in return. Anything he learned would probably come from the Bundeskriminalamt anyway, which seemed to be the FBI's primary source. All of which seemed uncomfortably alien to a man accustomed always to working by himself. But the time to operate alone hadn't come yet.

'Like I told you before, we're both on the same side here,' assured Lyneham, working hard to recover. Unhappy at having to make the concession, he added, 'You got any problem with that, Jamie?'

The younger American hesitated, nervous of the wrong reply. 'None at all.'

'Let's hope we all stay on the same side,' said Charlie.

'Can't see any reason why we shouldn't,' said Lyneham, knowing Charlie's remark had been aimed directly at him.

Charlie judged Lyneham's outburst to be the sort of irrational upset that arose for no good reason in the constricted environment of overseas embassies, particularly somewhere like Moscow.

Charlie strove at maintaining the special influence pretence and was mostly successful, although the Head of Chancellery remained aloofly unimpressed, which suited Charlie just fine because he didn't want any more contact with the man than was absolutely necessary. The ambassador, a white-haired career diplomat named Sir William Wilkes, personally welcomed him with the hope that he'd be happy and that everything would work out well, making Charlie wonder if the man really knew what he was there for, and Thomas Bowyer and his wife hosted a party to introduce him to more legation people. Their compound apartment of plywood and formica convinced Charlie he'd made the right decision by living outside. Fiona was a bustling, rosy-cheeked woman who shunned make-up, wore handknitted cardigans and taught elementary English at the embassy school. She also matched Charlie's whisky intake, glass for glass and without any noticeable effect, and Charlie liked her. Paul Smythe had obviously been the chief grinder at the rumour mill and Charlie found himself under as much scrutiny for imagined roles as he did for what he was officially supposed to be doing. To keep the personal mystique simmering, Charlie deflected both the outright questions and the heavy innuendo by saying he couldn't, of course, talk about his work and left people believing they'd come close to a secret.

He welcomed Bowyer's suggestion of their going together to two foreign embassy receptions and at both, the first French, the second German, he was sought out by the respective intelligence heads, both of whom announced they wanted close working relationships. He was additionally button-holed at the German party by Israeli and Italian *rezidentura* officers saying the same thing. After a lifetime of being the left-in-the-cold outsider with his nose pressed to the window, Charlie found the sudden popularity as curiously amusing as it was unusual. With absolutely nothing to lose but everything to gain, Charlie assured each he wanted the contact to be as close as they did, particularly the German, Jurgen Balg, from whom he anticipated the most benefit.

Charlie followed up the German encounter with lunch the following day, exchanging private and direct line telephone numbers and fixed luncheon appointments with the others over the course of the succeeding fortnight. Although Charlie considered the contacts, at this early stage, little more than finger touching, it gave a semblance of activity to report back to London, which he did methodically. He also wrote fuller memoranda to himself about the men and their discussions, which he left in the unlocked cabinets in his office for Bowyer to discover and use as he felt fit. Charlie also logged daily a much-inflated expenditure, particularly out-of-pocket items like taxi fares, phone calls, gratuities and casual, bar-level hospitality for Bowyer to find. He knew it wouldn't allay the inevitable challenge from Gerald Williams, but it gave Bowyer and the financial director something to talk about.

And most of all he waited for the hoped-for call from Colonel Aleksai Semenovich Popov. Which never came.

Charlie accepted in hindsight he'd invested far too much in what had, considered objectively, been little more than a diplomatic response that avoided outright rejection. But he *had* thought there was a chance. Maybe Popov had suggested it and been turned down. But Charlie would have still expected the man to come back to him, to tell him one way or the other. It would not, after all, have reflected upon him personally. Lyneham had even predicted such an outcome.

Charlie had to wait, with increasing frustration, until the beginning of the second week before he got an excuse to go against the imposed system and make a call to the Russian instead of waiting for Popov to contact him. It was scarcely sufficient and Charlie didn't doubt Kestler had the same information as he did, because the Bundeskriminalamt was clearly the source, but the impatient Charlie judged it reason enough. The British station in Bonn, with what looked like corroborative rumours in Berlin, picked up the suggestion of a nuclear shipment transiting Leipzig in the coming month. There was no indication of destination or source, although there was a hint it would originate from the Ukraine.

Popov's direct line rang interminably unanswered and the girl who finally responded didn't speak English and appeared unable to understand Charlie's groping Russian, just as he didn't get everything she tried to tell him. Despite the language difficulty Charlie attempted the main Interior Ministry switchboard, several times being plugged through to further unanswered infinity and twice reaching whom he thought to be the same secretary, on the second occasion understanding from her near-impatient insistence that Popov wouldn't be available 'for a long time'.

'The good old Russian runaround. I told you that earlier stuff was just so much bullshit,' insisted Lyneham, when Charlie finally confessed the failure. Charlie had developed the habit of practically daily visits to Ulitza Chaykovskovo, as much to get out of the British embassy and appear to the watchful Bowyer to be doing something as in the hope of gaining even a scrap of information from the Americans. That day Kestler confirmed they had virtually the same information about the possible Ukraine shipment and admitted that he, too, had been unable to locate the Russian colonel.

'You ever had difficulty like this before?' Charlie asked Kestler.

'A couple of times,' conceded the younger American. 'You leave a name and a number?'

'Finally, yesterday.' The atmosphere between the two Americans seemed easier.

'He's normally pretty good at calling back.'

The thought of a continuing delay depressed Charlie: having provided even limited information London would anticipate a Russian response. And wouldn't be impressed at his inability to reach the operational chief with whom he'd already told them he'd formed precisely the liaison he'd been sent to Moscow to establish.

Charlie accepted Lyneham's Happy Hour invitation – once it was extended to and accepted as well by Kestler, with the promise to join them later – because the alternative was another lonely evening in the echoing Lesnaya apartment. And he was passingly curious to see if the American mess was better than that at the British embassy.

It wasn't, but then the British building was far superior to that of the United States, which Charlie had always thought of as a bunker barriered by shutters and bars. Befitting such architecture, the American recreation facility was in the basement. The attempts to brighten it up with wall posters of American tourist scenes hadn't worked and the polished-leaf plants had lost their gloss in the struggle beneath the harsh strip lights that whitened everything, giving everyone a sickly pallor. A sign promising an extension of the cheap drink period was propped against a jukebox dispensing muzak and an occasional soul lyric. At the far end a white-coated black steward dispensed drinks with the conjuring skill exclusive to American bartenders. At the edge of the bar furthest from the music centre a hotplate and dishes steamed gently, offering complimentary snacks. Charlie declined any food and was relieved to spot Macallan among the bourbons and ryes. Lyneham had to make two trips to the hotplate to assemble a sufficient supply of buffalo wings, chicken legs and meat balls.

'Sure you don't want any?' pressed the FBI man, gravy speckling his chin.

'Quite sure.'

Lyneham emptied his mouth. 'Guess I was a little out of line the other day.' He hated the humiliation but after a lot of thought he'd decided he'd gain more brownie points clearing the nonsense up than by letting it drift. He'd made another decision, too.

'About what?' asked Charlie. He had, of course, to pretend he hadn't noticed anything.

'Sounding off like I did at Jamie.'

'None of my business,' said Charlie.

'Under a lot of pressure from Washington,' exaggerated Lyneham, hugely. 'They want results. This latest thing about the Ukraine isn't going to help, either.' He managed to get two buffalo wings into his mouth at once and started chomping.

'I know.' Despite Kestler's named appointment, he supposed Lyneham carried the ultimate responsibility. Why wasn't Bowyer as concerned then? There was no comparison between the length of time he and Kestler had been in Moscow. But Charlie, who rarely accepted the obvious, was far more inclined to think Bowyer had got some sort of back-channel assurance that he was absolved from any failure.

It was several moments before Lyneham had room to speak again. 'That's not the only problem in Washington. There's some internal shit.'

Confession time, guessed Charlie; confiding time, at least. He waited, knowing the FBI man didn't need encouragement.

'Jamie's connected,' announced Lyneham, enigmatically.

'To whom or to what?' demanded Charlie, attentively. So the Happy Hour invitation wasn't social after all.

It only took Lyneham minutes to sketch the Fitzjohn family tree in which Kestler had his special nest.

'You think he's fireproof?' asked Charlie.

'I think he's less likely to get burned than a lot of others.'

Charlie wasn't interested in a lot of others, only himself. The idea of working with someone more flame-resistant than himself made Charlie uneasy. It explained a lot of Lyneham's attitudes, too. 'He worry you?'

'He worries the hell out of me,' confessed Lyneham.

'You under orders to treat him with special care?'

'No,' replied Lyneham. 'Jamie himself has never once asked for any favours, either. But you know the way these things work?'

'Yes,' said Charlie.

'Just thought you should know.'

'I appreciate it,' said Charlie, who did.

The serious purpose of the encounter achieved, Lyneham made a head movement into the room and said, 'Kind of wish it was me they're interested in!'

Charlie was already conscious they seemed to be the object of fairly frequent attention from female embassy staff at several tables between them and the bar. 'What are they looking at?'

'*For*,' corrected Lyneham. 'Where I tread, others surely follow. Or rather one particular other. The female to male ratio here is completely skewed. So anyone with half a dick who knows it's not just to pee with is the most popular guy in town. Particularly if he's a bachelor. Which Jamie is.'

'Lucky Jamie.' The dangerously enthusiastic little sod seemed to have it all.

Lyneham was sure he'd pitched it just right. First the admission of being too hard on the eager bastard, then the family connection, now the begrudging admiration for his sexual prowess, neatly combined to portray a crusty, bark-worse-than-bite mentor showing concern about a protégé for whom he deep down had a lot of regard. 'He's got two ambitions: to hang scalps of nuclear smugglers from his tent pole and see fucking declared an Olympic sport.'

'Let's hope he achieves both.' He *had* been right about Lyneham, he decided.

'Sure as hell won't be for want of trying, on either count.' Perfect, Lyneham congratulated himself: he'd ended on the subtle reminder of Kestler's unpredictability.

The younger American's entry into the mess appeared timed just as perfectly, coming at the precise conclusion of the conversation between Charlie and the FBI chief. Forewarned and curious, Charlie closely watched the reaction of the assembled women, upon Kestler's arrival. A blonde at the nearest table positively preened and an older woman at another bench gave a finger-fluttering wave. Kestler greeted his audience with the panache of a matinée idol accustomed to adulation, noted Charlie and Lyneham's order as he passed and stopped at two tables on his return with the drinks, leaving both laughing too loudly at whatever he'd said. Charlie saw he'd been wrong imagining earlier that Kestler didn't drink. As well as their whisky the man carried wine for himself.

'See what I mean?' said Lyneham, maintaining the mock envy.

'What?' demanded Kestler, in feigned ignorance.

'I filled Charlie in on your one-man crusade to free the embassy of sexual frustration,' said Lyneham.

'It's a job and somebody's got to do it,' clichéd Kestler cockily, enjoying the approbation of the older man. It was a brief relaxation. 'Washington messaged us, about fifteen minutes ago. And then there was a call from Fiore, at the Italian embassy. Both are talking about fuel rods and Fiore thinks their Mafia are probably involved in a tie-up with a group here. It's not clear if it's connected with the Ukraine suggestion or whether it's something quite separate.'

Umberto Fiore was the Italian who'd approached Charlie at the embassy reception and with whom Charlie was lunching in two days. What Kestler had just passed on would be enough to convince London he had built up useful in-country contacts: hopefully, Charlie thought, he'd be able to pad it out with more after meeting the Italian. Abruptly there was a flicker of apprehension. If Fiore kept his reception undertaking, he'd have telephoned Morisa Toreza, like he'd called Kestler, giving Thomas Bowyer the opportunity secretly to advise London in advance of his being able to impress Rupert Dean. 'Did you try Popov again?'

Kestler nodded. 'I was told he wasn't available and that they didn't know when he would be. So this time, just for the hell of it, I asked where he was because I had some important information. And got told again he wasn't available but they'd pass a message on. So I left my name.'

'Like I said, the good old Russian runaround,' insisted the persistently cynical Lyneham, lumbering to his feet to get fresh drinks and calling Charlie a lucky son-of-a-bitch because mess rules prevented non-members buying.

Kestler played eye-contact games with the preening blonde and said to Charlie, 'You fancy making up a foursome? I could make a personal recommendation.'

'I might. But would any of them?'

'You haven't any idea of the desperation in this city!' Kestler realized what he'd said as Charlie was about to respond and said, 'Oh shit! I'm sorry, Charlie. That wasn't what I meant. What I meant . . .' He was flushed with embarrassment, redder than he had been under Lyneham's attack.

Charlie grinned at the younger man's confusion, unoffended. 'I need to get back to my embassy anyway.'

'What about later?' demanded Kestler, abandoning the available harem in his eagerness to make amends. 'Why don't we look around the town? Go to a few of the clubs where the bad guys hang out?'

Charlie was immediately attentive. It was something he had to do – he'd even argued the need during the London expenses negotiations – but he'd never considered either Lyneham or Kestler as his guide. The rumpled, elephantine Lyneham probably wouldn't have been allowed past the door and he hadn't imagined a fitness freak and wrongly believed non-drinker like Kestler venturing anywhere near unhealthy nightclubs. 'I'd like that.'

'It's a bit like watching animals in a zoo,' warned Kestler, enjoying being the man of experience like he'd earlier enjoyed being identified as the stud. 'Seeing them at play it's difficult to imagine they'd bite your head off.'

Which it was.

Lyneham said he was too old to go with them, freeing Charlie of one uncertainty, and he was relieved of another far more pressing concern when an urgent-voiced Bowyer said on the telephone that there'd been calls for him from both Fiore and Balg, both of whom had refused to leave messages. Charlie said he knew what it was about from other sources and that it looked big. He was fairly confident Bowyer would send some sort of message to London and the date would coordinate perfectly with whatever expenses he later submitted. He had to remember to get as many supporting bills as possible.

They used a US embassy pool car, a complaining Ford which looked very much the orphan among the Mercedes and BMWs and Porsches clustered around the Nightflight, in what Kestler insisted people still called Gorky Street, despite its post-communism name change. Charlie wasn't sure he would have been admitted if Kestler hadn't confidently led the way and Charlie mentally apologized for thinking it was only the shambling Lyneham who might have been a hindrance.

It was vast and cavernous and half-lit, a plush-seated and expansive balcony overlooking a heavy dance floor, a viewing gallery from which to watch fish shoal. Charlie contentedly followed the American's lead, ignoring the downstairs bar for the larger and better-lit one upstairs. A glass of wine and a whisky purporting to be scotch but which wasn't cost Kestler $80 and Charlie realized he hadn't negotiated his allowances as well as he'd thought.

They managed to get bar stools close to one end of the curved, glass-reflecting expanse, giving them a spread-out view. Each table was a separate oasis of competing party people. The predominant female fashion was bare shoulders or halter-necks, featuring valleyed cleavage and neon displays of what looked like gold and diamonds and which Charlie decided probably were. A lot of the material in the men's suits shone, like the gold in their diamond-decked rings and identity bracelets and the occasional neck chain that fell from open-collared shirts. Champagne bottles – French, not Russian – stood like derricks on the biggest oil lake ever struck and quick-eyed waiters ferried constant supplies to ensure the gushers never stopped bubbling. There were a lot of quickly smiling girls offering uplifted invitations at various stretches of the bar: two actually extended their attention to Charlie.

'You've got to be careful,' advised Kestler. 'They're virtually all professional. Anything ordinary runs out at about $400 to $500 a trick and that's practically a fire sale. And there's a lot of infection about.'

'I'll be careful,' promised Charlie, solemnly.

'You need to be,' said Kestler, looking past Charlie to the assembled tables. 'Make another sort of mistake and hit on someone's wife or regular girlfriend and you end up chopped liver. Literally.'

'I'll remember that, too.' Charlie thought Kestler's earlier description of a zoo at feeding time was very apposite: most of the men *did* look dangerously unpredictable and those who didn't were closely escorted by companions who did and a lot of whom sat slightly on the sidelines, waiting to be told what to do. *Capone country*, recalled Charlie. Lyneham's description was apposite, too: it was like being in the middle of every gangster movie Charlie had ever seen. He remarked just that to Kestler, as he gestured for refills. The American grinned back and said, 'That's *exactly* how it is. This is performance time, each strutting their stuff for the others. The jewellery is compared and the tits and the ass is compared and the macho is compared and even the size of the bankroll is compared.'

Charlie watched his $100 note disappear into the till. The receipt came but no change. 'You ever tried to make up case files?'

'Mug shots and criminal records and stuff like that?'

'Stuff like that,' agreed Charlie.

Kestler smiled at him, more sympathetic than patronizing. 'Ask me that at the end of the evening.'

They left Nightflight an hour and $200 later. There was an even larger cast posturing and performing at Pilot, on Tryokhgorny Val and it cost Charlie a further $300 to sit in the audience. 'I think I know what your answer's going to be,' said Charlie, as they left.

'Like they say in the movies, you ain't seen nuthin' yet,' parodied Kestler.

Upstairs at the Up and Down club a striptease dancer of breathtaking proportions was ending the tease as they negotiated their way past a shoulder-to-shoulder cordon of granite-faced men all of whom Charlie believed from Kestler's assurance to be former *spetznaz* Special Forces. The dance floor was downstairs. The two drinks at the bar there cost Kestler $200 before they went back upstairs to watch another stunning girl disrobe during the most sensuous dance Charlie had ever witnessed.

'Shit, that makes me horny!' declared Kestler.

'Think of the cost,' cautioned Charlie. He'd already fantasized about bringing Gerald Williams to the Up and Down if the inevitable reimbursement dispute ever brought the financial director personally to Moscow on a fact-finding enquiry.

'It's the only thing holding me back,' admitted the American. He looked, with obvious reluctance, from the gyrating girl, but swept his hand out in the embracing gesture of an ancient farmer dispensing seed. 'This is the *crème de la crème . . .*' The man hesitated, for the prepared joke. 'Or *crime de la crime*, if you really want to get it right. You do a bust here tonight, I guarantee you'd get someone from all the big Families . . . Ostankino . . . Chechen . . . Dolgoprudnaya . . . Ramenski . . . Assyrian . . . Lubertsky . . . All of them. And probably a few making up their international links with Italy and Latin America and the United States as well.'

'Has it ever been done?'

'Why should it have been done? There's no statute in Russian law to justify a raid. And all these motherfuckers know it . . .' Kestler looked around the room again. 'These guys would *love* it, if it happened. It would polish their macho image to be publicly hauled off and then be back on the street again, in hours. Giving the authorities the stiff middle finger.'

'Is that why there is so little action here? That there isn't legislation for the law to move in the first place!'

'One of the *excuses* why there's so little action. Along with about a hundred others, a lot of which I've forgotten.'

'Which is why you've never bothered with a mug shot comparison from any of the clubs?'

'They all laugh at me, Lyneham particularly, for running around in circles. But there are some circles that even I won't waste my time revolving in.'

A barman stood demandingly before them and their empty glasses. Charlie, who reckoned he had enough for just one more round, nodded. To Kestler he said, encouragingly, 'Things seem a little easier between you and Lyneham in the last few days?'

'He's OK,' defended Kestler, loyally. 'Just cranky, sometimes. Haemorrhoids or something.' He regarded Charlie with sudden intensity. 'Say, you don't jog, do you? I run most mornings. We could do it together!'

Charlie winced at the idea. 'No, I don't jog.'

Kestler shook his head. 'No, I guess you don't.'

Charlie watched the departure of his last $200. The situation between Kestler and Lyneham was not one for him to become overly concerned about, but definitely not one to be overlooked: squabbling children often upset their dinners over innocent bystanders and the way things seemed to be going Charlie was reconciled to having to stand pretty close to both men in the foreseeable future.

Charlie ended the evening having spent $850 but with carefully pocketed discarded till receipts of others as well as his own amounting to $1,200, a vague headache from drinking fake whisky and a difficulty in deciding what the evening had actually achieved. In positive terms, very little. But in the long term, perhaps a worthwhile investment. By itself – and essential to validate the expenditure – he had a lengthy report to London about the apparently blatant openness of organized crime in the city, which had genuinely surprised him. And an equally lengthy query to Jeremy Simpson in London to confirm the weakness of anti-crime legislation in Russia.

It meant he was fully occupied the following morning, although he managed to finish early enough for a brought-forward lunch with Umberto Fiore. Wanting to acquire as much as possible for the following day's report, he fixed dinner that evening with Jurgen Balg.

'I think I should come up!' insisted Natalia.

'You already know everything. But it's your choice, obviously.'

'I want to see for myself. Meet Oskin and this man Lvov.'

Popov had dutifully maintained the promised contact, calling her as often as three times a day – once five times – but as the indications had hardened of a genuine and large-scale theft, Natalia had grown increasingly frustrated by the feeling of being on the sidelines.

'I'm sure they're right about Kirov and Kirs being infiltrated by Mafia informers,' said Popov.

'I wouldn't go anywhere near any of the plants themselves. Or the regional offices.'

'Having got this far we can't risk a mistake which would ruin everything.'

'Don't you *want* me to come up?' demanded Natalia.

'Don't be silly!' said Popov, the quick irritation showing in his voice. 'This isn't a question of what I want or don't want. It's a question of what's best in an operational situation.'

'So what's best in this operational situation?'

'I think you should come up to Kirov,' said the man. Then he added, 'I've missed you. And Sasha.'

Because the routine worked so well Stanislav Silin again personally met the Berlin flight for them to talk in the car, which of course was not the identifiable, bullet-proofed and interior-partitioned Mercedes in which he customarily travelled, but the same anonymous Ford as before. This time the Dolgoprudnaya chief turned south on the outer ring road, satisfied he didn't have to stress any more loyalty reminders.

'All the banking sorted out?' asked Silin.

Instead of answering, the man handed the deposit books and validating identification documents across the car.

'When are you bringing the others in from Berlin?' asked Silin, accepting the package.

'Over the next two to three weeks.'

'They all know what they're supposed to do?'

'Absolutely. What about Sobelov?'

'He made a public apology at the last Commission meeting.'

'That must have hurt!'

Silin said, 'Not as much as a lot of other things are going to hurt!' and they both laughed. Silin added, 'I'm letting him be in charge of the interception.'

The other man frowned. 'You sure that's a good idea?'

'It amuses me to let him have his last delusions of grandeur.'

'The date is definite then?'

'It's got to be geared to their timetable. We'll be ready when your people get here.'

chapter 11

Natalia thought Kirov was small for a provincial capital and odd in the way it clung to the umbilical cord of the Vyatka. From their room she could see over the low dockside warehouses and timber yards to the sluggish river on which even slower boats hauled daisy chains of connected, lumber-laden barges with occasional fussy tugs encouraging the procession from the rear. Beyond the port complex the Stalin era apartment blocks stood in line, grey skittles all in a row. Only vaguely visible through the uncleared midday mist, the far-away fir forests that provided the town's wood industry had no colour either, deep black outlines against the dull skyline. Apart from the apartment blocks and the abrupt domed towers of the isolated cathedral everything was uninterestingly flat, as if the place was boxed up ready to be moved somewhere else.

By contrast, Popov's room gave an impression of permanent residence. He'd had to tidy the bathroom cabinet to make space for her things and rearrange the wardrobe for her clothes. He'd had an extra table moved in, for papers and two spread-out maps and his open briefcase was on a bordering chair. A glass held several pencils and a pen: other glasses from the same set ringed a half-empty vodka flask on a side table and a jacket was draped carelessly over the back of another chair. Two pairs of shoes were neatly arranged but outside the wardrobe, and the bed was made but bore the impression where he'd lain on top, before Natalia's arrival.

Incongruously, a small sled was upturned on its runners against the wall behind the door. A box was beside it. Seeing Natalia's look, Popov said, 'For Sasha. There's a whole farmyard of wooden animals in the box, as well. Do you think she'll like them?'

'I'm sure she will,' smiled Natalia. He really did treat Sasha as if she were his own.

'Who's looking after her?'

'The matron at the crèche. There's an arrangement. I'll call, later.'

Popov had kissed her, almost anxiously, when she'd arrived and he came close again at the window, folding his arms around her from behind with his face at her shoulder. 'I enjoyed telling the receptionist you were my wife. You didn't want a separate room, did you?'

'Is there really a need for an explanation?'

She felt him nod, into her shoulder. 'This *is* genuine: I'm convinced of it. So I'm not taking *any* chances.'

'When do I meet Oskin?'

'Tonight. Dinner. He's chosen the restaurant.'

'Lvov?'

'Tomorrow. We're going out to Kirs.'

Natalia pulled away from the man. 'So tell me about it.'

Popov took the larger of the two maps from the table, tracing by pencil the curved road to Kirs. 'The nuclear plant is on the outskirts of the town itself. It's being decommissioned: a lot of the technical staff have been transferred already. There are four silos, each holding an ICBM. And a warhead storage facility. There's also about 250 kilos of cassium and plutonium 239, most of it weapons graded. That's what they've told Lvov they want.'

'Who's "they"?'

'He's met four men, so far. He's sure two, at least, come from Moscow.'

'Names?'

Popov snorted a laugh. 'Of course not.'

'Not even talking among themselves?'

Popov shook his head. 'The first approach was from just one man; Lvov thinks he's local. There've been two further meetings since. That's when the others turned up. Each time there've been threats about what will happen to his family if he doesn't do what they want.'

'What *do* they want?'

'Guaranteed access. A plan of the facilities, with the storage complexes marked with what each contains. Code systems, to get into the complexes. Guard rosters and manpower strength. And complete details, including the electrical circuitry, of all the alarm systems.'

Natalia let out a deep sigh. 'They don't seem to have overlooked anything.'

'They haven't.'

'Any positive date?'

Popov shook his head. 'The one thing we haven't got. And can't do anything without. He's stalled them so far by saying it's difficult to get all they demand. They've given him two weeks, as of three days ago.'

'How do they meet Lvov?'

'He's never warned. It's one of the reasons he's so frightened. They're just there, unannounced. The first time was a Saturday. He was shopping and the man he thinks is local stopped him in the street. The second time he found people either side of him in the trolley car, going home from work. They made him get off to meet the other two in a park. The last occasion – that was three days ago – they arrived at his apartment when his wife was out, at the cinema with their daughters. They obviously watch him, choosing their moments. He says he feels like an animal, knowing it's being hunted but not when it's going to be shot.'

'It sounds as if he is.' Natalia looked down at the map, noticing a series of pencilled crosses between Kirov and Kirs. 'What are these?'

'Nonsense, for the benefit of curious hotel staff. I'm supposed to be a mining engineer, surveying possible mineral deposits.' Popov didn't smile at Natalia's amused grimace. 'It accounts for my staying here, for so long. And for driving around the countryside.'

Natalia was suddenly seized by a feeling of unreality going beyond that prompted by near-theatrical subterfuge and accounts of mystery men stalking a frightened nuclear security officer. She'd undergone the obligatory operational training during her long-ago KGB induction but never been called upon to use it. The major part of her previous career had been debriefing and interrogating potential defectors and sometimes recalled Russian field operatives whose psychological stability had become suspect. So all her experiences of practical danger and the fear it engendered had been second-hand, recounted and sometimes exaggerated by others. Now she was *involved*, living part of the subterfuge. She had secretly to meet men genuinely terrified of being murdered and hear and assess their story. And then to approve, in her name and under her authority, a way to defeat a robbery which, if it wasn't prevented, could potentially end with the slaughter of hundreds. Or even thousands. The feeling was more than unreality. Natalia was frightened. And not solely, or even predominantly, at the risk of failure, disastrous though that would be. There was an unease at the fear of the unknown, of being physically hurt, even. Natalia positively stopped the mental drift. She was being ridiculous. She was in no physical danger, meeting Oskin or Lvov. Aleksai would be with her: Aleksai, a Militia colonel who'd worked the streets and conducted criminal investigations and had six commendations for bravery that he didn't boast about, one of them involving a shoot-out in which a hostage-holding murderer had been killed. She smiled at him as he looked up from his map.

'What is it?' he frowned.

'Nothing.'

He smiled back. 'Yes,' he said, wrongly guessing what she was thinking. 'There *is* a lot of time before we have to meet Oskin. Hours. And it has been a long time for a hard-working mining engineer who's missed his wife.'

Natalia held her smile but wished he hadn't misunderstood. Of course she loved him and of course she wanted to go to bed with him and for him to make love to her because it was always so good because he was such a consummate lover and Natalia liked sex. But not now, not at this moment in these circumstances. She hadn't understood enough; been told enough. It would have been better later, when she'd settled in after the flight from Moscow and asked all her questions and met Oskin. But she *was* meeting Oskin, she realized. He was Aleksai's source and it was probably better if she heard everything herself from the regional Militia chief rather than entering the conversation with preconceived impressions from what Aleksai told her.

Aleksai *was* a consummate lover. Natalia couldn't remember a time when he'd failed her and often, like now, there was surprise as well as excitement because lovemaking to Aleksai was a complete pleasure to which he gave himself completely, arousing her to total abandonment. He loved her with his mouth and she loved him the same way and when she tried to pull him into her he held back until she mewed with frustration and slapped at him, hard, and said she was coming but still he refused. When he did, finally, she exploded almost at once and he did as well but he didn't stop and she came again and then clung to him, exhausted, panting 'bastard' over and over again into his ear, slapping him again, although not so hard, when he laughed back at her.

They slept as they lay and Natalia would have missed the meeting with Oskin entirely if Popov hadn't awakened her. As it was, she had to hurry to bath and repair her love-bedraggled hair. In the reflection of the mirror when she was doing that she saw Popov check the clip of the Markarov and settle the gun comfortably in the rear waistband of his trousers. She thought the gun looked enormous and felt another flicker of fear.

Popov became aware of her attention and looked back at her, in the mirror. 'It's best. Just a precaution. Nothing's going to happen.'

'If you say so.' Natalia was authorized to carry a weapon but had never done so and was glad her rank had for years now freed her going through the once-required range practice. She'd hated the noise and the weight of a pistol she could never hold properly or fire without squinting her eyes closed at the trigger pull, so that her score rate had always been appalling.

The restaurant was virtually in the shadow of the Uspenskii cathedral and their last three or four hundred metres were slowed by people making their way to the evening service. Natalia, who had followed her religion even under communism, hoped she would have time to go there before returning to Moscow.

Popov parked some way away, although there was space far closer, and further bewildered her by fully circling the square and even stopping to look into the window of a hunting equipment shop instead of going directly into the restaurant. Which was unexpectedly good, an ancient lop-sided and crannied place with a main eating area dominated by a huge central fireplace open on both sides with the chimney mouth hung with hooks and grids to smoke the meat and fish.

They were late because of the straggled churchgoers and their meandering approach but Nikolai Oskin was not there. Their reservation was at a corner table furthest from the main door. Popov ordered a flask of vodka for himself and Georgian wine for Natalia and told the waiter they'd delay ordering because there was a possibility of their being joined by someone else.

'Possibility?' queried Natalia.

'Oskin won't come if he thinks we were under any sort of special attention.'

'He was watching us?'

Popov nodded. 'There's a public kiosk near the hotel. If he doesn't show up tonight he'll phone there at eleven tomorrow.'

Natalia didn't smile, like she had at the criss-crossed map to account for his being a mining engineer. For several moments she stared fixedly at the door, at people following them in. 'Where was he?'

Popov shrugged. 'I don't know.'

'How do we know he isn't being watched? He's far more likely to attract attention than us, isn't he?'

'We don't. And yes he is. All this is for his benefit – and peace of mind – not ours.'

'But if he doesn't come it means . . .'

'. . . Nothing. He and I have been very careful: had our meetings like this all the time. So I'm absolutely sure no one has linked us, in any way. If he imagines anyone outside that's exactly what it will be, imagination . . .' He smiled, sadly, at her seriousness. 'We'll laugh about it when it's all over. But at the moment it's got to be done his way. Their way.'

It was a further thirty minutes before Nikolai Oskin came into the restaurant. He remained unmoving just inside the door and Popov's warning touch upon her arm enabled Natalia to study the man. He was extremely short and his fatness made him appear even smaller. Oskin's approach, having located them, was a strut of quick, jerky steps. He wore civilian clothes, of course. The suit had no tailored crease but was bagged and shiny from wear and neglect. The shirt was reasonably clean but did not appear to have been ironed. Natalia tried to remember the man from his Moscow headquarters posting but couldn't, although she knew from his personnel records, which she'd read before coming to Kirov, that he had served at Ulitza Zhitnaya until eighteen months earlier. He stood politely and virtually to attention during Popov's introduction and appeared surprised when Natalia offered her hand. It was only when she did so that Natalia realized he was deferring to her with the respect befitting the absolute head of his department. He sat, at her invitation, and accepted the vodka Popov offered. They did not attempt any conversation until they had ordered. Natalia disinterestedly chose quail, without any appetite.

'No trouble, then?' opened Popov.

'I don't think so,' said Oskin. Then, hurriedly, 'No. None at all. I made sure.'

Natalia wondered if he normally spoke in such a high-pitched voice or whether it was another indication of nervousness. He wasn't sweating now but as close as he was, Natalia could smell that he had been, very recently. And badly. She moved to speak, stopping just short of referring to her deputy as Aleksai. Instead she said, 'Colonel Popov believes there is going to be a genuine robbery attempt?'

'There's no doubt,' agreed Oskin, positively. The voice was still high.

'The man whom Lvov thinks is local, to Kirov? Have you any idea who he is?'

Oskin shook his head. 'There is one major gang here. Run by a man named Yatisyna, Lev Mikhailovich Yatisyna. If Lvov is right and there is a link with one of the big Moscow Families I think it would be through someone from the Yatisyna group. But it's only my guess.'

'Does Yatisyna have a record?'

There was another nod. 'A lot of petty stuff, when he was young. Two more serious charges, of physical assault. Cleared on both occasions. Witnesses were intimidated against giving evidence.'

'So there are photographs?'

The arrival of their food delayed Oskin's answer. Natalia was conscious of Popov's frown, at her question.

'The photographs aren't recent,' said Oskin. 'Eight, maybe nine years ago. That was the last time he was brought in.'

'Still good enough,' decided Natalia. 'Let's take them to Lvov tomorrow; photographs of everyone connected with Yatisyna, in fact. He might be able to identify someone.' Natalia went through the pretence of eating, rearranging the food on her plate. It looked very good. She wished she was hungry. She was conscious of Oskin looking towards the door at each new arrival.

'What are we going to do?' demanded Oskin.

'Stop it!' said Popov. 'What else?'

'How?'

'We don't know yet,' admitted Natalia.

'With people from Moscow?'

'Do you think that's necessary?'

Oskin swallowed heavily, clearing a mouth he'd overfilled with pork and red cabbage. 'Whatever you try to do will leak if you attempt it with local personnel.'

'I could hand-pick a Moscow squad,' Popov said, to Natalia. 'It would guarantee security.'

'When it's all over I want Kirov cleared up! And cleared *out*!' ordered Natalia, looking between the two men.

Oskin finished eating, neatly setting his knife and fork down but staying with his eyes on his half-finished plate. 'I have a particular request. Something that's very important.' The voice was still high-pitched but practically at a whisper.

'What?' asked Popov.

'I believe Lvov. That he and his family will probably be killed, either way. Coming to us . . . trying to get the people arrested . . . isn't going to protect him enough. Just as there won't be sufficient protection for me if I take part in whatever operation is mounted . . .'

'You mean you *don't* want to take part?' demanded Natalia.

For the first time Oskin smiled, a sad expression. 'That wouldn't protect me either. They know here I'm a Militia officer: know nothing could have been set up without my being involved. There'll be retribution afterwards, whatever happens.'

Oskin had a wife and two sons, Natalia remembered, from the personnel file. 'What then?'

'A transfer back to Moscow. If I am not withdrawn I shall be killed. My family too. It wouldn't just be the nuclear theft. I'd be blamed for the clean-up you've just ordered.'

Natalia was aware of the enquiring look from Popov. If Lvov were right and there was a Moscow Family as well as a local organized crime group involved then Oskin was hardly going to be any safer back in the capital. She let her mind run on, trying fully to assimilate what she was being told. Which was staggering – still difficult for her totally to believe – even if it were only half true. As it was equally impossible to believe that one provincial region and one provincial capital was unique in the corruption of its law and order mechanism. So there had to be others. Could the rot *really* be so bad? If it were – again, if it were only half true – the bad was inevitably going to overwhelm the good. Resulting in what?

Chaos, she supposed: anarchic chaos. Too sweepingly catastrophic, she thought at once, refusing the despair. The situation – of which she still had no definite evidence, just the insistence of one very frightened and possibly paranoid man – in one town couldn't be magnified by any over-active stretch of imagination into applying to a whole country, certainly not a whole country the size of Russia. Neither could, or should, the possibility of an enormous problem be overlooked. So what could she do? Hers was a specific division, in reality quite separate from the regular Militia and other law enforcement organizations, each of which had their own specific directors and chairmen ascending pyramid-fashion to the pinnacle upon which sat the Interior Minister himself. Did she have enough credible authority to emerge beyond her own department to make allegations other directors would inevitably infer to be criticism of their efficient control, organizational ability and honesty, both personal and professional? Natalia didn't know the full answer. What she was sure about, without any doubt whatsoever, was that if she failed with this nuclear investigation, her own efficiency and organizational ability would be so destroyed she wouldn't have any credibility left to achieve anything.

'Well?' finally prompted Popov, impatiently.

Natalia had been so immersed in her own reflections she momentarily had difficulty refocusing on what Oskin had asked. 'You'll be moved back to Moscow. You have my word.'

The tiny fat man straightened in his chair, as if relieved of a physical burden. 'I am not a coward. Or a weak man.'

'You've proved that already.'

'It's not easy to be honest in Russia. Much easier to be the other way.'

'I know that.'

Popov stretched out a reassuring hand to Oskin's shoulder. 'You see! I told you it would be all right!'

Oskin kept his attention upon the door but did appear to relax, slightly. Natalia decided on the spot to move in a

Moscow prevention squad hand-picked by Popov. To prevent any leakage of their movements, they would be helicoptered in at the last moment, although not to the airport. She and Popov would rely upon Oskin to designate somewhere close to the city or even nearer to Kirs itself, further to maintain the element of surprise. Trucks would be sent in advance, again from Moscow, for the final assault, with the helicopters kept on standby for any eventuality. Both men agreed Oskin could safely and without arousing suspicion get to Moscow for the final planning session by Natalia officially summoning him for reassignment talks, which was virtually the truth. Natalia agreed to the man's family accompanying him then, to get them away from the area before the robbery attempt.

Natalia found herself instinctively employing her old debriefing techniques to take Oskin from the very beginning of Lvov's disclosure, letting the man generalize as Popov had earlier generalized but then returning him to points of his story she wanted in more detail, hiding her disappointment at the final awareness that there was little more than what Popov had previously told her.

She didn't have to hide it from Popov. He broke in as soon as Oskin began to repeat himself and Natalia reluctantly agreed they'd taken everything as far as they could, at that stage. The cautious Oskin left first with assurances to provide all the available photographs of the Yatisyna clan before their meeting the following day with Valeri Lvov. With Popov totally familiar with the city, it took the two men only minutes to fix a handover rendezvous.

Natalia accepted there was no reason for both of them to keep it. Popov said it would take him about an hour and Natalia decided to go to the cathedral, briefly shutting herself off from talk of murder and mass slaughter amid the incensed-calm of the baroque and filigreed church. She lit a candle for Sasha and then, upon second thoughts, added one from Popov and another for herself. She prayed for all their safety and for guidance in the immediate weeks to follow and still with time to spare sat half-listening to a black-bearded, black-robed prelate incanting the creed. She actually stayed longer than she should, reluctant to quit a sanctuary in which she felt cocooned and safe from the uncertainties outside.

Popov was already at the hotel when she got back, briefcase between his feet. He started up, the annoyance obvious. Before he could speak she said, 'I've been to church. Prayed for us.'

Popov, whom she knew had no religion, said curtly, 'We're going to need more than prayers.'

'How much stuff did Oskin have?'

'Enough.'

Natalia accepted tension would be inevitable in all of them in the coming days. And just as inevitably probably get worse. 'Let's hope it is.'

The trip towards Kirs showed Natalia how thickly the region was forested. They seemed to drive, mostly in silence, constantly through canyons of tight-together trees. She supposed there were cleared areas in which helicopters could set down but driving along this road it was difficult to imagine where. It was, she recognized, superb ambush country. And then accepted the cover would be as good for those they were trying to trap as for themselves. Several times they were slowed practically to a walking pace by huge, flat-bed lorries piled high with chained-in-place cargoes of tree trunks. On four occasions Popov pointed out covered trucks marked with an insignia he identified as that of the nuclear plant, although there was no recognizable lettering: two vehicles in convoy were escorted by uniformed militia motorcyclists, headlights on to clear slower vehicles out of their way.

'Does that happen a lot?' asked Natalia.

'I've never seen it before.' Then, abruptly, Popov pointed to her left and said, 'There!'

There was no immediate, positive break in the trees but then Natalia saw a slip road with a barriered control post some way back from the main highway. And beyond, just visible through the tree screen, four chimneys and what looked like a tower block, although they passed too quickly for her to be sure.

'It doesn't have a name, just a number,' said Popov, formally. 'Sixty nine.'

'Where's the town?'

'Another four or five kilometres.'

Natalia guessed it was a further two, maybe a little less, before the treeline began to thin and finally straggle into a rolling plain. Almost at once Popov turned off to the right. The road was unmade and holed, jarring Natalia in her seat. It got worse when the hardcore trailed away into a dirt track, snarled with exposed roots and deeper holes. Very quickly the terrain became moonscape, undulating hills and low valleys with little ground covering until they came to a bowl-like core, an enormous open area sloping down for what must have been almost two kilometres to a lake at its bottom. Here there were a few stunted trees and when they got close to the water's edge Natalia saw a small jetty protruding into the lake from an old and lopsided hut. Popov carefully took their car around to the rear of the ramshackle building and parked as close as he could to it on the side furthest from the lake. Here the trees were substantially although oddly thicker, the last hair on a bald head.

As Natalia got out she physically shivered at the cold desolation. 'What happened here?'

'An accident a very long time ago, just after the Great Patriotic War,' said Popov. 'This was where 69 was originally sited. They had to move it.'

'Is it safe?'

'Lvov says so. They've carried out tests. People eat the fish from the lake, fishermen built this hut.'

'This is where we meet him?'

'His choice, like Oskin's last night. Anyone following would be visible for a very long way.'

Natalia shivered again, acknowledging the security. 'This is all so . . .'

'. . . Ridiculous?' suggested Popov, when she trailed to a halt.

'I wasn't going to say that. I'm not sure what I was going to say.' She started at a sound from inside the hut, jerking around to Popov.

'He had to be here first, to see it's safe,' said the man, gripping her arm for reassurance. 'If it hadn't been he would have left, through the trees back there.'

The hut was dark, a square box without any furniture apart from benches along two walls and closed cupboards along a third, and actually smelled sourly of fish. There were other smells, too: the rot and decay of dampness. There was a rod and a small bag along one of the benches, which Natalia assumed belonged to the man waiting for them.

Valeri Lvov was thick-set but not fat and his hair was turning from grey into complete white. The shirt was stained and sweat-ringed under the arms and the boots into which the rough work trousers were tucked looked uniform issue. He stood half to attention, like Oskin had the previous night, but with his hands cupped before him, holding the cap he'd taken off as a further mark of respect. He appeared as surprised as Oskin that Natalia offered her hand, responding hesitantly. Lvov's hand was wet and greasy. There was a nervous tic jerking near his left eye and his lower lip pulled constantly between his teeth.

Natalia didn't want to sit – she didn't want to be in the stinking hut – but did so in the hope of relaxing the man. He remained standing until she suggested he sit, too. He did so quite deliberately on the bench opposite and Natalia realized that from where he had chosen Lvov could see the track along which anyone had to approach through a split in one of the badly placed planks.

It was much more difficult than it had been with Oskin to urge the man through his story. He contradicted himself on the date of the first approach and on the day he was taken off the trolley car by the two strangers he was sure came from Moscow. When Natalia asked why, in contrast, he could remember their list of demands, Lvov said it had been written down: they had told him to memorize it. He didn't have the list any more because they'd ordered him to destroy it. That had been before he was able to tell Oskin and felt he had to do everything they told him, to keep his family safe.

'I know it was wrong. Stupid. I'm sorry.'

'It's done now,' accepted Natalia. Judging it fitted this part of Lvov's account, she took him through the Yatisyna Family Militia photographs. Lvov didn't hurry, holding several prints up to the better light from the single, unglassed window.

'No,' he said, finally, offering the package back to her.

'None at all?' pressed Popov.

'I'm sorry.'

'That's all right,' soothed Natalia, the expert debriefer. 'We only want what you're sure of. Don't tell us anything you think we *want* to hear that isn't true. Or exaggerated.'

'I'm sure they're going to kill me! Harm my family!' Lvov burst out, answering her literally.

Natalia remained silent for several moments, reaching a decision. 'You were in the Militia, once?'

'At the Kirov headquarters,' confirmed Lvov. 'That's how I met Major Oskin. He arrived a month before I left. I'd already resigned.'

'Why did you resign?'

'I wouldn't become part of the system. Become crooked. So they made it hell for me. No one talked with me, accepted me. I had to eat alone, in the canteen. Got all the worst shifts, all the time. They put shit in my locker, sometimes into my boots. There were phone calls to my wife at one or two in the morning with no one at the other end when I was working nights. Other times they were obscene: men saying they were coming around to screw my daughters while she had to watch . . .'

Positively, Natalia announced, 'I promise you that neither you nor your family will be harmed, for what you have done. And are doing, to help us. I will take you back into the Militia. Not here. In Moscow. I'll transfer you and your family away from here, to where you'll be safe.' I hope, she thought. She was aware of Popov's look of surprise but didn't respond.

Like Oskin the previous night, there was almost a visible lift of pressure from the man. 'Thank you! Thank you so much!'

Natalia coaxed Lvov on details, establishing there were two service roads into the complex other than the one she had already seen, also guarded by control posts operating road barriers. The plant was entirely circled by an electrified fence, which at night was permanently lit. The guard contingent had consisted of fifty men but that was being scaled down like everything else in the decommissioning.

Natalia picked on the word, risking the deflection. 'On our way here today we passed some lorries, going in the opposite direction. There was a small convoy with motorcycle outriders?'

Lvov nodded. 'That's part of it. A lot of stuff is being moved from Kirov, by special trains. Mostly to one of the closed-city sites around Gorkiy. It's going to go on for several months.'

'*Had*!' declared Natalia, realizing the mistake of going off at a tangent.

Both men frowned at her, bewildered.

'Had,' she repeated, to Lvov. 'You said the guard contingent *had* consisted of fifty men. But that it was being scaled down?'

'Yes,' agreed Lvov, doubtfully.

'So what is it now?'

'Fifteen. I'm the lieutenant in charge.'

'So how properly can you fill your rosters? Police everything?'

'We can't,' admitted Lvov, in a puzzled voice as if he thought Natalia already knew that.

Beside her Popov stirred and Natalia guessed the information was new to him. 'So what do you do?'

'We don't man the perimeter guard towers at night any more. Or mount the perimeter patrols we used to . . .' Defensively, Lvov hurried on, 'The bunker security . . . the entry combinations and the codes . . . are very good. They're changed, daily. That's enough, really.'

'What about the guard posts on the entry roads?' prompted Natalia.

'That's where I assign the officers I'm left with: the most obvious places.'

'Day *and* night?' she challenged, expectantly.

'When I can. I've sometimes got to come down to one man.'

Natalia felt the satisfaction warm through her. She looked sideways at Popov, surprised he didn't answer her smile. 'They want the codes and security strengths from you?'

Lvov frowned towards Popov, then back to Natalia. 'I told you that! I told Colonel Popov, too!'

'Not in the way we understood it,' said Natalia, sympathetically. 'So because you've got to set them, you know *in advance* the main and subsidiary gate entry codes?'

'Yes.'

'How *many* days in advance?'

'Two.'

'And you allocate, days in advance, the number of guards there'll be on the approach roads?'

'Yes. They've said they want one road unmanned. Some are, sometimes.'

There was a more positive movement from Popov. 'You never told me this!'

'I told you they wanted rosters and codes!' insisted Lvov, nervously.

'It doesn't matter now,' said Natalia, as if she were reassuring Lvov but in fact wanting to cut off any criticism from Popov. Because it *didn't* matter. They had it! She'd found how they'd know, ahead of the attempt, when the robbery was to take place. It would be the day of a special code number – which they would know Lvov had supplied – through a gate Lvov had to ensure would be unmanned. So their ambush was guaranteed.

'I suppose not,' agreed Popov, reluctantly.

'You've done very well,' Natalia told Lvov. 'Very well indeed.'

'You will protect me? And my family?' pleaded the man.

'You have my word,' promised Natalia.

There was a final meeting the following day with Nikolai Oskin to reinforce the need for closer than usual contact with Lvov and because she felt it necessary, Natalia repeated her safety assurances to the man. That night she and Popov ate alone but at the restaurant close to the cathedral. She chose quail again and ate it this time and agreed to the second bottle of wine, flushed with her success.

'I didn't expect you to bring Lvov to Moscow as well as taking him back into the service,' said Popov.

'We couldn't have stopped this without him. And don't we need to recruit honest men?'

'And we can stop it now, can't we?' smiled Popov. 'Nothing can go wrong.'

'Definitely.' If she hadn't personally questioned Lvov they might not have found the way, thought Natalia, allowing herself the conceit. She quickly cast it aside. 'I'm glad you didn't need the gun.'

Popov didn't take the remark with the lightness she'd intended. 'We might have done.'

There would be shooting, Natalia knew: people would be killed, wounded. 'I want everything planned very carefully.'

'What about the Englishman?' asked Popov, suddenly. 'He suggested participation, at the end of an investigation. For the American, as well.'

For the first time in days Charlie Muffin came into Natalia's mind. She was pleased the consideration was entirely professional. 'We *are* going to stop it,' she said, reflectively. 'It would be right to get the maximum benefit, not just here but abroad as well.' Reminded, she said, 'There've been several attempts to reach you, from both of them. The American's message was that it was important.'

'If it was it's been delayed,' said Popov, critically.

She should have mentioned it earlier, Natalia conceded, although only to herself. 'Nothing's more important than this.'

'What about them?' said Popov, finally allowing his own

satisfaction to surface. 'Do we include them? Prove how efficient we are, after all?'

'I'm not sure,' said Natalia. 'I think perhaps we do.'

The anticipated howl of protest at the size of Charlie's expenses came from Gerald Williams, culminating with the financial director's unequivocal refusal to reimburse them, under any circumstances. Savouring the fact that he was arguing from an unshakeable base, Charlie launched the sort of missile he was in Moscow to prevent being manufactured. In one single protest memorandum he invoked the amended Wages Act of 1986, the Trade Union Reform and Employment Rights Act of 1993, the Employment Protection (Consolidation) Act of 1978 and the Employment Protection Regulations of 1995, which between them made Williams' threat technically illegal. At the same time he appealed directly to Rupert Dean, who accepted Charlie's suggestion that Thomas Bowyer accompany him to the nightclubs for which he claimed and independently establish their cost. Bowyer covered it well but Charlie was sure the man was shellshocked at the cost by the end of the evening. There was no acknowledgment or apology from Williams, merely the authorization to Peter Potter in the embassy's financial office to settle the claims in full.

The argument provided the brief relief to what settled into a mundane round of routine contact with the American, German and Italian embassies and unsuccessful attempts, still with the Ukraine excuse, to contact Aleksai Popov. The only really positive development was Simpson's confirmation from London of the embassy's legal assessment that there was no proper, comprehensive Russian law to enable organized crime groups effectively to be targeted: under communism, the myth had always been that crime did not exist.

With so much time on his hands Charlie allowed the nostalgia of revisiting what had been some of their favourite places when he'd lived in Moscow with Natalia. With the advantage of foreign currency he shopped for food at the free enterprise market on Prospekt Vernadskovo and several times came close to going into the nearby State circus, remembering how much she'd enjoyed a birthday outing there. He subjected his feet to the botanical gardens on Glavnyy Botanichestiy Sad that they'd gone to several times and bench-hopped around the park on Sokol'niki. He had, of course, kept the find-me photograph and studied so hard and so frequently not the baby but the background he'd believed to be her suggested rendezvous that he ended unsure if it was, after all, the spot near the Gagarin memorial on Leninskaya.

Charlie intensely disliked the Lesnaya apartment for which he had fought so hard, feeling like the only bone-clattering ghost in a mausoleum large enough to be the waiting room into the Hereafter. Ironically, its only benefit was the enormous television he ordered from the embassy commissary and upon which he avidly watched the Russian language educational slots, gradually extending his viewing to the more general programmes to tone up his Russian. Apart from which he used Lesnaya like he had the box in Vauxhall, somewhere in which to sleep and shelter from the rain, which was actually becoming more frequent with the approach of autumn.

Otherwise he got out and stayed out as much as possible. Part of the routine was to go early to Morisa Toreza, before most of the embassy staff: in the very beginning he'd tried reversing the tables to get into the inner *rezidentura* to spy upon Bowyer as Bowyer was spying upon him, but it didn't work because none of the keys he had been given opened the necessary drawers. He ignored Nigel Saxon as much as possible, who ignored him in return.

It still meant he was entombed far more than he wanted to be in his catafalque office, wishing there was the diversion of crapping pigeons at which he could fire paper clips. He was actually fashioning the prototype of such a weapon when the telephone rang. He recognized at once the voice of the anonymous woman in Popov's secretariat.

'The colonel would like a conference on Thursday, at noon,' she announced. 'It's important.'

Charlie had to wait to be connected to James Kestler. When he was, the American said, 'That's why you had to hold; she must have called me immediately after you.'

Stanislav Silin supposed they would be using the Ulitza Razina apartment regularly when other robberies were planned after this first one. So he'd have to do something about furnishings and decoration: it offended him to be in surroundings like this. Marina could help. She'd enjoy doing that, like she'd enjoyed working with the interior designers who'd turned the two mansions into far better palaces than they'd been when they were first built. And it would be safe, remain their secret, if Marina was the only other person to know. Although he'd defeated Sobelov's challenge it had still unsettled him. More even: frightened him. The conduit to unlimited nuclear materials and even more unlimited money was his absolute protection. So his knowledge had to remain a total secret and this apartment, where the conduit was to operate, an essential secret with it.

The two arrived on time and together again and on this occasion accepted the offered drink, both choosing genuine imported Scotch whisky, and the one who always did the talking said, obviously rehearsed, 'We can afford to become accustomed to what we can really afford.'

Taking his cue, Silin slid their respective bank deposit documents to each man. Neither spoke for several moments, clearly overwhelmed by the size of their fortune.

'Just the beginning,' reminded Silin.

'Just the beginning,' echoed the spokesman. 'You've already got buyers?'

'Of course.'

'Who?'

There was protection in their not knowing, decided the newly cautious Silin: he himself only knew the nationalities, never the names. He only knew the Iraqi middleman as The Turk. 'Does it matter?'

'Not in the slightest,' said the second man. Tapping the bank documents he said, 'This is all that matters.'

'How soon should we meet, after the robbery?' asked the first man.

'How about a month?' suggested the Mafia head.

'There'll be the rest of the money then?' asked the greedy man.

'With a deposit slip to prove it,' assured Silin. 'Will that be too soon to discuss another robbery?'

'I don't see why it should,' smiled the man.

chapter 12

The Interior and Foreign ministers before whom Natalia was summoned, separately and then during a following day joint session, agreed the political benefits of foreign involvement. Their agreement was, however, weighted with conditions. There were repeated warnings that jurisdiction should be kept strictly separated from foreign observer status and equally positive insistences that while both could participate in final planning, it was out of the question for either to be allowed on the ground at Kirs during the interception.

Natalia led every meeting but ensured she was accompanied to each by Aleksai Popov, to whom she deferred during any operational discussion. But in which he, with equal consideration in front of their superiors, took care to include her as if she was as experienced as he was in practical policing. Natalia was impressed by the speed and comprehension of Popov's organization and knew both ministers were, too. Within a day of their return from Kirov he'd supplemented his personally chosen squad of Militia rapid response commandos with two platoons of *spetznaz* Special Forces and taken over disused army barracks close to Moscow's Vnukovo airport for cohesive group training. Air Force helicopters arrived the following day, to be assimilated into the planning.

Natalia's pride at the politicians' obvious admiration jerked into immediate alarm when, in answer to a question from Interior Minister Radomir Badim at the joint ministerial session, Popov announced he would be the overall ground commander.

'There'll be shooting?' she said, when they returned to her office.

'Almost inevitably, although when they realize what they're up against they might just give up. It'll be amateurs against professionals. They'd be annihilated. If they've got any sense they'll realize it.'

'Where will *you* be?'

Popov frowned. 'There! That's what I said at the meeting.'

'I know what you said at the meeting. You could get killed.' Her throat almost blocked at the word.

'I have to be there.'

'I don't think you do! Not actually taking part! You're the *director* of operations, not the commander of them. Stopping what's going to happen at Kirs is different! A specialized job for specialized, trained people. Killers in uniform.' She couldn't risk losing him! She'd lost twice, for other reasons, and was determined she wouldn't – couldn't – lose again. She wouldn't get another chance, not with someone as special as Aleksai. Not with anyone.

'I've done it before,' he reminded, lightly. 'Do you want to see my medals?'

'I'm not joking!'

He came around the desk, putting both hands on her shoulders and holding her at arms' length. 'Hey, calm down.'

'I won't have you in a war situation!' she said, frightened anger driving the careless exaggeration.

But it wasn't the hyperbole he picked up on. '*Won't*?'

'You heard what I said.'

'I wish I hadn't.'

Natalia hadn't intended it to become a matter of superior authority, of her rank superseding his; hadn't meant to shout or argue irrationally or create the confrontation building like a wall between them. The only obstruction of rank had been at the beginning, which had held Aleksai back from making the first move until Natalia had agreed to dinner after an embassy reception and accepted a second halting invitation when there wasn't the excuse of an official function to justify it and about which they had often laughed, since. Natalia wondered how long it would take them to laugh about this. 'I don't want an argument,' she said, willing to retreat.

'Neither do I.'

'I can't . . .' she started badly, changing in mid-sentence. '. . . you can't take the risk. It's ridiculous. Unnecessary.'

'You're being ridiculous,' he said, openly challenging. 'It's this conversation that's unnecessary.'

'I don't want officially to forbid it,' she said, refusing to retreat any further.

'Then don't.'

'We should have talked about it!'

'I didn't think we had to.' Popov smiled, a satisfied expression. 'This conversation *is* unnecessary. It's already decided: the ministers have approved.'

'No!' Natalia refused, wishing her voice had not been so loud. '*You* decided, without discussing it with me. And then you *announced* it to the ministers.'

Popov had taken his hands from her shoulders some time before. Now he stood looking steadily at her, letting the accusing silence grow. 'To countermand it would completely undermine my position. And my authority.'

'It would do nothing of the sort! There are *two* operations, one at the plant, the other to seize as many of the Yatisyna Family as possible. You're the *controller* of both. If you concentrate on one – the nuclear complex – you neglect the other.'

'One's more important than the other.'

'No! I will not undermine your authority; embarrass you in any way. A memorandum of today's meeting has to be prepared, for the understanding between us and the ministers to be confirmed. Mine will state, as you stated, that you will be in overall charge. But from a central command position coordinating both separate actions. Which is where, and how, you should be.'

'Which central command position? Where?'

Natalia didn't know. Desperately she said, 'Militia headquarters in Kirov.'

'Which we've already decided to be corrupt and which

you have already ordered to be cleared out, the moment this is over. So any security will be breached, before the first move is made against anybody . . . headquarters in which there are not, to my understanding, electronic or radio facilities adequate for three-way communication between me and the two separate forces.'

'There would be even less facilities if you were with just one force.' She recognized it was only just an argument.

'Where then?' he pressed, isolating the weakness.

'A command helicopter!' she said, recovering. 'It will have every sort and type of communication equipment and give you complete mobility.'

'I am asking you not to do this,' said Popov, with quiet forcefulness.

'I am asking you not to oppose me.'

'I know why you're saying this. You know I love you, too. And I love you *for* saying it . . . for wanting to do it. But you're mixing our private lives with what we have to do, officially. And that's wrong.'

He was correct, of course. Not totally but with a stronger argument in his favour than she had in hers. Natalia's awareness did nothing to lessen her determination. 'I don't want – won't have – you in the middle of a battle.'

'Regulations permit me to send a separate memorandum to the ministers, protesting your decision.'

'Which would be you embarrassing yourself. Create uncertainties at the very top, when there's no need and where none exists at the moment. And possibly endanger what we're trying to achieve.'

'This is wrong, Natalia,' he insisted.

'It doesn't endanger anything professionally,' she said. 'Or you, personally.'

Popov left the office tight-lipped and without any talk of that evening, which he rarely did any more unless he was involved in some chess activity that took up a lot of his leisure time. Natalia waited later than she normally did but he did not contact her and when she passed his office the engaged or disengaged slide on the door was marked closed.

The wooden toys Popov had bought her were Sasha's favourite of the moment. She'd taken them to the crèche and unpacked them for a fresh farmyard the moment they got back to the apartment.

'Ley coming?' asked the child, from the floor. 'Ley' was the closest she could get to Aleksai. It had been Sasha's choice, getting over their problem of how she should refer to the man whose presence she never questioned.

'Not tonight.'

'Why?' Communication with Sasha very much revolved around 'why?'

'He has to work.' She wondered if he would send a contrary memorandum. Hers, to the ministers, was marked for a copy to be sent to Popov so courtesy as well as regulations required he should duplicate any protest to her.

'Why?'

'He's very busy.'

'Why?'

'Because he has to look after a lot of people.' Me most of all, Natalia thought. She wanted to be cared for by Aleksai Popov more than anything else she had ever imagined or dreamed of.

'Look!' demanded Sasha, proudly.

'Clever girl!' praised Natalia, scooping Sasha up for her bath but leaving the animals lined up as the child arranged them. Natalia had a vague recollection of Charlie telling her of all the animals of the world being saved from drowning by a vengeful God when they'd once discussed religious mythology, but she couldn't remember enough to turn it into Sasha's bedtime story. It had been right, referring her intention about Charlie and the American to the ministers, although she had been, and still was, totally off-balanced by the dispute that arose after it with Popov. She was quite confident she wouldn't be off-balanced by the outcome of her second decision. She knew she would be quite able, without the slightest nostalgic difficulty, to come face to face again with Charlie Muffin.

That was why she was going to conduct the meeting to

which he and the American James Kestler had been summoned the following day.

When Sasha was asleep Natalia swallowed her pride and telephoned Popov. There was no reply to that or to the succeeding two attempts.

chapter 13

The self-serving courtship of others, whom unashamedly he'd courted in return and for the same if not greater self-serving reasons, became an irritating claustrophobia for Charlie Muffin, the perpetual loner unwilling to become a team player in anything. Charlie lost count of the approaches from the uninvited German and Italian in the intervening days, impatient with Kestler's defence for having told them that both were owed the cooperation for what they'd provided about the possible Ukrainian shipment and the separate rumour about fuel rods. Charlie insisted that Balg and Fiore would have limited what they shared, casting as little bait as necessary upon the waters, and was proved right when both supplied more in their desperation to learn all they could about the Interior Ministry encounter: Fiore confided the Italian Anti-Mafia Commission were targeting a Sicilian clan headed by Gianfranco Messina for conventional weapons smuggling and Balg provided named identities of three Russians the Bundeskriminalamt suspected of setting up a smuggling cell in Leipzig.

Charlie, who'd never had a problem with professional hypocrisy when it was to his benefit, was quite happy to ferry the new information to the Interior Ministry and after initially deciding against a night-before planning session with the over-zealous Kestler, changed his mind because there was potential benefit in his doing that, too. Lyneham sat nodding approvingly as Charlie, careless of the condescension, lectured on the danger of offering everything at once.

'Let's trickle it out, a little at a time. Which shouldn't be difficult because that's all we've got. A little.'

'They're not calling us in for nothing!' said Kestler.

'We don't know *why* they're calling us in,' Charlie pointed out. 'Everyone's far too excited for no good reason.'

'Listen to the man,' Lyneham urged the other American. Jesus, he thought, the frenetic son-of-a-bitch needed a brake; actually what Kestler needed was his foot nailed to the floor.

'We've got enough,' argued Kestler, unpersuaded.

'What?' demanded Charlie, unknowingly as worried as the FBI chief at Kestler's unbridled enthusiasm and wishing he was going alone to the following day's meeting. He held up his hands, to count off points. 'All we've really got is an unsubstantiated rumour, about a possible theft from an unknown site in an unknown place of an unknown quantity of nuclear material! Which might or might not involve fuel rods. Grafted on to that rumour there's another that it just might be coming out of the Ukraine. Which if it is, makes tomorrow's meeting academic because Russia doesn't rule the Ukraine any more, even though the contents of its nuclear arsenals belong to them. Fiore's additional contribution is about the *possible* smuggling by the traditional Mafia of *conventional* weapons, which the traditional Mafia has been smuggling since conventional weapons were bows and arrows. And if they are, so what? Fiore wants to trade with what we're being called in for and in my view has thrown the Messina rabbit into the pot for us to invent a connection. Which is what you're doing. And Balg is trying the same shell game, giving us the names of three Russian villains who might, but then again might not, have set up a smuggling business in Leipzig. Again, so what? He's not saying it's nuclear. You are. Germany – Europe – is full of Russian organized crime smuggling everything from condoms to coffins. So tell me! What have we really got, to bargain with if we've got to bargain at all?'

'A bucket of spit,' concluded Lyneham. If the English had had a few more sneaky bastards like this guy a couple of hundred years back, America would still be a British colony and they'd all be drinking warm beer.

The crestfallen Kestler looked between the other two men. 'You're throwing away what we've got!'

'That's exactly what I'm *not* doing,' argued Charlie. 'Put forward properly, it sounds like something. Dump it in their laps all at once and it looks like what it probably is: shit.'

'Trickle it, the man said,' endorsed Lyneham. 'Listen first, speak later.'

'Maybe I'll follow you,' Kestler conceded, to Charlie.

Bingo! thought Lyneham, relief lifting off into euphoria. There was a God after all and He cared about old guys taking six-packs to go fishing off the Florida coast and piss over the side when they felt like it.

'That's fine by me,' accepted Charlie. It was anything but fine by Charlie because whatever his new role was it certainly wasn't playing nappy-changing nursemaid to a politically well-connected sex machine who couldn't sit still for more than three minutes at a time. But despite his realistic refusal to invest the following day with unjustified expectations, there had to be some valid reason for a summons that both Lyneham and Bowyer were adamant hadn't happened before. And whatever it was, he didn't want it fucked up by a caped crusading Kestler trying to fly faster than a speeding bullet. So for the moment he'd take the nursemaid's job.

'We'll go to the ministry together, then?' suggested Kestler.

Shit, thought Charlie. 'Why don't you pick me up, on your way?'

Charlie's final impression of cloying claustrophobia came with the repeated-phrase lecture from Nigel Saxon to maintain political awareness at all times and which Charlie was tempted to duck but didn't, preferring to endure the pointlessness than to have the envious Head of Chancellery add separately to whatever nit-picking Bowyer was channelling back to London. Which wasn't Charlie modifying the independent habits of a lifetime, just adapting them to the needs of the moment for the purposes of the moment.

Kestler was predictably early but Charlie was ready anyway. As the American picked his way through the traffic, he said, 'I've got five bucks that says I'm right. And that today is going to be something you didn't expect.'

'You're on,' accepted the financially flushed Charlie.

He lost.

The first person he saw when he entered the small conference room, thirty minutes later, was Natalia. Which was the very last thing in the world he expected.

Charlie's shock was absolute and numbing. He was aware of almost missing his step, close to faltering, and was glad he was following Kestler, who might have hidden it. By the time he cleared the doorway he had recovered and was sure his face was set.

The Russian group was assembled opposite places ready for him and the American: leather-encased blotters, with notepads and sharply pointed pencils and individual bottles of mineral water, with accompanying glasses. Popov invited them to sit and Charlie took the chair directly opposite Natalia, separated from her by no more than two metres. Popov was to her right, with a grey-haired man next to him. A younger, moustached man sat to Natalia's left. There was a gap of two chairs before a bespectacled clerk already hunched over a notebook, several pencils laid out to minute the meeting. There was a tape recorder, to the man's right.

'Good morning,' greeted Natalia, in English. 'I am General Natalia Nikandrova Fedova and I am in charge of the special division within the Interior Ministry specifically formed to combat the stealing and smuggling from Russia of nuclear material . . .' Her brief sight of him, in the corridor, hadn't really prepared her for what Charlie looked like, after five years. He had changed, apart from the pressed suit and crisp shirt, in both of which he seemed vaguely uncomfortable. She thought there was more grey in the hair, which was disordered despite the obvious tidying attempt, and he might be slightly fatter, although she wasn't sure. He hadn't shown any recognition – any facial reaction at all – but she thought he might have stumbled coming through the door: it was difficult to tell from the way he normally walked.

Charlie responded to the greeting slightly after Kestler. Her voice was quite level and controlled. Natalia looked exactly as Charlie Muffin remembered, that last day he'd watched her wait expectantly for him to snatch her away from the Russian delegation that had been her excuse to get to him in London; watched her at the same time as looking for the squad, hidden like he had been hidden, waiting to grab him when he made his approach. Which he never did because he hadn't been brave enough – hadn't loved her enough – to trust her. The hair was the same length and just as dark, with no visible greyness and coiled in a businesslike chignon at her neck, and she'd been sparing as she could afford to be with such flawless skin with her make-up, just an outline of her eyes and lips. The grey dress was as businesslike as the hair, high-buttoned and long-sleeved and full, with no hint of the figure he knew to be beneath. The dark-stoned ring was new: on the small finger of her right hand, he noted.

'My colleagues . . .' she continued, turning her head first right and then left '. . . are Colonel Aleksai Popov, my deputy, whom you both know, and representatives, respectively, from this and the Foreign Ministry. Observers.' She didn't provide names. She nodded further, to the note-taker. 'An official record is being made. It will be available, if you so wish.' She spoke, looking directly at Charlie, who held her eyes. He wasn't trying to discomfort her, Natalia knew: he'd always been able to focus his concentration to the exclusion of anything and anyone around him, seeing everything, even what people didn't want him to see. Would he be aware how easy it was for her to confront him; that it didn't matter any more?

So Popov was her deputy. Which made Natalia the higher authority to which the man referred at their first meeting. She must have known he was in Moscow, been aware of his coming even before he'd arrived. Known, too, that he was officially working through the embassy, where she could have contacted him if she'd wanted. Beside him Kestler was saying he would appreciate a transcript and briefly Natalia switched her attention before coming back enquiringly to him. Instead of simply accepting, Charlie said, 'So there must be matters of significance to discuss?'

He hadn't changed there, either, Natalia recognized. When they'd been together – after he'd admitted his Moscow defection was a sham but it hadn't mattered because by then she'd loved him – he'd taught her more about her craft than any instructor. Words had been a creed. Bait, he'd called words. Lures. Which was the way to use them all the time, every time: always make people come to you, never go to them. Words and then silence, like now; silence that people felt they had to fill and made mistakes by rushing in to compensate. 'If there hadn't been, this meeting would not have been called.'

Charlie was briefly conscious of the immaculate, full-bearded Popov looking curiously sideways at her. Here it was, he thought, dismissing the Russian. He was face-to-face again with Natalia, the never-believed-possible moment he'd rehearsed a thousand times in a thousand different ways – although none of them like this – and imagined a thousand different feelings. So what *was* the feeling, now that it was happening? Nothing like he'd imagined. There really was a numbness, a dead, difficult-to-move sensation in his arms and legs. And a hollowness, as if his stomach had been scooped out to leave a void that ached, almost as much as the ache that had begun in his feet. All of which combined into a disorientation initially far greater than that he'd felt when the Director-General had announced the assignment which made this moment possible. There'd been a lot of operational times when he had forced himself to go that extra mile – or more accurately, that one extra inch – but Charlie could not recall it ever being as difficult as it was now to push himself forward to proper, thinking reality. Even as he did so, he recognized the effort was inextricably linked to his emotions for Natalia. He wanted to perform for her, in front of others who didn't know: to impress her. With a head movement to include Kestler, he said, 'It's difficult to think of anything more important than what we've been sent here to help in preventing. So we welcome *being* involved. And hope we are.'

He was good, conceded Natalia, like he'd always been. She hadn't begun with any positive intention, apart from personally controlling the encounter at all times, but she had thought of taking her time, which she admitted to herself would have been to let Charlie fully appreciate her position and authority now. But his response had taken control away from her, making her the person who had to respond, not lead. 'Involvement is what we're here to discuss.'

Natalia sat, waiting, looking at him.

Charlie sat, waiting, looking at her.

Beside him, Kestler shifted, restlessly. Don't! Charlie thought, anxiously; don't for Christ's sake say anything! We haven't got anything yet! In front of him there was another frowned look from Popov towards Natalia. Who was the first to concede.

'We are sure of an intended nuclear robbery. Which we of course are going to prevent. The decision has been made . . .' Natalia hesitated, moving her head positively towards Charlie. '. . . following your suggestion, to include both of you, under strictly limited and clearly understood conditions, in that prevention.' There, you bastard! Natalia thought. Now I'm back in command. Like I'm going to be in command of everything else while you sit on the sidelines and watch.

But it wasn't Charlie who spoke. Kestler said, 'Where is this attempt to be made?'

For the first time Natalia took her attention from Charlie, looking invitingly sideways to Popov.

'To the northeast,' said the man.

Charlie had tensed, nervously, at the sound of Kestler's voice but it had been a perfectly valid question. Before the American could speak further, Charlie said, 'Northeast of where?'

'Moscow,' said Popov, unhappy at not having made himself clearer in front of Natalia and the two officials who were both members of their minister's secretariat.

'In Russia, then?'

'Of course it's in Russia!' said Popov, glad the Englishman was talking inadequately so soon after him.

Natalia knew Charlie's question hadn't been careless. 'Where was *your* information that it was happening?'

He'd taught her to interrogate like that, recalled Charlie. Not *exactly* like that – the question assumed a fraction too much – but always to convey more knowledge than she possessed to lessen the guilt or importance of what her interviewee had to offer so they would provide even more. 'There are widespread rumours in the West of an intended robbery. The Ukraine has been mentioned. Fuel rods, too.'

'No,' rejected Popov, shortly.

'Would you know, if it was the Ukraine?' demanded Kestler.

Cunt! thought Charlie, anguished. Why, when they were being led by the hand into the promised land, did the complete and utter asshole have to use their previous evening's rehearsal to denigrate the colonel in front of his superiors! As Popov's face tightened, Charlie hurriedly said, 'Any material would, we know, be Russian. I think my colleague's question was to confirm the liaison between yourself and Kiev.' The attempted recovery could have been a thousand times better but it was preferable to leaving the rudeness hanging in the air. Calling Kestler a colleague had stuck in Charlie's throat. He wondered if the pain in his feet would worsen if he kicked the American like he wanted to, right in the crotch.

'Of course there is excellent liaison,' said the grey-haired ministry official, as annoyed as Popov.

'I didn't intend to suggest there wasn't,' mumbled the American, agonized by his thoughtlessness.

Natalia welcomed the diversion, although she didn't take her attention away from Charlie. He'd be furious, she guessed: writhing inside. He'd told her once that was why he hated working in any sort of group or even with another person: he took full responsibility for his own mistakes but refused to inherit those of others. He had every cause to be upset today: the American, whom she half-suspected of sexually appraising her, was badly displaying his inexperience. Moving to lessen the hostility but not to excuse the man, Natalia said sarcastically, 'There were messages, about information? Was that *it*?'

'Quite obviously nothing to do with what we're here today to discuss,' seized Charlie, gratefully. He allowed a hopeful smile towards Natalia for the first time.

She didn't respond. 'It would seem not.'

'Then perhaps we should concentrate upon what we *are* here to talk about?'

'That would be a sensible idea.' Natalia delivered that line to Kestler, completing the rebuke.

'Where, in the northeast?' Charlie demanded, directly.

'Near Kirov.'

Which wasn't a straight answer, Charlie recognized. It probably didn't matter: most of the Russian nuclear sites were known by Washington or London so it could be identified by a process of elimination. 'When?'

'Within the next month.'

Didn't know or wouldn't say? wondered Charlie. Or was she intentionally making him beg for crumbs? If she was, he was content to do so: he wasn't in any hurry to end the meeting. What he was in a hurry about was to have another one, as soon as possible. Just the two of them. He wanted to reach out, to touch her, feel her softness and her warmth and have her touch him back, like she'd done when they were together, a reaching out to know one was with the other. 'How, exactly, is our involvement to be limited?'

Natalia was enjoying playing with him, showing him how much she remembered of what he'd taught her, hoping he'd realize she was taunting him. He'd tried to out-fence her with that question but it wouldn't work because she could use it to demonstrate how secondary he was going to be. Charlie had never liked being secondary in anything. 'You will not, of course, be allowed to take any part in the actual interception operation: to go anywhere near the site, in fact. Your involvement will be restricted to that of observers, during planning. You will be informed of the identities of the criminals concerned, after their arrest. And attend any trial, if you so wish.'

He might as well be sitting with a begging bowl in front of him instead of a blotting pad, thought Charlie. Hoping against hope that Kestler wouldn't butt in and ruin the possibility of her saying more, Charlie delayed his response by pouring himself water.

You'll have to do better than that, thought Natalia; you were too good a teacher. Ask, Charlie; ask humbly.

Kestler spoiled the contest. 'I am authorized by my Bureau to offer any technical assistance you might require,' the man blurted.

In front of him Charlie saw Popov reach out for Natalia's arm. She bent her head towards the man and then nodded. Coming back to them Popov said, 'We appreciate the offer, but I think our facilities are quite adequate.'

Charlie's concentration wasn't fully upon the predictable rejection. There was nothing unusual in the man getting Natalia's attention by touching her arm, but Popov had remained holding it as he'd talked and Charlie thought Natalia had begun but then stopped an impromptu movement to cover Popov's hand with hers. Ridiculous, Charlie thought: in the bewilderment of being confronted by Natalia he was trying too hard and seeing significance where none existed. The colonel had been surprisingly over-familiar and any shift by Natalia, if indeed she had stirred, would have been a gesture of displeasure. Discarding the unnecessary reflection Charlie said, 'I'd like to make clear that I am extremely grateful to be included. And although I naturally accept the limitation of an observer I would appreciate the opportunity to contribute during the planning.' There, he thought, I'm practically on my knees. And talking like a recorded message, which should read well in the transcript he intended sending back to London to prove to everyone he was behaving exactly as he had been told.

Natalia felt Popov go forward, to respond, but quickly spoke ahead of him. 'I'm sure we would welcome any worthwhile contribution.' Charlie was far too clever to be ignored: besides which, the idea of virtually having Charlie work *for* her appealed to Natalia. She hoped he'd interpret it that way, too. Beside her Aleksai was doodling squares within squares along the edge of his blotter. She'd indulged herself, Natalia conceded, enjoyed too much the unexpected ease of meeting Charlie again and of proving to everyone – herself most of all – that she was the person to whom they all had to defer. Which she'd proved enough. Now it was time to defer herself, to let Aleksai take over. Things were still strained between them and she wanted to make amends, not worsen the situation by dominating everything. She pulled back, physically withdrawing, and said, 'Mine is, of course, the overall responsibility. Colonel Popov is the operational director.'

The renewed introduction appeared to surprise Popov, who hesitated for several moments, once looking at Natalia as if for guidance before coming back to the two men. It was Kestler who responded to Popov's invitation for any further questions. Charlie decided, quickly, the American's mistakes had come from the younger man being over-impressed at the echelon with which they were dealing. He'd adjusted now, probing generally to begin with rather than snatching isolated points out of the air and Charlie withdrew, too, letting the meeting briefly move away from him. His apparent attention upon Popov, as the man spoke, hid his absorption with Natalia. She, too, deflected to Kestler and occasionally to the two government officials, but a lot of the time she remained looking directly at him.

Where was the sign? Charlie accepted, as the anxious thought came to him, that it was ridiculous to expect her to behave in any way other than with strict formality – just as it was impossible for him to do anything else in front of the men by whom she was surrounded – but he wanted *something* from her, a signal or a hint. A signal or a hint about what? That she was glad to see him; that everything was going to be all right? That wasn't just ridiculous. That was downright bloody madness; the utter delusion of a rambling mind. He was being irrational. Fantasizing, like a lovelorn schoolboy. Charlie didn't like being irrational or letting himself fantasize and most certainly not thinking like a schoolboy, lovelorn or suffering any other sort of dementia.

The reflection was shattered by Popov's revelation of the size of the intended haul. Charlie was so startled he exclaimed, 'How much?' and didn't give a damn that his shock was obvious.

'250 kilos,' repeated Popov.

'A bomb the size of that which killed 40,000 people in Nagasaki can be made from five kilos of plutonium,' recited Charlie, dead-voiced. 'Which means 250 kilos could kill about 2,000,000. And mutilate and injure millions more.'

There was echoing silence in the room for several moments before Popov said, 'We've had the same estimate from our nuclear experts. We know *why* we've got to stop it.'

'I think we all do,' said Charlie.

'And we will,' insisted Popov. 'I will contact both of you, in advance of the final planning meeting.'

Charlie wrote hurriedly on the provided notepad while Popov talked. As the man finished, Charlie slid the sheet of paper across the table more towards Natalia than her deputy. 'My home number here in Moscow, if it has to be out of embassy hours.' It wasn't good – in fact it was bumping along at schoolboy level again – but it was the best he could think of.

'I've already got that, too,' reminded Popov.

'Then we don't need it again, do we?' said Natalia, picking up the note and crushing it into a discarding ball.

Charlie remained annoyed at the American's gaffes but the fury-of-the-moment had gone and there wasn't any benefit in further belittling the man who apologized anyway the moment they got into the car.

'Just wanted to get things clear,' said Kestler. 'And I was *told* to make the technology offer.'

'No damage done,' dismissed Charlie, who wasn't dismissing the experience entirely: he really would have to be careful he wasn't caught by the fallout of anything the other man might do.

'I was right, wasn't I?' demanded the relieved Kestler.

'I owe you $5,' accepted Charlie.

'This is going to be commendation stuff! Bureau performance medal even!'

'Let's hope.'

'We've got a problem, though. What about Balg and Fiore? You think we should tell them?'

'No!' said Charlie, immediately alarmed. 'They start feeding stuff back through their own agencies it could leak out to whoever the customers are in Europe and completely screw the cooperation we've been offered today. And keep us permanently on the outside in the future.'

'So what are we going to tell them?'

'Bugger all!' determined Charlie. 'We were told Moscow had heard of the Ukraine business and were in contact with Kiev. We'll let them know if we hear anything more and in the meantime we'd like to be told whatever else they get from their sources.'

Kestler frowned. 'That's pretty shitty.'

'Life's pretty shitty,' insisted Charlie.

'They'll know we lied to them, when it all comes out.'

'You want to risk losing two hundred and fifty kilos of weapons graded nuclear explosives!'

'Of course not!'

'Then the Germans and the Italians don't get told.' He very definitely had to guard against Kestler, Charlie decided again.

'You debriefed him, all those years ago?'

'Yes.'

'He didn't show any sign of recognition.'

'I scarcely recognized him.'

The ministry observers had agreed it was a good meeting but Natalia welcomed the private review between herself and Popov. He was still aloof, restricting himself to the examination of the earlier conference. She still hadn't received his threatened dissenting memorandum but Natalia was determined not to ask if he still intended to submit one. Just as she was determined not to be the first to cross the line into their personal relationship in anything she did or said. It had been more than a week now since their argument.

'You even identified yourself, by name!'

'It was hardly likely he'd draw attention to himself and to what happened in the past, was it?' Aleksai's curiosity was entirely understandable.

'He must know we'd have a file!'

'Not necessarily. A lot of the KGB files went with the end of the organization. He didn't know until today it would be me he was meeting.' Which was true, Natalia thought. He'd handled the surprise very well, professionally. It was personal situations he'd been incapable of dealing with. Not her problem any more. Natalia had been surprised at herself; surprised how easy it really had been for her.

'I don't think he's very good!'

Charlie's best trick, Natalia remembered: getting people to despise him. 'He's only observing. He can't cause any problems.'

'I didn't expect you to accept his contributing, at the planning sessions to come.'

'Why not? He can contribute. We don't have to act on anything he suggests. It's simply giving them the impression of involvement.' Was there any point in letting the distance remain between herself and Aleksai? She'd imposed her will and he had every right to be offended. But it wasn't a game between them, a contest with a winner and a loser.

'We can't guess what the American would be like under pressure: he could be unpredictable,' said Popov.

Natalia wondered what description Aleksai would have chosen for Charlie if he'd known the man as well as she did.

'They'll both be totally under our control, at all times. They can't disrupt anything at Kirs.'

'I still think this is a mistake; one we'll regret,' insisted Popov.

'It's the decision of two ministries, one of which imposed both men upon us.'

'Proposed by you.'

'It can always be rescinded.' She hesitated. Then she said, 'I'm not doing anything this evening.'

Popov stayed for several moments looking steadily at her, as if making up his mind. 'Neither am I.'

'I could make dinner,' suggested Natalia, allowing the final concession.

'All right.'

Natalia wished the acceptance hadn't been so begrudging.

'I thought one thing was odd,' said Popov, reverting to the meeting. 'His offering the contact number like he did, when he knew I already had it.'

'An easy thing to forget.'

'He didn't strike me as the sort of man who forgot things.'

Charlie wasn't, Natalia knew. Any more than she was, although she'd write down the telephone number she'd memorized from the piece of paper before screwing it up in perhaps her most positive and almost too extreme act of disinterest. She had no real reason to keep it, of course. But then there was no real reason why she shouldn't have it, either.

chapter 14

The reaction from London and Washington was even more frenzied than Charlie expected. Charlie's assessment of the meeting was longer than the actual transcript itself and took the rest of the day and most of the evening to transmit: even before he'd finished the Director-General telephoned to withdraw him immediately for a personal briefing. Charlie successfully argued that there could be as little as an hour's notice of the next summons, which had as much to do with his hope of a personal approach from Natalia as it did for a professional one from Popov. There was no good reason for his being recalled: being taken back to London verbally to tell people what they'd already been told in print was a classic bureaucratic knee-jerk. Rupert Dean ended by thanking Charlie for doubting the assessment of the scientific mission.

Charlie's summons from the ambassador came early the following morning.

Sir William Wilkes, who was accompanied by the stone-faced Nigel Saxon, used phrases like 'amazing information' and 'catastrophic potential' like the ones that had confettied his London briefing and Charlie recognized the familiar routine of everyone wanting from the safety of the sideline to get involved in the best career act in town. Which Charlie willingly provided to be part of the same career act himself. He didn't expect any favours from the disgruntled Saxon, but it didn't hurt for the ambassador to refer to him by his christian name.

It was, unsurprisingly, Saxon who introduced the rebuke

the moment Charlie finished the briefing. 'You should have advised the ambassador before London!'

'I did not consider a robbery that hasn't happened as urgent enough to approach Sir William. I would naturally have provided an account.'

'You were wrong! Let's not have any mistakes in the future,' said the Head of Chancellery.

'Considering the potential of what we're discussing we can hardly afford mistakes, can we?' retorted Charlie, refusing to be bullied. Heavily he added, 'Like the recent scientific mission appears to have misjudged things.'

'In future we want to know ahead of London,' insisted Saxon. 'And don't forget it.'

'No,' said Charlie. Bollocks, he thought; my rules, not yours.

Dean's subsequent reply to Charlie's specific query was not as good as Charlie had hoped. There were, responded the Director-General, three possible nuclear installations in Kirov's administration area, at Kirs, Kotelnich and Murashi. Kirs and Kotelnich were believed to have manufacturing capabilities, but Murashi was classified as a storage facility. Charlie decided against sharing the inadequate information with Kestler: the American was potty trained, old enough to vote and a supposedly trained investigator who should be able to work out the cross-check for himself. And if Kestler did, it would be a test of the promised cooperation if he offered what he got back from Washington. Charlie was totally untroubled by his own hypocrisy: another cardinal Charlie Muffin rule was that rules by which he expected others to abide never applied to him.

Charlie accepted Balg's luncheon invitation when he telephoned the German to say the Interior Ministry meeting had been about the supposed Ukraine activity, wanting to maintain the link because Germany was the major route along which nuclear components were channelled. Balg was a thick-bodied, blond-haired man given to heavy jewellery – a chunky identity bracelet and ornately marked ring – and wore the sort of calibrated astronaut's watch that told the time on Mars. The man chose a Georgian restaurant on Novodevichy Proyezd, overlooking the Moskva.

'So it was a wasted meeting?' said the German, immediately after they'd ordered.

'Not at all,' frowned Charlie, gauging a challenge. 'It maintained our contact with Popov. And proved the Russians intend to work with me.'

'Just Popov?'

Charlie sipped the heavy Georgian wine, needing thinking time. Balg didn't believe him. Charlie wouldn't have believed Balg, if the circumstances were reversed, but he would have disguised the disbelief better. Cautiously, he said, 'Not just Popov. His director, a woman general. Natalia Fedova.'

'No one else?' pressed the German intelligence officer.

Charlie used the wine delay again. 'There were ministry officials. We never got their names.'

Now it was Balg who let silence into the conversation. Eventually the man said, 'The head and deputy head of a division – and ministry officials – convening a conference to discuss so little!'

'I'd been calling them. Kestler, too. Both of us said we had something important, without setting out *what* it was. It was logical for them to think we had more than they did.'

'They must have been disappointed.'

'It was confirmation of what they had.'

'But nothing more?'

Why didn't Balg come right out and call him a lying bastard! 'They said the working relationship with Kiev is excellent.'

'If they didn't know in advance from either you or Kestler, it must have been from Kiev that they got their information.'

A suspicion of his own flickered in Charlie's mind, firing the first burn of anger. 'Obviously.' He lay down his fork, pushing the *satsivi* away only half-eaten.

'So how was it left?'

'That we'd keep in the closest touch, passing on whatever

we got to build up a fuller picture.' Jesus, it even sounded like the lie it was!

'And what have you been able to pass on since?'

That was a karate kick straight in the balls, assessed Charlie, a reminder where the Ukraine information had first come from with the clearly implied threat it could be withheld in the future. 'Nothing,' Charlie conceded.

'So unfortunate when a useful source dries up, don't you think?'

Charlie was quite prepared to acknowledge the German had good enough cause for the scarcely veiled hostility. But he was buggered if he'd let Balg trample all over him. Pointedly, he said, 'Unfortunate for everyone.'

'It depends upon the number and veracity of the sources.'

You weren't looking where you were going and just stepped in the dog's shit, Jurgen my son, thought Charlie. He'd expected the German to be cleverer than that: too anxious to launch a blitzkrieg instead of firing a sniper's shot. 'It does indeed depend on just that! Which is why I'm glad you and I have reached the understanding we have.'

Charlie's chirpiness confounded the other man. Unable to rise to it, Balg instead continued ponderously, 'Which is why I protect and respect my sources.'

'Most of us do,' agreed Charlie, still brightly. He'd had enough. He was convinced he knew what his problem was and was glad now that he'd delayed protesting it sufficiently; if push came to shove he could play dirtier than Balg. Which the man was a bloody fool if he didn't realize. Like he'd be a bloody fool if he didn't recognize which professional to stay with. 'I grade my sources, not just on the level of what they tell me but on their long-term value. Don't you do that?'

Balg remained confused. Hesitantly he said, 'Yes. That's what I do . . . try to do.'

Umberto Fiore was adamant the short notice wasn't an obstacle to dinner that night and was waiting in the bar when Charlie got to the Savoy. The Italian worked from practically the same script as Balg. The disbelief was far more subtle although just as swift and Charlie accepted that since midday

Balg would have rehearsed Fiore. Better prepared himself now, Charlie introduced the flippancy much earlier to cut off Fiore's attempted warnings about continued cooperation. Charlie ended the evening quite convinced he was right and glad he'd arranged the visit to the American embassy the following day.

Charlie refused to join the much-repeated insistences about how good everything was turning out, unresponsively waiting to see if Kestler would reveal that he'd run a nuclear check in the Kirov region. Which Kestler did, as soon as he'd stopped anticipating their soon-to-occur career benefits.

'So we're going to shift a satellite into geo-stationary orbit right over the goddamned place: cover all three sites to see what's going on.'

'You already told Balg that? And Fiore? Like you told them everything that happened at the Interior Ministry!'

Kestler blinked at the sudden accusation mid-stride through a lap of the FBI office. From behind his desk Lyneham elbowed his bulk into a more upright position.

'What?' tried Kestler.

'You heard what I said.'

'What's going on here?' demanded Lyneham, apprehensively.

'A fuck-up's what's going on here,' said Charlie. 'And it risks the deal we've got with the Russians . . .' He paused, looking directly at Kestler. '. . . And all because you want to be everybody's best friend. Instead of which you're a total, utter prick!'

Charlie had no proof, although he was sure he was right, and if he'd kept his nerve Kestler could have called the bluff. But he panicked, speaking ahead of thinking, as he had to Popov. 'I just . . . I mean I didn't . . . there's no harm . . .'

'What the fuck's the idiot done?' demanded Lyneham.

Lyneham came fully upright as Charlie told him, elbows on the desk with his face cupped in his hands. When Charlie stopped, Lyneham looked across at the other American and said, 'Jesus H. Christ!'

'I didn't tell them everything!' protested Kestler.

'What, precisely, did you say?' pressed Charlie, the quietness of his voice belying the anger.

Kestler paused and Charlie wondered if it was for recall or to prepare an acceptable excuse. 'That it wasn't the Ukraine business,' stumbled the man. 'I said the Russians thought something might be going on, within Russia itself. And that they'd asked us in to see if we'd heard anything to connect outside.'

'And you told them as well who the Russians were at the meeting!' pressed Charlie.

'That, too,' admitted the man.

'That all you told them?' demanded Lyneham.

'On my life!'

'I don't give a fuck about your life: it's mine I'm worried about,' admitted Lyneham, openly for the first time.

'*Why*?' moaned Charlie. 'If you weren't going to tell them everything, why tell them *anything*?'

'Germany's important,' argued the man, desperately. 'Italy, too. We can't afford to piss them off.'

'So now they know half a story of which we only know half to start with,' said Lyneham, wearily. 'So they've cabled Bonn and Rome and they'll have investigators all over their goddamned countries beating down the doors of every snitch, informer and grass there is and knocking shit out of them. And every snitch, informer and grass is going to go running straight to the bad guys to tell them why the heat's on. And by the end of the week there won't be a yak herder in Outer Mongolia who won't know about it. You *any* idea what you've done, you asshole?'

'They said it wouldn't be like that!' protested Kestler, weakly.

'What control have either of them got over *how* it's going to be?' pointed out Charlie. 'They're just lighting the touch paper.'

Ignoring the younger man, Lyneham said to Charlie, 'You think you should warn Popov? And the woman?'

Charlie was uncomfortable at Natalia being referred to as 'the woman'. He said, 'I think I should. But I'm not going to.

It would be closing the door on myself.' The separation of himself from Kestler was intentional.

Continuing as if Kestler wasn't in the room, Lyneham said, 'I know it doesn't count for a row of beans, but I'm sorry, Charlie. Truly sorry.'

'Yeah,' said Charlie, not wanting to be rude but not wanting to acknowledge an empty apology, either: like Lyneham said, it didn't count for a row of beans.

'I'd like to say . . .' started Kestler but Charlie stopped him. 'Don't! I don't want to hear anything you say. I'm pissed off with everything and anything you say.'

Back at the embassy Charlie spent more than three hours formulating the protest to London, reminding the Director-General of the concern about Kestler in the summary that he'd sent with the official transcript of the Russian meeting and going into itemizing detail of what the American had done since. He concluded by advising London of Kestler's family connections.

In London Peter Johnson silently read each sheet Dean handed him, looking up stone-faced when he'd finished. 'This is terrible!'

'That's a conservative judgement.'

'What are we going to do about it?'

'Nothing,' said Dean, mildly.

'Nothing!'

'Nothing premature and ill-considered.'

'I think it should go before the committee.'

'I'll decide what's to be done.'

Johnson shifted irritably in his seat. The bloody man treated them like school children. And he knew why: it was Dean's way of concealing his own inadequacy. 'This is too important to ignore!'

The Director-General wondered, unconcerned, which way the committee would split in their support between him and Johnson, if ever they were called upon to do so. 'I didn't say I was going to ignore it. I said I wasn't going to do anything premature or ill-considered.'

Johnson wished the innovative idiots who'd decided a

reorganized agency should have someone like Dean at its head could have heard this conversation. Moscow had been such an opportunity to achieve so much! Fenby had been honest about the problem with his Moscow appointee so why hadn't he put some minimal curb on the stupid little sod. 'I really must recommend a committee discussion on this.'

'I'll think about it.'

Which was what worried Johnson. If Dean took some arbitrary decision, which he had the power to do, it would be several days before he knew what it was.

In the solitude of the echoing apartment and the straitjacket embassy cell – leaving neither for any length of time unless it was absolutely necessary – Charlie went over every word and every gesture and tried to find every nuance from his meeting with Natalia, sinking as he had after the initial elation of the Moscow assignment into the swamp of despair at deciding for the second time, and upon stronger evidence now, that she really didn't have any interest in him any more. She could have made contact if she'd wanted. She'd have known of his posting; had a far easier way of reaching him than before. But she hadn't. Like she hadn't shown anything at the meeting. Charlie tried to buoy his hopes by telling himself there was no sign she could have given, in the circumstances and surroundings of the encounter. But then punctured the attempt by convincing himself she could have shown *something* – he didn't know what, just something – that would have had a significance only to him. Instead of which the most personally significant gesture had been the contempt with which she'd discarded his pitiful effort with the Lesnaya telephone number. It had, he supposed, epitomized what she'd intended to achieve by hosting the gathering: showing throughout it by her very lack of any sign her utter disdain for him.

The agonized conclusion greatly altered Charlie's perception of everything.

With the chance of being with Natalia again he could imagine no better city in the world than Moscow from which to work in a job everyone else in the old firm would have given their eye-teeth to get. Without her, Moscow was a grey, gritty Mafia mecca of the soulless preying on the helpless and the job was one he was being hindered from doing properly by restrictive officialdom and everybody's-friend amateurism. The recollection abruptly came to him of the knocker's van disappearing up the Vauxhall Bridge Road with all his worldly possessions. Moscow, without Natalia, was all he had: there was nowhere else to go, nothing else to do.

Charlie was on his third Macallan and the damp floor of rare self-pity when the telephone jarred in the Lesnaya apartment.

'You have a right to see Sasha,' announced Natalia.

'I'd like to,' Charlie managed, dry-throated despite the whisky.

'A moral right. Nothing more. Nothing legal.'

'No.'

'On my terms.'

'Of course.'

'She's never to know.'

'Of course.'

'That's all it is. The chance to see Sasha.'

'I understand.'

'There's a lot you have to understand.'

Hillary Jamieson wore a skirt Fenby considered far too short, a sweater that was far too tight and wasn't treating him with the sort of respect an FBI employee should show and he didn't like it. Or her. He wasn't happy, either, that for once his likes or dislikes, so important to anyone's career, couldn't affect anything: in addition to having the slenderest legs and the pertest breasts he'd ever wanted not to see, Hillary Jamieson had honour and distinction passes in every applied physics and molecular scientific degree it was possible to achieve and an IQ rated at genius level, which meant he was stuck with her to advise him about what was coming out of Moscow.

'So 250 kilos is sufficient to build a bomb?'

Hillary frowned at the apparent naivety. 'Lots of bombs: enough to start a full-scale war.' She agreed with the considered Bureau judgment that Fenby was a prick – the word that came into her mind – and guessed he couldn't make up his mind whether to look up her skirt or concentrate on her tits. Hillary enjoyed making the silly old fart feel uncomfortable.

'It was a serious question,' said the Director, stiffly.

'It was a serious answer. But weapons-graded uranium or cassium or plutonium isn't gunpowder: you just don't pack it into a cartridge and fire it, bang! It needs a highly technical facility staffed by highly trained scientists to manufacture an atomic device.'

Fenby was undecided whether to mention the way the girl dressed – as well as his irritation at her lack of respect – to the head of the Bureau's scientific division. She definitely needed bringing into line but he'd become a joke in the Bureau if word got out that he'd initiated the censure. 'According to the CIA a lot of displaced Soviet scientists have been employed in the Middle East.'

'If they've got facilities then you've got trouble.'

'What about fuel rods?'

'Nothing to do with weapon construction, although plutonium is a uranium byproduct. Someone's trying to jerk someone else off. A con.'

Jerk off! thought Fenby, agonized. And he was sure she'd shifted in her chair to make her underwear more visible. 'I want you to get rid of anything you're currently working on. I want you solely available on this; let the Watch Room know where you'll be out of office hours. And that includes weekends. I'll send memoranda this afternoon to everyone who needs to be advised.'

'Yes, sir!' said Hillary. She hadn't intended it to be quite as mocking as it had sounded.

He wouldn't complain, Fenby determined: it wasn't important enough to risk being laughed at. He was sure her pants were pink. Maybe with black edging, although that could have been something else.

It was an hour later that the call came from London. 'Good to hear from you, Peter!'

'I'm not sure it is,' said Johnson, from the privacy of his South Audley Street townhouse.

The skyscraper on the Ulitza Kuybysheva was one of the newest in Moscow, visibly modern as Stanislav Silin had tried – and was determined to make – the Dolgoprudnaya modern like the established Mafias of Italy and America, with which he intended strengthening their already tentative links. Through one of their many registered companies they owned the entire penthouse floor, which was normally over-large for their Commission meetings but necessary today for the final planning meeting to which Silin had additionally summoned the middle echelon and group leaders from every Family involved in the robbery. Everyone listened in total admiring silence to what was going to happen and for several minutes afterwards just looked from one to the other, a lot in disbelief.

'Any questions?' demanded Silin.

No one spoke.

'In fact,' the Dolgoprudnaya chief finished, 'our part could be considered minor . . .' He gestured towards where the Commission sat, separate from the rest, wanting to end on a note for his own continued amusement. 'Sergei Petrovich Sobelov will ensure everything goes as intended, at the scene . . .' He smiled, bleakly. 'Which is the only way it can go, exactly as we intend it.'

He was anxious to get home to hear what Marina had decided to do to the Ulitza Razina apartment.

chapter 15

Charlie didn't know what to do. Or say. It would have been wrong to try to kiss her, which was his first impulse. And to offer to shake hands seemed ridiculous. Which it would have been. So he just stood at the apartment door, waiting for Natalia to do or say something.

Natalia didn't know what to do or say either and stood on the other side of the threshold, looking to Charlie for the first move. Which didn't come. Finally, unspeaking, she stood aside. Charlie went in but stopped immediately inside.

'At the very end,' she said. She wished she hadn't been thick-voiced.

He walked down the small corridor but halted again directly outside the door. 'You'd better go in first,' he said, like a courteous visitor outside a sick room.

Natalia did, calling Sasha's name as she entered. The child squatted rubber-legged by the window, tending her wooden farmyard. She looked up, blank-faced, at Charlie's entry.

'This was my friend, from a long time ago,' announced Natalia. Charlie's Russian was good enough now: *Was my friend.*

'Hello,' said Sasha and smiled, looking at the gift-wrapped package in Charlie's hand.

Charlie hadn't known how to prepare for Natalia but he'd imagined he would be ready for Sasha. But he wasn't, not at all. She was dark, like Natalia, the hair frothing in natural curls to her shoulders, and chubby-cheeked, although she wasn't fat. The eyes were blue, again like Natalia, but the nose was bobbed, upturned at the tip, which was like neither of them, but she did have Natalia's freckles. In the photograph she'd been a baby and babies to Charlie all looked the same: now she was a tiny, real thing, a person in miniature. The dress was red-checked, with bows on the bodice, and there were patent shoes with white socks and Charlie thought she was the most perfect, fragile, prettiest creature he'd ever seen. Mine, he thought, his throat clogged. Not a *creature*! I'm looking at my own daughter, baby, child, girl: someone I made. Mine. Part of me. He coughed to say more clearly: 'It's for you.' He'd relied entirely upon Fiona, who'd recommended the doll and even chosen the paper to wrap it in. She would obviously have told Bowyer, and Charlie was curious what had been relayed to London.

Sasha hesitated, looking to Natalia for permission. Natalia nodded and said, 'All right.' The child stopped smiling as she came up to Charlie, solemnly accepted the gift and said: 'Why?'

Charlie blinked, nonplussed. 'I thought you'd like it.' Christ, his feet ached. Everything ached: feet, body, head, everything. He felt lost.

'Why?'

'I thought you'd like a baby to look after.' This was terrible! He was floundering, about to go under.

Sasha looked uncertainly back to her mother. Natalia said: 'Why don't you open it?'

Sasha did, with difficulty, because Fiona had been liberal with the tape and the child began by trying to unpick it: eventually, exasperated, she tore at the paper. For several moments she held the doll at arm's length, seriously examining it, before finally smiling.

'She has dark hair, like you,' said Charlie. How did you speak – what did you say – to a child! His child. His baby. His daughter. His *own* daughter. Mine.

'What's her name?'

'You give her one.'

'Why?'

'Because she's yours.'

'Why?'

'Because I want you to have her. Look after her.'

'Why?'

'Because I do.' Child logic for a child.

Sasha continued to consider the offer gravely, looking first between the doll and Charlie and then to Natalia, who nodded permission again. 'Anna,' the child declared.

'That's good,' said Charlie, not quite sure what he was approving. 'Anna's yours now. Look after her.'

'Sasha!' prompted Natalia.

'Thank you,' said Sasha. She waited, for another nod that the thanks were sufficient, before returning to the window. There she set the doll on the chair so it overlooked the still-life farmyard and said something to it that Charlie didn't hear.

Conscious of the child's early hesitation, Charlie said to Natalia: 'I hope that was all right. Something from someone she doesn't know. I didn't think . . .'

'It's all right,' said Natalia, clearer-voiced. She appeared to become aware they were both still standing. 'Why don't you sit down?' Charlie was uncertain, she recognized. It surprised her because she didn't remember him confused about anything. She wasn't, Natalia decided, positively. There *was* a feeling: nothing more – nothing worse – than discomfort, unease at the oddity of something difficult to believe. It would have been unnatural if there hadn't been something at their meeting as bizarrely as this, neither knowing what to do or what to say with their child – the child he'd never seen, a complete stranger – playing innocently between them. But she was quite sure that was all it was, a perfectly acceptable reaction to the peculiarity of the situation. He was heavier, although not by much, and he'd tried very hard. The sports jacket was new and the trousers had a crease where a crease was supposed to be. Only the footwear was the same and he'd shuffled several times as if he were embarrassed he hadn't done something about that as well.

There was a chair just inside the door, separate from most of the other furniture, and Charlie chose that. Natalia sat, too, on the window-fronting couch close to where Sasha was playing. It put them practically as far away from each other as it was possible to get, virtually on opposite sides of the room. Charlie pulled his feet under the chair, as if to hide them.

It could not have been long, just seconds, but to Charlie the silence seemed interminable. Again it was Natalia who broke it, although with near-cliché. 'Would you like something . . . a drink . . . ?'

'No. I'm fine.' Hurriedly he added: 'Thank you.' He would have liked a drink – liked several drinks – but didn't want her leaving the room, her doing anything but sitting there, opposite him; their being together. He didn't know what to expect or how today was going to end but for as long as it lasted he just wanted her with him, doing nothing else, thinking about nothing else. Just there. Speak! he told himself: say something. Sasha was the reason for his being there, the swaying bridge between them. He babbled: 'She's very pretty . . . beautiful . . . like . . .' He brought himself up short before adding 'like you', which would have sounded crass. There *was* a similarity which Natalia must have recognized, so the remark would not have been too out of place. Today Natalia wore a loose, long sweater and a skirt and her hair was looser than at the formal meeting, although still bunched at the neck. She'd been irritated, sometimes genuinely so, when he'd called her beautiful, complaining her features were too heavy and her nose too pronounced, but Charlie thought she *was* beautiful. The freckles – the freckles Sasha also had – were more obvious today so she must have worn more make-up than he'd thought before, to cover them.

'Yes.' It was an acceptance of an obvious fact, not a mother's conceit. He seemed enraptured with her, which was understandable, too. More worrying than understandable.

Unthinkingly they'd reverted to English. Briefly Sasha looked up, frowning, but then started playing again. It was as if the language was familiar to her, Charlie thought.

'You must be very proud.' Banality piled on banality: the way strangers talked, anxious to get away from each other.

'I am.'

'It's marvellous . . . incredible . . . being able to see her.' Edith had been devastated at not being able to have children: the guilt she'd felt – which Charlie could never understand, because it wasn't her fault, not anybody's fault – had been an obstacle in their marriage in the beginning. He suspected she'd never fully believed it wasn't important to him and that he didn't blame her or think she'd failed him in some way. But it really hadn't mattered to Charlie: it was something that couldn't be, and with the job he'd done it was probably better that it couldn't. Which was what he and Edith had decided when they'd discussed adoption. And by the time he'd met Natalia he'd so accepted the fact of childlessness that the idea of Natalia becoming pregnant had never once occurred to him. Or to her, he didn't think. Certainly they'd never talked about it.

'She's mine, Charlie!' declared Natalia, warningly. 'All mine! Legally.' The bubbling discomfort was still there – growing if anything – but easier to appreciate now. She wasn't going to tolerate any threat to the unthreatenable, to herself or Sasha. He had to accept that. Properly acknowledge it.

'I know.'

Not enough. Too glib. 'I mean it! There isn't any way you can interfere. Upset anything.'

'Why should I do that? Do anything? Want to. Don't be silly . . .' He shouldn't have called her silly, but it was too late now. And it was ridiculous for her to regard him as a danger. God, how much he wanted to interfere and upset, although not in the way Natalia meant! Interfere and upset their lives by becoming part of their lives, caring for them, protecting them, so that Natalia would stop worrying any more about danger.

'Your solemn promise!'

'My solemn promise.'

'Don't ever break it!' The hissed demand, heavy with all his broken undertakings and commitments of the past, hung between them like a curtain. Natalia flushed, visibly, with what Charlie inferred to be anger.

'I came,' announced Charlie, seizing the opening, in a hurry to tell her and start putting things back as they had been between them and he wanted them to be again. 'Virtually to this very place . . . !' He pointed beyond her, beyond the window. 'I *got* the photograph. And was sure I recognized the background out there, on Leninskaya. Close to the Gagarin monument. I came and I waited . . . !' He looked briefly towards Sasha. 'It was her birthday, wasn't it! That's what I was supposed to understand: that I was to be there on her birthday – August the eighth.'

He had to be lying: cheating her like he'd cheated her so many times and in so many ways before! She *knew* he hadn't been there, because she *had*. And not just that first year, when she'd prayed he'd turn up. The following year as well, on the same date and at the same place, and she'd lingered there for hours.

'Don't, Charlie! I know it's not true. It *was* August the eighth. And it was the Gagarin obelisk. But you never came. I waited. For hours. But you never came.'

'I *did*!' implored Charlie, so vehemently that Sasha looked up at him, startled, and uttered a nervous whimper.

'It's all right,' soothed Natalia, stretching out an arm towards the girl. 'Play some more, darling.'

Charlie burned with embarrassment at frightening the child and with frustration at Natalia's dogmatic, unmovable disbelief. He took all the fervency out of his voice and quietly, reasonably, said: 'Natalia, listen to me! Please listen! I *did* come. And when you didn't arrive I decided I'd misunderstood. So I came on other days . . . four or five other days in case I'd got the date wrong, which I knew I hadn't. And I went to the old apartment and tried to find you but they said they didn't know where you were. And then I decided you hadn't tried to contact me after all: that you hated me and that the photograph was to let me know just how deep that hate was . . .' It was a different type of nagging foot pain now, the sort that came when he made a mistake and didn't know what it was. Which was what it should be because somewhere, somehow, there had been one of the worst mistakes he'd ever suffered in his life and he couldn't work out how or why it had happened.

Natalia sat shaking her head, not in denial or refusal but in matching incomprehension. 'None of it makes sense. You got it right: what I meant by the picture! Her birthday . . .'

'No!' stopped Charlie, softly. 'Oh no . . . !'

Natalia sat slightly open-mouthed, bewildered.

'What's today's date?' demanded Charlie, flat-voiced in the gouging, bitter relief that he knew what the mistake was. Why! Why hadn't he remembered her belief in a God?

'The twentieth,' she said, her face clouded, still bewildered. 'October the twentieth.'

Charlie nodded. 'That's my date too: because you've adjusted. Automatically.' He smiled sadly towards the playing child. 'Is she christened, Natalia?'

'Of course . . .' started the woman, then stopped, finally realizing. In a whisper, she finished: 'Oh my God, yes.' Her fault! Her terrible, stupid, ridiculous mistake – after being sure she'd planned how to find him so cleverly and so carefully and *had* got through to him – that had ruined so much that might have been. Because he *had* come to her.

'Eleven days,' murmured Charlie, disbelievingly. 'We missed each other by eleven days.' The difference between the Gregorian calendar by which the West worked and the Julian calculations of the year's length that Russia followed: followed particularly in its orthodox church ceremonies in recognizing births, deaths and marriages. And he'd missed it! He'd ponced around thinking he was so bloody smart, Jack the Lad who always got everything right, and he hadn't had the nous to calculate the difference, to be by the space-shot monument on both dates. Charlie couldn't believe it: he really couldn't believe he'd overlooked something so simple and so obvious.

'My fault . . .' they each began at the same time, and then stopped. For the first time Natalia smiled.

'Both our faults,' said Charlie, actually laughing, his spirits in flight. 'But it doesn't matter, darling, not any more. We've made it, finally!'

Natalia's smile faltered, then died. 'Things are different, Charlie.'

Charlie sat, emptied, as Natalia talked, haltingly and at times changing her mind in mid-sentence to start again. While she was talking, Sasha tired of farming and clambered on to her mother's lap. Now Natalia sat with both arms wrapped protectively around the child, who'd left Charlie's doll on the chair but still clutched the wooden model of a cow from her farmyard set.

'But you're not married!' Charlie wondered who the man was: he thought she'd been about to tell him several times but changed her mind with those mid-sentence breaks.

'He's asked me.' Seeing Charlie look around the apartment Natalia said: 'No, he doesn't live here.' The unsaid 'not yet' hung in the air.

'Are you going to? Marry him?'

'I haven't decided.'

Charlie felt a pop of hope. 'Don't you love him?'

Natalia hesitated, wanting the words to be right. Then, holding Charlie's eyes, she said: 'Yes, I love him. I love him very much.'

Charlie's mind blanked, momentarily, no more words to say or thoughts to think. Sasha stirred, on Natalia's lap, snuggling tiredly into her chest. Looking at the child Charlie said: 'Does he know about Sasha?'

Natalia's hold tightened, perceptibly. 'My husband is registered as the father. The dates just worked. He's dead now.'

The drunken womanizer from whom she'd been separated for years, remembered Charlie. With it came a more current thought. There really wasn't any proof or trace of his being Sasha's father. Abruptly aware of her consternation, Charlie said: 'I didn't mean anything, by that! Nothing . . . nothing difficult. Believe me!' From the look on Natalia's face, Charlie wasn't sure that she did.

'He loves Sasha,' she said. 'He's very good to her.'

With an umbilical intuition between mother and daughter

Sasha held the wooden animal out towards Charlie and said: 'Ley's.'

'Leys?' Charlie supposed it could be the Russian word for 'cow'.

'That's the closest she can get to his name.'

'Who is he?' asked Charlie, directly.

'Aleksai Semenovich,' she said. 'Aleksai Semenovich Popov.'

'My boy negotiated all this?' demanded Fitzjohn.

'It's classified, you understand,' said the FBI Director. Covering himself against the thought of indiscretion, Fenby smiled and said: 'I checked your security clearance.' Which was true.

'It's on his records, though?'

'Bold and clear,' assured Fenby. That was true, too. The stupid son-of-a-bitch didn't deserve it. If it hadn't been for his too-important family connections, he'd have hauled Kestler out of Moscow – even if he'd made the mistake of putting him there in the first place – and posted him somewhere like Montana or North Dakota, snowed in where he couldn't do any more damage. He was profoundly grateful for Peter Johnson's warning. He could move quickly now, if he had to.

They were at the Four Seasons again, Fenby's parade ground. The House Speaker waited while their plates were cleared and said: 'What about the physical danger, sir?'

'Strictly involved in the planning,' said Fenby, in further assurance. 'No physical involvement whatsoever.'

Fitzjohn stirred the ice around his bourbon with its cocktail straw, gazing down into the drink. 'Jamie's part will be made known, though? When it's over?'

'Of course.'

'Obliged to you, sir. Greatly obliged.'

At that moment, five thousand miles away in Moscow, the telephone rang in the apartment in which Natalia was now alone, except for Sasha.

'There's been a message from Oskin,' reported Aleksai

Popov. 'He wants to come to Moscow to discuss his re-assignment.' It was the code they had arranged in the Kirov restaurant to announce a date for the robbery.

As Natalia replaced the receiver, Sasha said: 'Why are you crying, Mummy?'

'I'm not crying,' said Natalia. 'Your hair flicked in my eye.'

chapter 16

Aleksai Popov occupied centre stage – literally, from a slightly raised dais – and clearly enjoyed it. There were maps and charts on display boards and he held a short pointer, like an army baton, in readiness. Natalia sat with the same unidentified ministry officials who now had a bank of individual advisors behind them and the note-taker of the previous meeting was supplemented by four others, as well as by a man operating recording equipment. At a separate bench there was a very short, fidgeting man in a creased uniform of a Militia major and two other men in black, military-style belted outfits devoid of insignia of rank, service or unit. Again there had been no introductions, but to Charlie they were unquestionably *spetznaz* Special Forces. Directly behind the black-suited men were more aides in anonymous black fatigues. The table for Kestler and Charlie was away from the main grouping, relegating them to the sidelines.

Where he was being kept in more ways than one, Charlie accepted. In the intervening twenty-four hours since his encounter with Natalia he'd gone through the helpless anger and the why-me self-pity and the how-could-it-have-occurred despair. Now he was concentrating upon being objective, which wasn't any easier than the other emotions but necessary for the catharsis. What there had been between him and Natalia was over, like he'd warned himself in London it might be. She'd thought he'd failed her and was about to make what would probably be a better life than the one she might have known with him. Which, after all the shit she'd suffered, she deserved. She had to know he accepted that:

most of all that she had nothing to fear from him about Sasha. Natalia might have stopped loving him but he hadn't stopped loving her. So it was inconceivable he'd cause her any problems about Sasha. He'd have to make her believe that more than she'd believed him the previous day. Sasha *was* hers, hers alone, no one else's. He had no right to intrude. Popov loved the child, Natalia had said, was very good to her. So Popov would be the surrogate father. Natalia would marry him and Popov would care for Sasha as if she were his own.

Maybe for the benefit of the military men – or maybe just because he liked occupying the podium – Popov reviewed what Charlie and Kestler had been told at the first encounter; certainly the military aides, behind their commanders, scribbled furiously as if they hadn't heard it before. Abruptly, dramatically, Popov declared, 'The attempt is to be made in three days' time,' and a stir went through the room. Charlie was aware of Natalia's eyes upon him and smiled towards her. Although she didn't respond, there was a softening in her face.

Popov retreated to the display boards, naming the Kirs plant for the first time and disclosed the two-pronged intention to seize both the intruders to the installation itself as well as to round up the Yatisyna Family. Indicating the black-suited men, Popov said the Special Forces would be helicoptered into the area on the day of the attempt: the group assigned to the nuclear facility would be split, half dispersed inside in advance of the illegal entry, the remainder held outside. The radioed command for the outside group to complete a pincered ambush, once the entry had been made, would simultaneously trigger the house-to-house round-up of the second independent group on standby in Kirov. The two units would comprise 350 men, with another fifty making up a communications, supply, medical and transportation support force; trucks to ferry the *spetznaz* throughout the area were leaving Moscow that night. Popov hesitated, looking towards Natalia, before saying that he would coordinate both seizure operations from a central command helicopter, which additionally would have continuous, open-channel links to the ministry in Moscow. Popov brought the two military commanders on to the platform before inviting questions, which he pointedly did to the ministry group, not to either Kestler or Charlie.

The ministry queries were inconsequential, the determination of bureaucrats to be included in the official transcript, so instead of listening absolutely to the answers Charlie concentrated on Popov himself. To hate the man, dislike him even, would be ridiculous. It hadn't been a may-the-best-man-win contest, both of them evenly competing for Natalia to make her preferred choice. She hadn't had a choice until the previous day. And by then it was too late. He'd lost his chance but Natalia still had hers. Sasha too. So any personal like or dislike for Popov didn't feature. If he felt anything it was that Popov was the luckiest bastard in the world, whom he envied more than any other man in the world. Which was coming back to self-pity and he had to stop that.

Charlie snapped back to full attention upon the briefing at the sound of Kestler's voice. It was a contribution-to-the-transcript question – whether there could be any doubt about the actual date of the attempt – but it brought Popov and the two officers round to them, giving Charlie his cue. He waited for Popov's condescending reply that they were quite sure of the timing and then said, immediately, 'A total of 400 men, at least? With helicopters and ground transport?'

'Yes,' frowned Popov.

'Even though you're bringing in the helicopters and the bulk of the interception force at the very last minute you won't be able to hide that amount of movement,' insisted Charlie. 'You'll frighten them away. They won't go anywhere near the place.'

Natalia shifted uncomfortably. It was a valid observation but she hoped there wasn't an element of challenge to the man Charlie knew she loved.

Popov smiled, more patronizing than he'd been to the American. 'Large-scale army manoeuvres throughout the Kirov region are being publicly announced today, both from here in Moscow and from Kirov itself. By Thursday an actual tented army camp will have been erected eight kilometres from Kirov. In today's announcement Thursday is being given as the arrival day for the major troop contingent, with their helicopter transport: large-scale movement will be *expected*.'

Good enough, conceded Charlie. 'How *many* helicopters?'

Popov deferred with a gesture to the taller of the two commanders, a shorn-headed, chisel-featured man whom Charlie guessed would resent being professionally questioned by a Westerner, certainly by a non-military Westerner.

'Adequate. The Kamov Ka-22 has a one hundred-man capacity,' said the man, dismissively.

Charlie said, ' "Adequate" was the word used in the official report into the failure of the American operation to get their embassy hostages out of Teheran. Or rather "inadequate" because they didn't allow back-up for accidents or engine failure.'

There was a brief and huddled consultation between the two officers before the taller man said, 'There are allowances for a standby Kamov for rapid redeployment. And four smaller Mi-24 reconnaissance machines.'

Charlie thought they'd made that provision up on the spot but it didn't matter, providing they made the addition. Across the other side of the room Natalia thought don't, Charlie; don't compete.

'There will be a lot of radio traffic, once the operations begin,' intruded Kestler. 'And there will be delays no matter how simultaneously everything is coordinated. How secure . . .'

'Totally,' cut off the second, shorter officer, in impatient anticipation. 'The liaison between the two separate forces and with the ministry here in Moscow will be over a restricted military wavelength, sealed against any outside interference or eavesdropping.'

'Everything is to be confined to Kirs and in Kirov?' demanded Charlie.

Popov frowned again, more in rebuke at the apparently repetitive question than in confusion. 'I don't understand.'

Charlie went from the bearded man to the ministry officials among whom Natalia was sitting and then back to Popov. 'I fully accept all the obvious reasons – Russian legal jurisdiction being the most obvious – but has any consideration been given to letting the robbery run?'

'*Run*!' echoed Popov, the frown more genuinely one of confusion now.

Charlie tilted his head towards Kestler. 'Nuclear smuggling is an international crime, that's why he and I are here. An interception at source blocks that source, admittedly. But it doesn't destroy the intermediary couriers or the European middlemen or expose the recipient countries.'

It was one of the unnamed ministry men who responded, incredulously, ahead of anyone else. 'Are you seriously suggesting letting two hundred and fifty kilos of radioactive bomb-making equipment out of one of our facilities and then attempting to follow it across Europe?'

There were smiles and open sniggers from every Russian in the room except Natalia. She thought stop it, Charlie; for God's sake stop it!

'No,' answered Charlie, quite relaxed. 'Two hundred and fifty kilos of something that *looks* like radioactive bomb-making equipment. You've got until Thursday before a robbery by people who won't be nuclear experts: their proof that what they're stealing is genuine is simply that it's *in* a nuclear facility. Why not substitute the real thing with something that's phoney and which won't matter if it does get lost while we try to follow it? Why not play the same con game that the villains play all the time?'

Natalia felt the inward tension ease away, recognizing the familiar Charlie deviousness. To prevent the Kirs theft was going to be sensational enough. But to extend those arrests throughout Europe and expose the purchasing countries would turn it into a truly spectacular international coup. It wouldn't happen, she knew. From the ministry men flanking her and from others with whom she'd discussed Kirs in detail and nuclear smuggling more generally Natalia knew – like Popov knew – that Moscow was determined that this operation was going to be an all-Russian affair entirely confined to Russian legal authority and for Russia to be internationally eulogized for its commitment to smashing the illegal nuclear trade. Which put political cynicism higher than the commitment but which would be lost in the general euphoria.

'It would be unworkable,' dismissed Popov, although no longer condescending. 'There are at least three hundred kilos of weapons-graded material stored at Kirs. Because we don't know which they'd steal, we'd have to switch all of it. We don't have sufficient time or alternative, safe facilities to which to transfer it . . .' The man paused, looking to the nervously shifting Nikolai Oskin. '. . . We also have grounds for believing that the people who are attempting this robbery have informants inside the plant: there has to be, for them to have stipulated to our informant precisely what they want. It would be impossible to replace the material without it becoming known to those planning the robbery. The operation has to be carried out this way.'

Quite independently, both Charlie and Natalia had thought Popov had been going to conclude his rejection by saying 'my way' instead of 'this way'.

There would have been safe alternative storage sites at Kotelnich and Murashi, Charlie remembered. But the time limit and the security inside the Kirs plant were valid enough objections. But created another, in his mind. 'Half the interception force is being moved into the plant *before* the attempt. If internal security is that bad, they'll be warned ahead of their attempt. And not make it.'

Popov hesitated and then went sideways for a huddled conversation with the two *spetznaz* officers and Charlie was sure it was a danger they hadn't anticipated. Across the room Natalia had the same suspicion.

Popov said, 'The installation will be sealed, from the moment our forces go in. No employee will be allowed out. Nor will any outgoing telephone calls be made.'

'Won't that cause a problem in itself?' came in Kestler, discerning the weakness. 'Regular workers will be expected home at regular times. When they don't arrive, people are going to start asking why.'

'*Unsupervised* outgoing telephone calls,' qualified Popov. 'Communication specialists will be among that initial entry force, to take over the switchboard. Incoming as well as outgoing calls will be monitored.'

Not a bad recovery, Charlie gauged. He hoped Natalia didn't imagine there was anything personal in the exchange: something else he'd have to make clear to her when the chance arose. He had her telephone number as well as her address but he'd left Leninskaya without any talk of their meeting again. Certainly not until after Thursday. She wouldn't welcome any distraction and he had to concentrate on what he was officially in Moscow to achieve.

Beside him Kestler was trying to establish their own logistics for Thursday, arguing Washington's gratitude for the degree of cooperation so far to justify their being allowed close access to what happened at Kirs. It was the man whom Natalia had identified as a representative of the Foreign Ministry who responded.

'There has been some discussion today about security,' said the sparse-haired, square-featured official, looking first to the note-takers to ensure everything was being recorded and then directly across the room at Kestler and Charlie. 'Just as there were understandings about security at our first meeting. Since which time there have been a number of enquiries to our embassies in both Rome and Berlin concerning nuclear shipments into Europe.'

Inheriting the mistakes of others, Charlie recognized: a problem in which he had no intention of getting caught up. Kestler was the one who couldn't keep his mouth shut. So let the eager little bugger talk his way out of the obvious suspicion. At once came the contradiction. Neither of them were on their own: Charlie only wished they were and that he didn't have Kestler around his neck, like an albatross. The Foreign Ministry man had pitched the inferred accusation very cleverly, clearly making it an accusation but leaving it very general, for Kestler or Charlie to condemn themselves by their own reactions. Quickly Charlie said, 'The information we passed on, about the Ukraine and fuel rods, emanated from Germany and Italy. I would have expected both countries officially to be in contact with you.'

'The enquiries weren't about Ukraine shipments or fuel rods,' refused the second ministry man.

Shit! thought Charlie. Separation time, he decided. The alternative was to be sucked down in a swamp of obvious lies and Charlie had no intention of letting that happen. 'At our earlier meeting I gave an undertaking. Which I have kept. I have discussed nothing of that meeting, nor will I of this briefing, with anyone other than my superiors in London. Certainly not with any representatives here of either Germany or Italy.' In the old days the permanent surveillance would have logged his encounters with Jurgen Balg and Umberto Fiore, making that insistence impossible to sustain even though it was true. Charlie hoped the old days were well and truly over. He wanted very much to see how Kestler was visibly responding but to turn would have indicated complicity. He'd given the younger man a way out, for Christ's sake! All he had to do was take it hopefully to save both their asses! Lie a little, mentally urged Charlie, at once correcting himself. Not a little: lie a lot.

'I also gave undertakings at that meeting,' began Kestler, strong-voiced. 'And I kept them. The only people to whom I communicated anything were those at FBI headquarters in Washington . . .'

Go on! thought Charlie; don't stop!

'. . . I made the need for security quite clear to Washington, even though it should have been obvious. I do not believe rumours could have leaked from there. But I will today reinforce my earlier warning . . .'

'We are proving our commitment to cooperation by making transcripts of our meetings available,' reminded the Foreign Ministry man, heavily.

'I will, of course, provide a copy of today's memorandum,' undertook Kestler. 'And of my earlier message.'

The attention switched to Charlie. 'Of course,' he accepted, at once. It wouldn't involve much work, revising and backdating a few phoney messages to London. Which was what they'd expect him to do, after all. But they'd have a provable official piece of paper, that ever-essential bureaucratic asbestos.

There was a momentary, uncertain silence. Then the Foreign Office official who'd clearly been appointed their chief accuser said, 'If there were to be a problem with this operation my government would consider the fault to be external, not one originating from within the group we've assembled to prevent it.'

Everything was getting a bit heavy-footed, Charlie decided. Unctuously he said, 'Having had the preparations outlined today, it's very difficult to foresee how anything *could* go wrong . . .' He allowed the pause for the oily words to sink in. 'But there is still *our* unresolved logistical position?'

'Here, at the Interior Ministry,' announced Natalia.

'What was that crack about the American failure in Teheran?' demanded Kestler, on their way back from the ministry.

Charlie, who usually accepted American transport to make taxi-fare profit on his expenses, looked across the car at the younger man. 'It's a fact. Teheran was a fucked-up mission.'

'What about this one?'

'I'll tell you on Friday morning.'

Kestler looked across the car to Charlie. 'You sure as hell don't seem very enthusiastic about this!'

You've got enough – and more – enthusiasm for both of us, thought Charlie. 'Don't you have an expression in America – something about nothing being over until the fat lady sings?'

Kestler appeared to consider the question. 'I'm not sure it fits.'

'That's always the big worry, something that doesn't fit.' Charlie couldn't think of anything the Russians had overlooked or failed to make allowance for. But his feet ached worryingly.

There had been a secondary conference after the departure of the Westerners, the outrage at their inclusion strongest from the two *spetznaz* commanders unable to comprehend any reason for Western outsiders being involved. Close behind came the antipathy of Aleksai Popov, fuelled by the anger at being wrong-footed by some of Charlie Muffin's demands: he was fairly confident he'd covered himself from most of the people in the room but knew he hadn't with Natalia because they'd discussed and analyzed every preparation he'd made in advance. The Foreign Ministry man's weak and personally unfelt justification of political necessity for the Western involvement didn't placate any of them. The belief that the leak to Germany and Italy had emanated from Moscow was virtually unanimous.

Popov arrived at Leninskaya earlier than Natalia had expected, less than half an hour after she'd returned with Sasha. He held the towel and helped dry the child after her bath and afterwards solemnly examined the animals she'd drawn that day to accompany the letters of the alphabet she'd been taught at the crèche and declared they were the best he'd ever seen. He sat easily at the kitchen table while Sasha ate.

'There was a lot of posturing today,' said Popov.

From everyone, thought Natalia. 'Yes.'

'I said it was a mistake to include them, didn't I?'

'It hasn't proved to be, not yet.'

'It's something we should give serious consideration to in the future.'

How much I wish I knew what was going to happen in the future, thought Natalia. 'Perhaps.'

'You all right?' he demanded, suddenly. 'You seem . . . distracted about something.'

'I am thinking about Thursday,' avoided Natalia, easily.

'When you handled him before . . . Muffin, I mean . . . was he this arrogant?'

Not then. Nor today, Natalia thought. Every point Charlie made had been valid, although she remembered being unsure at the beginning. 'The first time he was acting a part.'

Sasha scrambled down from the table and disappeared into the corridor. They remained where they were. 'Why did you suggest they come to the ministry on Thursday?'

'To ensure we knew where they'll be,' replied Natalia, at once.

Popov smiled, approvingly. 'That was very clever.'

Sasha re-entered the kitchen loudly demanding they look and Natalia was glad that Popov did because it prevented his seeing her alarm at the sight of the doll Charlie had brought the previous day.

'Anna,' announced Sasha, proudly, offering it for Popov's closer inspection. 'My baby.'

Natalia watched helplessly as Popov accepted the doll, still smiling. 'A very pretty baby.'

'The man gave it to me,' said Sasha. 'The man that made Mummy cry.'

Unthinkingly holding the doll on his lap as he would have held a real child, Popov frowned across the table. 'What . . . ?'

'The man who talks like you and Mummy do sometimes. Funny talk.' She giggled, involved in a grown-up conversation.

Popov seemed to become aware of the doll. He handed it back to Sasha, all the time looking steadily at Natalia, waiting.

Natalia had to plumb the absolute depths of the debriefing expertise that had taught her how to respond instantly to a situation while at the same time remaining in control of it, knowing the essential requirement was to minimize the lie as much as possible. 'He came here, yesterday. Unannounced . . .'

'WHAT?'

The fury roared from Popov, even making Natalia, who

expected it, jump. Sasha gave a tiny shriek of fright and then a whimper, like she had the previous day. She clutched out for Natalia, who lifted the girl on to her lap. Calm, Natalia told herself: she had to feign just the right amount of affront, at Charlie Muffin's impudence, but above all stay calm. 'Their embassy obviously have records on us, like we have upon their sensitive people. He had the doll for Sasha. His excuse was having been here before. To Moscow . . .' Desperately she tried to remember every detail of the sanitized records she knew Aleksai had read far more recently than she had. '. . . He wouldn't have known, of course, that it was me who exposed his defection as a deception. He said he hoped I hadn't been caused any trouble. That it wouldn't affect our working relationship now . . .' Enough! Don't lie too much or say too much!

Popov stayed staring at her, unspeaking, for so long that Sasha made another tiny mewing sound and clawed up to bring her mother's arm tighter around her. 'Natalia!' said the man, finally, his voice whisper-thin. 'How did he know you *had* a daughter!'

The abyss opened before her, black and bottomless. 'The same records where he got this address from, I suppose . . .' She strengthened her voice. 'I didn't bother to find out! I asked him to leave and he did. It obviously had nothing whatever to do with the past. Apart, perhaps, from his thinking he might be able to use it to get an advantage the American hasn't got. Which would have been ridiculous . . .' Inspiration came abruptly to her. 'But then you were surprised today by his arrogance, weren't you?'

There was another long silent appraisal. 'Why didn't you tell me?'

Gentle mocking, she decided: a reminder of priority. 'Darling! It happened yesterday evening! Immediately after which we got the definite date for the robbery. Which meant people had to be told . . . the military summoned. And today's conference arranged. Don't you think one was just slightly more important than the other? This is when and where you were going to be told. As you are being told.'

'She said you cried.'

Natalia forced the snorted laugh, holding back from tightening her hold of Sasha and praying for the child not to understand and try to contribute. 'She says your farmyard animals talk to her. The longest conversations are with the horse.' Don't say anything, darling! Just sit there without saying anything! There was no sound from Sasha apart from the occasional slurp of her sucked thumb.

'What are you going to do about him?'

Natalia forced the quizzical look, like she was having to force everything else. 'Do? Why should I do anything? He overextended himself and ended up looking foolish . . . being humiliated. That's enough, isn't it?'

'I think there should be something more public: that his embassy be told.'

'No,' refused Natalia, feeling the ground firmer under foot. 'Making the rebuke public would give the episode an importance it doesn't have. His embassy – or more likely his people back in London – might *expect* him to try something like this . . .' She smiled for the first time. 'With luck he might have even told them he was *going* to try it. Having to admit failure to them himself would be far more humiliating than our making an official complaint. That would make *me* look stupid.'

'And you're going to let her keep that?' he demanded, nodding to the doll the near-sleeping Sasha still held.

'Aleksai! It's a toy! You expect me to throw it away? Or send it back to the embassy? Come on! This was a silly little incident of no importance.'

The atmosphere, of Popov's making, lessened and finally died during the evening. They opened a second bottle of wine during dinner and there was no reserve at all when they made love, but then Popov never made love with any reserve. Afterwards, when she thought he'd drifted into sleep, he suddenly said, 'I overreacted, earlier. I'm sorry.'

'Let's forget it.' How much I wish I could, she thought.

chapter 17

During the subsequent forty-eight hours Natalia only saw Popov, and almost always among a crowd, by going along their communal corridor to his suite, into the adjoining dressing room in which he had a cot moved to avoid quitting the building at night.

The suite itself was transformed virtually into a war room. The map and chart display boards were brought from the conference hall and the double doors to an ante-room thrown back both to enlarge Popov's normal quarters and to accommodate the radio link equipment. The command helicopter went to Kirov as soon as the phoney army manoeuvre camp was established for a series of test transmissions, all of which worked flawlessly. The *spetznaz* commanders were invariably with Popov, as well as various people from the Foreign and Interior Ministries, usually accompanied by the permanent secretaries who had attended all the planning sessions. Nikolai Oskin was also in constant attendance, as well as Petr Gusev, head of the Moscow Militia under whose authority Oskin was being transferred. Natalia reassured the Kirov commander of his protective transfer and issued instructions for temporary Moscow accommodation for his family. It was only when she was personally discussing the agreed move with Oskin that Natalia learned it would be impossible to bring Valeri Lvov to the promised security of the capital until after the raid: at the meeting at which its precise date and timing had been established Lvov had been told by the men terrorizing him that he had to be at the plant to enable their unimpeded entry.

If he wasn't there his wife and daughters would be killed by other gang members watching their apartment.

'I've already organized a *spetznaz* unit to look after them,' promised Popov, when she raised it with him at the end-of-the-day review session.

'They won't be able to go anywhere near the apartment until after everything has begun.'

'I've thought of that, too,' guaranteed Popov. 'Our people will be in an enclosed van, less than a street away. With a radio tie-in to me. Everything will be secured before there's a chance of anyone getting harmed.'

Natalia felt the latest threat to Lvov proved the wiseness of her banning Popov from the actual interception but didn't remind the man. She was glad he hadn't after all officially protested her ruling, which was why she in turn didn't question the constant reviews and replanning sessions Popov repeatedly conducted. She personally felt some were unnecessarily excessive, like living in the ministry building was excessive, although she conceded such attention to detail made their planning virtually foolproof. She actually felt pride-by-association, too, in how it personally established Popov not just in their own ministry but in the higher echelons of the Foreign Ministry, as well.

The frantic activity was not confined solely to Moscow. Kestler's long explanatory message why he had to provide the Russians with two supposed warnings to Washington – both false and one back-dated – on the need for total security prompted a series of urgent and direct personal telephone calls from the nervously unsettled Director himself. Fenby initially forbade either being sent. When he fully realized the commitment Kestler had already and publicly made – confirmed unarguably by the faxed transcript of the planning meeting at which Kestler had given the undertaking – Fenby insisted on revising both messages to include Kestler's supposed doubt about how the British would utilize the atomic smuggling information. When Kestler, uncomfortably reminded of his confrontation with Charlie and Lyneham, honestly protested he had no such doubts, Fenby snapped that it was an order that had to be obeyed. After getting the hopefully absolving cables entirely to his satisfaction, Fenby fabricated responses in which he gave apparent assurances from both the FBI and the State Department that the information would not be dispersed or shared with any other organization and most certainly not with any third country. Fenby's second faked reply pointedly referred to the doubt about Charlie Muffin he'd had Kestler introduce into his cable. Only then did he return the courtesy of Peter Johnson's earlier warning by calling the deputy British Director at home to advise what he had done.

In Moscow, Kestler complained to Lyneham, 'Everything's being dumped on the Brits.'

'That it is,' agreed the local Bureau chief, more interested in how far he was from any firing line. Lyneham was personally very sorry but professionally acknowledged that life – their life – was more frequently a bowl of dog dirt than a bowl of cherries.

'That's not fair. It was my fault,' moaned the younger man.

'I keep telling you fairness hasn't anything to do with anything,' reminded Lyneham. 'If you feel that bad about it, 'fess up to the Director and resign. That way you get a squeaky clean conscience without a single Hail Mary.'

Sometimes, thought Kestler, the fat slob tried just a little too hard for the cynic-of-the-year award. 'You know I can't do that. It wouldn't make anything right, anyway.'

'Then shut up and do what you're told and accept what's known as political reality. I would have thought you'd learned all about that from your uncle.'

'What's my uncle got to do with anything?'

Lyneham's eyebrows came close to his hairline. 'You work it out! It's all too complicated for me!'

By comparison, the forty-eight hours for Charlie were relatively uncomplicated. He had, of course, to prepare the bogus security restriction messages to comply with the Russian demand but his explanatory memo to Rupert Dean simply needed cross-referencing with his earlier complaint about the American, which he specifically ensured it did. His ostracism by Balg and Fiore, jointly designed to frighten him into realizing how great his isolation, if he didn't include them, saved him the chore of lying to them any more: during one of their regular telephone conversations, Kestler told Charlie he was averaging two calls a day from both the German and the Italian. Kestler swore he'd said nothing.

Popov's expanded office, which Charlie recognized from their introductory encounter, was crowded when Charlie and Kestler arrived precisely at the time stipulated by Popov before his departure to Kirov. There were about half a dozen women, the rest men. Seating was directed towards the radio bank at which two headphoned operators sat, their backs to the room. The equipment glittered with power and sound level lights and there were several dial needles twitching in unison, like heart beat monitors, but there was no sound. In Popov's absence, it was Natalia who resolved the doorway uncertainty, guiding them to seats once more separated from the general grouping. She did so quite detached, not looking directly at either of them or saying anything after the initial, automatic greeting until they got to their seats. There she indicated an open side door through which they could see long, white-clothed tables with attendants behind. There were urns and cups and saucers and salvers of sandwiches, with a gap separating wine and vodka and glasses.

'If you wish,' she said, with stiffly correct politeness, and then walked back to her own seat in the very front without waiting for either to respond. Apart from the open door, the hospitality room was distinctly separated from where the events at Kirs were to be relayed and was deserted, although a few people sat with glasses they'd carried back into the main office. Charlie and Kestler ignored the invitation.

With flashing lights and flickering needles the only other diversion, Charlie and Kestler were momentarily the objects of curiosity. Although it had minimal practical purpose, Charlie inherently gazed back even more intently, trying to fix faces for later indentification from embassy photographs to advise London who the audience had been.

When the sound did come a lot of people jumped, even though it was what they were waiting for.

'Sighting!' Popov's voice was very clear, without any distortion, although slightly too loud.

One of the operators made an adjustment.

'Definite sighting!' A pause. 'Timed zero one twenty-three.'

Instinctively several people checked their watches. The room hushed into utter silence.

The unreality heightened for Charlie. It was like – it *was* – listening to a radio drama where everything was real but you still had to create your own mental imagery. Charlie's was of blackness: black figures in black forest, then the installation a dazzling blaze of light. A perimeter fence, of course. More likely walled than impermanent wire. But barbed wire somewhere. Maybe control towers. A gate. Large, big enough for large transporters.

Popov's commentary was staccato, pared to essential words solely for their benefit. The detailed conversations between the man and the military units were being separately recorded for transcription later.

'*Three lorries. No, four. Four lorries and two cars. No lights.*'

Right about blackness, wrong about people: black vehicles in black forest. Moving slowly. Unseen road. Drivers straining for the illumination of the plant. No one talking in the cars or lorries. Silence, like here.

'*Halted. Lead car going on alone. Mercedes. Driver and one other man.*'

Cautious. Checking security, entry codes.

'*It's the unmanned gate. Inside unit alerted. Kirov group on standby.*'

Nerves wire-tight. Both sides. Hunters and hunted. Listening, looking. Charlie's hands were wet, squeezed tight.

'Gate's opening. Flashlight signal. Convoy moving. Lorries are canvas-covered: indications of men inside, impossible to count how many. Last vehicle is another Mercedes. Four men. Everything going into the complex.'

End of the outside visual surveillance. How long before the internal changeover? Minutes, according to the planning sessions.

'In view of inside unit. Straight to storage depot. Men in each lorry. Sixteen . . . twenty . . . twenty-five. Twenty-five including cars. Outside unit closing in. Kirov round-up group launched.'

Nothing rational now; legs, arms, minds, bodies all automatistic. Value of rehearsal and training. Movement without thought. Macabre dance.

'Back-up unit in. Gates sealed. Engagement! Kirov seizure squads meeting resistance. There is shooting! There is shooting.'

A chair scraped. Hisses for silence. A cough. More hisses. Charlie realized he was breathing shallowly, as lightly as possible.

'Engagement inside! Automatic fire! Grenades. Grenade response. Storage facilities penetrated, providing cover. Casualties! There are casualties! Casualties inside the installation and at Kirov.'

Charlie saw Natalia was tensed towards the flat-voiced, emotionless commentary, her neck corded, hands clasped on her lap. Tensed for her lover. Worried.

'Surrender! There is isolated surrender inside the plant! Still resistance. Medics going in. All known Kirov addresses secured. There are casualties. Medics moving in at Kirov.'

Practically all over. Too quick. After so much time and planning it seemed all too quick. But successful. Casualties were inevitable but the robbery had been prevented. Natalia had eased back in her chair, relieved.

'Inside resistance over. Full surrender. Fifteen dead. Some severe casualties. Lev Yatisyna among those detained. Eight dead in Kirov. Some severe casualties.'

The room was relaxing now. Chairs scraped without

hissed protest. People coughed. Began smiling to each other. Nodding. Charlie's feet hurt. His shoulders and neck ached, from the tenseness with which he'd held himself. He stretched up, trying to ease it. Beside him Kestler did the same.

'*Plant 69 and Kirov targets totally secured. The robbery has been prevented with the seizure of all involved. Timed zero two forty-five.*'

The initial applause was isolated but quickly became overwhelming. The self-congratulatory charade of people scarcely involved degenerated embarrassingly into handshakes and even back-slapping. Natalia stood apart but smiling, nodding effacingly at the personal praise and appearing discomfited having to accept the offered hands. By common consent the room began to empty into the hospitality area. Charlie watched Natalia become intently engrossed in a closed-circuit radioed exchange with Popov: she held the earphone pad to one side of her head and smiled all the time.

'They did it!' enthused Kestler. 'Wrapped the whole thing up and tied it in a ribbon! Guess we should celebrate, too.'

'I guess we should,' agreed Charlie.

Natalia was moving ahead, oblivious to them, but Charlie manoeuvred them closer so they arrived inside the adjoining room virtually together.

'Congratulations.'

She actually appeared surprised to find him beside her. 'Thank you.'

Some attendants were standing with already poured champagne. Kestler hurried to get glasses for them, momentarily separated Charlie and Natalia from everyone else and Charlie said, hurriedly, 'You must understand everything's going to be all right . . .'

'No!'

'Please!'

'No!'

Kestler bustled back, champagne flutes cradled between entwined hands. 'It was a first-class operation,' he congratulated, raising his glass.

'By Colonel Popov,' qualified Natalia.

'By everyone,' insisted the American.

One of the few women who'd been in the audience came up behind Natalia, familiarly cupping her elbow and smiling apologies to guide Natalia towards a waiting group of officials.

Kestler looked around the developing party, where most were drinking with the traditional Russian throw-away-the-bottle-cap abandon and said, 'Gonna be a lot of sore heads tomorrow. And why not?'

Charlie, who didn't like the acidity of champagne, moved his tongue over his teeth and decided to change to vodka for the next drink. 'Why not?' he agreed, disinterestedly. Outsider in the planning and outsider at the party, he decided: his contribution – their contribution – amounted to absolutely fuck all. Late though it was he decided to make up lost ground by calling both Jurgen Balg and Umberto Fiore before they heard from anyone else. They'd imagine they'd frightened him into line, but he didn't give a damn about that. He was keeping doors open for himself, not pushing them ajar for them. As he went towards the bar Charlie saw one of the radio operators whisper briefly to Natalia, who frowned and followed him immediately back to the radio equipment. Charlie kept his attention on the connecting doors as he returned to Kestler with fresh drinks.

Natalia reappeared at the doorway but stayed there, seemingly uncertain. Finally she clapped her hands, calling out in a cracked voice for attention. Haltingly, in disbelief, she said, 'There's been a robbery . . . from Kirs . . . it could be as much as two hundred and fifty kilos.'

She finished, looking directly at Kestler and Charlie, and Charlie guessed the sudden wide-eyed consternation was at her realization, too late, that she shouldn't have made the announcement in front of them.

chapter 18

Charlie knew their expulsion was only minutes away: the taller of the two known ministry men actually started to move towards them. Charlie was later to decide Fred Astaire never danced a quicker quickstep than the fast-footed verbal performance he staged that night.

'Use us! Don't exclude us!' A chameleon adapter to the concealment of crowds, Charlie abruptly found himself in the unaccustomed and uncomfortable position of addressing one, not hiding in it. The room was still hushed, people unmoving; even the ministry man stopped, uncertainly. Natalia remained gazing at him.

'You can't exclude us!' challenged Charlie. 'From this room and this ministry, of course you can. But we *know*! And we are going to have to act upon what we know, although it isn't sufficient to advise Washington or London properly. If something's gone – however it's gone – then it's going into the West. Where, with proper cooperation, it still might be possible to stop it. For *something* to be done! But not with each of us working separately, no one knowing what the other is doing. The only outcome of that will be chaos . . .' He still had them! Maybe only just, but there was still complete silence and no one was moving and they were listening to what he was saying. 'If anything like this quantity of nuclear material has gone, then recovering it or stopping it supersedes any national pride. It's a simple choice: responsibility or irresponsibility . . .'

For several moments there was a complete hiatus, everyone suspended in a time warp of indecision, a lot of other-way looking for the escape – for *anything* – of higher authority. Charlie's concentration was upon the official he knew and who had started out towards them. The man moved again, finally, but not in their direction but to a crinkle-haired, thick-set man whose slightly bloated bull-necked appearance Charlie had earlier registered for the embassy photograph comparison. The man made a dismissive hand gesture and people moved away to create a confidential cordon for the two to talk.

It was a very brief exchange, with a lot of head movement, the thick-set man for emphasis, the ministry official of acceptance. It was impossible to anticipate anything from the blank-faced approach of the official. 'You are to wait.' Behind him the room was emptying back into Popov's office, very obviously now at the command of the thick-set figure of authority.

Charlie waited until the door closed firmly upon them – but with an attendant standing guard against it on their side – before going to the bar. He downed two vodkas one after the other, each in a single gulp, and emptied half the third before pausing. It wasn't the booze that made him breathless.

'Charlie!' said Kestler, in slow-voiced admiration. 'I don't care what the outcome is, that was fucking marvellous!'

'If we don't get some sort of entry it was a waste of time.' Two hundred and fifty kilos, he thought; fifty Nagasaki bombs, 2,000,000 dead, millions more maimed.

'They haven't thrown us out,' reminded the American.

'Yet.'

'What the fuck can have happened?'

The younger man was picking up Lyneham's conversational style, thought Charlie. Or maybe his. He shook his head, in matching bewilderment. 'We *heard* Popov say everything was secured; that nothing had been taken! We got a body count! Everything!'

'You think they'll try to swing whatever went wrong on to us, after what was said at the planning meeting?' asked the conscience-pricked Kestler.

Charlie took another drink, shrugging. 'Nothing practical

to be gained speculating down that road, until we know what did go wrong.'

Kestler teetered on the edge of admitting to Charlie what the FBI Director had ordered him to do. 'If this much has gone, the search for scapegoats will be awesome.'

'Let's wait and see what's happened,' urged Charlie, again. There would be a scapegoat hunt: it was part of the algebraic formula after every cock-up, as enshrined as Archimedes' Principle and the Theory of Relativity. Much more relative, in fact, than anything Einstein ever had in mind. How exposed would Natalia be? He had no way of knowing or even guessing, but she headed the specific department trying to defeat the business and at the moment it looked like that business had just got away with the biggest nuclear heist in history. But she had another friend to go to: someone far more closely involved and able to help than he was. He looked to the American. 'Let's hope to Christ your satellite picked up something useful.'

Kestler flushed slightly, at having forgotten the one practical thing they had been able to do. 'You think I should offer it?' he deferred.

'No!' said Charlie, at once. 'A robbery from Kirs, after the preparation and force that went into stopping it, would have had to be brilliantly planned. So our chances of picking up any sort of trail in the West isn't good . . .' Charlie hesitated, jerking his head towards the guarded door. 'We've got to hope that in their panic they don't realize that. But if they do cooperate, anything your satellite picks up is our ace-in-the-hole to keep us in the game.'

'So we sit on it whatever they decide tonight?'

'Sit on it very tightly,' confirmed Charlie. 'If we are thrown out, it'll be all we've got.'

'I'll . . .' started Kestler and then stopped as the linking door opened.

They couldn't see who relayed the message but the inner attendant called, 'You are asked to go in.'

The room had been virtually cleared. Only six people remained, the two known officials, the man to whom everyone deferred, Natalia and the two radio operators still at their light- and needle-flickering equipment. The official group were assembled around Popov's pushed-aside desk and the thick-set man occupied Popov's chair. The man said at once, 'I am Viktor Sergeevich Viskov, deputy Interior Minister . . .' A sideways gesture. 'General Fedova you already know. Mikhail Grigorevich Vasilyev . . .' The taller of the two officials straightened slightly. '. . . is my executive assistant. Yuri Petrovich Panin represents the Foreign Ministry . . .'

Names for the first time, freely offered: it looked promising, quickly assessed Charlie. And they'd been *asked* to go in.

There was another gesture. 'Sit down.' Natalia and Panin were already seated; Vasilyev remained standing in the presence of his superior.

'Plant 69 was not the only target,' announced Viskov. 'There was also the train.'

'What train?' demanded Charlie. It was a risk, interrupting the man, but a greater one would be obediently to accept prepared information and not question what was being kept from them.

The minister looked to Natalia. She said, 'Plant 69 is being decommissioned. You were told that. Material was being moved to other installations. By train.'

Holy shit! thought Charlie. Why should anyone go to the trouble of breaking *in* to an installation when stuff was being moved *out* of them! But a gang *had* broken in. 'Tonight's attempted robbery, actually at the plant? That was a genuine attempt?'

'Unquestionably,' confirmed Viskov. 'All those arrested inside the depot are known Kirov criminals. You heard Lev Yatisyna himself was seized. He heads the main Mafia group in the city: he was leading the group at Kirs.'

Charlie's feet began to throb. 'Are you suggesting that tonight – on the *same* night – there were two quite separate robberies from the *same* installation? One in fact acting as the unintended or unwitting decoy for the other!'

Viskov sighed. 'That could be one conclusion.'

The leader of a criminal group wouldn't set himself up as an intentional decoy. How had one been used to the benefit of the other then? A defector in the Yatisyna clan going across to another, Charlie guessed.

'The train was in Kirov?' queried Kestler, entering the discussion.

'No,' said Natalia. 'It left at nine tonight, when the lines could be closed in advance to general traffic with the minimum of inconvenience. Because of what the cargo is, great care is taken in its transportation: it travels very slowly. The interception was at Pizhma.'

'It left *precisely* at nine?' demanded Kestler.

Well done, Charlie mentally applauded: they'd need as much detail as possible accurately to access whatever the satellite might have picked up.

'Why is the precise timing important?' queried Viskov.

'Every known fact is important,' insisted the American and Charlie thought, you're learning, my son; you're learning.

Natalia crossed to the radio operators, picking up a clipboard. Reading from it, she said, 'Nine-ten is the exact time given.'

Before Natalia could return to her seat, Kestler said, 'What time was it stopped at Pizhma?'

'Twelve thirty-five. As I said, it moves extremely slowly, because of the great care necessary.'

After what had happened, how the hell could Natalia talk about great care being taken in its transportation! Charlie thought she looked very strained, grey-faced, concentrating upon every word and gesture from the deputy minister. 'How was it intercepted?'

Natalia waited, for Viskov's permissive nod. 'Signals set at stop. Men in rail service overalls on the track, warning of a derailment.'

'Weren't the freight cars sealed? Guarded?' asked Kestler.

'The guard commander and several of his men came out, to see what the hold-up was,' said Natalia, dulled by the recitation of disaster. 'It seems the doors were left open: a blatant security breach. They were simply shot down, six of them. Two more were killed inside the cars themselves; three others are likely to die, from their injuries. The two signal box operators were found shot dead.'

'There is need for concerted and quick Western help,' conceded Viskov, anxious to hurry the meeting on.

Not so fast, thought Charlie. 'The men seized at Kirs? Where are they being questioned?'

'There, initially,' said Natalia, returning to her seat. 'All will be flown here to Moscow, during the course of the day. The main interrogation will take place here.' The curiosity with which she looked at Charlie barely covered her inner anxiety, for some sort of guidance. All she had been able to do so far was accept the criticism, direct or implied.

It didn't conceal it at all from Charlie, who knew her so well. Quite brutally he decided he wouldn't make his point now: he needed readmission, solely for the job, nothing at all to do with how he wanted to see Natalia again. So she had to infer he had something to offer, something they couldn't afford to dismiss. If Natalia had to suffer for him to achieve that, then that was the way it had to be. 'Will transcripts be made available?'

Viskov sighed again, at what he saw as hard bargaining. 'There could be consultation,' he offered, limiting the concession.

'From both sides,' accepted Charlie.

'Have you a point to make?' probed Viskov.

'Not until I know more,' lured Charlie, ambiguously. The man was practically on the hook, about to bite!

'Use us, you said,' reminded the deputy minister, hopefully.

Because I couldn't think of anything else to say, thought Charlie. Aloud, exaggerating hugely, he said, 'I will be fully briefed on London's input by this afternoon.'

'So will I,' promised the American, following Charlie's example.

'We'll be waiting,' said Viskov. Heavily, he added, 'And expecting no public announcements, of anything.'

There was already movement on the streets of Moscow when Charlie and Kestler left the ministry. Kestler said, 'You sure we'll have anything to offer, as soon as this afternoon? It's going to take for ever just getting this report together!'

'Fuck the report!' said Charlie, urgently. 'Telephone your Watch Room: whoever or whatever can make things move as fast as possible. We need everything there is from that satellite.' Sometimes, he conceded, there were advantages after all from working as a team. Particularly when the other player had access to things he didn't have.

Everyone had remained awake throughout the night at the Ulitza Kuybysheva penthouse, too. With forced humility it was Silin who poured the celebration drinks from the table with the city view and who took Sobelov's telephone call and who proposed the toast after which he stayed silent for the repeated congratulations which each of the remaining five Commission members were anxious to offer individually.

He'd make them all watch when he put Sobelov to death, Silin decided. Let them see what happened to anyone who believed they could overthrow him. Maybe, even, insist on each of them inflicting some torture upon Sobelov themselves to prove their loyalty.

chapter 19

With their only negotiating benefit whatever – if anything – the repositioned American spy satellite might have detected Charlie's initial intention was to gatecrash the US embassy personally to witness the exchanges with Washington, and be kept out of nothing, gambling that both Americans were so accustomed to his presence by now neither would challenge his intrusion. But Charlie wasn't entirely sure he could con a done-it-all professional like Barry Lyneham and even a friendly, do-me-a-favour objection would have created friction Charlie didn't want at such a delicate juncture. He was reasonably confident the Americans would share sufficient with him if there was anything to share and even more confident he could isolate what they might try to hold back from what Kestler offered at the ministry that afternoon. So there was much more to be gained returning immediately to Morisa Toreza to initiate the other moves he'd already decided.

The night duty watch were still staffing the embassy when he got there but Bowyer hurried in, unshaven, within minutes of Charlie's arrival, which Charlie found both illuminating and irritating. He'd accepted Bowyer's monitoring but hadn't realized the man was employing others on the task as well. 'Didn't know you worried about me staying out late!'

'What happened?' demanded the station head, ignoring the sarcasm.

'At the moment the score is won one, lost one. With the bad guys leading by a mile.' Charlie used the recital as a template for what he had to tell London. It didn't take as long as Kestler had forecast.

'Jesus!' said Bowyer, aghast.

'Right! We should all start praying.'

'What are you doing?'

'Preparing a full report! What else?'

'I think we should alert the Watch Room at once.'

'*I* think *I* should be left to do the job I have been specifically assigned here to fulfil, as *I* think fit. It's only four in the morning in London. Panic only generates more panic.' He was pissed off as it was having the other man constantly looking over his shoulder: he was fucked if he was going to be told what to do by someone who'd openly admitted being glad he wasn't involved.

'I was simply trying to be helpful?' flushed Bowyer.

'The biggest help you could provide at the moment is telling me what time the canteen opens, so I can get some coffee.' Enough, he told himself: it really wasn't the time to fight petty battles.

'Eight o'clock, as a matter of fact.'

The literal response was so absurd Charlie had difficulty not laughing outright. 'Thank you. I'll have to wait then.'

Charlie was almost finished by that time, which usefully coincided with the start of the first cipher-clerk shift. He dumped the bulk of his account for London transmission on his way to the canteen and carried the slopping cup back to his cubicle to finish off, which only took him another thirty minutes. Having added it to the first dispatch, Charlie kept to his buffet-room decision and telephoned Jurgen Balg, once more easily dismissing the hypocrisy. Until this moment he hadn't needed the German; now he did. He said nothing about the American satellite: circumstances hadn't changed that much.

'Does this mean we're cooperating at last?' demanded Balg.

'Germany's the most obvious route.'

Balg laughed, openly and unoffended. 'So I have my uses?'

'And benefit because of it.'

'Who knows you're calling me?'

'You.'

'I see.'

'Fiore has no need to know. About anything.'

'No,' agreed the German, at once.

'Or anyone else.'

'No,' agreed Balg again.

Charlie waited patiently for a reciprocal contribution.

At last Balg said, 'I'm not sure where Pizhma is: how long things might take?'

'Northeast of Moscow,' supplied Charlie. 'Beyond Gorkiy. Nothing's been said but Gorkiy was a closed city under communism, so I'm assuming the transfer was intended for some nuclear depot there . . .' He hesitated, committing something to memory for later. '. . . The most direct route, skirting Moscow to the north, would be through Belorussiya, across Poland and into Germany. If it goes more southerly, then it transits the Ukraine. From which you've already had suggestions of nuclear movement. If the Ukraine is the way, then it could go through what was Czechoslovakia . . .'

'. . . Or through Hungary to get into what was Yugoslavia,' cut off Balg, impatient with the geographic dissection of Europe. 'In unpoliced Yugoslavia they could spend as long as they like negotiating a purchase price.'

'The entire deal for this much was negotiated and agreed before the first move to take it,' insisted Charlie. 'This was stealing to order; highly organized, highly sophisticated, highly professional.' He'd suggested all that in his account to London. Almost nine o'clock there now. Alarm bells would have been sounded, the Director-General himself alerted. Maybe even the Prime Minister's cornflakes had grown soggy from a breakfast interruption. Possibly not just as a result of his messages but additionally from Washington as well. Christ, they needed something from that bloody satellite! Charlie was particularly hopeful that Britain's GCHQ – which during the Cold War worked in the closest cooperation with America's National Security Agency – would have picked up something. He'd attached the highest priority to his request for London to pressure the Gloucestershire facility.

'Whichever way it goes, it's going to take a few days.'

'Which means we've only got a few days to pick it up!'

'Just like that!'

If they'd been talking face-to-face Charlie knew the other man would have snapped his fingers, to enforce his scepticism. 'You happy to wave it goodbye, as it goes along the autobahn?'

'Of course I'm not!'

Charlie managed to fetch more coffee from the canteen – but not to avoid spilling it during the journey – before Rupert Dean's anticipated call. 'What on earth's happened?'

'At the moment you know all that I do.'

'They fully recognize the sort of crisis they've got on their hands; *we've* got on our hands!'

'If not fully during the night they will by now.' And Natalia would be in the eye of every storm, although not in the airless calm: tossed and buffeted between every responsibility-avoiding squall.

'I've alerted GCHQ. Anything else you can think of?'

'Not at the moment: I'm hoping for a lot more this afternoon.' That was an exaggeration. Charlie didn't know what to expect that afternoon.

'I want to be updated immediately from now on, no matter what time of the day or night.'

'Of course.' Tiredness was at last pulling at Charlie, wiping his mind with moments of blankness. If the pale autumn sun hadn't been vaguely visible through the window grime, he wouldn't have known whether it was day or night.

'I'm briefing the Foreign Secretary and the Prime Minister in an hour,' disclosed Dean.

So there had been soggy cornflakes. 'I'm not due back at the ministry for hours yet.' Before which he hoped to get something about the satellite. Best not to promise what he didn't have.

'How is it locally with the Americans?'

'No more problems: he's settled down.'

'You think they'll share everything from the satellite?'

'I don't know. GCHQ might be a useful cross-check.'

'I've met the FBI Director. I don't trust him.'

Always expect the worst from people and you won't be disappointed, thought Charlie: paramount personal survival rule. 'I'll be careful.'

'Make sure you are. Get back to me as soon as you can. And to *me*, personally. I'm taking over direct control.'

'Understood,' accepted Charlie, happily. He was so deeply asleep, slumped precariously in his upright office chair, that it took several rings to awaken him and he actually dropped the handset in his delayed anxiety to pick the telephone up.

'I think space technology is a wonderful thing, don't you?' greeted Kestler.

'I'm looking forward to being convinced,' said Charlie. He was glad he was awake when Saxon appeared at the door.

'What the hell are you playing at?' demanded the Chancellery head.

The crèche arrangement had only been for one night so Natalia used the break in the continuous emergency meetings from Viktor Viskov's chairmanship to that of the Interior Minister himself to extend Sasha's care indefinitely. Radomir Badim took personal control around 8 a.m. after which it was always he or his deputy in direct radio communication with Kirov, denying Natalia any chance of speaking to Popov. With every exchange being automatically recorded, it could only have been an officially restricted conversation but Natalia, mind-fogged by lack of both sleep and any proper understanding of how the disaster could have occurred, was desperate just for the sound of his voice. A mid-morning crisis cabinet convened by the President gave Natalia the brief chance to sleep, which she did in Popov's cot. It was more exhausted collapse than sleep and her last conscious thought was that when she woke up Aleksai would be back in Moscow: Badim's last instruction had been to suspend the on-the-spot interrogation and return to the capital, with the prisoners, for a full debriefing that afternoon.

She awoke after only three hours, gritty-eyed and aching, grateful there was a bathroom and shower adjoining her suite. She alternated the shower between hot and cold and got rid of some of the cramp but not all. The most important improvement was to feel absolutely clear-headed. She'd come the previous day with a change of clothes, expecting to be up most of the night although not for it to be as long as this, so she was able to change into fresh underwear and an uncreased, muted check suit. She critically surveyed her appearance in the full-length bathroom mirror not for her own satisfaction but for that of Aleskai, when he arrived. Bringing a change of clothes had been the best precaution, the shower completed the freshness and her face didn't show the weariness of someone who had been up all night.

Charlie Muffin was very much an afterthought and nowhere in any reflection was how she might physically impress or appeal to him. Natalia didn't want any more personal meetings with Charlie Muffin but she personally believed there was every reason to listen to the man professionally. She'd already experienced enough that morning to know what the agenda would be in the afternoon: it would be an inquest and inquests were always into the causes of a disaster, rarely to find a resolve for one. Only Aleksai had any practical, investigative experience, the knowledge and the expertise to know how to look forward, not backwards. Badim and Viskov and Vasilyev and Panin were bureaucratic politicians and the *spetznaz* officers were specialized soldiers and she was a former intelligence officer whose life had been spent trying to get inside people's minds. Charlie Muffin was also a former intelligence officer but one whose life had been as far removed from hers as it was possible to be or to imagine. He'd *always* been operational, in the field: always expecting to be cheated, always prepared for the worst, always ready for the first prick of the knife in his back, literally or otherwise. In many ways, Charlie was more able than Aleksai, although she would never have admitted that opinion to either and was even embarrassed to think it herself.

Aleksai had always been governed by legal regulations, widely interpretive though they may have been. Charlie never had. In the name of his country – and therefore justifiably – he'd worked with only one remit. Get done whatever was required in whatever way was necessary and don't get caught doing it. Charlie *thought* bad, never good. Which was how he'd think now because he didn't know any other way to think. She'd recognized snatches of that instinctive rationale during that panicked discussion in the middle of the night. Which was why she'd successfully argued with the deputy Interior Minister for Charlie to be included. But that had been in the first minutes and the first hours of non-thinking panic and in the middle of the night. Now it was bright, clearer-thinking daylight. And there was a pass-the-parcel session – the parcel marked 'responsibility' – being conducted by the President himself. And shortly there would be arriving military commanders who'd been dumbfounded to find themselves not just facing Western civilians at a Russian military debriefing but Westerners with the impudence to question tactics and about whom Natalia was sure by now there would have been official complaints to the Defence Ministry. Whose minister would have been at the current cabinet gathering.

So middle-of-the-night promises could very easily be reversed, by the weight and prejudice of higher authority. What would she do, if that happened? She'd have no power to overturn a higher decision. There was only one thing she could do. And she wouldn't be able to explain it objectively or rationally to Aleksai: it was hardly rational – although there was some objectivity – to herself. But Aleksai wouldn't accept any argument or persuasion about Charlie's criminal think-alike professionalism: he'd only see it as a direct slur upon his ability and resent it – and her – more than anyone else. But could she do nothing? Her argument inside last night's room, to gain the admission of himself and the American, had been Charlie's argument outside. There was far too little chance of recovering anything *with* Western help: without it there was no chance whatever. And if two hundred and fifty kilos of bomb-making material was lost, she was lost with it. There couldn't be the remotest possibility of her remaining head of her division if it wasn't retrieved and she didn't need to think about the personal implications of being removed because she'd thought through each and every one from each and every angle and approach.

Natalia's afterthought had become her most dominant thought, focusing her mind upon survival. Charlie's creed, she remembered: *always find the back door and leave it open, just in case*. Natalia didn't think she had a back door: she didn't think she had doors at all to flee through.

In temporary limbo, Natalia arranged the larger conference room that would be necessary for that afternoon and ensured a simultaneous transcript was available of all the preceding twenty-four-hour radio communication.

The Interior Ministry delegation swept back into the building like a whirlwind, Badim and Viskov encircled by a swirl of aides and advisors: Viskov and his executive assistant, Mikhail Vasilyev, denied the chance of any rest by the cabinet meeting, were dough-faced with exhaustion and stress, their blinking a frequently more drawn-out squeezing together of their eyes in apparent bewilderment at the chaos around them. Natalia didn't understand Viskov's head-shake towards her as she joined the group flustering into the conference. She tried to sidetrack the deputy's assistant to get some idea of what had emerged in cabinet, but got more helpless shoulder shrugging from Vasilyev than information, although he did blurt that officials from the Foreign Ministry and the President's secretariat would be attending and that another cabinet session was planned directly after the personal accounts of Aleksai Popov and the *spetznaz* commanders. The warning enabled Natalia to answer Badim's impatiently snapped demand that the Kirov group had already arrived at Vnukovo and were expected at the ministry within thirty minutes.

In the event the journey only took twenty minutes. Popov and the special force officers actually arrived ahead of the outside observers – the drained Yuri Panin, from the Foreign Ministry and an austere listening but untalking man from the President's office – thrusting into the room with controlled urgency. None of them showed the slightest effect of sleeplessness or of what they'd gone through in the previous twenty-four hours: his beard saved Popov even appearing unshaven. Natalia smiled towards the man. Popov simply nodded back, but looked at her long enough for Natalia to know he'd seen and liked her crisp composure.

Natalia had only arranged seating on the dais for Badim, Viskov and Vasilyev, unprepared for Panin and the President's man, but both appeared content to be in the body of the room with everyone else.

Popov at once adopted the role of spokesman. His opening – 'The operation I personally coordinated, the interception at Plant 69 and the seizures in Kirov, was one hundred per cent successful' – showed the man's anticipation of the responsibility-ducking situation to which he had returned in Moscow. No nuclear components of any sort had escaped from the plant. They had lost six men, with four more seriously wounded, two only slightly. In the plant itself there had been twelve civilian deaths, with nine more during the Kirov round-up. At this disclosure, Popov hesitated, looking briefly to Natalia. One of the deaths at Kirs had been that of Valeri Lvov, their initial and pivotal informant. A protective unit had been assigned to the man's family but had not expected gang members to be present inside the apartment in advance of the attempted entry: by the time they'd forced entry Lvov's wife had been murdered. She had been raped first. So had both of their surviving daughters, who were now under medical care.

Popov snatched another look at Natalia, who remembered a twitching man in a stinking fishermen's hut and her promise of protection and felt a surge of sadness. She thought of Sasha and wondered how old Lvov's girls were. She'd ensure they had every medical care: psychiatric counselling, too, if necessary. If there was no other family to which they could go, she'd make orphanage or care provisions, here in Moscow.

Popov continued that of those arrested eighteen were, from their criminal records, members of the Yatisyna Family. There were six other men whose identity documents gave Moscow addresses. It was not known to which criminal organization they were attached but their fingerprints and photographs were being compared with Moscow criminal records. No proper interrogation had been possible but none so far questioned had said anything apart from denying any knowledge or involvement in the separate Pizhma robbery.

'Which is far more serious than we imagined,' declared Popov, dramatically. 'It was obvious for us to put down there on our way back from Kirov, for an on-the-spot examination. Which was impossible. As a preliminary measure we have left the majority of the special forces group in the area, to seal it . . .'

'Seal it?' demanded Badim, impatience surfacing again. 'Why couldn't you make an investigation?'

'Several protective containers have been breached. The entire area, at the moment over a radius of two to three kilometres, is contaminated. At the moment Pizhma itself isn't affected but it could be if the wind changes. 2,000 people live in Pizhma. I have ordered experts into the area, initially from Kirs and Kotelnich . . .'

Badim looked accusingly at Natalia, then back to Popov. 'Why weren't we told of this before? The radio . . .'

'The area is sealed, every possible precaution taken,' repeated Popov. 'I considered it too sensitive even for a restricted channel. The delay in your knowing is literally less than three hours: everything necessary to be done is – or has already – been put into place.'

Natalia turned at the scrape of a chair and saw the presidential aide gesture Badim as he hurried from the room. Virtually every other face was frozen in an expression of horrified disbelief. Natalia was stretched virtually beyond any comprehensive thought, punch-drunk from the unfolding catalogue of disasters.

'This certainly should not become public knowledge,' declared Yuri Panin, from the floor. 'Most definitely not public knowledge abroad. Chernobyl is still too recent in Western memories.'

'Too much of what was happening in Kirov and Kirs became public knowledge abroad,' picked up Popov. 'I believe the Pizhma robbery was possible as the result of those foreign leaks.'

Badim said; 'A conclusion of this morning's cabinet was that it was a mistake to have allowed the Englishman and the American to remain, after what happened at Pizhma. And particularly to have included them in any discussion . . .'

It had been her persuasion, acknowledged Natalia. The four men who had agreed would have sacrificed her to defend themselves. It was the only thing they could have done. She would be destroyed, Natalia thought, desperately. And Sasha would be destroyed with her.

'. . . The decision was also reached this morning to cancel the Western cooperation and in future to exclude any but authorized Russian officials in nuclear matters . . .' The minister paused. 'In view of what we have just learned about the radioactive contamination I would expect that ban to be confirmed by presidential decree.'

'I gave an undertaking,' reminded Viskov, his voice cracked by fatigue and despairing inability to avoid responsibility.

'Which has been rescinded,' pointed out Badim, in a reminder of his own.

'Who will tell them?' asked the deputy.

'I am officially their liaison,' offered Popov. 'It should be me.'

'Then do it!' ordered Badim. 'Let's do *something* to start recovering an initiative! Make it clear everything is suspended. They can get the positive cancellation through the Foreign Ministry.'

She *had* been right – Charlie had been right – in arguing their need for Western help but there was not the slightest point in protesting. The decision was irrevocable, like her dismissal would be irrevocable.

Popov's heavy combat boots clattered over the floor but Natalia was too dulled even to look around at his re-entry. It was Badim's frown towards her lover that concentrated Natalia's attention.

'What is it?' demanded the minister, discerning Popov's uncertainty.

'The American says they know how it was done: how many vehicles were involved, the number of men in the ambush. Even the road they took, to escape! And that containers are strewn around the train!'

Kestler was early picking Charlie up from the embassy, with things to talk about. 'Popov started to tell me everything was suspended!' he announced. 'That we were out!'

'I agree with you,' said Charlie. 'Space technology is a wonderful thing.'

'You are directly impugning my ability!' protested Johnson.

'I am doing nothing of the sort. And you know it,' said the Director-General. 'I'd be failing in my responsibilities if I didn't take over personal control.'

'It's a matter for the full committee!'

Dean regarded the other man quizzically. 'Under your personal control it can be handled alone! Under my personal control, it requires a committee!'

'Of course that wasn't my imputation! I would have convened the committee.'

The man was letting his bruised pride cloud his reasoning. 'Which is *precisely* what I intend doing. As and when there is sufficient reason to call everyone together and to whom I shall be the conduit of every development.'

chapter 20

It was the American's game so it was right Kestler should run with the ball. Which suited Charlie fine. His most recent embassy confrontation needed thinking about. Charlie had no doubt the ambassador himself would have accepted the explanation that he was waiting until after this meeting before making a full presentation, which was the easy excuse Charlie offered, but the defence had been weakened by his not having arranged an appointment – and giving a reason for it – with Wilkes. The censure had been a double act masterpiece, the Head of Chancellery mouthing the words with Bowyer providing a lot of the feed lines. It had culminated with the threat of an official protest to Peter Johnson, whom Saxon said had already asked for any indication of insubordination. Had he not immediately before the bollocking spoken to the Director-General, Charlie would have been more concerned than he was. He nevertheless determined to do better in the future, which did not mean conforming, just getting his story better next time.

Far more worrying was Kestler's embassy arrival remark that Popov had been about to shut them out until hearing what they had to trade. That was warning enough that post-mortem blame was already being apportioned and that a lot was being dumped on them. What he didn't know and couldn't guess was how much Natalia was getting. Charlie doubted the recrimination fallout could have moved so fast in so few hours, but Natalia was the most obvious internal target and there'd be a lot of flak flying. If she were absent it could mean she was the first casualty. What about Popov? The man was hardly endangered at all. The Kirov and Kirs interception appeared to have gone perfectly and the man's approach to the American put him still very much at the centre of things. That call itself was interesting. Why to Kestler and not to him? Careful, Charlie warned himself. There were a hundred possible answers to each uncertainty with as many chances of his not getting any of them right: the danger of spinning the conspiracy carousel too fast was ending up too giddy to think straight.

It was a good feeling not to be any longer apprehensive about Kestler. The brash gaucherie wasn't there any more. Kestler hadn't been overawed in the presence of the deputy Interior Minister during the night, seeming to think of what he was saying before he said it. And Charlie was reasonably confident the younger man was not trying any sort of shell game. He believed Kestler's isn't-space-technology-wonderful call had come within minutes of the man being told what the satellite had picked up. Just as he believed Kestler had shared everything that he had been told. And hadn't held back during their initial preparation discussion during that telephone conversation and again during the car journey.

As they were escorted up to the executive floor of the by-now familiar ministry, Kestler grimaced to Charlie, 'Trickle it out, a little at a time.'

'It's down to you,' agreed Charlie, standing back for the American to enter first.

The tension in the room was palpable. So was the ill-concealed hostility: like preparing to do root canal dentistry on rattlesnakes with toothache. The relief Charlie felt seeing Natalia was brief. The freshly neat appearance in a suit she hadn't been wearing earlier was belied by her expression and her physical attitude. She sat slump-shouldered, her usually unlined features creased by what Charlie guessed to be a combination of fear and despair. Natalia stared directly at him and Charlie would have liked to think it was an imploring look for help, but didn't allow himself the fantasy. By comparison Aleksai Popov appeared positively vibrant, clear-eyed and thrust forward half out of his seat towards them. Charlie thought a Superman cape might have complemented Popov's action-man outfit and at once stifled the sneer: personal jealousy didn't have any place in this room, this afternoon.

From the top table arrangement Viskov clearly wasn't in charge any more. Having carried out his intended embassy photographic comparison after Kestler's wake-up call, Charlie recognized Radomir Badim in the chairman's role, which was hardly surprising in the circumstances. He quickly surveyed the rest of the room, seeking more identities from the previous night's scrutiny. There was no one else he could positively label but a tall, austerely dressed and austerely demeanoured man directly in front of the Interior Minister looked similar to Dmitri Fomin, a member of the President's secretariat.

Badim waved them towards a table yet again set apart from the rest of the room and demanded, 'You have information!'

'I hope we both have information to exchange with each other,' said Kestler and Charlie decided he couldn't have done better himself.

The minister's face tightened. 'You have already been accorded access to a considerable amount.'

It was to Popov that Kestler briefly turned before coming back to the minister. 'As you will have already been told, we have a considerable amount of data collected at the actual moment of the robbery at Pizhma. A complete documentary record of everything that occurred will, of course, be made available to you.'

Made available after detailed photo-analysis and image enhancement, Charlie knew. It would be up to Rupert Dean to make certain they got all that from Washington separately, to match what the local Bureau office made available to him.

Popov's impatience at Kestler's offer was so obvious that Badim looked enquiringly towards the man, who inferred it to be an invitation. 'How?' Popov questioned, loud-voiced. 'Quite obviously you had advance intelligence that there was to be a second robbery; advance intelligence intentionally withheld from us, enabling the theft to take place!'

Battle-lines were being drawn, recognized Charlie, contentedly. But drawn badly. The intention not to intrude on Kestler's presentation didn't preclude him from any general discussion, certainly not when it was a full frontal attack which had to be just as quickly resisted, before it gained any dangerous support: Popov had made the accusation half looking at the presidential official, either for approval or effect. 'That would have been very difficult, wouldn't it?' Charlie suggested, mildly.

'Why?'

'We didn't know anything about material being transferred by train from Plant 69 until *after* it had been stopped and robbed at Pizhma, did we?' pointed out Charlie, intentionally keeping Popov on the back foot with another luring question. 'All our meetings here have been recorded, verbatim. By the people making the recordings this afternoon. It would be quite easy for you to confirm that. They might even have transcripts with them . . .' Charlie looked towards the note-takers and let the suggestion trail away, before he patronized too far. It was tough shit if Popov ended up looking a prick in front of his superiors and Natalia: Popov had picked the fight, not him. Charlie couldn't decide if Natalia has straightened slightly in her seat.

'How *was* your data obtained?' demanded Badim.

'An American reconnaissance satellite was positioned in geo-stationary orbit over the area,' admitted Kestler, simply. 'As I made clear at every meeting, my Bureau – my government – is prepared to offer every facility.'

'A spy satellite!' The accusation came from the austere man and Charlie became even more convinced it was the presidential aide whose photograph he'd studied earlier that day. They were making a lot of premature mistakes in their anxiety to make accusations that hardly mattered.

'A surveillance facility the information from which we always had every intention of freely sharing with you, fulfilling our understanding of the official agreement between us,' corrected Kestler, perfectly pitching the formality. His conclusion was just as perfect. 'Which is what I am here today to do.'

Now it was Dmitri Fomin who flushed. Charlie's satisfaction at their so far rebutting any criticism was marred by a concern that their very success in doing so would add another layer to the discernible hostility. There was nothing they could do about it now. Bridge-building had to come later. He hoped they had the opportunity.

'Photographs?' came in Badim again.

'A total of 150, all time-sequenced,' confirmed the American. 'Each frame is individually timed, providing a chronological record of every stage of the robbery. On the assumption that the drivers remained at the wheels of their vehicles, a total of eighteen men were involved . . .'

Steady, thought Charlie, glad the man beside him had paused; don't forget the trickle affect.

'How sharp is the detail?' asked Badim.

'Extremely good,' assured Kestler, which Charlie knew to be an exaggeration: on their rehearsal-packed way to the ministry Kestler had admitted they wouldn't know the clarity until after the technical evaluation.

'It was the middle of the night!' protested Popov, anxious to recover.

'Our infra-red and image-intensifying technology is highly developed. So is our analysis: we can identify a person's height, stature, weight . . . a full profile,' said Kestler. 'I am told, for example, it is possible to identify which of the attackers carried out the killings of the train guards.'

Charlie showed no surprise at hearing something he had not been already told. Despite the conversation with the Director-General he didn't automatically believe it was something deliberately withheld, either. Instead, his mind followed the tangent he'd opened up with his GCHQ request to London. Kestler had found the denial easy because of the Russian's clumsiness, but the American satellite *was* a spy in the sky, an overhang – literally – from the Cold War. And the technology *was* sophisticated: as long ago as Brezhnev, the Americans had a device miles high over Moscow capable of listening in to the Russian leader's car telephone conversations. It was virtually certain the Kirov satellite – years in advance of what was available during Brezhnev – would have had a listening as well as a photographic capability. Kestler hadn't mentioned the possibility. Maybe it hadn't occurred to him. Or maybe he hadn't been told. Or then again been told but instructed to say nothing.

'So the detail is extremely good?' insisted Badim.

Charlie, to whom verbal subtlety was like the scent of prey to a famished lion, wondered if there was any significance in the Interior Minister virtually repeating himself.

'Extremely so,' assured Kestler.

'What else do the photographs show?'

'The vehicles, to which the canisters were visibly transferred. There were three lorries, one canvas topped, the other two solid bodied. And two cars. One is certainly a BMW. The other is foreign to Russia, too: most probably a German Ford.'

'You talked about knowing the escape road?' demanded Popov.

'The most obvious route,' said Kestler. 'Southwest, towards Gorkiy. Presumably continuing towards Moscow.'

'Presumably?' queried Fomin. 'Can't your satellite continue to track it?'

Kestler shook his head. 'It was geo-stationary: held in one position by the counter-revolution of the earth. And that one position was over Kirov. Pizhma was at the very edge of its "eye".'

Abruptly Fomin crossed the narrow gap to the table at which Badim sat and for several moments there was an unheard, head-bent exchange between the two men, with Viskov leaning sideways to listen although not contribute. Fomin had not resumed his seat before the Interior Minister said, 'If the photographs are a consecutive time sequence, it will be an easy calculation to establish precisely how many canisters were taken?'

Charlie assumed Kestler's brief hesitation reflected the

same surprise he felt at the question. It was an even easier and more immediate calculation to establish how many canisters had gone to have subtracted the number remaining on the train from the figure of those loaded at Kirov.

'Of course,' said the American. If he was surprised it didn't sound in his voice.

'Do you have that figure available?'

The first twitch came to Charlie's left foot.

'Not of those transferred. But it would be easily obtainable in advance of the hard data arriving,' offered Kestler. In what he later admitted to Charlie to have come automatically, the American added, 'But I can tell you there were five canisters left lying beside the train.'

'I can assure you the entire area has been sealed,' said Badim, hurriedly.

The disclosure was like the tolling of a huge bell, so deafening it made the senses reel. In an instant Charlie understood the repeated queries about detail: perhaps the overwhelming reason for their being admitted at all. The Russians believed the photographic detail already sufficient – which it most probably would be, after enhancement – to show that the abandoned canisters were opened and leaking their radioactivity. Which was why they had so far been unable to establish precisely what had been stolen: the area was too hot to go anywhere near. Just as quickly, not wanting Badim or anyone else to realize the premature revelation, Charlie said, 'That's obviously a very necessary precaution. What is the extent and degree of the contamination?' Another response came to him, but he decided to wait for his answer.

'About two to three kilometres in area. Experts are there now assessing the degree.'

Turning directly to Popov, Charlie said, 'London and Washington have had this information for more than twelve hours: information of a serious radioactive leak. The fact that there has been no public disclosure or announcement must prove our total discretion to anyone who continues to doubt.'

Dear God, thought Natalia, there wasn't any place for him

as a lover any more but she needed Charlie as a defender, unwitting though that defence had been. It was her only rational impression: she was confused – disoriented even – by everything Aleksai had said and done.

The attitude change towards them throughout the room was almost imperceptible but Charlie was sure it had changed and in their favour, although not from everyone. He didn't expect any lessening of the military antipathy and Popov would surely remain on the other side of the fence. The importance was the shift of those in higher authority, the minister and the man with the ear of the President whose orders others – even the most hostile – had to obey. Where in the equation would Natalia be? Although her judgment should be businesslike he guessed she'd side *with* Popov.

Radomir Badim, the professional politician, certainly appeared to pick up the vibrations – or maybe decided to generate them – and almost immediately began making conciliatory noises. 'I think we can appreciate that undertaking. And we're grateful for it.'

Never leave an advantage until all the pips were squeezed out, thought Charlie. 'I would hope that in the future there will not be any further misunderstandings.'

'I'm sure there won't be.' It was Badim who looked pointedly at Aleksai Popov, not Charlie, but Popov who hurried back into the discussion.

'You must concede the circumstances are utterly extraordinary?' invited the bearded man.

Charlie, who'd made it a lifetime's practice never to concede anything, allowed that Popov had balls even if he'd so far worn them around his neck. But he was buggered if he was going to make easy the man's attempted rehabilitation in front of his peers. 'Or utterly – even admirably – understandable.'

'*Admirably*!' The astonishment came from Dmitri Fomin.

'The robbery at Pizhma was brilliantly conceived and carried out,' insisted Charlie. 'It would be a great mistake to underestimate or despise an adversary clever enough to have done it.'

'Think like your opponents think?' She shouldn't stay silent any longer, Natalia determined. In little over an hour she'd been brought back from the abyss – now the person to be praised, not condemned, for keeping Charlie and the American so closely involved – so it was time she made a positive contribution instead of sitting there, letting everyone guess her relief. And it *was* intended as a positive contribution. Charlie was more expert than anyone else in the room in putting himself in the mind of his opponents and she wanted to hear something practical, not more inquest avoidance.

Popov showed the most visible surprise at Natalia's intervention, turning sharply towards her. Badim frowned, although Charlie couldn't understand why. Or why, for that matter, Popov had reacted as he had.

'It's a tried and trusted methodology,' suggested Kestler. 'Taught even, at Bureau academies.'

Charlie was glad of the space the American's response gave him. He might not know what Natalia's personal attitude was but her outward appearance was most definitely changed. She wasn't slumped any longer and her face wasn't as care-worn as it had been, just perhaps showing the tiredness they all showed and in Natalia's case even that not too noticeably.

'We need to know, and know quickly, who they are, not how they think!' rejected Popov.

Party time, decided Charlie: for him perhaps with more fun than he and Kestler had anticipated. 'One could give you the other,' he crushed, relentlessly. 'And you've already got the way to find out. More than one way, even.' A pause. 'Haven't *we*?' Ask, you bastard, thought Charlie; I'm not going to help you. Radomir Badim didn't help this time, either.

'How?' Popov was finally forced to enquire.

'The most obvious, first,' set out Charlie. 'Two possibilities. You've rounded up the Yatisyna Family: the leader himself. Run a criminal records check first, to find out who of the Yatisyna Family you *haven't* got. They are your lever. The best guess is that they have gone across to a rival group who used the attempt at Kirs as the decoy it was . . .'

'You might even be able to narrow it down tighter,' picked up Kestler, choosing his moment according to their rehearsal on their way to the ministry. 'To have known about the Kirs attempt sufficiently far in advance, someone would have had to be pretty high up in the Yatisyna organization. It doesn't matter, though, if that doesn't show up. You won't have got everyone. Mock those you have with the names of those you haven't, sneering how they were sold out. Someone will break, trying to even the score by naming the Moscow Family to which the Yatisyna are most closely affiliated . . .'

'Which there's another way of finding out, anyway,' resumed Charlie. 'Who, among those you've picked up, *isn't* Yatisyna but from Moscow, representing the people with whom the Yatisyna were working? That's easy enough to discover, once you've got your Moscow identities: a simple check on Moscow criminal records. One records comparison will give you the most important lead you need, the name of the Moscow Family rivalling that to which the men you've got in custody belong. Which will most likely and most logically be the Family that attacked at Pizhma. Your interception at Kirs would have been the best and most humiliating bonus they could have imagined.'

The Russians were being inundated with theory – all of it practical and feasible, the sort of basic investigatory process that *should* be followed – but an avalanche nevertheless, calculated to appear a far greater contribution than it was to set in concrete the right of Charlie and Kestler to remain part of everything. From the majority of the expressions confronting them, Charlie guessed they were winning.

'Which shouldn't be the only approach to the investigation,' Kestler pressed on. 'There might not even be a connection between Kirs and Pizhma, unlikely though that is: just conceivably the two could be a complete coincidence. In which case the information that made Pizhma possible wouldn't have come from the north at all. But from the south, from wherever the components were being transferred *to*. The receiving installation would have had every detail of the train, wouldn't they? Routes, schedules, quantities, timings. The receiving plant should be blanketed, to discover if the leak came from there . . .'

The American's pause, whether intentional or otherwise, gave Charlie his entry. Smiling to Popov, as he'd smiled frequently towards the man in seeming friendliness, Charlie said, 'That would have been our immediate operational reaction. But then I'm sure you've set everything like that in motion already.' A final pause. 'Haven't you?'

Charlie didn't expect it would be easy next time. But at least he was reasonably sure there would be a next time.

The photographic enhancement, which Fenby got within an hour of Kestler's breathless telephone link from Moscow, went far beyond confirming the radioactivity leak. Refusing to believe what he was told at first, the FBI Director summoned the photo analysts to the seventh floor and had them take him through the montage to prove that not only were the canisters visibly breached but that, viewed in sequence, the only possible conclusion was that they had been intentionally forced. There were at least fifteen shots showing men with either crowbars or cold hammers, prising and smashing at the seals.

'That's incredible .. it's . . .' stumbled Fenby.

'. . . Suicidal madness?' suggested the photographic chief.

Hillary Jamieson didn't agree when she arrived at Fenby's office, fifteen minutes later; the skirt was as short but at least the shirt was looser. Impressively, she instantly and mentally calculated from the time-stamp on the relevant frames that the men would have only been exposed for a maximum of six minutes and said, 'Enough to make them sick, maybe. Better if they changed their clothes and showered, but whatever it is in the containers I doubt it would be terminal.'

'But look at the timing!' insisted Fenby. 'That stuff's been there leaking for getting on for twenty-four hours now! We're looking at another Chernobyl!'

'No, we're not,' corrected Hillary, not bothering to soften the rejection. 'Chernobyl was a melt-down, a China Syndrome. And it was an *entire* reactor: the amount was hugely much greater. But it's still dangerous. Those poor bastards posted around it are in real trouble if they haven't got the proper protective clothing and unless it's sealed pretty damned quick Pizhma – I presume it's a town or a village – is going to be affected. Other places, too, if there are any, the longer it remains unsealed. I can't be any more precise until I know positively what was in the canisters and the extent and degree it had been irradiated.'

Fenby's concern was such that he did not even notice Hillary's careless cursing.

He had a big one here – the biggest of his career so far – of international consequence with the added burden of the House Speaker's very personal attention. Everything had to be right, exactly right, with no wrong moves and certainly no oversights. Overkill didn't matter; overkill was fine, in fact, because too much not too little got done in overkill.

He smiled across the expansive desk at the girl who sat, as she'd sat before, with her legs crossed to display practically the whole length of her thigh. 'I want to be on top of this, one hundred per cent,' he said, unthinking of the *double entendre* that broadened Hillary's smile. 'I want you in Moscow.'

'Me! Moscow!'

'As soon as you can,' said Fenby. 'I'll get State to arrange the visa as quickly as possible.'

The conference, which continued after the departure of Kestler and Charlie, broke up in near disarray and with Natalia as exposed as ever although with more chance to influence decisions for which she was ultimately accountable. The Interior Minister insisted Natalia chair the immediately convened and following meeting to prevent the Pizhma haul getting out of the country, which was technically her responsibility as the department head, although Natalia thought there was an element of inferred criticism of Aleksai and suspected he thought so too. The impression increased, spreading, she believed, to the military commanders, when the meeting ended with the belated investigation following virtually every suggestion put forward by Charlie and the American. That second session was expanded, again on Radomir Badim's orders by internal division commanders from the Federal Security Service, the new intelligence service formed from the old KGB, and the Federal Militia to provide as much additional manpower as possible to secure borders into Europe and the West. A further ministerial edict was that every planning decision be channelled to the minister through Natalia, which kept her the inevitable focus for mistakes as much as for successes. And realistically she recognized the risks of mistakes were far greater than the benefit of successes.

Ever conscious of that, Natalia questioned and examined every proposal, relegating to secondary importance the chauvinism of the military and the other male division chiefs and Popov's barely concealed impatience at her operational experience. Natalia rigidly limited her questioning to the practicalities of stopping the stolen nuclear material reaching the West, but was not reluctant to challenge Popov.

She was as annoyed with him as he appeared to be with her. She'd been very vulnerable at the beginning of the minister's inquest and Aleksai had done nothing to help: indeed, he had led the denunciation of Western involvement with which she would have been culpably linked if it had been judged ill-conceived, and she'd felt satisfaction as well as embarrassment for her lover when the attack had blown up in his face.

It was a resentment Natalia intended privately to let him know beyond what he'd doubtless already assumed, but she acknowledged the opportunity wasn't going to be easy that night. As pointedly as Natalia felt able when she left to report to the minister, she demanded Popov contact her with the street-level, city-by-city details of the regional and outer border closures upon which they had decided.

She returned uneasily to Leninskaya, hoping Popov would assume the contact insistence a relayed demand from Radomir Badim that had to be complied with. Which it virtually turned out to be anyway from the point-by-point interrogation to which she was subjected by the minister, as well as by Viskov and Fomin, before they agreed every proposal. Because of the uncertainty, Natalia left Sasha in the care of the crèche staff.

It clearly was Popov's assumption from the formality with which he telephoned, an hour after she arrived back at the apartment.

He recited the demanded details in a flat, expressionless tone, scarcely making any allowances for her to take notes. She didn't ask him to slow or repeat anything. 'Is there anything additional you want?' he concluded.

'I don't think so.'

'I shall stay at the ministry tonight.'

Objectively Natalia accepted it was right he should remain in the ministry building: the need was greater now than when he was preparing for the Kirov interception. 'Call me immediately there is any development.'

'Of course. Anything else?'

'I would have liked more support this afternoon.' If she couldn't tell him to his face she'd tell him this way.

'So would I!'

'You were too anxious to criticize!'

'And you to approve!'

'I wasn't approving! Just showing practical common sense to practical common sense suggestions!'

'Which no one was left in any doubt about that I should have had and already initiated!'

'You're assuming a criticism nobody made!'

'Your Englishman made it.'

'He's not *my* Englishman! And you asked him what he would do in the circumstances, didn't you!'

'I was made to look a fool!'

By yourself, nobody else, thought Natalia. Aloud she said, 'Blaming Western involvement, which you set out to do, could have cost me the directorship!'

'That's an exaggeration.'

'I don't think so. I don't have to tell you what that would mean . . . not just to me. To Sasha, too.'

'And I don't have to tell you how much I want properly to look after you. And Sasha.'

Natalia hadn't expected him to turn the conversation like that and for several moments could not think of a response. She recognized it as the olive branch to end their argument but she didn't want so quickly to take it. He hadn't done enough to help her. So it was right he should know how deeply she was annoyed: too deeply to be mollified in a five-minute telephone conversation. Reverting to the formality with which he'd begun, Natalia said, 'Call me, if there is anything.'

Rebuffed, Popov said, 'I will,' and replaced the telephone without any farewell.

Natalia remained by the receiver, gazing at it. She hadn't said what she'd wanted to say and knew what she had said hadn't been right. She felt confused and angry, at herself and at Aleksai and peremptory ministers and presidential aides and at whatever they were involved in, about which she felt most confused of all. She grabbed the receiver when it sounded, anxious to hear Aleksai apologize.

'We *should* talk,' suggested Charlie.

'Yes,' agreed Natalia. 'We should.'

'What's the seriousness of the leak?' demanded Patrick Pacey.

'We need far more information before any proper assessment can be made,' said Dean. 'There's a scientific team being assembled at Aldermaston. We're feeding them the raw information as it comes in. Washington is cooperating fully: the President telephoned Downing Street an hour ago. I've had three separate telephone conversations with Fenby.'

'Is it a Chernobyl situation?' persisted Pacey.

'We don't know enough to answer that.'

'The fallout, from Chernobyl, reached England!' Simpson pointed out.

'This can't possibly be as big,' guessed Dean.

'Chernobyl was a reactor,' reminded Pacey, unnecessarily. 'This is weapons-graded. Surely that will be more powerful?'

'I don't know!' repeated the exasperated Dean.

'Why break open the canisters deliberately?' said Johnson.

'It's beyond belief!' said Pacey.

'It all is,' agreed Dean.

'What are the Russians doing about public warnings?' asked Johnson.

'There's still the insistence on a news blackout.'

'They've never given a damn about endangering their civilian population with their nuclear programme,' reminded Pacey.

'We could have a catastrophe,' said the deputy Director, pointlessly.

'I'm not sure what we have got,' said Dean. There was one thing he was sure about, though.

chapter 21

The doorstep greeting wasn't as awkward as the first time but Charlie thought it was close. He halted again at the inner door, for Natalia to precede him to where he expected Sasha to be.

'She's being looked after. In case something urgent comes up,' explained Natalia, without being asked.

There was a moment of uncertainty. 'I'm glad you agreed. It's right.'

'I know.' She hoped he believed her about Sasha and didn't think she'd done something ridiculous like hiding the child away. Or be offended by what she had half decided to suggest.

'Last time didn't work out very well, did it?' She'd changed again, into a one-piece trousered outfit not unlike that which Popov and the *spetznaz* officers had worn, although Natalia's was made of a silky blue material. He wasn't sure if she'd tried with make-up but if she had she'd failed: her eyes were hollowed and dark-ringed and her face was pinched.

'That's hardly surprising, in the circumstances.' She waved him to a chair. He didn't choose the one by the door this time. 'I've got some Scotch. It isn't Islay.'

He smiled, briefly. 'A long memory!'

'About a lot of things. But just memories, Charlie.'

'You already told me,' he acknowledged, disappointed she'd felt the need to reiterate the rejection. 'And Scotch would be fine.'

He studied the room in her absence, caught again by the complete absence of anyone's occupation but her own, although she'd stressed Popov didn't live with her. At once Charlie extended the scrutiny. Sasha did live with her but there wasn't any trace of the child, either. Natalia had always been obsessively neat, chiding him for his untidiness. Memories, like Natalia had reminded; out-of-place memories. She carried wine back for herself. When she handed Charlie his glass she said, 'The toast used to be "Death to the enemy." '

'It still is. They're just more difficult to find these days.'

Natalia settled herself on the couch where she'd sat with Sasha, leaning back as if she needed the support of the cushions. The whisky was smooth enough and Charlie began to relax, too. His initial doorway impression had been wrong. Tonight things were much easier. So far, at least.

'Well?' Now that he was here – now that she had reversed all the resolutions – Natalia felt too tired to force things as they probably should have been forced. She wasn't sure any more that she would go through with it. She'd let him lead, maybe make up her mind as things went along.

'I want to make a lot of things clear,' began Charlie. 'I promise you I won't do anything to cause you any embarrassment. Or difficulty. You. Or Sasha.' Charlie paused, momentarily unable to say what he felt he had to. 'She'll be Popov's daughter, if that's what you want . . .'

Natalia wasn't sure – not committed-for-the-rest-of-her-life sure – that's what she did want. Not that Charlie's reappearance affected any uncertainty. She *was* sure that was over. She knew she needed Charlie professionally and it was easy sitting here with him now and it would even have been pleasant imagining times like it in future. But what there had once been with Charlie could never be again. 'You really mean that? . . . that you'd let Sasha think of someone else as her father?'

Charlie supposed that's what he did mean but it didn't sound right put as direct as that. 'Popov's more to her than I am. Isn't that best for her?' He wasn't accustomed to selfless decision and didn't like this one.

'Yes, but . . .'

'And let's get something else clear. I didn't set out to force a confrontation between him and me this afternoon. There was nothing personal.' Charlie meant it, although it was the truth according to Charlie's rules. Popov had been shown up to be all the things Charlie had mentally labelled him and Charlie had felt then and felt now a satisfaction at having done it in front of Natalia.

Natalia pushed the fatigue away, making her decision, moving aside the wine that wasn't helping the tiredness. 'I know. It was unnecessary: achieved nothing. I don't know why he did, not like that.'

'It could have been personally difficult for you.' He never expected the reaction the remark achieved.

Natalia came abruptly forward, elbows on her knees. 'I took a huge chance with you once, Charlie. More than once. Risked everything . . .'

' . . . I've said . . .'

' . . . I'm not opening old wounds,' overrode Natalia, refusing his interruption in her anxiety to get out what she wanted to say. 'You must be totally honest with me!'

'I will be,' promised Charlie, hoping she believed him.

She hesitated, knowing she couldn't extract any assurance beyond that. 'What are you here for? Here in Moscow?'

Charlie looked blankly at her. 'You know what I'm doing here!'

'Do I?'

Charlie understood. 'It's all changed, Natalia. Like it's changed here. We're becoming like an FBI now. I'm here because of nuclear smuggling. That's all. I promise.'

She remained silent for several minutes, seeking the courage to say the words. 'I'm going to take another chance. The risk isn't as great, not like before. I know I need help, your help, Charlie, if I'm to stay where I am. Which I have to do, for Sasha . . .' It wasn't coming out as she wanted. 'You saw what it was like this afternoon. The resentment. And not just Aleksai. All of them. But they won't be held responsible for failure . . .'

'Stop it . . .' Charlie halted just short of calling her darling. 'Stop it, Natalia. You don't need to explain. You know you'll have everything . . . anything . . . you want.' It was instinctive for Charlie to think that to fulfil that undertaking he'd have to get everything from Natalia in return but he didn't feel embarrassed about it. Professionally, it put him in a spectacular position.

'I'm trusting you again.'

'I know that.' He caught the sad resignation in her voice.

'Every time I've done it before you've let me down.'

'I won't this time.'

'You've got to mean that, Charlie.'

'All I can tell you is that I *do* mean it and all I can do is ask you to believe me.'

'It isn't that simple . . .' Natalia began.

'Yes it is,' anticipated Charlie. 'Aleksai will never know. *No one* will ever know.'

'Now it's me being utterly selfish, thinking only of myself. Myself and Sasha.'

'It's your turn.' Where the hell was he now? Professionally on the inside track, ahead of everyone. But personally it would need Machiavelli with a slide rule and compasses to work it out. He was going to do all he could to keep in power the mother of his child whom he'd just agreed to surrender to her new lover who couldn't be allowed to find out what was going on. It was almost too much for a soap opera novel. 'Have you really thought it through?'

'No,' Natalia admitted, honestly. 'Neither have you.'

'I don't have to.'

'I know it won't be easy!' she accepted, abruptly belligerent. 'Give me just one other choice!'

If he'd been able, Charlie wouldn't have told her. He wasn't offended by the obvious inference that if there *had* been another choice she would have taken it. 'How strong is the resentment?'

'Total, in most cases. Strong in others.'

'So we could be excluded if our usefulness dries up?'

'Of course,' agreed Natalia. 'You always knew that, surely?'

'It wouldn't be wise for you to protest.'

'And I won't, unless I'm sure of the grounds for doing so.'

Had he not known and now trusted Natalia so completely, Charlie would have suspected this extraordinary episode to be a brilliant con trick for the Russians to close them out but at the same time learn everything being fed in from the West. 'Don't, even if you think you are sure.'

Natalia *hadn't* thought through the complications of what she was asking. She shook her head in another abrupt mood change, this time despair. 'It *won't* work, will it? If you and Kestler are kept out, how *can* I introduce something I've no way of knowing!'

She *was* too tired to think properly: if she hadn't been, perhaps she wouldn't have sought his help in the first place. 'We'll make the approach in such a way they'll have to meet with us. It won't be down to Popov alone now, will it?'

'Probably not,' said Natalia, uncertainly. She brightened. 'I'm the official link between the operational group and the ministry and presidential secretariat.'

A mixed blessing for her, incredible for him! As the idea came to him, Charlie said, 'But you *must* openly campaign for our inclusion, when I tell you.'

Natalia's exhausted reasoning was ebbing and flowing, each and every thought difficult to hold. There was an overwhelming relief, at there being someone upon whom she could rely. Trust *and* rely. The contradiction snatched at her. How could she feel relief and trust and reliance for someone who had so consistently let her down? She just *did*. Natalia didn't want to think or consider beyond that simple decision. 'How?'

'All you have to do is judge the moment. Which you will always be able to do, from what I tell you in advance. And from knowing who's going to be at your meetings. *Always* wait until Badim or Fomin or someone in higher authority is involved. At those sessions press as hard as you can for our inclusion. Your judgment, to those in authority, will be proven right, every time, because you'll know in advance everything we've got. And the opposition and resentment of those arguing against you will be proven wrong, every time. When there aren't people in higher authority, don't push. Wait.'

Natalia's relief became a blanket, the sort of blanket she wanted now to pull up over her and sleep. She stood, unsteadily, needing physical movement to keep herself awake. From the window she could just see the Gagarin monument where they'd both so hopefully waited, forever separated now by a nonsense of religious history. '*How* will you be able to tell me? You can't call the ministry. And here . . .'

'. . . Popov will too often be,' Charlie completed for her. 'I don't keep in touch with you. You keep in touch with me.'

Natalia turned from the tower block view, with another pendulum swing. 'It *could* work, couldn't it?'

'It *will* work,' guaranteed Charlie. Because he'd make it work; work better and more successfully than any scheme he'd ever orchestrated before. He'd fantasized of coming back to Moscow to care for her and for a child he didn't know. Now he was going to. Not in the way he'd imagined – what they were devising was beyond any imagination – but sufficient. Whatever followed – whatever could be built on – was a bonus. Natalia looked obviously at her watch and Charlie hurriedly said, 'So let's start now.'

It was a superhuman effort to focus her concentration. 'How?'

'The leak at Pizhma was intentional,' he disclosed. His mind more than ever upon cooperation, Charlie found it interesting that he'd been told direct by Kestler of what the expertly analyzed photographs showed just fifteen minutes before Rupert Dean's call, relaying the same information Washington had made available to London. And which – but with Dean's permission – he'd relayed to the ambassador.

The shock was sufficient to rouse her. 'What?'

It took only seconds for Charlie to outline the unarguable discovery from the enhanced image intensified satellite photographs. Desperately Natalia said, 'I don't understand! Why?'

'I don't understand or know why, either. Not yet.'

'I won't have to argue your participation yet: we'd obviously have to meet to discuss the photographs.'

'Tell me something!' he demanded. 'Kirov was planned as a military operation. And military operations have code names?'

'*Akrashena*,' she supplied at once.

'Does it have a meaning?' queried Charlie, not recognizing the word.

Natalia smiled, bemused. 'It means "wet paint". Aleksai thought it fitted. Remember "*mokrie dela*"?'

The phrase translated as 'wet jobs' and had been the old KGB euphemism for assassination. 'I suppose it does,' agreed Charlie.

'Why is it important?'

'I don't know that it is,' avoided Charlie. 'It was just something I wanted to know.'

'I'm very tired, Charlie.'

'I'm going,' he said, standing.

They stood, momentarily, looking at each other. Then Natalia said, 'I don't love you, not any more. But I do love you. Does that make sense?'

'As much sense as anything tonight,' accepted Charlie. What had transpired was more than enough, that remark – denial though it was – most of all.

The Director-General had apologized during their last conversation that there was still no confirmation from GCHQ of any voice interception from the satellite and Charlie felt too exhausted after leaving Natalia to go back to the embassy to make a further check. Instead he telephoned the London Watch Room from the Lesnaya apartment for a traffic check, pleased to recognize the voice. George Carroll had been with the department practically as long as Charlie.

Carroll seemed as pleased to hear him. 'I was bloody glad to hear you'd survived, Charlie. Even if it is Moscow.'

'Good to think I have. Still learning to adjust, though.'

'Aren't we all?'

Charlie frowned. 'How *did* you hear?' The Watch Room was a message relay and alert facility, with no operational function. And as he'd had no contact with it since his posting there was no way George should have known he was still with the department and even less that he was in Russia.

'You've got Red Alert classification.'

The designation required the Watch Room immediately to transfer an operative personally to his case officer on a secure line, irrespective of the time. In the circumstances it was hardly surprising, but Charlie didn't consider the check he was making justified bothering Rupert Dean. 'It's not worth going through to the Director-General tonight; it can wait until tomorrow.'

'It's not the Director-General,' said Carroll. 'It's Peter Johnson. I'll put you through.'

'No,' stopped Charlie. 'There's no point in troubling him, either.'

He was still staring curiously down at the instrument when it rang again, so quickly after he'd replaced it that he thought Carroll had made the connection anyway. But it wasn't London.

'We're getting cavalry in skirts,' announced Kestler. 'Washington is seconding a nuclear physicist here. And it's a woman!'

'She might be ugly,' warned Charlie.

'Every woman is beautiful in her own special way, even the ugly ones.'

Charlie fell asleep wondering what Christmas cracker Kestler had got that aphorism from. Before that he'd spent a lot of time going over the conversation with George Carroll.

There was a large panel of mirrored glass set into a wall of the interrogation cell, enabling Natalia to watch unseen from an adjoining observation room as Lev Mikhailovich Yatisyna was brought into it. One of the guards was a blonde, heavy-breasted girl, the most attractive Natalia had been able to find in the time available. Her selection was just one of several hurried-together psychological devices to disorientate the man far beyond his realizing how little Natalia had to work from. Fingerprints of three of the six arrested Moscow gangsters linked them to the known Agayans' Mafia group forming part of the larger Ostankino Family. Her only other advantage was knowing, from the inadequate criminal records, that there'd been bloody turf battles in the past with the Shelapin Family, which formed part of the Chechen Mafia.

Natalia was encouraged by the view from her hidden vantage point. Yatisyna had been wearing overalls when he'd been seized but she planned a lot from the reported search of his Kirov apartment. There'd been fifteen suits, in addition to six sports jackets and casual trousers and twelve shirts had still been in their wrappers, in addition to another twenty pressed and folded in the dressing bureau. There'd been ten pairs of shoes. Everything was imported, either from Italy or France. Dispassionately gazing through the glass, Natalia acknowledged that the dark-haired, swarthy Yatisyna was physically handsome; he would have looked good in any of his designer clothes. Most important of all, he would have known it.

Now he looked ridiculous, which was precisely what Natalia wanted, because he would know that, too. The prison-issue uniform was intentionally three sizes too large, the trouser cuffs puddled around his ankles and the sleeves practically to his fingertips. Regulations required the trousers to be self-supporting, without either belt or braces, but the waistband was much too big and Yatisyna had constantly to hold them up. They were unwashed, from previous use, and the dirtiest it had been possible to find. There was only one chair in the room, for Natalia. There was obvious relief when the man sat on it, able for the first time to let go of his trouser band. Natalia guessed the attempted swagger was almost instinctive but it failed totally because of the scuffing trousers and made him look even more ridiculous. The effort to loll with his arm over the back of the chair didn't work, either. Natalia had primed both guards. The man made a remark to the girl who laughed, loudly. Natalia hadn't bothered with the sound system so she didn't hear what Yatisyna said, although from the facial snarl he was obviously angered. The wardress laughed at him again.

Before going into the room Natalia carefully placed at the top of the file the photographs she'd had taken earlier of the scowling Yatisyna in his engulfing uniform. She entered briskly, apparently in the act of closing the dossier she'd been studying to remind herself who she was seeing. She maintained the distracted, impatient attitude, flicking her hand towards the man. 'Get up! Stand at the other side of the table. Properly!' She thought Yatisyna would probably have ignored her if she hadn't extended the gesture for the male warder physically to remove him. As it was, the gang leader rose very slowly, as if it were his decision to vacate the seat. Having to keep his trousers up again ruined that bravado. Natalia heard the primed laugh, from behind. Before sitting Natalia very obviously examined the seat, as if expecting Yatisyna to have soiled it. When she finally looked up directly at him, Yatisyna's face was a blaze of fury. Natalia let her eyes slowly go the whole length of his body. At the puckered ankles she smirked, going briefly to include the wardress in her amusement. The girl smirked back. Still smiling, Natalia depressed the start button of the recording equipment on the table beside her and said, 'So this is what a great big gangster looks like!' The disdainful, nose-wrinkled sniff wasn't forced. He stank. She half opened the dossier, just sufficient for Yatisyna to see the photographs of himself. She saw his eyes flicker to them.

'Fuck off.'

'You even *look* the idiot you were, getting set up like that by the Shelapin's . . .' She picked up the photographs, shuffling them through her fingers. 'I can't make up my mind which to issue to the newspapers when we announce your arrest. They're all so good!'

'Motherfucker!'

'That's what Ivan Fedorovich called you! A lot of other things, too. He used amateur a lot: idiot fucking amateur.' She'd decided Ivan Fedorovich Nikishov, from their sparse records the most senior of the arrested Agayans' Family, would have been the one with whom Yatisyna would have had most dealings. Nikishov had told her to go to hell thirty minutes earlier, although he had boasted of his clan's Chechen connections. She'd been shocked by the man's total disregard as to where he was and of what he was being accused, the only inference being that he never expected to appear in a court. Would Yatisyna have the same attitude? It was always difficult to gauge how someone would respond to questioning. During the period when she'd been with the KGB she'd had meek-looking, clerk-like men resist interrogation for days and supposedly trained professionals – like Yatisyna was a professional – crumble in minutes.

'What's that bastard know?'

'He knows you all got set up and the leak must have come through your people. And he knows he's going to die, like you all are. Which he's cooperating to avoid. But you should be glad the death penalty is automatic for you: it should be quick. I don't think you'd live longer than a week in any prison, after the damage you've done to so many people.'

'Nothing leaked from me. Or my people.'

He was talking and he shouldn't have done: the first concession, Natalia realized. 'That's not what the Agayans people are telling us, in signed confessions and with promises to give evidence against you . . .'

'Liar!' erupted Yatisyna, managing something close to a sneering laugh. 'No one's going to give evidence against me!'

'Yes they are! They *want* to give evidence against you . . .' She pulled a sheaf of papers from the file and began to read what she herself had written, thirty minutes earlier. ' "Lev Mikhailovich planned everything, said all we had to do was follow his instructions." ' Natalia looked up. 'Chernenkov attested that.' Nikita Chernenkov was one of the Agayans group identified by fingerprints. Natalia selected another personally written sheet. ' "We thought he knew what he was doing. He came to us in Moscow, with this big plan. We were going to make millions. He wanted to become big time in Moscow, not just the provincial punk he is. Said he had contacts and that it would be easy." ' Natalia came up again. 'That's part of Nikishov's confession . . .'

Yatisyna shook his head. 'No one's going to give evidence. And I mean no one. There's going to be an amazing loss of memory.'

The arrogance again, recognized Natalia. She had to prevent it hardening. 'From men who know the alternative is going before a firing squad . . .' She quickly stopped, frowning, a person who had said something inadvertent, which she hadn't. She hurried on, 'Did you recognize any Militia personnel?'

'I don't have to recognize them; they recognize me.'

'*Every* Militia officer came from Moscow: there wasn't a single man from the entire Kirov region. And the main contingent weren't Militia anyway: they were *spetznaz*. Nothing can keep you from the firing squad. Nikishov, maybe. But not you. You're dead.' Had he missed what she'd tried to make seem a mistake?

The flush, which had begun to subside, was returning but the remark registered as well as her contempt. 'What about Nikishov?'

'What about him?' she asked, hopefully.

'You said men who knew the alternative was going before a firing squad. They doing deals!'

'It's none of your business.'

'They are, aren't they?'

It was going much better than she'd expected. 'I said it's none of your business.'

'He's lying! It was an Agayans job: Yevgennie Arkentevich himself!'

'We've got scores of witnesses you can't intimidate. What Nikishov and the others are giving us fills in all the details. And we've got *all* the details. Times, dates, who was at the meetings, everything.'

'Is Nikishov going to get clemency?'

'I don't know what he's going to get,' said Natalia in a voice that clearly indicated that she knew very well indeed.

'So he is!'

Natalia patted the sides of her dossier into a neater pile: she'd assembled it to look impressive largely with statements from past and quite unrelated investigations with less than a quarter, including her fabricated confessions, connected with the Kirs attempt. The very top folios were the formal record of the criminal charges brought against the man, which were some of the few genuine documents and which, under Russian law, had to be officially accepted by a defendant. 'We've talked enough. But you have to acknowledge understanding of the charges.' She held out a pen towards him, reversing the pages for his signature. She was careful to make the ridiculing photographs more visible as she did so.

He made no move to take the pen. 'Perhaps there is a reason for us to talk more.'

Natalia felt a warm satisfaction; one of the early ones to collapse, she thought. 'What reason?'

'I know a lot of things.'

'So does everyone else talking to us.'

'No they don't. Not what I know.'

'So tell me.' The room was becoming filled by the stink from the prison uniform.

'You can't show clemency, not yourself, can you? It has to come from the Federal Prosecutor.'

Natalia's expectation wavered, off-balanced by his challenge. Very briefly she considered lying but decided against it. 'It has to come from the prosecutor.'

'Get his agreement. I want a positive undertaking before I'll say anything.'

'Don't be stupid,' rejected Natalia. 'I haven't got anything to go to the prosecutor *with*. You've got to tell me what you're talking about first.'

'No,' refused Yatisyna.

Unspeaking, Natalia reoffered the charge sheet and the pen.

Yatisyna still didn't take it. 'I want to think. I won't acknowledge the charges until I've had time to think.'

She'd lost it, conceded Natalia. Not for ever, but certainly today. She did have things to say at the soon-to-start conference but there was a wash of disappointment at their not being as much – or as dramatic – as she'd hoped: as impressive as Charlie insisted she had to be, in front of higher authority. 'We can proceed without your signature. It's only a formality.'

'I have the right to a lawyer.'

'At the discretion of the prosecutor.'

'See if he's prepared to deal.'

'Not until I know what I'm talking *about*.'

Yatisyna nodded towards the tape recorder. 'Without that next time.' There was another head gesture, towards the guards at the door. 'And them.'

She *was* going to get more, Natalia decided. It would be wrong to abandon her adopted approach. 'I'm not going to keep coming here for nothing. Make your mind up. When you have, let me know.' She stood, abruptly, collecting up her mostly contrived file.

'I have a request!'

The bombast was going: he was an early breaker. 'What?'

'This prison overall stinks. I have the right to a clean one.'

Natalia remained standing, smirked as she again examined the man from head to toe. 'You haven't *any* rights that I don't choose to allow you. You're not getting any change of uniform and you're not getting any deal. All you're getting at the moment is a trial that will be little more than a formality and then a firing squad. No one's frightened of you any more, Lev Mikhailovich. You haven't got any power, can't frighten anyone, not any more.'

The attractive wardress laughed again, exactly on cue, and Natalia decided it had been a good early morning's work. And there was a whole day left.

In the hills was definitely best. There were a lot of places in Moscow – he personally owned a linked section of houses and apartments on Ulitza Dvorsovaya, in addition to the two mansions where no one would have dared to see or hear anything – but Silin wanted the death of Sobelov and the two shits who'd supported him to be the most dramatic example possible for everyone. Which meant making it last – for as long as Sobelov could survive the torture – so the country estate was where he'd arranged everything. Even announced, when he'd issued the summons, that it was going to be a special occasion.

Silin smiled to himself, enjoying the irony that no one else yet knew but soon would: a far more special occasion than any of them had ever known. His people – the few Dolgoprudnaya people he knew he could trust, like Petr Markov – had called from the dacha, confirming they were already there, waiting. Confirming, too, that it was all arranged, in readiness.

The rest of the Commission would be setting out soon, Sergei Petrovich Sobelov one of them. With no idea what he was heading for – the most delicious irony of all – in that ridiculous American car, probably with the head of some girl whose name he didn't even know gurgling in his lap.

Silin rose at the knock on the study door, almost reaching it before it was respectfully opened by Markov.

'The cars are outside.'

'Good.' Silin wanted to be there at least an hour before the rest, to enjoy their unsuspecting arrival, miss nothing.

Marina waited beyond, in the corridor, neat as she always was, attentive as she always was. 'The kitchen want to know if you'll be back tonight.'

'Not to eat,' said Silin. The dinner at the dacha was going to be the highlight. The boar would probably already be cooking – prepared, certainly – and there was going to be French wine. He'd be at the head of the table and whatever happened he wanted Sobelov to be kept alive to be strapped into a chair to watch them eat what would be for him the last supper. He'd have insisted Bobin and Frolov inflict their torture on Sobelov by then, so they'd be strapped in chairs, too, on either side of the man they'd backed, knowing what was going to happen to them; shitting themselves, crying, begging for mercy, lying. Maybe he should have brought a doctor in, to keep them alive; there were a lot he could have chosen from. Too late now. A minor oversight. Didn't affect the main objective. That no one else in the Commission – no one else *anywhere* – would ever dream of challenging him after today.

'What time then?' She kept in step with him towards the main entrance.

Silin stopped there, turning towards her, while Markov checked the street outside. He smoothed the greying hair that didn't need smoothing, just wanting to touch her. 'It'll be very late.'

'I'll still wait up.' She raised her face, expectantly, for him to kiss her, which he did, softly.

At Markov's gesture Silin hurried to his customized Mercedes directly outside. There were escort Mercedes in front and behind, with four guards in each. Markov settled himself in his customary seat, beside the driver of Silin's car. Without having to be asked, Markov raised the screen between himself and the driver and Silin, in the rear. At the same time Markov took the Uzi from the glove compartment and placed it more conveniently beside him: one of Silin's modernizing insistences was that the Commission never carried personal weapons themselves, like the American Mafia heads never risked moving around armed. Like all the glass in the Mercedes, the screen was bullet-proof.

The Pizhma robbery had been brilliant, Silin thought. And the best part of all was that there would be more, as big or maybe even bigger. It was going to be difficult counting the money! He'd make the announcement at dinner that night, so Sobelov would hear with everyone else. So the man would die knowing it. Give them all another example of how reliant they were upon him.

The motorway crossed the outer ring road intersection and Silin looked expectantly for the Dolgoprudnaya direction sign, smiling at its familiarity. Which was something he'd have to guard against from now on, comfortable familiarity. There wouldn't be any more nonsense again, not after today, but Silin admitted to himself that it had still been a lesson well learned. He wouldn't relax in future, like he had in the immediate past. Today would show them and . . .

Silin's mind trailed away, the thought never finished, at the blurred sight of a Mytishchi direction sign which shouldn't have been on this road at all because it wasn't the way to his dacha. That realization came with the awareness that this *wasn't* his road at all but one he didn't recognize. He pressed his console button, to bring down the separating screen. Nothing happened. He pressed it harder. When still nothing happened he jabbed at it again and again and then rapped at the glass behind Markov's head. It was the electrics: something had gone wrong with the electrics. The man in front of him didn't turn. Neither did the driver. Silin shouted, although the rear of the car was soundproofed by its protection. They still didn't turn. Silin twisted to see that the escort car was behind, like the one in front remained with him, then hammered and shouted at the screen and tried the button again. It still didn't work. Neither did the controls for the windows. Nothing worked.

The turn into a driveway he didn't recognize was abrupt,

throwing him sideways and momentarily full length on the rear seat. When he thrust himself up Silin saw they were approaching a wooden villa he didn't know – like he didn't know anything – an old-fashioned building girdled by a verandah. There were people on it, arranged like an audience: Bobin and Frolov were there with the rest of the Commission, with Sobelov at the head of the steps, a smiling host. Silin snatched out for the console again, to lock all the doors.

Very slowly, prolonging every movement, Sobelov descended the steps and tapped lightly, mockingly, for Silin to open his door. Silin actually shook his head, whimpering back across the car to get away from the other man. And then he whimpered even louder when Sobelov, even more mocking, opened the door anyway from his side, clearly knowing it would not be locked.

'We're throwing a party for you, Stanislav Georgevich: everyone's coming,' smirked the man. 'We're all going to enjoy it. You especially. We've got a lot to talk about: *you've* got a lot to talk about. To me.'

chapter 22

Expectantly Charlie watched the wired-to-electricity shock go through the assembled Russians at Kestler's announcement that the photographs proved the breaching of the nuclear canisters to be intentional.

There were two additional Russians, one in recognizable Militia officers' uniform, the other a slightly built, anonymously dressed civilian whom Charlie's like-for-like antenna at once recognized. They, like everyone else in the room, gave reactions similar to the ministers and the presidential aide. Natalia managed to look convincingly surprised. She showed no trace of tiredness. She was sitting with the *spetznaz* officers separating her from Popov, who'd abandoned the black tunic for one of his immaculate suits. The man had nodded and relaxed his face into the beginning of a smile at Charlie's entry. Charlie had nodded and smiled back more openly.

Predictably the discussion began with the Russians, led by the *spetznaz* commanders, challenging the American photo interpretation. When that dispute ended with their reluctantly agreeing it was the only possible conclusion, Charlie let the increasingly wilder theories swirl about him but didn't contribute, even when invited, unwilling to lose a strengthening idea among the general here's-what-I-think eagerness to voice an opinion. As the discussion trailed into silence Popov abruptly announced that the weather had favoured them, with no disseminating wind, and that containment experts from Kirs and Kotelnich had capped the smashed housings and sufficiently water-suppressed the contamination not just around the site but throughout the carriages to enable the train to complete its journey with the rest of its untampered cargo. A comparison between the loading manifest and what remained on the train put the loss at nineteen canisters, not the American assessment of twenty-two.

'And we have located the lorries and the cars used in the robbery,' announced the operational director, triumphantly. With theatrical timing, he added, 'Here in Moscow.'

Popov deflected the top table attention of Fomin and Badim to the uniformed Militia officer, who coloured although clearly prepared for the introduction, which he completed by naming himself to be Petr Tukhonovich Gusev, colonel-in-charge of the central Moscow region. In a pedantic, police-phrased account, Gusev said that at precisely 4.43 that morning a Militia street patrol had located three lorries and a BMW parked in central Moscow, close to the Arbat. The lorries were empty. The German Ford had been found thirty minutes later, abandoned on the inner Moscow ring road, empty of petrol.

'In view of the Pizhma contamination, both areas have been sealed pending an examination by nuclear inspectors,' picked up Popov, on cue. 'No one involved in securing the areas has been told what the lorries contained, of course, to avoid a nuclear theft of this magnitude becoming publicly known. The initial Militia patrol carried out some preliminary general checks on all the vehicles. The engines of the lorries and both cars were discernibly hot, to the touch . . .' He hesitated, for the implications to be realized. 'They had clearly arrived in the city within an hour, maybe less, of their being discovered!' Popov nodded to the Militia commander. 'By six o'clock this morning, all major routes out of Moscow were sealed. In the five hours since, extra Militia and Federal Security Service personnel have been drafted into the city. *Any* vehicle attempting to move beyond the outer Moscow ring road is being stopped and searched . . .' The man smiled towards the minister. 'I think we can confidently say that the proceeds of the Pizhma robbery are contained within Moscow and that it will only be a matter of time before they are recovered. Certainly nothing can get through the cordon we now have encircling the city . . .'

The palpable relief went through the room like a communal sigh. Charlie passingly noted the look on Natalia's face and then saw Fomin, smiling broadly, turn towards Popov. Before the man could speak Charlie said, 'I don't think we can confidently say anything of the sort!'

Popov's face closed. Fomin turned to Charlie, the intended praise unspoken. 'You have an observation to make?'

'Several,' promised Charlie. 'There's no reason at all to suppose the contents of the lorries were transferred *where* they were found. If an hour elapsed before their discovery – thirty minutes even – the transfer vehicles could have got way beyond the city limits before any checks were in place. So your cordon is useless. Dumping vehicles used in a theft is basic robbery practice. But why abandon the four vehicles where they're bound to be found so quickly? Or leave the Ford on a no-stopping ring road where its being immediately found was even more assured? The thing's got a petrol gauge. Knowing that it was running out of fuel, why wasn't it abandoned in some back alley somewhere? Like the other vehicles could have been split up and left in places where they wouldn't have been found or aroused suspicion for days. Everything was left for exactly the same reason that the canisters were breached. It's all decoys: the breaching to delay the beginning of any proper investigation – which it did – and the vehicles to concentrate everything *within* Moscow. Which it did. Making it that much easier to get the stuff into the West.'

'A fascinating theory, without any supportive facts,' sneered the taller of the two *spetznaz* officers.

'Establish some facts then!' Charlie knew he'd get six buckets of shit knocked out of him in a stand-up fight with the Special Forces officer but in a stand-up discussion of deception it wasn't a contest.

'How?' asked the other soldier, sparing his colleague.

Charlie gestured sideways, to Kestler, 'From the American photographs we know *exactly* what time the train was stopped: twelve thirty-five the night before last. And we know precisely the time the trucks were found at the Arbat and the Ford on the ring road. They would have been driven fast from the scene of the robbery. So let's try an average speed of sixty kilometres an hour. Drive the trucks – once they've been cleared by your nuclear people and by your forensic examiners – between Pizhma and Moscow to see if the journey takes almost twenty-nine hours! They'd have had to be going *backwards* to take that long! Fill the Ford up with petrol and see if it can make the journey on one tank. It won't be able to. See how many times it has to be filled up to get directly from Pizhma to Moscow. The petrol left, on arrival here, will indicate how large a detour they took to offload the canisters before dumping the vehicles in Moscow.'

'I think we must accept those as valid qualifications,' conceded Badim, reluctantly.

'There could be a number of explanations for so much time elapsing,' tried Gusev, tentatively and badly.

'That's surely the point!' came in Kestler, at once.

'Nothing has been scaled down outside Moscow,' insisted Popov. 'The maximum state of alert is still in operation. The discovery of the vehicles is clearly the most *practical* way to proceed.'

The defence was greeted with agreeing nods from the minister and the presidential advisor. Natalia frowned, questioningly, towards Popov, who raised his eyebrows in return and Charlie wondered what the hell the exchange meant.

'I've been authorized to offer any scientific assistance that might be necessary,' declared Kestler, unexpectedly.

'Scientific assistance?' queried Badim, cautiously.

'With Foreign Ministry agreement a senior FBI scientific officer has been assigned to our embassy here. A qualified nuclear physicist.'

The attention switched abruptly to Yuri Panin and from the expression not just on Natalia's face but that of the Interior Minister Charlie guessed neither had known until that moment. Panin's reaction confirmed Charlie's impression. The Foreign Ministry official flushed and said, 'I intended to explain today, for everyone to be told at the same time.'

Dmitri Fomin moved quickly to defuse the tension. 'We benefited from the positioning of the satellite.'

'An outside scientific opinion would provide independent confirmation of the findings of our own experts,' suggested Popov.

'She is already here and available,' assured Kestler.

'The interrogation of those arrested at Kirs has been productive,' declared Natalia, entering the discussion at last. 'I personally participated earlier today in the initial examination of Lev Yatisyna.'

Better late than never, thought Charlie, relieved.

'A total of twenty-four people were arrested, either at Plant 69 or in the Kirov round-up,' reminded Natalia. 'Each is being detained separately, to prevent rehearsed stories being prepared. All have been told they face trial for murder, of those Militia, Special Forces and security guards killed in the operation. The four men seized in the apartment of Valeri Lvov have been specifically charged with the murder of his wife and the rape of the girls. All have also been told they will be charged with the attempted robbery of nuclear material.'

It was right she should set the facts out as she was doing but he hoped she'd soon get to the promised results, to hold their attention.

'. . . It has also been made clear that the death penalty will be demanded and that clemency is never exercised in murders of Militia or soldiers . . .' Natalia's pause was every bit as theatrical as Popov's presentation earlier. '. . . except in very rare and exceptional circumstances. None is in any doubt what that means. Each has been left, totally alone, to decide how to save his own life . . .'

The taller of the *spetznaz* officers said: 'Will clemency be shown to anyone providing the sort of cooperation you want?'

It was Fomin who answered. 'No,' said the presidential aide, positively.

The officer looked more towards the note-takers. 'I would like the request recorded now, for later reference and discussion with the Federal Prosecutor's office, that the executions are carried out by Special Forces firing squads.'

'I give my personal assurance to raise the matter with the prosecutor,' said Fomin.

Charlie's mind began to slip sideways during the interruption. What they were talking about and trying to resolve now naturally had the utmost and undivided priority. But it was the beginning, not the end, of his Russian posting. Which – quite irrespective of any arrangement he'd made with Natalia – he didn't intend fulfilling permanently cap-in-hand, with a sign around his neck begging for Russian handouts. He'd need Russian approval for the proposal germinating in his mind. London's permission, too. And Gerald Williams really would be driven to apoplexy by the amount of money it would need. Worst of all, everything could go disastrously wrong and end up with him impaled by his testicles atop one of the Krelim tower stars, the most reluctant Christmas tree fairy ever. But the idea that had come to him seemed a good one. Something to consider more fully later, he decided.

'We have confirmed, initially from fingerprints and through fingerprints from criminal records, the identities of the six arrested men from Moscow,' resumed Natalia, bringing Charlie's concentration back to her. 'All belong to one of the major clans attached to the Ostankino Family. As I've already said, I personally interrogated Lev Yatisyna earlier today. I let him conclude we'd established the Moscow connection from confessions we'd already obtained and he confirmed the Kirs robbery was set up by Yevgennie Agayans, leader of the Ostankino clan. An arrest warrant was this morning issued for the man . . .' Natalia allowed a long pause. '. . . We've also established from interrogating those of the Agayans group we have in custody that the Chechen are their chief rivals, in particular the Shelapin Family, with whom they dispute control of the area around Moscow's

Bykovo airport. We've independently confirmed, again from records, that in the past nine months five men have been killed in shootouts between the Agayans and Shelapin Families. Arrest warrants, alleging nuclear theft and attempted nuclear theft, have been issued against both groups . . .' Natalia hesitated again, looking this time first towards the military officers and then to the anonymously dressed man, confirming Charlie's instinctive arrival empathy. '. . . Special Forces units are assisting Militia, as well as contingents from the Federal Security Service, in swoops upon all known addresses and locations used by the two Families.'

Charlie fleetingly wondered if any of the clubs he'd been to would feature among the known locations. Judged with the necessary impartiality, Natalia had performed better than Popov. And personally questioning Yatisyna – and so quickly confirming a lead to who might have carried out the Pizhma robbery – had been a brilliant move.

Natalia knew she'd done well, although she kept any awareness from showing. Her satisfaction did not last long.

Popov said: 'There are clearly members of the Yatisyna Family still free. Or maybe the retribution was exacted by the Agayans mob. Our initial information about the intended robbery at Plant 69 came from the Militia regional commander at Kirov, Nikolai Vladimirovich Oskin. Without his contribution, the intrusion at Kirs would have undoubtedly succeeded. And we would now be dealing with an unthinkable nuclear loss twice as large as that we face now. Nikolai Oskin knew the risks he was taking. He asked for protection. He and his family were transferred to Moscow . . .'

Asked *me* for protection, thought Natalia, in growing apprehension.

'. . . Their bodies were found this morning, in the apartment that had been provided for them. Each had been tortured. Oskin was bound in a chair. From the position in which it was placed and the way in which the bodies of his wife and children were left it would appear he was made to watch while they were mutilated and finally killed – each by being decapitated – before being physically tortured to death himself.'

Perhaps, thought Charlie, his most recent idea wasn't such a good one after all.

With an ingrained determination to be part of everything, even if he was not invited, Charlie hung around while Kestler approached Popov to arrange the American scientific examination of the recovered lorries and, when it emerged the Russian team were already at the Arbat, went unchallenged in the Militia car to collect the telephone-alerted woman from the American embassy compound.

Hillary Jamieson was waiting for them at the compound entrance, wearing one-piece overalls Charlie accepted to be scene-of-crime official issue from the colour and the foot-high FBI lettering on the back, but which owed more to designer-inspired alteration than to government seamstresses. The trousers were tapered to show legs which Charlie would have thought, in other clothes, reached her shoulders but visibly and delightfully stopped at a tightly displayed ass so perfect that Michelangelo would have gone into artistic if not lustful rapture and in this case might just have converted from the sexual proclivities of a lifetime. He would certainly have modelled the breasts, even more provocatively displayed as bra-less both by the tightness of the material and the insufficiently closed zip, for a statue that would have reduced the Venus de Medici to an effigy of someone's washerwoman grandmother.

Kestler was briefly and literally speechless, actually stumbling as he hurried from the car to hold open the rear door for her. Prick teaser meets prick teased, thought Charlie, watching the performance. She shook her head against Kestler taking a large plastic workbox and a thick plastic suit-carrier type sheath from her, following both into the rear and directing to Charlie a sculpted-toothed, favoured-mortal-to-local-aborigine smile as she did so. She gave an apologetic hand flutter to Kestler that her equipment took up too much room to allow him in the back as well. As the disgruntled Kestler got into the front she said, 'I'm still not sure what the fuck I'm doing here but I hardly expected to hit the ground running! What have we got?'

Kestler noticeably blinked at the 'fuck'. He said, 'You haven't met Charlie. Assigned like I am. From England.'

Hillary twisted back in the rear seat. 'Hi! I thought you were local!'

'They're different from us: they wear animal skins and grunt a lot,' said Charlie.

She laughed, unrebuked. 'I thought they did that in England, too! And painted themselves with woad.'

'Not in London. Only out in the country.'

The car began to slow, impeded by the congestion from part of the inner ring road as well as the Arbat being simultaneously closed off. The driver asked Kestler which scene they wanted and when Kestler identified the Arbat, turned on his emergency siren and lights and overtook the stalled traffic on the wrong side of the road, flashing for street patrol Militia to clear intersections ahead of them, and Charlie was glad they had accepted Popov's suggestion to take an official vehicle. Knowing the closeness of the Arbat Charlie became serious, answering Hillary's initial question while Kestler was engaged with the driver.

She listened, just as seriously. 'What's this Arbat place?'

'Tourist quarter. Largely pedestrianized.'

'How wide an area has been cleared?'

'Extensive, from what we were told this morning.'

'It had better be, if these lorries are contaminated.'

'Not predominantly because of the health risk,' qualified Kestler, from the front. 'The chief concern is that the general public – abroad as well as here in Moscow – will find out what's happened.'

'Tell me you're kidding me that no official warning has been given!' demanded the girl.

'We're not kidding you,' assured Charlie, flatly.

'This isn't a joke, for fuck's sake!'

'Welcome to the real world,' invited Charlie.

'This isn't the real world! It's the *un*real world!' She

looked searchingly around the car, then back to Kestler and Charlie. 'Where's your protective stuff?'

Kestler and Charlie exchanged looks. Kestler said, 'We don't have any.'

Hillary said, 'This isn't happening! I just know this isn't happening!'

'It is,' argued Charlie. 'Look!'

The scene ahead was like one from a surrealist movie. For fifty yards in the direction they were approaching the road and the surrounding pavements were crowded with milling, other-way focused people and protesting, horn-blasting vehicles cut off from a view of absolutely unmoving and unpeopled emptiness, as cleanly as a sharp knife separates one side of a cake from the other, by metal-fence barriers hedged by shoulder-to-shoulder Militia. As far as they could see beyond the barrier there were no cars. There were no trolleys. The windows of every building and shop were blank. There was a fountain which didn't spout water. It looked exactly like the desolation Charlie imagined *would* follow a nuclear explosion.

'Just an ordinary, downtown Moscow street investigation, folks!' mocked Hillary, making an up-and-down hand cupped masturbating gesture. 'Nothing to see! Just move along now; all go home!' The mockery stopped. 'How's this going to be kept quiet, for Christ's sake?'

Charlie had had the same thought listening to Natalia itemizing the arrest warrants at that morning's meeting. Instead of answering he physically pulled Hillary against the seat as they reached the barrier. 'Sit back! Don't go forward!'

Unprotesting Hillary remained where Charlie had hauled her. As the barriers were briefly moved aside there was the pop of flash bulbs and the sharp whitening of television lights. Obediently pressed against the seat, Hillary said, 'I just know there's got to be a reason for what you've just done!'

'Three letters a foot high all over your back,' said Charlie. 'God knows who the media were back there but it's supposedly free here now. How'd you think they'd interpret an FBI scene-of-crime scientific officer, especially one looking like you do, in an ordinary, downtown Moscow street?'

'Buried deep down somewhere I'm sure there was a compliment,' grinned Hillary.

'Buried deep down under a lot of practical common sense, maybe,' half confirmed Charlie. He was surprised to see the bearded Aleksai Popov already at the scene, which was around a sharp curve in the approach road and completely out of sight of the road block. Popov was surrounded by uniformed and plainclothed officials, grouped about ten metres from the neatly parked, side-of-the-road cluster of vehicles. None wore any sort of protective clothing. Charlie counted four men around the lorries. All appeared to be wearing cotton overalls, like Hillary, but with their faces obscured with hamster-pouched air-filtering masks.

'Doesn't look as if I'll need this,' said the girl, patting the suit-carrier. 'Maybe an idea for your guys to stay with the others, though.'

'You speak Russian?' challenged Kestler, simply.

Hillary grimaced. 'Can't think of everything. Wait until I check for levels.'

Kestler identified Popov as they approached on foot and Charlie was uncritically aware how long it took Natalia's lover to get his eyes up to the American girl's face. Popov greeted her in English and said the Russian technicians were expecting her.

From the way she bent her body away from it, her equipment box was heavy. When she was about five metres from the lorries she put it down and took out what looked like a hand-held mobile phone and a mask quite different from those the Russians were wearing. There were no side filters but it was looped to a back-pack canister she slipped expertly on as she continued towards the vehicles. The Russian scientists stood together as a group, watching her, and there was a flurry of hand language when she reached them. Hillary vaulted lightly into the rear of each truck, disappearing for what seemed a long time in every one. After the interior check she went crab-wise beneath them, her hand-held device raised aloft and afterwards checked each cab and finally the BMW before gesturing back to them. Once more, uninvited, Charlie tagged along. There was no objection from anyone. Popov went with them. By the time they got to the lorries, Hillary had the mask unclipped, hanging loosely at her throat.

'Clean enough to take the kids to school,' she greeted. To Kestler she said, 'Ask them what the reading was when they got here.'

Kestler did and a balding technician with a grey, chin-fringed beard said five, offering a much larger instrument for Hillary to look. Charlie attached himself to them as she established, through Kestler, the exact time of their arrival, the scale of dissipation since then and the precise places in each vehicle, including the BMW, that had given off a radiation reading. Hillary ended the scientific exchange with a smiling handshake and Popov said, 'I'll let you have the written forensic report.'

'I'd like to see it as soon as possible,' accepted Charlie.

'I can tell you already there's not a single fingerprint, anywhere,' said Popov. 'The canvassed lorry was stolen three months ago, in St Petersburg. The other two from a Moscow haulage company, at the same time. The Moscow registration on the BMW is false: it belongs to a Lada owned by an air traffic controller at Sheremet'yevo. The plates on the Ford abandoned on the ring road were stripped off a genuinely imported Ford parked at Kazan railway terminal.' Looking directly at Charlie, Popov said, 'We are going to take all the vehicles on the check run to and from Pizhma tomorrow.'

Charlie decided Popov enjoyed showing the efficiency in front of Hillary, who looked suitably impressed. The man with the beard fringe offered that they'd already checked the Ford, which had shown no radiation whatsoever, and that the vehicle remained isolated on the ring road solely for their examination. Hillary shook her head as Kestler translated and said: 'Not unless you guys want to.' Neither did.

Kestler manoeuvred himself next to Hillary in the rear of the Militia car, putting Charlie in the front. He sat turned towards the American, his arm over the seat, so he was instantly able to squeeze the girl's leg in warning when she started; 'Well, the story so far . . .'

She stopped, grinning at Charlie. 'You trying to tell me a secret?'

'No!' he said, pointedly. 'Maybe keep one.'

She remained silent until they transferred at the ministry into the embassy car. Because Kestler had to drive it put Charlie in the back with Hillary again. At once she said; 'Sorry. But everything with the driver was in Russian; I didn't think he could speak English. And anyway, aren't we on the same side now?'

It was Kestler who explained their acceptance on sufferance, which Charlie finished by saying that if he'd arranged their transport, like Popov had for them, he would have ensured the driver was fluent in English. 'So what would he have heard?'

'The level of radiation when I got there was virtually non-existent,' reported Hillary. 'If the Russians' curie reading is accurate to within a degree, any contamination was entirely residual and from *outside*, from when they smashed the containers. That's why I checked the outside and underside of the lorries and confirmed a reading. The inside of the trucks gave me a lot, though. It's not shown in any of the satellite photographs, but each truck had some sort of hydraulic lifting device, to bring the canisters on board. Near the tailgate of each there's extensive scratching and on the metal floor of one of the covered lorries there are clear circular markings of the sort you get from rubber pads at the end of support legs. The canvas lorry is flatbed and wooden decked: the wood here has been positively depressed for maybe a millimetre. From the satellite shots of the smashed open containers Washington's already made weight calculations from height and thickness measurements. The floor markings on the lorries are consistent with the containers being pretty standard, hard outer casing, two-inch thick lead lining. In my opinion the floor markings prove that the containers were *full* when they were lifted inboard. On our estimate of twenty-two being stolen, that puts the total nuclear graded loss at just under two hundred and forty nine kilos . . .'

'. . . According to this morning's meeting, they only lost nineteen,' interrupted Kestler.

'We'll have Washington recount,' said the girl, at once. 'I can't see how our picture analysts were wrong, but on the lesser figure the loss will be two hundred and forty two kilos, forty minimum.'

'Five kilos makes one bomb,' remembered Charlie. 'They've got enough to make forty-eight, at least.'

Hillary hesitated. 'Only with proper laboratories staffed by properly qualified technicians and physicists. But you're right – the bad guys have got enough to rule the world.'

'Unless they're stopped,' said Kestler.

'I think the most significant thing is that the housing isn't in the lorries back there any more, either,' said Hillary, answering the question as Charlie was about to ask it.

Instead he said; 'So it was transferred, to go on supporting the canisters in the trucks into which it was transferred.'

'Obviously,' agreed the physicist.

'From the timed satellite sequence we know it took an hour to move the containers from the train into the trucks,' said Charlie.

Hillary took up the calculation. 'Where the egg box was already prepared. This time the support frames had to be transferred, along with the containers. I'd say two hours, minimum. More likely three. Longer than that if they did it in the dark.'

'So it wasn't done at the Arbat,' concluded Charlie, positively.

'Who said it was?' demanded the girl.

'That was the suggestion at a briefing this morning.'

'On the street back there!' exclaimed Hillary. 'Bullshit! No one taking the trouble these guys did would have risked that.'

'You think there could have been an expert – a physicist even – involved in the robbery?' queried Kestler.

'Advising, maybe,' she judged. 'What I am damned sure about is that they didn't intend losing what they got. Or being caught, getting it.'

Natalia called Lesnaya within an hour of Charlie returning from the embassy, listening without interruption to everything he recounted. She said, 'There must be a connection, between the two! Kirs *had* to be a decoy!'

'Prove it, from the people you've got in custody,' urged Charlie. 'You did well, personally involving yourself in the questioning.'

'I'm pretty sure Yatisyna will break quickly.'

'Did he give you any indication of what he's got?'

'If he's telling the truth about Kirs being set up by Agayans, he might know who the intended purchasers were.'

'That could take us a long way forward,' agreed Charlie.

'I almost promised it at today's meeting.'

'Don't promise what you haven't got,' warned Charlie. 'And don't tell anyone else. If you get it, keep it for a higher authority meeting. And get all the credit yourself.'

'I didn't know anything about the lorries and the cars being found,' Natalia admitted abruptly.

'Popov didn't tell you before the meeting?' queried Charlie, recalling the look on her face. He could hear Sasha in the background, singing tunelessly.

'I didn't get up from the interrogation cell until fifteen minutes before it began. There wasn't time. For me to be told about Oskin, either. I personally promised the protection!'

In the solitude of his apartment Charlie frowned. 'It's work, Natalia! Don't get personally involved. You couldn't have anticipated what was going to happen.'

'I should have done.'

'Stop it!' he insisted, sternly.

After several moments' silence, she said, 'They're obviously very well organized, particularly here in Moscow.'

Charlie hesitated. 'I wasn't personally challenging Popov. He was assuming too much.'

'You don't have to keep apologizing.'

'I'm not apologizing. I just don't want you to misunderstand.'

Beyond the sound of Sasha's tiny, unformed voice Charlie heard a man's shout. Natalia said quickly, 'I have to go.'

'Yes.' Popov must be in the hallway: it was obvious he would have his own key.

Charlie replaced the phone feeling emptied. It was a feeling he was to experience a lot in the coming days, increasingly about events involving Natalia. Which was not Charlie allowing an intrusion because invariably those events were professional. He actually wished they hadn't been.

None of which, however, was his immediate concern. That was – finally – the public disclosure of the robbery.

The metal hooks and shackles had probably been fitted into the basement walls when the dacha was first built, to hang meat or support gardening equipment. The bands around Silin's wrists and ankles were very tight and wide apart, so that he was spreadeagled with his arms and legs widely outstretched. He was trying very hard not to show any fear to Sobelov, who stood directly in front of him.

'I fixed the Pizhma robbery my way,' said Sobelov. 'I even started the war between the Chechen and the Ostankino just the way you planned, to send everyone around in circles. So there's only one thing I want . . .'

Silin shook his head, not trusting himself to speak. He was very frightened, knowing he'd totally lost.

'I want the Moscow contacts, to the nuclear material.'

'Go to hell,' managed Silin.

'That's where you're going. But not until I've had my fun. You're going to tell me what I want, you know. You won't be able to stop yourself.'

He wouldn't, determined Silin. Whatever they did to him he'd beat the bastards over that.

chapter 23

Charlie was first alerted at Lesnaya by the night duty officer at the British embassy, relaying a message from the London Watch Room. He and Kestler both jammed their phones trying to reach the other until Charlie realized what was happening and left his line free, for the American's call. Charlie said, philosophically, it had been inevitable and that he was surprised it hadn't broken sooner. The more subdued Kestler hoped it wouldn't screw the Russian cooperation and promised to be in touch the following day. Which he was, by nine, already at the embassy.

'It's incredible,' Kestler insisted. 'I had a round-up sent overnight. There isn't a newspaper or a media outlet in the West that hasn't made it their major story. The comparison with Chernobyl was inevitable, I suppose. Like the death tolls in Japan in 1945. Washington's going to make some announcement during the day; maybe the President himself.'

Kestler was as quiet-voiced as he had been the previous night, which Charlie supposed was natural if the usually ebullient younger man believed things had reached presidential level. 'Where did the story origininate *from*?'

'Reuter. Under a Moscow dateline.'

Which wasn't really the answer to his question but Charlie accepted, philosophical still, it wouldn't ever be answered because the source would be impossible to trace. If the American reaction was anything like Kestler was suggesting, it would be mirrored in London with more soggy cornflakes. Despite the time difference, he should be at the embassy. 'You tried contacting Popov?'

There was a pause from the other end of the line. 'Still too early.'

Forcing the thought, Charlie wondered if the Russian would still be with Natalia at Leninskaya. The apartment didn't give any indication even of overnight stays but he hadn't seen enough of it properly to judge. 'I'll try him from the embassy; let you know what happens.'

'Likewise.'

Rupert Dean's call came thirty minutes after Charlie got to Morisa Toreza, while he was still collating the coverage from the news agency services monitored at the embassy; as well as breaking the original story Reuter had assembled a media round-up which showed Kestler had not exaggerated the worldwide reaction. Chernobyl was invoked in practically every story. So was Japan.

'This going to create a problem for us?' demanded the Director-General.

'They could make it into one,' assessed Charlie, realistically.

'What's their advantage?'

'Externally, nil. Internally we've still got a lot of buck-passing and the resentment of that earlier business at our inclusion.'

'What about the damned investigation?'

'Secondary, to keeping jobs at the top. This will be used, somehow, by anyone wanting to cover themselves.' He had to reach Natalia somehow, to find if it was being used against her.

'This is too serious for buck passing, for God's sake!'

'It's *because* it's so serious that everyone's trying to get out of the firing line.' Dean wasn't accustomed to bureaucracy, Charlie remembered.

'You spoken to the Americans?'

'Briefly. There could be a statement from Washington later, maybe by the President himself.'

'There's going to be a parliamentary announcement here. I need guidance, for the Foreign Office briefing.'

The uncertainty about job security wasn't confined to

Moscow, remembered Charlie. 'Anything going to be disclosed about my being here?'

'I don't see any reason for there to be,' said the Director-General.

'Was there any voice transmission picked up at GCHQ from the American satellite?' demanded Charlie, abruptly.

There was a silence from London. 'What's that got to do with what we're talking about?'

'Maybe a lot if I've got to have a reason to go on being included by the Russians.'

'There *was* some audio pick-up. I don't think it was complete; it's being translated and analyzed now. You'll get it before the day's out: original text and translation.'

'I called the Watch Room last night,' embarked Charlie, cautiously.

'Why?'

'To find out if there was a voice transcript on its way,' He allowed a silence. 'The Watch Room said there was a Red Alert but that my control was Peter Johnson. I thought you were supervising everything personally?'

Now the silence, much longer, came from the Director-General. 'I don't know anything about this. It was a mistake, obviously.'

By whom and for what reason, wondered Charlie, recalling the appointment antipathy rumours and familiar enough with internal politics to know the personal danger of getting his balls caught between a rock and a hard place. 'I'm worried about mistakes with two hundred and fifty kilos of atomic material running around loose.'

'So am I,' sighed Dean. 'I'll look into it.'

'I am to continue to report to you?' Was he choosing the right side, if internal battles were being fought? Upon whose side was the industrious Thomas Bowyer?

'*Solely* to me.'

The stress was sufficient for a man as nuance-conscious as Charlie. It had been a comforting impression imagining a similarity between Sir Archibald Willoughby and Rupert Dean. But at the same time there'd been some things which hadn't settled quite so well in his mind and now Charlie didn't feel as comforted any more. He was suddenly aware of Bowyer lingering at the cubicle door. 'I know, sir, it's clearly inappropriate at this moment but I think we should have a detailed discussion about various aspects of my position here.'

'I think we probably should,' accepted the man. 'Let's talk first about what guidance I'm going to give the Foreign Office.'

'How much time do I have before your briefing? And the parliamentary statement?' asked Charlie, pitching the entire exchange as much for his hovering observer as for Rupert Dean.

'Six hours, maximum. I'd like to hear earlier.'

The station head hurried into the room the moment Charlie replaced the secure telephone. 'That the DG?'

'Morning!' greeted Charlie, brightly.

'Was that the DG you were talking to?' repeated Bowyer.

Charlie was a man of many dislikes: high on the list was calling things or people by acronyms or initials. 'Who?'

'Dean!' capitulated Bowyer at last, exasperated. 'What's happened?'

'Yes,' said Charlie, replying in sequence. 'Reuter broke the news of the robbery.'

'It seemed serious,' said Bowyer, actually nodding towards the telephone.

Which is what I wanted you to imagine, you snide little bugger, thought Charlie. 'They'll probably try to pin the leak on us: us or the Americans. Or both.' He guessed Bowyer would go through the tiny office with a toothcomb and vacuum at the first opportunity.

'What are you going to do?'

The perennial question, identified Charlie. Which naturally led to thoughts of *re*action and *pro*action and from there to the idea which had come to him at the previous day's briefing, adjusted and refined to Charlie Muffin rules. 'Wait to see what the Russians do,' he said, reluctantly.

Charlie tried to get it by telephoning Popov, but the

personal number rang out unanswered on the first two occasions and on the third the woman whose voice he recognized insisted Popov was not available and she did not know when he would be. Charlie left his name. With nothing else practical to do, Charlie called the American embassy and was told James Kestler was momentarily out of his office and wasn't responding to his bleeper. Neither was Barry Lyneham, who was also absent from his office. Briefly Charlie considered asking for Hillary Jamieson but didn't. Instead he retrieved the original Reuter message to dissect with a surgeon's care. Here, as so often elsewhere, Chernobyl and Japan were mentioned but Charlie ignored the references, expertly recognizing the cuttings library additions to expand a major story to its maximum. He also scored through the other background material and speculation about the size of the Russian nuclear stockpile, the agreements and difficulties of recovering it from former satellite republics and the smuggling trade that had followed the end of the Cold War. He was left with the barest details of the failed attempt at Kirs, with the number of arrests and the identification of the Families to which the arrested men belonged, and an equally sparse account of the successful robbery at Pizhma of a special Kirov to Murom nuclear cargo train, with the loss of nineteen containers of plutonium 239. An unknown scientific source was quoted insisting no serious or long-lasting danger had been created at Pizhma by the abandoned containers being breached.

Charlie made a careful list of what he considered the salient points, double-checking and then checking again to ensure he'd missed nothing before sitting back, quite content. By themselves what he'd itemized were insufficient proof of anything, although perhaps good enough for a defensive argument if he was called upon to make one, but Charlie felt a familiar satisfaction at isolating colours that just might match in an intricate jigsaw. He was curious if he'd find any more when he succeeded in speaking to Natalia. Although it would probably have been meaningless, Charlie shredded his itemizing list in advance of any later office search by Thomas Bowyer.

Charlie was actually about to try Popov again when his own telephone rang.

'You want to come across, Charlie?' invited Kestler.

'What is it?'

'I just got back from a full briefing at the Interior Ministry.'

'*Who*, specifically, excluded me?'

'I guess it was a committee decision: that's the way they're working now. All the usual people.' Kestler was flushed, sweating slightly, moving around the FBI office more quickly than usual.

'But who actually *told* you?' persisted Charlie.

'Popov, when he called about a meeting. Said you weren't to be included any more . . .' The younger man pulled his lower lip several times through his teeth. 'I didn't want to endanger our own access. I'm sorry . . .'

'My decision,' volunteered Lyneham. 'I said he had to go ahead without telling you. Damage limitation. This way we're still in the game. All of us.'

Charlie shook his head against the apologies. It was the only thing the Americans could have done. It would be wrong to ask outright if Natalia had been present. '*All* the usual people, except me?'

Kestler nodded.

'No discussion about my not being there?'

'At the beginning,' said Kestler. 'Popov said it had been decided the British were not being allowed to participate any more. And Badim and Fomin kind of nodded and that was that.'

'I was not positively connected with the leak?'

'Not by name, no.'

'Anything said about our working together?'

'Not in as many words. After the meeting Popov told me our continued liaison – between me and the Russians – was being reviewed.'

'So we could be out too,' added Lyneham. 'My guess is that we will be. It's a bastard.'

Not for him it wasn't, mused Charlie. Because he wasn't out. Through Natalia he was very much in. 'They can't afford to exclude us! That stuff's on its way into the West.'

'They don't think so,' disclosed Kestler. 'That was the purpose of today's conference. They've got some back and think they're going to get the rest. So they *don't* need us.'

With difficulty Charlie stifled the anger: practically a whole fucking hour before they'd told him, almost as an afterthought! 'I'd really like to hear all about getting stuff back!'

What was so far known appeared to support Popov's insistence that the Pizhma haul was still in the Moscow area, said Kestler. The promised round-ups of the Agayans and Shelapin Families had gone on, after the previous day's conference and throughout the night. At 8 p.m. the previous evening – ironically around the time the Reuter story of the robbery was breaking – a combined Special Forces and Militia squad had raided an apartment block at Ulitza Volkhonka, near the metro station, where it was believed some members of the Shelapin Family lived. Three gang members had been shot dead, resisting arrest. One Militia officer had died and two more were injured, one seriously. In a basement garage belonging to one of the dead men were three containers from the Pizhma train. They were still being checked but if full they would contain several kilos of enriched plutonium. Radomir Badim was holding a press conference for the international news media that afternoon at which they hoped to display the recovered canisters. Before that, assurances were going to Western governments through the Foreign Ministry.

'Assurances about what?' demanded Charlie.

'That wasn't made clear.'

'They talked of assurances?' Each and every word was essential if he was to advise the Director-General properly.

'Yes.'

'What, *exactly*, was said?'

'That Western ambassadors were being called in . . .' Kestler looked at his watch. '. . . about now. To be told of the recovery before any other official announcement.'

'It's clever,' admitted Charlie, begrudgingly.

'Classical,' agreed Lyneham.

'You've got to concede it's pretty damned good,' suggested Kestler, misunderstanding.

'Three from twenty-two leaves nineteen,' said Charlie, impatiently. 'So where's the great recovery, with nineteen containers still missing! From the markings Hillary found in those trucks yesterday we *know* it wasn't transferred anywhere near Moscow!' To Kestler he said: 'Didn't you make that clear?'

The young American momentarily stopped his office wanderings. 'They're not accepting those marks came from a support frame. Or from any heavy lifting gear. According to Popov, and the Russian forensic report, everything could have been caused by the normal use to which the trucks were put, before they were stolen.'

'They can't be serious!'

'That's what they're saying; what they want to believe,' said Kestler.

'They've let Hillary go to Volkhonka,' said Lyneham. 'That's where I was when you called: running her there.'

'Where is she now?'

'Still there.'

'The containers are sealed?'

'I specifically asked,' said Kestler. 'There's no danger.'

'So it's part of the smokescreen,' judged Charlie.

'Thicker than a donkey's dick,' agreed Lyneham.

'What's Volkhonka like?'

'Like every other apartment block you've ever seen and loved in Moscow,' said the Bureau chief.

To Kestler again Charlie said, 'You ask about the cordon beyond Moscow?'

Kestler nodded. 'Everything's still in place, according to Popov.' The man paused. 'But the search is very definitely being concentrated in Moscow.'

The repeated phrase caught Charlie's attention. 'Popov appears to have done most of the talking?'

'Virtually all of it,' confirmed Kestler. 'But he is the operational commander. It's his responsibility.'

'It's wrong!' insisted Charlie. 'All wrong! Kirs was a decoy and dumping the lorries in Moscow was a decoy and finding the stuff at Volkhonka is a decoy.'

'I'm prepared to believe it,' said Lyneham. 'No one else is.'

London would, determined Charlie. Sir William Wilkes would be one of the ambassadors getting the reassuring bullshit. 'I'm going to do my best to see that as many other people as possible believe it.'

'I'd like you to explain it to me,' invited Dean. For once the delivery wasn't staccato: instead the words were measured, spelled out to prevent any misunderstanding. The worry bead spectacles moved through his fingers. 'I told you quite clearly that I was assuming personal control.'

Peter Johnson laughed, dismissively, settling himself languidly in the chair opposite the other man. 'A simple oversight. Until all this business blew up he was my responsibility. I set up the Watch Room link as part of the detailed briefing, which again if you remember you asked me to complete. I simply forgot to rescind it.'

'Forgot, about something that's assumed the importance that this has!'

The bloody Watch Room clerk had breached regulations, but in the circumstances he couldn't use that as the reason for dismissing him, thought Johnson. He'd have to wait for a month or two and find some other cause. 'Assumed an importance in what, the last three days? During which time I've been concerned specifically about that importance, rather than a system that's practically automatic . . .' Johnson allowed the patronizing smile. 'We're on the same side, aren't we?'

The Director-General stopped playing with his glasses.

'That's an interesting question. Why don't you answer it for me?'

Johnson felt the first bubble of unease. 'I don't understand.'

'I'm not sure that I do,' said the shock-haired academic. 'Because of the short time I've been here – and my background – I wasn't even familiar with this out-of-hours contact procedure. With the security of our telephone system as a whole, in fact. I didn't know, for instance, how many conversations are automatically recorded. Or that *all* outgoing and incoming telephone calls are logged. Would you like to tell me about that?'

Johnson shifted in the chair, no longer languid. He wasn't going to damn himself out of his own mouth. 'I'm not sure that I understand that, either.'

'Our records show dated and timed telephone calls to the FBI headquarters in Washington from your office on a number of occasions during the past three months. There was one on the day we made the Moscow appointment, for instance. Another on the very day I *did* take over control. There are also several incoming calls logged to be from the Bureau Director: calls that did not reach me.'

Johnson felt the warmth rise through him, sweat actually pricking out on his back, and hoped it hadn't reached his face. He shrugged, trying the dismissive laugh. 'Of course I've spoken to Fenby! This is virtually a joint operation, isn't it? I can only assume you weren't available when he called.'

'The times are logged,' reminded Dean. 'I was available on every occasion.'

'Then I'm afraid I can't explain it.'

'We *are* supposed to be on the same side,' said Dean. 'Why didn't you tell me you were talking to Fenby?'

Johnson blew his nose, using the gesture to mop the sweat gathering on his upper lip. 'I don't remember anything of consequence that made it necessary.'

'University lecturers do need to remember,' said Dean, intentionally mocking the other man's earlier remarks. 'I can remember, for instance, your telling the first full committee meeting after Muffin arrived in Moscow that the Americans had expressed gratitude . . .' He paused. 'Not to me they hadn't. And then there was the intentional breaching of the containers at Pizhma. You announced that to the committee, before I'd had the chance.'

Johnson made an ineffectual waving motion with his hands. 'I had a lot of dealings with Fenby, when we used the American special relationship to achieve the appointment to Moscow. They've simply continued . . .' He tried the laugh again. 'You make it all sound sinister.'

'I am not the one who's allowed things to appear sinister.'

Johnson's hands fluttered again. 'I don't think I can respond to that.'

'I don't want you to. What I want you to do instead is make a decision, about your future. I will not tolerate resentment or ridiculous back-alley manoeuvrings. What we're dealing with now is far too important for digressions like that. I will have a loyal team. If I don't get it, I will create another one. Have I made myself clear?'

'I think so,' said Johnson. He knew his face was burning and there was nothing he could do about it. He *did* feel like a schoolboy found cheating at exams.

'Then let me know your decision very soon.' The magnitude of the Russian situation was far too great for the disruption of an enforced resignation, which in turn would have required a replacement, but Dean hoped he hadn't made a mistake in not demanding the man's departure. And demanding, too, to know what Johnson and Fenby were discussing during their telephone calls.

This time Natalia did check the back-up connection to the observation room, prepared if necessary to turn off the table-mounted recording system to entice Yatisyna into the promised revelations. Through the glass she saw Yatisyna had done his best with the prison issue. He'd rolled the trouser and sleeve cuffs up and left the fly open to tie the two ends into a supporting knot at his waist. The superfluous material actually formed a penis-like protrusion and as he sat down Yatisyna feigned masturbation with it and asked the big-busted wardress what she would like to do with it. The rehearsed girl jeered that she'd probably catch something groping through the fetid uniform even before she was infected by what he had between his legs. The sound was perfect. Yetisyna still looked foolish but with the adjustments to the overall was better able than before to play the mafiosi braggart. She attached particular significance to his not losing his temper at the wardress' clumsy derision. She guessed he'd decided to cooperate and believed that what he had to tell would be sufficient to negotiate a prison sentence from which he could either escape or bribe his way to freedom.

Natalia listened and assessed everything with part of her mind still upon the meeting from which Charlie had been excluded. The American wasn't sufficiently adept by himself. With Charlie at his side Kestler hadn't appeared overawed by his surroundings but alone he'd hardly said anything, certainly not making sufficient contribution to justify his continued inclusion. She wasn't sure how to read this new development. She still had their private link – more relieved now than ever that she'd established it – but she'd welcomed his presence at the open sessions, although not what had become the almost inevitable clashes with Aleksai. She was increasingly concluding, and wishing that she weren't, that the fault was Aleksai's. Determinedly she put aside what had already happened that day, thrusting her way along the connecting corridor to where Yatisyna waited.

He was in her chair again and actually grinned up when she entered. She made the impatient shooing away hand gesture without bothering to speak and the expression faltered. He got up as slowly as he had the previous day. As she sat she started the visibly placed recorder and said peremptorily, 'Your message said you had something to say. So say it.'

'There's a lot to talk about first. You speak to the Federal Prosecutor?'

'No,' said Natalia, at once. 'And you knew I wasn't going to, until there was something to be discussed.'

He said, 'That wasn't very sensible,' but Natalia thought the braggadocio flaked away, just slightly, at her rejection. She gazed up at him from the table, unspeaking. His smell had become noticeably worse.

'I don't like being recorded.'

'I don't like being kept waiting.'

'I want it off.'

It would be making a concession, which wasn't good psychology, but she'd anticipated it. Natalia was surprised he didn't suspect a back-up system. She reached out, snapping the machine off. 'You've got two minutes.'

'And them,' said the man, jerking his head to the prison escorts.

Another concession, although she was prepared for that as well. 'Leave us but stay directly outside.'

'I'd like to sit down.'

'You've wasted thirty seconds.'

'I want a guarantee!'

'You're not getting one.' It was time to regain superiority.

'I want to trade!'

'Forty-five seconds.'

'Take what I give you to the prosecutor! Tell him there's more! A lot more. But he won't get it unless I get an understanding.'

There'd have to be something among the bluff. 'All right.'

'You got Agayans?'

'There's a warrant.'

'But you haven't got him yet?'

'No.' There was no danger in that admission.

'He *did* set it up, all of it. He needed us because it was our territory; the Militia were ours.'

'So you thought.'

Yatisyna grimaced, accepting the correction. 'That's something else I'll give you. All the names.'

Important but not *the* most important. 'So Agayans approached you?'

'Six months ago. Said he had buyers for nuclear stuff and that he knew there were three installations around Kirov where it was available. Which we already knew. We already had people inside Kirs. What we didn't have were buyers. So it was the perfect partnership.'

'Agayans had buyers?' isolated Natalia.

'Yes.'

'Not just one? Several?'

'Yes.'

Natalia fought against the excitement, knowing if she gave the slightest indication Yatisyna would believe he'd provided enough. 'How many?'

'Three. Maybe four.'

Too vague: he was lying. 'Names?'

'I never knew any names.'

'What was the deal, between you and Agayans?' With his sleeves rolled back Natalia could see Yatisyna had a bird tattooed on the forefinger of his left hand; she'd heard some Russian Mafia Families affected skin decoration as a mark of recognition.

'Twenty million dollars, minimum. And affiliation with the Ostankino.'

'You were going to get twenty million dollars and join one of the six leading Mafia Families in Russia but they didn't trust you enough to meet one single buyer!'

'I did meet a buyer. Three months ago. Here in Moscow, in a club.'

'What nationality?'

'Arab.'

'Which country?'

'I don't know. He had a European with him: French, I think, who could speak Russian.'

'Did Agayans know the name?'

'I think so.'

'How did everyone refer to each other, when they talked?'

'They just talked, without using names.'

'Could you identify the Arab again?' Natalia decided to bypass the operational group and go direct to the ministers:

warn them in advance for Dmitri Fomin to attend, from the President's secretariat.

'I think so.'

'And the Frenchman?'

'I think so.'

'Could you describe them, for an artist to make an impression?' He'd had twenty-four hours to invent this story. There was no guarantee of any of it being true, until they could confront Agayans, but a lot of it sounded convincing enough.

'I could try.'

Arab, reflected Natalia: with a French intermediary. How would that balance against Aleksai's insistence of the material still being in Moscow. She was immediately annoyed with herself. With Yatisyna she was discussing a robbery that *hadn't* succeeded. And Aleksai had never argued against the West or the Middle East being the final destination, just that it hadn't moved in that direction yet. 'I'll arrange it tomorrow.'

'And see the Federal Prosecutor?'

'Yes.' Dmitri Fomin had already made the decision but there was everything to be gained by stringing the man along.

'That's a nice dress,' said the gang leader. 'Nice watch, too. You like nice things?'

'Very much,' said Natalia. If he wanted to go on she certainly wasn't going to stop him. 'You know a lot of Militia people in Kirov who like nice things?'

'Not just in Kirov,' said Yatisyna, pointedly.

'Moscow, too,' she anticipated.

'Agayans is very proud of his special friends. He's introduced me to a lot of them.'

'Who?'

Yatisyna smiled. 'After you've talked to the prosecutor.'

chapter 24

Even before he left the American embassy Charlie worked out the priorities to achieve the maximum advantage, the most important of which was getting his side of every story to London first. So he was relieved that Sir William Wilkes's Rolls wasn't in the forecourt when he got to Morisa Toreza. He avoided Bowyer's office and his own cubby-hole, skirting directly to the cipher room. He was connected instantly to the impatiently waiting Director-General, who said at once the Foreign Office briefing had escalated to Downing Street and the Prime Minister's chairmanship. Charlie promised, page by page, information he insisted was essential before any parliamentary statement was made. Aware that all telephone communications with Moscow were recorded and would later be available for examination, Charlie accepted that if he'd misinterpreted by a jot his balls would within twenty-four hours be fluttering in the wind like the British pennant from the ambassadorial Rolls, which still hadn't reappeared outside.

'You made any protest?' demanded Dean, sharply, when Charlie announced his exclusion.

'Nothing to object *to*,' reminded Charlie. 'We were always accepted on sufferance.'

'But the Americans are still in?'

'They don't think they will be, for much longer. While they are, we're covered.' There was, of course, no question of his ever telling London of the arrangement with Natalia.

'Full cooperation locally.'

'It's working well.'

It was time he brought Fenby down to earth, Dean decided. 'We'll discuss it more fully later.'

Charlie remained in the cipher-room hideaway, handing his written account a promised page at a time for simultaneous encryption and transmission, careless of mistyping in his eagerness to get his views and opinions in London before any others. He'd finished most of it before Bowyer appeared, flushed, at the door. 'Where the hell have you been? The ambassador's going mad, trying to find you! Everyone is!'

'Working,' said Charlie, not looking up.

'Stop what you're doing and come with me!'

'I'm going to finish this.'

'I told you to come with me!'

'Call the Director-General and ask if he wants me to stop.' Charlie held back, just, from referring to Dean as the DG: there was the specific London instruction about Bowyer's seniority down the drain, he reflected. But there was a purpose in his doing it, like there was in every move he was making now.

'Are you . . . !' started the outraged station chief.

'. . . Fifteen minutes,' stopped Charlie. 'Call London.' He went on writing while Bowyer stood for several minutes at the doorway before turning abruptly to stomp back into the main embassy building. Charlie refused to meet the conspiratorial attention upon him from the clerks. It actually took him twenty minutes to finish and a further ten to retrieve his full, un-encrypted report, which was a leaving-the-room afterthought. Charlie found Thomas Bowyer sitting rigidly in the official *rezidentura*. Charlie was sure Bowyer would have sought London adjudication and that the stuffed-animal demeanour was the result but didn't press it. He said, 'Sorry to have kept you,' wishing the cliché hadn't sounded so mocking.

'The ambassador's waiting,' said Bowyer, moving jerkily out into the corridor. They went in total silence to the ambassador's suite.

Wilkes waved away Bowyer's hurried apologies for lateness but Nigel Saxon sat tensed forward in a chair bordering Wilkes's desk, impatient to strike. 'You've been in contact with London before consulting us!' accused the Chancellery head. 'That's directly against the instructions you were given. You were told to report to senior authority at all times.'

'The ambassador was not available,' said Charlie. 'It was a matter of urgency.'

'It was the ambassador's responsibility to respond to this!'

'Which is being delayed by this conversation,' pointed out Charlie. It sound stronger than he intended. Saxon pulled his lips into a tight line.

'I do think it's important to get on,' prompted Wilkes. 'It seems the Russians have pulled off quite a coup.'

Whatever he'd lost here at the embassy he'd made up for by getting his views to London first, Charlie decided. 'I'd advise caution with that assessment.'

Wilkes's frown was to Bowyer. 'According to the briefing I've just had at the Foreign Ministry, they've recovered a lot of material. And expect to recover a lot more.'

'They actually said that?'

'They inferred it.'

'I don't believe there are any grounds whatsoever to think that,' said Charlie. 'They're trumpeting a success to cover a failure: there's still an enormous amount missing . . .' He stood, putting his dispatch on the ambassador's desk. 'This is my opinion.'

'Reached upon what grounds?' demanded Saxon.

'The facts, as we so far know them. And common sense,' retorted Charlie. 'The Russians are mounting a containment exercise, blowing up as much smoke as possible. Which I don't blame them for: any government would do the same, in the circumstances in which Moscow finds itself. I just think we should see through the smoke.'

'Which you can do!' said Saxon.

Charlie looked directly at the man for several moments without speaking, making the disdain clear. 'Which everyone *should* be able to do, looking at the situation objectively.'

Wilkes came up frowning from Charlie's report. 'You

certainly disagree with the guidance I got, that there was little risk of anything reaching the West: that it was still in Moscow.'

'Total rubbish,' insisted Charlie. 'The majority remains missing and are on their way to the West.'

'Where's your *proof*?' insisted Saxon. 'Are you seriously suggesting the ambassador *ignores* what he's just been told? That the Russians are lying?'

Sometimes, thought Charlie, *Alice Through the Looking Glass* seemed like a treatise in irrefutable logic. 'The Russians are doing exactly what every government does when there's a potential disaster: mislead to fool the people they rule and as many outsiders as possible that they *can* handle it. In this case they're trying to fool other governments, too.' And from Wilkes's attitude, Charlie guessed they'd succeeded.

A discernible shift ran through the room at the cynicism. 'I think that's an extreme opinion,' volunteered Bowyer, entering the discussion. 'And one not necessarily shared by everyone.'

Charlie looked sideways at the other man, the irritation surging through him. He'd need something positive, some evidence, upon which to complain to London, but he didn't think it would be too hard to achieve. And when he did he'd openly confront this situation. At first it hadn't worried him – he'd even thought it potentially useful – but now he found it a downright bloody nuisance.

'I asked you for proof, upon which you base your opinions,' repeated Saxon.

If I had it I wouldn't offer it to you, thought Charlie. 'And I gave you my answer.'

'Then I think we should rely upon official sources rather than base a reaction upon the opinion of someone with little knowledge or awareness of diplomacy.'

'Why don't you do just that?' suggested Charlie.

The ambassador came up from Charlie's account a second time, the affability gone. 'You seem to make a practice of expressing yourself very strongly.'

Charlie supposed that was a diplomatic slap on the back of his legs. He looked pointedly at his watch. 'In a few hours from now an official statement is going to be made in the House of Commons. If it's wrong or misguided, within a very short time – days even – it could prove to be extremely embarrassing. Most embarrassing of all for the people upon whose guidance that statement was made.'

'As it could if it is based upon your guidance and your opinion is wrong,' challenged Saxon, immediately.

'Unquestionably,' accepted Charlie, just as quickly. 'You asked for my input. That's it, lying on the table there. I am not asking you, not even suggesting, that you take any notice of it. I am prepared to stand and be judged by it. I am not asking anyone else to be.'

The ambassador blinked at the forcefulness, which silenced Saxon and Bowyer, as well.

'You must have information that we don't know about to be as positive as this?' said Saxon.

'I have been doing the job I was sent here to perform.'

'Does that mean you're refusing to give us your sources?' demanded Bowyer.

Fucking right it does, thought Charlie. The bastard was trying to exacerbate a positive confrontation for the ambassador to invoke his ultimate authority! And Charlie didn't want to go as far as having to refuse outright, which he would do if necessary. 'You have everything I have sent to London.'

Instead of making the demand Bowyer, and possibly Saxon, had hoped, Wilkes said, 'You're sure of your information?'

'Judge it on the facts!' urged Charlie, again. 'Nineteen canisters are still missing! Recovering some is good but there's no cause for any upbeat reaction from London. Or from anywhere else.'

The ambassador nodded, an accepting gesture, and said, 'Thank you, for your opinion,' and Charlie knew he'd got away with it. Saxon and Bowyer knew it, too.

As they walked back through the embassy corridors,

Bowyer said, 'That was unforgivable! You were insubordinate!'

He had been, by diplomatic standards, accepted Charlie. 'You going to complain to London?'

'I'd be surprised if someone doesn't. Leaving me to provide an explanation.'

'And what would that be?' asked Charlie, directly.

Bowyer halted, in the corridor outside his office. 'It would be very difficult for me to defend your behaviour back there.'

'So I'm cast to the wolves,' mocked Charlie, who'd decided what to do during the walk from the ambassador's suite.

'You cast yourself,' said Bowyer.

The full transcript of what was available from the satellite audio-transmission was waiting when Charlie got back to his cubicle. The word *akrashena* appeared three times, although no specific importance was attached because in the context it read as if in the eavesdropped conversation between the nuclear thieves 'wet paint' was a mocking sneer at the contamination from the leaking containers. Which couldn't have been better.

Charlie sat back with his hands cupped contentedly over his stomach, allowing himself the self-congratulation. It had taken a long time but at last he was where he always preferred to be: on his own and unencumbered, with an inside track that was going to keep him ahead of the game and already with something that no one else would realize the significance of. He hadn't worked it out totally himself but he was getting there.

It took Charlie much longer to realize the significance of other disparate words, but when he did there was even more self-satisfaction. It was an over-familiar, incomplete reference and it wouldn't have meant anything if Charlie hadn't worked twice in Warsaw, in the old Cold War days, and heard the legend of the *Zajazd Karczma*. So there was the possibility it wouldn't mean anything to the analysts either in London or Washington, who'd be dissecting everything vowel by vowel, although he preferred to think they'd get it in time. But in time it would be too late.

Charlie endured five minutes of Jurgen Balg talking of the ambassadorial briefing before declaring, 'The rest – or a percentage at least – is moving through Poland. I don't have any timings or routes but it's Warsaw.'

'You're sure of Warsaw?'

'Yes.'

'Then it's more likely to be routed through Germany than the Czech Republic.'

'That would be my guess, too.'

'What's Moscow doing about it?'

There was no reason to tell the German he'd been excluded: it diminished his usefulness to the other man. 'They aren't aware of it.'

There was a momentary silence from Balg. 'What about America?'

'I don't know.'

This time the silence was longer. 'Between ourselves?'

'That's how I'd like it to stay.' Balg might have a reason to break the undertaking, so Charlie supposed he'd have to say something to Kestler. But there was no immediate hurry: self-preservation – with the new addition of protecting Natalia – was always the paramount consideration. And it was, after all, American information which they already had in Washington: probably in full, not intermittent like he had it.

'I'll be in touch,' promised the German.

'I'd like to be involved.' It was a lot to expect but if you don't ask you don't get, thought Charlie. So it was worth a try.

Having dealt with things in order of priority, Charlie came back to the decision he'd reached on his way back from the ambassador's office. He wrote steadily for half an hour, leaving until the end the final inscription on the fronting page and was actually putting it into his desk drawer when Thomas Bowyer appeared at the door.

'You're being recalled to London,' announced Bowyer, triumphantly.

'I hoped I would be,' replied Charlie, spoiling the other man's moment. But not until the following day, Charlie decided: he couldn't leave without talking to Natalia.

'We've been excluded,' announced Dean. As he had at the still-unconcluded confrontation with Peter Johnson, Dean spoke extremely slowly, measuring out his anger in every word.

'I'm sorry to hear that, sir.' Unthinkingly Fenby had picked up Henry Fitzjohn's unctuously polite mannerism: it was not unusual for him to copy speech affectation he admired.

You're going to be, determined Dean. He didn't yet fully know how, because it had to be to his maximum benefit and advantage. All he had at the moment was an implacable determination to overturn with as great an upheaval as possible whatever the water-drinking, salad-eating, ego-driven bastard imagined he was doing. Today was a simple declaration of war, which he expected Fenby was too stupid to realize. 'So was I. The nonsense about governmental leaks didn't justify it.'

'You think that was the reason, sir?' The FBI Director sat with his chair tilted away from the foot-resting desk of his top-floor office, gazing up Pennsylvania Avenue towards the Capitol with the telephone cupped loosely into his shoulder. Fenby's mind was only half on the conversation: my town, he was thinking; my town and I'm a central player.

'Can you think of another one?'

'I thought we gave a satisfactory explanation from here. Guess you did, too, from your end.'

'We gave an explanation,' agreed the Director-General. Heavily he added, 'An explanation for ourselves, that's all. In fact I think you should see it. The sanitized version and what really happened. I'm shipping both over in the diplomatic bag from your embassy today.' Charlie's itemized complaints against Kestler were already in front of Dean, isolated in an unusually cleared space on his desk.

In Washington Fenby frowned, at the 'what really happened' remark. 'Much obliged, but I really can't see the need.'

'In return, I'd be interested to see how you handled it, to find where I went wrong. We're treating the whole thing as a joint operation, after all.'

Fenby brought his feet down from the desk. 'Happy to send it over, sir; try to get it in your embassy bag tonight.' It would involve another morning creating another phoney response, that was all.

'It'll make both our records as complete as possible.'

'Politics is the art of the possible, isn't that what they say?'

The ill-fitting response momentarily silenced the Briton with its absurdity, although not by its significance. Rupert Dean *did* have the excellent memory of which he'd assured his deputy. Whom he remembered paraphrasing that very same axiom of his revered Bismarck at their briefing review just before Charlie Muffin had gone to Moscow. Another indication, which he didn't need, of how closely and how much Peter Johnson had maintained his back-door communication with the American. Would Johnson have already warned Fenby? He was still waiting for Johnson's response to his ultimatum. Briefly Dean considered taunting Fenby about the inane remark, sure the American knew nothing whatsoever about the statesman who'd unified Germany. Instead he said, 'Of course, ironically, I'm glad it's happened.'

'Glad?' Fenby frowned, beginning to concentrate.

'I'm temporarily withdrawing my man, obviously.' Dean wished it had been a face-to-face confrontation: he would have liked to see Fenby's complacency begin to crumble.

The FBI Director swivelled away from his powerhouse view. 'I'm not sure I'm following you on this, sir.'

'Well, I know you haven't swallowed that reassuring nonsense put out by Moscow.'

Fenby smiled in the solitude of his office. 'Got a very balanced account from my people.'

'Then you'll know there isn't a hope in hell of the Russians getting it all back: maybe none of what's still missing. We're going to have a major crisis – maybe more than one – on top of an already major disaster. With the Russians frantic to put blame on everyone but themselves. So the best place to be at the moment is as far out of it as possible, wouldn't you say?' Dean spoke looking at the muted television set already focused on the House of Commons chamber, in readiness for the prime ministerial statement. He'd have to congratulate Charlie Muffin, after the way the Downing Street briefing had gone: there couldn't be any doubts about the Moscow posting, from today. Or of the snipe-free security of the department.

In Washington Fenby felt the cold breath of uncertainty. He actually shivered. 'It's certainly going to need a lot of care.'

Dean grimaced at the inadequacy. 'Thought we should talk things through, to ensure we agree the scale of the problem.'

'I've already spelled it out to my people,' lied Fenby. But he was going to, the moment he got this damned man off the telephone.

'I look forward to getting your package,' said Dean.

'Like I am to getting yours,' said Fenby.

You won't when you read it, thought Rupert Dean. When the need arose – particularly if that need was to protect Charlie Muffin and the Russian appointment – he intended utilizing it through every media and diplomatic outlet to reverse their Moscow expulsion. The threat alone should be sufficient to bring John Fenby to heel, which by itself was a pleasing thought.

The first praise came from Dmitri Fomin, who'd entered the Interior Ministry prepared to be annoyed at the abrupt summons but whose attitude changed within minutes of Natalia giving a précis of her interrogation of Lev Yatisyna in advance of playing the full account to the ministerial group. The presidential aide called it outstanding and there was a brief discussion about reconvening the operational committee in advance of the following day's planned session before it was decided to be impractical. Natalia said she had already arranged for an artist to make the promised sketches and pointed out ahead of anyone else there couldn't be any question of their being publicly issued until after Yevgennie Agayans was in custody. Radomir Badim said if necessary he would actually get an official clemency document prepared to extract everything there was from Yetisyna, assuring Fomin at the same time it would be rescinded or simply torn up when they'd got all they wanted. Fomin said that politically, most particularly to avoid embarrassment in the West, any mass trials of corrupt policemen would have to be held quite separately from hearings involving the attempted or successful nuclear thefts. Badim pointed out that would be difficult if Militia officers were actually named in connection with nuclear thefts. The encounter ended with Fomin increasing his earlier praise by promising to identify her in a memorandum to the President.

Natalia decided, apart from Charlie Muffin's expulsion, it had been a hugely successful day. That was how she set out to describe it to Aleksai Popov but when she got to their office level he'd gone. There was no reply from his apartment and she replaced the telephone, anxious to make the other necessary call.

They'd used pulleys to raise him into a sitting position with his feet outstretched and there was nothing to sit upon, so all Silin's weight was supported by his wrist bands and his arms became dislocated first at the shoulder and then at the elbows by his writhing in agony from what they did to him.

Sobelov himself began beating the soles of Silin's feet, pausing periodically to repeat the one question he wanted answered, and when he grew tired he gave the metal rod to each of the Commission until Silin's feet swelled into footballs. He screamed over and over again and his bowels collapsed but he didn't give Sobelov the names. They crushed Silin's feet then, slowly, between gradually tightened vices. He lapsed into unconsciousness several times and Sobelov became impatient with the delay in reviving him. Still Silin said nothing when the torture started again. They used the bar with which they'd beaten his feet to break both his legs and his kneecaps. Silin screamed but didn't talk.

Finally, exhausted, Sobelov said, 'Remember, you're responsible for what's going to happen now.'

chapter 25

Charlie was back at Lesnaya in time to see the CNN transmission of the statement from both the Prime Minister and the American President, as well as the cable network's round-up of the rest of the Western reaction. The British was by far the most reserved, the concentration upon the amount of material still missing rather than upon that recovered, a fact that was seized upon by the Russian television commentary, which Charlie considered the biggest bonus of all.

He considered calling Kestler, wanting to know anything additional to what he'd already seen and heard on Russian television that Hillary Jamieson might have found at Ulitza Volkhonka, but decided it could wait until the following morning when he talked to the American about the satellite voice pick-up at the same time as announcing his London return. It would probably have been difficult to locate either of them anyway: even this early in the evening Kestler would probably be working hard to add Hillary's pubic scalp to his collection. He thought of packing for the following day but dismissed it as unnecessary preparation and instead poured a glass of Macallan, raised it to himself in lonely congratulation and said, 'Well done, Charlie. Keep it up.' He looked at his watch a lot, which was how he knew it was exactly seven-fifteen when Natalia finally rang.

'Yetisyna broke, like a baby: the easiest ever,' Natalia declared, needing to boast.

Nothing about his being closed out, thought Charlie: her speed, her priorities. 'Totally?'

'Enough. Classic bully persona, collapsing under the

slightest pressure.' Natalia used her account to Charlie as a rehearsal for the presentation the following day. She was glad now she hadn't been able to contact Aleksai. She wanted him to hear it first with all the others: most of all to hear the repeated praise and congratulation from higher authority. Aleksai had been accorded his: now it was her turn.

When she finished Charlie said objectively; 'How much do you believe?'

'Most of it. He's exaggerating, not actually lying.'

'Who knows?'

'Minister level. Fomin has promised a named reference to the President.'

'Very good,' acknowledged Charlie. 'No one else?'

'It's going to be announced at a full meeting tomorrow.'

Not so good, thought Charlie, although he didn't say so. 'To which I am no longer admitted,' he prompted.

'I didn't know it was going to happen,' Natalia said at once, anxiously apologetic.

Charlie frowned, curiously. 'Kestler thought it was a committee decision. I assumed you would have been present.'

'I didn't know in sufficient time to tell you,' Natalia clarified. 'I had to appoint interrogators to question the people arrested with the canisters: I was going to do it myself but then I had the message from Yatisyna that he wanted to see me, so everything had to be rescheduled. Everyone was assembled by the time I got there. Aleksai told me they thought it had been made public by the British and it had already been decided to withdraw all cooperation.'

'By the British,' pressed Charlie. 'Not by me personally?'

'No. You weren't mentioned by name.'

'And it was Popov who told you?'

'Yes.'

Which was who it logically should have been, acknowledged Charlie. It was time he made his contribution. 'The leak came from Moscow.'

'How do you know?' demanded the woman.

'According to the Western count, twenty-two canisters were stolen, not nineteen, which was what the Reuter story said. It also identified Murom as the train's destination: Kestler and I always assumed it was Gorkiy. We'd never heard of Murom. And what was taken has never been positively identified to us as plutonium 239. But it was in what Reuter put out.'

'What are you going to do?'

Charlie didn't want to cheat her but he had to lie: what she didn't know she couldn't inadvertently impede and what Natalia had just told him from her side increased the danger. So in ignorance she – and Sasha – would remain safe; he strained for any sound of his daughter in the background but couldn't hear her. He had to move Natalia onwards and away with a scalpel-like finesse to prevent any experienced suspicion. 'I have to go back.'

'Back where?' she asked, confused.

A good start, Charlie decided. 'London.'

'Ordered?'

'Yes.'

'How long for?'

Charlie detected no hesitation or voice change. 'Re-evaluation, I guess. I don't know.' Did he have to be this brutal, after everything else he'd done to her? Cruel eventually to be kind, he tried to convince himself. And wasn't convinced.

This time Natalia did hesitate. 'Could it be permanent?'

Enough, Charlie determined. 'No.'

'Can you be sure?'

'Permanently pulled out from something as big as this? You've got to be joking!'

'There aren't any jokes here, Charlie.'

And didn't he know it! Risking that she'd been sufficiently deflected, he said, 'I've got to leave tomorrow. So I need to know about the recovery now!'

It came disjointedly, a hurried, second-hand account of the Agayans and Shelapin Family purges to get to the interrogations in which she was personally involving herself. But Charlie refused to be hurried, breaking in to bring Natalia specifically back to everything she knew about what had happened at Ulitza Volkhonka. Which wasn't much. It had been one of several addresses checked of known members of the Shelapin Family. It was a rabbit warren of apartment complexes, so a surprise approach had been impossible. By the time the Militia and Special Forces had closed around the identified address, it was barred against them: the demand that the door be opened had been answered by a scatter of Kaleshnikov fire that injured two Militia officers. The door had been blown in by a grenade. The first Militia man across the threshold had been killed instantly and it was in the resulting fire-fight three gang members had died. It was only later, after all the arrests, that the canisters were found in the basement garage of one of the dead men, who had been named as Anatoli Dudin, an acknowledged Shelapin gang member who had a criminal record stretching back almost twenty years. The canisters had been intact and concealed only by a tarpaulin thrown over them. Every arrested Shelapin man denied any knowledge of the canisters or of the Pizhma robbery: their lawyers were already demanding their release.

'You still haven't got Agayans or Shelapin themselves?'

'No.'

'Agayans is important, after what you got from Yatisyna.'

'Charlie!'

'Sorry,' he apologized. 'What about forensic, at Volkhonka?' It had been a mistake not trying to speak to Hillary Jamieson. 'Have the canisters been checked for Dudin's fingerprints? Anyone's fingerprints?'

'It's hardly relevant, is it? The man's dead. And they were on his property. Petr Tukhonovich didn't say anything about forensic examination.'

'Petr Tukhonovich?' queried Charlie.

'Gusev,' completed Natalia and Charlie remembered the Moscow Militia commander who'd announced the finding of the lorries in the Arbat.

Charlie was disappointed Natalia didn't see the point of a forensic examination. 'Provable fingerprints, even of a dead man, would show that the Shelapin people were lying, wouldn't it? Like any prints could have led you to people with records for whom you haven't issued warrants yet.'

'My mistake,' admitted Natalia.

'Not your mistake. The mistake of the investigating scene-of-crime officer.'

'I think the containers have been moved to Murom.'

Handled by everyone and his dog by now, guessed Charlie. 'Nothing that can be done about it. Who's convinced everything else is still in Moscow?'

There was a pause. 'It just seems to be the general consensus,' offered Natalia, at last.

'Aleksai led the chorus the other day?'

'He's one of them,' she agreed. 'Gusev, too. Fomin and Badim seem to have accepted it, as well. Yatisyna's information was about Kirs, not Pizhma.'

'I believe some of it, maybe all of it, is being shipped through Warsaw. Probably even *gone* through Warsaw,' announced Charlie, flatly.

Charlie waited patiently for Natalia to recover and when she did she matched the professionalism of Balg, earlier, in not demanding proof or sources. 'It's already being acted upon?'

'Of course.'

'You sure of an arrest? A recovery?'

'No.'

'What can I do?'

'Nothing, practically,' cautioned Charlie. 'But use it, carefully. Go on as you did today, with people like Fomin and Badim. At that level – but not the operational group – argue as strongly as you can that Russia can't operate in isolation; that you need Western involvement and cooperation.' What he was hoping to achieve would need more than Natalia's lone voice, although she would have impressed people who mattered by what appeared to be the result of her interrogation of the Kirov gang leader.

There was another brief pause. 'That excludes Aleksai.'

'No, it doesn't,' said Charlie, reluctantly. 'Of course I expect you to talk about it to him.'

'He'll oppose it, privately as well as publicly. You particularly. He thinks you've picked arguments at the meetings.'

For once Charlie was uncomfortable with pillow talk because of whose pillow the talk came from. 'You know that's not true.'

'*I* do,' Natalia accepted, pointedly. Then she said, 'I feel I should do more, something practical! I just can't leave it, like that!'

'You haven't got a choice,' said Charlie, objectively.

'I don't feel I'm doing enough!' Natalia protested.

He hadn't felt that about himself, until the last two days: maybe even less. And he still had a lot to prove to himself, before he even considered trying to convince others. 'That's ridiculous! If half of what you got from Yatisyna is true you've taken the investigation a long way forward, with further to go when you get Agayans. You're being brought to the attention of the President, for Christ's sake!'

She didn't appear convinced. 'I'm not comfortable with this.'

'You could find the key to everything!' he insisted.

'I didn't mean the questioning. I meant this: you and I. Doing this . . . I feel I'm deceiving Aleksai. Which I am.'

A flurry of responses came to Charlie's mind. He didn't want to lose her: lose this link. And it wasn't just personal, not any more. He needed this back channel. Without it, now that official cooperation was denied him, he couldn't gauge the moves to make. 'We're not deceiving Aleksai: not in any proper meaning of the word. We're protecting you. And Sasha. And doing everything we can – more than anyone else with whom you're working – to solve a robbery that could cause a catastrophe. Where's the deceit, *real* deceit, in that?'

'I suppose you're right.'

'You know I'm right. Think about it.'

'Any idea how long you'll be away?'

'Just a few days.' There was an intake of breath from the

other end of the line and he expected her to say something. When she didn't he added; 'I'll have to call you, when I get back. It won't be difficult for you to let me know if it's inconvenient.'

'All right,' she agreed.

'We haven't talked about Sasha.'

'No.'

She was still uncertain, Charlie recognized. 'She all right?'

'Fine.'

'Good.'

'Learning numbers,' Natalia volunteered, at last. 'Not very well,' she added.

'She's only . . .'

'. . . I know how old she is, Charlie.'

'I . . .' he started and then stopped abruptly, before saying he'd like to see her again. Natalia had to trust him a lot more before that would be an easy request. Instead he said, 'When I get back maybe we should meet: not rely always on telephoning like this?'

'Why?'

He didn't like the immediate sharpness. 'I'd like to.' Not like: want to. He should have said something better; far better.

'This is professional.'

'I know that.'

'So this way is good enough.'

Was it that she was frightened of meeting him alone, not trusting herself? Careful, he told himself. 'So Sasha's all right?'

'I already told you.'

'There's nothing wrong in talking about her, is there?'

'I'm sorry, I . . .'

'. . . This is getting confused,' he stopped, although he didn't want to cut her off. 'I'll call you when I get back from London.' And persuade her somehow, some way to meet him again. But not with Sasha. By themselves. He had to take away her apprehension about the baby. He could lie, about London: invent something that sounded professional to get her to agree. He'd cheated her far worse in the past and this wasn't cheating. Was there any point, he asked himself. He didn't need to rationalize it, not yet, not now. Just not give up.

'Do that,' said Natalia and was the first to hang up.

Charlie was pouring the second scotch, no longer in quite the celebratory mood as before, when the telephone rang again. Hillary Jamieson said, 'What's a gal do for fun around here!'

'Go up and down,' said Charlie.

'That sounds interesting.'

'It's the name of the best club in town.' And if everything worked out in the coming weeks, one in which he hoped to spend a lot of time. So tonight was as good a time to start as any. But what was this call about from Hillary Jamieson? More confusion to add to that he already felt.

Hillary Jamieson entered the bar looking sensational in a mid-thigh sheath dress that didn't waste a single silk thread and a contrasting blue matador jacket, completed by just a single strand gold choker: several glasses stalled between table and lip as she eased towards him. Charlie couldn't remember seeing anyone move like her and didn't want the distraction of trying. Eased didn't describe it: poured was better but still lacking. He was at the bar because all the tables had been occupied when he arrived and poured still fitted the way she got on to the stool. She asked for vodka and said, 'When in Rome,' clinked glasses and then said, 'Here's to a new day,' and Charlie decided it was certainly going to be very different from a lot he'd known for a long time.

'What's left of this one's looking good enough.' Charlie was totally bemused and happy to be so. He still needed to know about Ulitza Volkhonka so he even had the excuse that this was work, not pleasure. There weren't, he told himself, any limits to which he wouldn't go for the job.

'Let's hope,' she smiled.

'So how are you scoring Moscow, out of ten?'

'Embassy compound accommodation nil. Socially, three and only then when the sun shines. Workwise, ten.'

He hadn't tried to rush anything, but it was all right with him if she wanted to get work out of the way. 'The canisters were OK?'

'Perfectly safe.' Then, at once, 'But I was right.'

'Right?'

'About their being held in racks, in the lorries. The outside of every one was scored at exactly the same height, where they'd shifted slightly during the drive from Pizhma.'

'So how was Volkhonka itself?'

'Charlie, you wouldn't believe it!'

He thought he probably would. 'Try me.'

'Even though I'm classified a scientist I've gone through the courses at Quantico, right? Done the basics. This wasn't even Keystone Kops. By the time I got to the garage there were at least eight guys, all standing around looking at each other doing fuck all but hoping to get into the television pictures that were being set up; their scientific guys – the same ones that were at the Arbat, I think although I'm not sure – had come and gone. It might have been them who'd put one of the canisters on its side but I'm not sure about that, either. There was a Militia man actually *sitting* on it, smoking a cigarette: if there'd been a leak he'd have been frying the balls he was trying to prove he had!' She needed a breath, after the outrage. 'And don't worry. I left before the cameras started shooting and I wasn't wearing FBI cover-alls anyway.'

Although he already had the lead from Natalia he still wanted to hear it from Hillary. 'What about forensic?'

She snorted a laugh. 'Nothing. And I mean just that: *nothing*. No dusting, no fibre checks, no positional diagrams, no ground casts, no scene-of-crime measurements, no nothing. Is there such a word as evidence in the Russian language?'

Charlie wished he had been at Ulitza Volkhonka, to have overheard the conversations among the posing policemen: he was surprised a Russian-speaking old timer like Lyneham hadn't hung around with Hillary. There was a crowd building around them, with Hillary the attraction, so Charlie pushed their way through the linking corridor to the Savoy restaurant, confident he wouldn't lose the momentum. The more he thought about it, and he was thinking about nothing else now, the more he realized how important Hillary Jamieson was and could be to him. Charlie didn't hurry with the comparison he wanted with what he'd been told on his first day at the British embassy. He went along with the predictable enthusiasm for the baroque decor and translated the menu and agreed it would be interesting to have the beluga before the sturgeon and took care over the imported Montrachet. Only then did he say, intentionally obtuse, 'I'm not really sure what we're up against here.'

Hillary looked at him blankly. 'You want to help me with that?'

'I don't mean the chaos and the inefficiency. What's plutonium and all the rest of it *do*? Where's the danger?'

Hillary smiled, nodding her head in a gesture Charlie didn't immediately understand. 'It's what makes the atom go bang: what splits it. By itself it emits rays you can't see – the radiation like X-rays – which burn and cause several kinds of cancer. It destroys bones literally within the body. And mutates unborn foetuses.'

'I wouldn't sit on it,' agreed Charlie.

'It's best not to.'

'How many weapons could be made from what's missing?'

She smiled again. 'Everybody's question: it was one of the first that Fenby wanted answering. I can't give one, specifically. Depends what sort of tactical weapon you want. If you're talking Hiroshima, Nagasaki size and we've still got more than 200 kilos missing, then a minimum of forty.'

'Minimum! You mean there could be more?' queried Charlie, who'd thought the lower figure was inconceivable.

'Nuclear technology has come a long way in half a century, Charlie!'

'How endangered are the men who breached the canisters at Pizhma? And the soldiers who cordoned it off, later?'

'The thieves, hardly at all. I've gone through our picture sequences: their exposure was very brief, less than ten minutes and that wasn't concentrated. The soldiers would have been stationary for a much longer time, just standing around being subjected to the contamination. They'll need a lot of monitoring: it could already be in their thyroids. They'll all be on iodine treatment. Or should be.'

This could all be academic, acknowledged Charlie. But if he succeeded in what he intended to propose the following day, it could literally be the difference between life and death: maybe his life and death. 'Could the Russians have hosed the contamination away from where the train was stopped? And the train itself, like they said they had?'

'They should have been able to, although I hope to Christ their nuclear people are better at what they do than their police are.'

'How long's the danger last if they aren't?'

She made her curious head-nodding movement again. 'We're talking plutonium 239 here, right?'

'Right.'

'So here's your question, for the kewpie doll on the back row. What's the life span of plutonium 239? You get one clue: give it your longest shot.'

'A hundred years,' guessed Charlie.

She laughed at him over the iced vodka he'd ordered with the caviare. 'Two hundred and forty thousand years. Not even Methuselah would have been safe; he only made it to 969.'

'You saying that's how long Chernobyl's going to be dangerous!'

'And a lot of that time lethal. Some nuclear scientists reckon the final death toll is going to be 500,000. But let's not stop at Chernobyl. After exploding their first atom bomb in 1949 the Russians concentrated a lot of their nuclear research around Sverdlovsk and Chelyabinsk. And used the Techa river as their radioactive disposal sewer. The current casualty figure is 100,000 . . .' She gave a resigned shrug. 'But it's not only Russia that deserves the finger. There's been more fuck-ups, cover-ups and outright murderous criminality in every country in the world developing nuclear technology than any other supposed science. In America we contaminated hundreds of people and hundreds of acres around Hanford, in Washington State; babies were born deformed. In Oregon Penitentiary American doctors paid lifers five bucks a month to let them do what that stupid bastard could have been risking at Volkhonka this afternoon, subjecting their testicles to radiation exposure to see what happened. Your people did fuck all to clear the aborigines out of your Australian test sites . . .'

'Whoa!' stopped Charlie, abruptly aware of the growing vehemence. 'Are we getting a statement here?'

She flushed, which surprised him. 'There are mistakes with every new discovery: they can't be helped. We developed nuclear fission fifty years ago. The mistakes should have stopped by now. And the nuclear power lobby shouldn't have been allowed to grow so strong or remain unchallenged, like they're too strong to be challenged now.'

'That why you're not part of it?'

She flushed again. 'Shouldn't I have a bright light shining into my face, with you hitting me with a rubber truncheon?'

'That isn't an answer.'

'Maybe,' she finally conceded. 'Now my question for you.'

'OK.'

'Have I passed?'

It took Charlie a moment to reply. 'You think I was testing you?'

'Weren't you?'

'No!' At last he understood the head nodding.

She regarded him doubtfully. 'I thought you thought I was a dumb-assed bimbo.'

'I don't think the FBI would include a dumb-assed bimbo in an investigation into a nuclear robbery of this size.'

'Sometimes people get the wrong impression.' It was an observation, not a defence.

'I haven't formed one yet.' Which wasn't true. Charlie had already decided she was anything but dumb-assed and wanted her to be very much part of what he had in mind, although he hadn't worked out how or what. In addition to which, he was enjoying the closeness of a woman, which was something he hadn't known for a long time. The continued envy of the other men in the restaurant, like that of others in the bar, wasn't hurting his ego, either.

'So far this hasn't been what I expected.'

'Me neither.'

'Didn't you say something about up and down?'

'It's a place, not an activity,' reminded Charlie.

Despite the designer-dressed, diamond-shined, coiffure-controlled competition, the reaction to Hillary's arrival at the Up and Down club matched that earlier at the Savoy bar, which Charlie decided was precisely because the competition was designer-dressed, diamond-shined and had every hair concreted in place. They had to try. Hillary didn't. She flowed alongside him utterly self-confident but seemingly unaware of the head-turning and for once Charlie welcomed the envious attention from the equally detail-perfect men. This *was* very much work and this the workplace. Which, he supposed, qualified as a tool the Roederer Crystal he ordered in preference to Dom Perignon with the anecdote to Hillary that it was the favourite champagne of the Romanov family to whom it was delivered in crystal bottles.

'These real life Mafia?' It was an objective although detached question from a person neither overly awed nor overly frightened.

'Real life and real death,' said Charlie. The two seemed to be a recurrent reflection.

'Lot of influence from Central Casting.'

'This is show-time.'

'Every night?'

'There's a circuit. Thought you might have gone around it with Kestler.'

'He suggested it.' The dismissiveness came down like a shutter.

Nervous of the downstairs dance area, the very definitely non-dancing Charlie remained on the upper level. The stripper was a different girl from Charlie's other visits but just as good and Hillary watched without any discomfort.

'There's a girl who knows what she's got.'

'Now I know it, too,' said Charlie.

She looked directly at him. 'That do anything for you?'

Charlie didn't reply at once. He *had* formed an impression, before tonight. And been wrong. He didn't any longer think Hillary Jamieson was a prick teaser. Taking his judgment beyond her cleverness, Charlie decided she was someone totally sure of herself and of how and what she wanted to be: so sure – arrogant about it, even, although not offensively so – that she genuinely didn't give a damn what anyone thought of her. Which made her, in fact, totally honest. She knew she had a spectacular body, as spectacular as the performer on stage, and saw no reason to be embarrassed about it and she said 'fuck' not for effect but because it suited what she wanted to say. There hadn't been any apology in her misunderstanding about his testing her. She'd gone along with it because it amused her. If it hadn't she would have closed him off like she appeared to have closed Kestler off, which was something else he had to find out about. Keeping her believed honesty in mind, Charlie finally said, 'Yes, it does something for me. She's exciting.'

'Isn't she demeaning herself – her sex – doing that?'

Another statement? wondered Charlie, surprised by the familiarity of the question. 'She might be exploited: if the Mafia control is like it's supposed to be she probably is. But she looks very professional to me: she wasn't snatched off the street yesterday. I think she's stripping because she wants to, not because she's being forced to.'

'So that's all right?' Hillary demanded.

She had him on the back foot, Charlie realized, demanding

attitudes and prejudices. 'Yeah, I think that's all right. It's her body and her decision how to use it. This way's more preferable, I would have thought, than doing it on her back. That's what she's got, beauty: her asset.'

As if assessing his replies she said, slowly; 'OK.'

'Have I passed?'

Hillary smiled. 'The marks are looking good.'

They both looked up at the arrival of a waiter at their table. Ignoring Charlie, the waiter said to Hillary, 'The gentleman at the table second from the bar wants you to join him.'

To Charlie, Hillary said, 'What did he say?'

Charlie had already identified the table. There were two men and one girl, all looking in their direction. A thick-set, very heavy man was smiling, expectantly. As Charlie looked, the smiling man said something to the girl, who smiled too. Tightly behind them and obviously part of the same group were two unsmiling men. Most of the suits had a sheen. Shit! Charlie thought.

'What did he say?' repeated Hillary.

'The man in the grey suit, two tables from the bar, has invited you for a drink. Actually, it was more than an invitation. The word was that he *wants* you to join him.'

'Oh,' she said. Then, 'You think you could help me out of this?' There wasn't any nervousness in the question.

'If I sit down with them, you sit. It won't be friendly. Very quickly tell me you've got to go to the bathroom so I can tell them what you said if they don't speak English. Then leave. If the girl comes with you, get away from her as best you can: let her go into a cubicle while you only do your hair or something. Anything. Just get away from her. And then get out of the club and back to the compound as quickly as you can: there's always cabs outside.'

'And leave you with them?'

'Do what I say, don't examine it. Smile when we go to their table.' Charlie wasn't frightened, not yet, although he knew he would be. At that moment he was angry, at not anticipating what could happen, because this could screw up everything.

It was when he stood that Charlie remembered the photographs of the body on the Berlin lake and what the bodies of Nikolai Oskin and his family had looked like, in the Militia pictures taken in their supposedly safe Moscow flat and the sick feeling lumped in his stomach. He began to smile some way away and hoped Hillary was doing the same: to have checked would have made him look nervous. The grey-suited man kept smiling but tilted his chair to say something to the minder directly behind him. Both protectors came slightly forward in their chairs. The smiling man looked only at Hillary, pushing out just one chair. Charlie took its back, to lean on, hoping they didn't realize how much he needed its support. Nodding to Hillary, Charlie said, 'She doesn't have any Russian, but thanks for the invitation. We'd like to accept it but we've got to keep a prearranged meeting with a business associate: if Yevgennie Agayans couldn't get here he's coming to the apartment.' Charlie smiled. 'It seems he can't guarantee his movements.' Christ it sounded thin: transparent. The only thing he was sure about was that the head of the Agayans Family hadn't been picked up yet, because Natalia had told him so. The arrest warrants had been reported in some of the Moscow newspapers but whoever these people were might not have read it, which left him dangling from the underworld grapevine. The size of the Pizhma robbery should have ensured the gossip but there was no guarantee here, either, that they would have heard it. He wasn't definite, even, that they *were* underworld. If they weren't, all he faced was an ugly row with a man who needed two bodyguards, which was scarcely reassuring. He was turning, to cup Hillary's elbow to lead her away, when the grey-suited man said, 'You know Yevgennie Arkentevich?' Close up he was even larger than he looked across the room, a bear of a man with very thick dark hair and with no break in his eyebrows, which made a black line across his forehead, and there was hair matted over the back of his hands, as well.

Charlie stopped, turning back. 'I intend to. That's the purpose of tonight's meeting. Arranged by mutual friends.'

'Where are you from?'

'England.' Time to move, Charlie knew: to get out. He took Hillary's arm.

'What business are you in?'

Before Charlie could reply another shiny suit came up from behind and whispered to the man, who nodded without looking away from Charlie.

'Import. Export. All commodities.' Charlie started to move and said, 'We will be here again. We like it. Maybe we can drink next time.' He walked with forced slowness, tensed for another halting remark, leaning sideways to Hillary. 'I'm supposed to be saying what an interesting chance meeting that was so nod and smile back at me and for fuck's sake don't hesitate,' and she responded brilliantly, even turning back with a half-wave at the door, which Charlie thought was going almost too far. There was the usual motor show of Mercedes and Porsches and BMWs and Charlie ostentatiously gave the doorman $20 and said he wanted a Mercedes taxi, which he got at once. Inside he warningly squeezed her thigh before she could speak and when she did she said, 'That wasn't you making a pass, was it?' And Charlie said it wasn't. He used the movement of putting his arm around her to check through the rear window but there was too much activity around the club entrance and the street outside to establish if they were being followed. Charlie said, 'This isn't a pass, either.' At Lesnaya Charlie added another $20 tip and settled the fare in the taxi to avoid any delay getting into the apartment, although there was no obvious vehicle behind.

Hillary didn't speak until they got inside. Then, erupting, she said, 'JESUS!' and the tension drained from Charlie so quickly he felt as if his strings had been cut.

'What the fuck happened back there?' she demanded.

Charlie emptied the Macallan bottle between them before recounting the nightclub exchange. Hillary listened with her drink untouched, elbows on her knees. 'Jesus!' she said again, although much quieter, when he finished.

'I don't think they followed but I obviously couldn't take you back to the embassy.'

'I'm not shouting kidnap.' For the first time she looked positively around the apartment. 'Which room's the Tsar got?'

'It's not the usual embassy apartment,' agreed Charlie.

'You any idea what embassy compound accommodation is like?'

'That's why I live here.' He hesitated and then said, 'There are two bedrooms.'

Hillary looked steadily at him, head to one side. 'Don't be stupid, Charlie!'

He'd never before had the practical experience of the aphrodisiac of fear but Charlie was surprised how long and effectively it lasted. Afterwards Hillary murmured: 'Don't ever risk sitting on a plutonium container, will you?'

'Never,' promised Charlie.

Peter Johnson's request for a meeting came at the very end of the day, when Dean was on the point of summoning his deputy to resolve their dispute ahead of the following day's meeting with Charlie Muffin.

'I think there has been a gross misunderstanding,' said Johnson.

'On whose part?' demanded Dean, refusing the man an escape. The fury he'd felt during his conversation with the FBI Director hadn't diminished, still so strong that he'd changed his mind about the inconvenience of internal disruption. If Johnson wanted to stay it would only be on his terms and the bloody man would know and have to accept it.

Bastard, thought Johnson. 'Mine. And I must apologize.'

'Yes,' agreed Dean. 'You must.'

'It was never my intention to be disloyal. At all times I had the best interests of the department and its new functions in mind.' The deputy Director had to force the words out.

'It's obvious how our exclusion has come about, wouldn't you agree?' Dean had checked the telephone log and knew there had been no incoming calls from Washington since he'd spoken to the FBI Director.

'Yes.'

'Did you have any knowledge, in advance, what Fenby was doing? Or might do?'

'No!' denied Johnson, who hadn't. 'That's unthinkable! I would have been undermining my own organization!'

Dean allowed his scepticism to show in the immediate silence. Then he said, 'I asked you to make a decision about your future.'

At that moment Johnson actually considered resigning rather than grovel as low as Dean was demanding. But then he thought of the conversations he'd had with the Bureau Director and of their conviction that Dean couldn't last in a job the man himself had indicated he didn't regard as permanent. And of their equal conviction that he was the natural and only possible successor to the directorship. 'I would like to remain with the department.'

'And I would like acknowledgment of that in writing.'

The disordered office and its disordered incumbent blurred in front of Johnson's eyes and he had to squeeze them tightly several times to refocus. No! he thought; dear God, no! No matter how ambiguous the wording, an official acknowledgment of a resignation consideration on his personnel record would make him a permanent hostage to the other man. 'I have apologized.'

'Verbally.'

'I consider you are asking too much.'

'I am asking for the support and loyalty which I don't believe I have so far had.'

'I give you my solemn undertaking of that.'

All or nothing, decided Dean. 'I want from you a memorandum telling me that having considered your position, you have decided to stay as deputy Director. I will consider that sufficient. Alternatively I will write my own memoranda of this and our earlier meeting.'

'I understand,' totally capitulated the deputy.

Johnson had shown himself to be a weak man by not telling him to go to hell, Dean decided.

'NO!'

No torture had torn such a scream from Silin, the anguish bursting from the crushed and mutilated man as Marina came into the cellar between two men, with Sobelov following and she turned at his cracked voice, seeing him for the first time and she screamed the same word, over and over and just as desperately.

Sobelov came around her, putting himself between Silin and his wife. 'It's your choice. Tell me what I want to know and nothing will happen to her. If you don't, you can watch.'

'Don't tell him!' Marina's voice was abruptly calm, without any fear. 'They'll kill us anyway. They've got to. So don't tell him . . .'

Sobelov slapped her back-handed across the face, stopping the outburst, all the time looking at Silin. 'Your choice,' he said again.

'Go fuck yourself,' Silin managed.

'No. I'll fuck your wife instead.'

Marina kept her eyes shut while they undressed her and while Sobelov raped her and didn't open them when Markov and then another man raped her, too.

After the third rape Sobelov came very close to the bulging-eyed, bulging-cheeked Silin and said, 'That was just the start. You want to stop what's going to happen to her now?'

Silin spat at the man, an explosion of blood and flesh hitting Sobelov in the face and chest. The man staggered back, gagging.

Markov went to Silin, jerking his head back. He turned to Sobelov and said, 'He can't tell us anything now. He's chewed his tongue off.'

'Hurt him!' ordered Sobelov. 'Hurt them both. As much as you can.'

chapter 26

Charlie hadn't expected the one-to-one session with the Director-General before going in front of the full committee. Or that it would carry over into Rupert Dean's private dining room with lunch and the best Margaux Charlie had ever tasted.

Charlie decided things were very definitely on an upswing, which he wanted to continue because he had a lot to achieve. Dean's remark that he'd done better than they could have hoped caused Charlie to work out for the first time that he'd only been in Moscow for three months. It seemed months longer and Charlie realized it had begun as an unconscious impression even on his way in from the airport and in everything that had happened since. London appeared strange, somewhere new and unfamiliar, a place he'd visited a long time ago and didn't properly remember any more. And brighter, a clean, freshly washed brightness that made the grass and the trees positively green compared to the grimed buildings and threadbare open spaces of the Russian capital, green only in its designated parks. It showed, Charlie supposed, that he was doing what he'd been told, adjusting to Moscow being his home.

The reality of that wasn't as inviting as it had been the last time he'd been on the seventh floor of this Embankment building. At least he'd returned to congratulations and not the threatened summary dismissal, although the Director-General made an unspecified reference to embassy difficulties, which Charlie tried to turn into his protest about Bowyer. He didn't, obviously, do so by naming the man. Or even by making a positive complaint because he had no proof, but if Bowyer's instructions hadn't come from the man himself the Director-General would certainly have had to know and approve the internal spying. Instead, Charlie talked in generalities of embassy supervision and of uncertainty about chains of command superseding diplomatic seniority. And ended wondering if he'd generalized too much because instead of being as positive as he'd previously been on their telephone links the Director-General merely said it would be interesting to expand the problems with the committee.

Charlie didn't get any better guidance on the operational suggestion he intended to push as hard as he could that afternoon. There was, in fact, a total *lack* of reaction. Dean was neither openly surprised nor outrightly dismissive, again called it interesting and said in his hurried voice that he looked forward to hearing the opinion of the full group about that, too.

All of whom were waiting, in the same seats as before, when he followed Dean into the office-linked conference room. Today the bald but moustached Jeremy Simpson was staring directly at him instead of at the river, which Charlie took as another sign of approval, like the smiles that came with all the nods from everyone except Gerald Williams, who gazed at him tight-faced and slightly flushed. Charlie pointedly smiled at the man, curious how much higher the colour would go before the end of the afternoon.

'I think we're all agreed the Moscow posting is working extremely satisfactorily,' began the Director-General, to assenting movements from everyone apart from the financial director.

Peter Johnson tapped his dossier, as if bringing the encounter to order, and said, 'Aren't you interpreting a lot from the GCHQ voice pick-up?'

Proving time again, Charlie recognized: and he had to impress them probably more than he'd ever before impressed a control body. 'There's a positive reference to "the *Zajazd Karczma*". Which is Polish, not Russian. It's an hotel in Warsaw. I've been there. On the GCHQ tape there are two references to Napoleon: in fact the full name of the hotel is *Zajazd Karczma Napoleonska.* It's supposed to be an historical fact that Napoleon stayed there en route to Moscow with his Grand Army. The first reference is garbled, apart from ''Napoleon's room''. The second is also incomplete – ''*. . . this Napoleon would have won . . .*'' I think it was a joking remark: they'd just carried out the biggest nuclear robbery ever and they knew it. Whoever it was – which will be provable, timing the photographic frames to the voice recordings – was showing off: releasing the tension. I think the full phrase would have been something like *''if or had he had this Napoleon would have won . . .''* Poland is the shortest route from Russia into the West: according to the Germans, it's been used before to transit nuclear material. And there are over two hundred kilos still missing from the Pizhma robbery.'

'The assumption seemed sufficient to alert the Polish and German authorities,' supported Dean.

Dean hadn't told him that earlier. Charlie hoped Jurgen Balg was properly appreciative of the six-hour head start he'd given the man, to get in first.

'Why should we ignore the Russian belief that the plutonium is still in the Moscow area?' challenged Williams.

'You've already got my arguments for that,' said Charlie, gesturing to the dossiers before each man, undecided whether or not to disclose the Arab buyer/French middleman claim from the Yatisyna interrogation. 'It has no *value* in Moscow. The West is the market place.'

'Why?' persisted Williams, the opposition prepared. 'Why can't the buying and selling be done in Moscow?'

It was the obvious introduction for his new operational suggestion, but the time wasn't right: he had to convince them more, about everything else, even confuse their thinking slightly, if he could. 'The buying and selling *is* done in Moscow! And in St Petersburg and in a lot of other cities and former republics as well! Buying and selling but for *delivery* in the West. That's the way the system works.'

'What system?'

Williams *had* prepared himself, Charlie acknowledged. 'The system that previous investigations have established.'

'Nothing's carved in stone. This robbery is different; bigger than any other. Why can't it be moved differently from anything in the past?'

'No reason whatsoever.' Charlie didn't like having to concede the admission and not because of the enmity between himself and the other man. He was agreeing that he could be wrong and he didn't want anyone apart from Williams – whom he knew he could never convince – to believe he could be wrong about anything. 'But from what we know about Warsaw, the probabilities are that it's being taken – or more likely *been* taken – out along an established route.'

'*Think* we know about Warsaw,' disputed Williams. 'I'm not prepared to be as easily persuaded. Nor should anyone else.'

'Several of us might be,' suggested Dean, mildly.

'What have the Polish authorities come back with?' questioned Williams.

'Nothing,' conceded the Director-General.

'And the Germans?'

'Nothing,' the man repeated.

'While the Russians, following standard police investigatory procedure, have recovered several kilos *and* made arrests!' said Williams.

Standard investigatory procedure he'd urged upon them, reflected Charlie. There wasn't any benefit in pointing that out: it would look as if he was boasting – and in some desperation – because he was being out-argued by Williams. And he was being out-argued. He'd have to do very much better than this to carry the other men with him. 'You already know what I feel about that: that I believe what was found in Moscow was a false trail.'

'Deliberately laid?' queried the Director-General.

'I believe so, by those who carried out the successful robbery at Pizhma.'

'So they knew in advance of the attempt at Kirs?' said Simpson.

'They had to,' argued Charlie. 'It's inconceivable there would be two robberies on the same night from the same plant.'

'Why couldn't it have been a deliberate decoy, two separate acts of the same planned robbery?' demanded Williams, ineptly.

'One of those arrested inside the plant was the leader of the biggest Mafia group in the area. If the decoy had been deliberate, those taken at Kirs would have been disposable, street-level people,' said Charlie, watching Williams' colour rise. It was another obvious moment to talk of the Yatisyna interrogation but still he held back.

'So one crime group, with inside knowledge of another, set that other Family up. Using their further inside knowledge of the nuclear installation itself?' set out the Director-General.

'That's my assessment,' agreed Charlie.

'Why would they have had to have inside knowledge of the plant itself?' asked Patrick Pacey. 'Knowing an entry attempt was being made would have been sufficient, surely?'

Charlie shook his head. 'They had to know the material was being moved, because of the decommissioning. And how and when and at what times it was being transported. Whoever it was at Pizhma knew it was being taken to *them*. All they had to do was wait and intercept it at Pizhma.'

'Someone with a very special inside knowledge, then?' pressed Dean.

'Very special,' accepted Charlie. It wasn't a speculative road down which he wanted to go. He had no intention of offering what he believed to be the significance of *akrashena*: of even disclosing the importance of the word. It would seem disjointed, but Natalia's interrogation would provide the deflection. He said, finally, 'Those who went into Kirs believed they had several buyers already established. The arrested local Mafia leader claims to have met an Arab and a Frenchman in a Moscow club.' He'd have to get a name from Natalia, he thought, remembering the episode with Hillary Jamieson.

There were frowned looks from the Director-General and Johnson and Williams shuffled through his documents, confirming Charlie's impression the bundle consisted of everything he'd sent from Moscow. Williams said, 'We haven't been told of this!'

'I only learned about it an hour before I left Moscow,' lied Charlie.

'What's the Russian response to it?' asked the legal advisor.

It was probably the best chance he'd get to bring the FBI into the discussion and maybe understand some of the Director-General's enigmatic remarks, which was something else the man had refused to enlarge upon during their lunch. 'I don't know, now that I'm excluded because of what the Americans leaked.'

Charlie was curious at the look that passed between the Director-General and his deputy, before Dean spoke. 'Which brings us to the reason for this meeting and the principle reason for your recall. Our level of protest.'

It's not my principle reason, thought Charlie. He hadn't scored sufficiently against Williams' sniping but there didn't seem any purpose in delaying any further: there certainly wasn't any purpose in discussing a protest he didn't want made. 'I don't see how we can argue against it. I've not officially been given any reason: not officially told my cooperation has been withdrawn. And we've got to accept that we were only ever admitted to what the Russians chose to include us in. I don't believe we've arguable grounds for complaint.'

'You mean you don't *want* us to protest?' frowned the deputy Director.

Charlie breathed in deeply, readying himself: for the moment the FBI mystery had to remain unresolved. He looked to each of the men facing him, once more assessing Williams' colour. 'No, I don't,' he agreed, simply.

'What?'

The demand came from Pacey, but everyone else was regarding Charlie with matching astonishment.

'What the Russians initially offered appeared precisely the sort of liaison we hoped to achieve,' allowed Charlie, cautiously. 'But there was always a strong, underlying resentment. The American leak gave a focus for that resentment, until now I believe the Russians think sharing with us was a mistake . . .'

'Are you admitting you haven't established what you actually advised us you had?' tried Williams, anxious not to miss any imagined opportunity.

'The arrangement always made us dependent upon the Russians,' said Charlie. 'They needed us – or the Americans, to be more accurate – because of the satellite. But we had no control or practical participation in what they did or how they used whatever they got from us. We were just sources, nothing else . . .'

'You weren't supposed to be anything else!' interrupted Wiliams, triumphantly. 'You were *specifically* forbidden to seek or attempt anything else.'

'Always Russian jurisdiction,' reminded Simpson, reluctant though he was to support the financial controller.

'Depending on the size of the weapon, enough plutonium has been stolen and is still unrecovered to manufacture at least forty nuclear devices,' reminded Charlie. 'If Moscow always leads and we always have to follow there will be other robberies as big, maybe even bigger. Russian silos and storage plants aren't controlled. Police who aren't totally corrupt are woefully inefficient, ineffectual and operate with antiquated methods and equipment. We have to get some agreement – an arrangement – to be proactive. It isn't a question of national pride and nit-picking jurisdiction. It's a question of stopping madmen – or the Mafia or warring Latin American drug cartels, all of which could easily afford the asking price – getting as many atomic devices as they want . . .' Charlie hesitated, wanting them to assimilate every word, but before he could continue the eager Williams cut across him once more.

'And Charlie Muffin has a way to stop it all!' The attempted sarcasm was too blatantly hostile and both Dean and Pacey frowned at the man.

Here we go, thought Charlie. 'No. Not all. Maybe only a very small percentage: maybe *none* at all. What I do think is that I could infiltrate the business, to a degree. I want to try to isolate the big traders, in Moscow. And their contacts at the plants and their negotiating middlemen in Europe and their buyers . . .' Charlie looked directly to the legal director. 'You've already confirmed law doesn't even *exist* in Russia to assemble the sort of criminal intelligence I'm talking about: criminal intelligence we could supply to Moscow, to preserve that all-important jurisdiction. But perhaps more essentially criminal intelligence we could use ourselves and share with other countries *outside* Russia, which is, after all, where the trade really operates . . . where the real danger really is.'

'How?' prompted Dean, simply, knowing already.

'By setting myself up in Moscow as a no-questions-asked broker, a dealer in anything and everything. There are dozens of such middlemen all over Russia already, a lot of them from the West. The Germans have mounted sting operations, although in Germany to retain their legal authority. Why can't we? And take it one stage further, by setting ourselves up at source?'

'You seriously think it would be possible?' demanded Peter Johnson.

'Yes,' insisted Charlie. 'Easily possible. In Moscow crime rules, not the law. It's wide open: flaunted. If I didn't believe I could infiltrate in some worthwhile way I wouldn't be suggesting it.' He shrugged. 'And if I don't we can kill it off as an idea that didn't work. At least we would have tried something positive.' And I might have satisfied a lot of personal as well as professional uncertainties, he thought.

'Aren't you overlooking the personal risk?' demanded the thin-featured deputy Director.

'Not at all,' assured Charlie, even more insistent. 'I'd need protection. Every one of the traders I'm talking about has his own guards: I wouldn't be taken seriously if I didn't have the same. Which Moscow could provide. It would represent their participation. I'm suggesting a joint operation, not usurping or overriding Russian authority.' The nightclub confrontation had convinced Charlie how essential *spetznaz* would be if he persuaded these still-unconvinced men. The reflection made him think of Hillary. She'd awoken in Lesnaya without any of the first-morning-after awkwardness and made love and then breakfast as if there had been a lot of mornings-after. Charlie hoped there would be. Which wasn't just a personal anticipation. He'd need her in what he was trying to get agreed today, if it worked out successfully.

'What would all this cost?' asked Williams, his face relaxing slightly in expectation.

He'd have to go for broke, Charlie knew. 'The expense would be substantial. To fit the part I would need an impressive car, something like a Mercedes or BMW: vehicles like that are virtually tools of the trade, like having bodyguards. A Russian, not just as one of those bodyguard but as a chauffeur. An office. And I'd need to trade, in whatever I'm asked to buy or sell, to establish credibility. The department would have to be my supplier and buyer, but there'd be a financial loss: the need would always be to do the deal, not make a profit.'

'It would cost thousands – tens of thousands even – and take months without the slightest guarantee of your ever being approached to broker any nuclear deal,' objected Williams. 'All we'd end up with is a warehouse full of stolen or black-market goods.'

The vehemence had gone out of the other man's voice, judged Charlie, curiously: that last remark had been an observation, not a challenge. 'It's worked in Germany. In America the FBI have frequently trapped criminals – up to and including the Mafia – with *exactly* the sort of phoney-front operation I'm proposing. We've even done it ourselves, before our role was expanded. The cost would be extremely high. But I'm not suggesting we run it for months. We give it a *reasonable* period.'

'There's certainly precedents,' encouraged Dean. 'The problem I have with it is that it could only be done *with* Moscow's cooperation. And the reason you were brought back is that they've withdrawn just that.'

The most difficult barrier to get around, Charlie acknowledged. 'I've been rejected from a working group dealing with a specific situation at a specific level. This proposal would have to come officially and formally from here, not from me in Moscow. And if it comes from London it would obviously have to be in the same way and at the same level as you proposed my going there in the first place.' Which he knew, from Natalia, had been to a level of the Foreign Ministry higher than her. But one to which she now appeared to have access. Which, by carefully rehearsing her, opened another channel of persuasion.

'Going over the heads of the people you've been dealing with?' accepted Johnson. 'Which would surely increase the resentment you've already talked about.'

I hope so, thought Charlie; that was the major object of the exercise, although not the one he wanted them to believe. He said, 'If those people are involved at all it will only be peripherally. So their resentment won't matter.'

'What has this proposal got to do with what we should really be discussing: the theft of enough plutonium to make God knows how many weapons?' demanded Pacey.

'Nothing, in any practical way of getting it back,' admitted Charlie. 'But then again, maybe a lot. The Russians are insisting what was stolen at Pizhma is still in Russia and can be retrieved. I'm not as convinced. But I'd like to be proven wrong: what I'm suggesting might just give me a lead.'

There was a shocked silence. Pacey said, finally, 'You *really* think it's already out?'

'I think it's a strong possibility,' said Charlie. 'I'm looking beyond Pizhma: looking to stop a robbery of that sort of size being repeated. Pizhma, surely, was enough!'

'Dear God!' said Johnson, hollow-voiced.

'Which is a further argument – the strongest argument – to

put to Moscow for their agreeing to what I'm suggesting,' added Charlie.

'Are the police really as corrupt as you say they are?' asked the deputy Director, stronger voiced.

'I think so.'

'Then there's the risk of the Mafias you want to infiltrate learning the whole thing is phoney?'

'It's a risk,' conceded Charlie, uneasy with another admission. 'But again, making the approach as I've suggested should restrict the knowledge to a limited number of people.'

'Has anyone thought the information that enabled the Pizhma robbery could have come from the Kirs interception operation?' demanded Jeremy Simpson.

I don't think, I know, thought Charlie. 'It's a strong possibility. But it would be impossible to narrow it down. There were at least four hundred *spetznaz* and Militia personnel involved. Not all of them knew precisely what they were assembled for, although there were some hurried exercises. All the officers and NCOs certainly would have been aware of it.'

'You are officially accredited to the British embassy,' reminded Patrick Pacey. 'I'm not comfortable politically with someone with diplomatic status setting himself up as a conduit for crime, even if it's known about and approved by the Russian government.'

'During the time I would be running the operation, I wouldn't work from the embassy,' insisted Charlie. 'If you remember, my argument for having outside accommodation was because I might have to mix with criminals.'

'Which means you wouldn't be under embassy supervision,' said Johnson.

It couldn't have been better if it had been rehearsed, thought Charlie: it was even the word he'd used to the Director-General. '*Am* I under embassy supervision?'

'There has been a complaint from the Head of Chancellery,' disclosed Pacey, the political officer.

'I'd like to know what sort of complaint?'

'Insubordination.'

'Made on the day the nuclear theft became public?' asked Charlie, expectantly.

'Yes.'

'I was responding to specific instructions,' defended Charlie, cautiously, wanting the discussion to run as long as possible for him to gain as much as possible. 'There was an urgency . . .' Abruptly, in mid-sentence, Charlie didn't continue about the time-saving benefit of giving Sir William Wilkes a written account, which was a weak part of his argument anyway. Instead, recalling his impression walking from the ambassador's office with Bowyer, Charlie switched to concentrate specifically on time. 'The ambassador still had several hours before the Prime Minister spoke to the House.'

It was the over-anxious Williams who responded too quickly, the ammunition for his intended attacks already set out before him and believing he'd found his next ambush. Looking up from his hurriedly consulted papers, the financial chief said, 'Not according to the Head of Chancellery's message . . .'

'. . . Timed at what?' broke in Charlie, tensed for a reluctant apology if he had been wrong the previous day.

'Eleven in the morning, precisely,' said Williams, smiling in anticipated satisfaction. 'Four and a half hours, for a statement of the magnitude that the Prime Minister had to make, was totally insufficient for the Foreign Office to brief Downing Street in the detail required.'

Charlie looked around the assembled men, thinking again how much redder Williams' already pink face was likely to become, conscious of Dean's second frowned look at the man. He'd been lucky, Charlie accepted: hugely, wonderfully lucky in a way he'd never imagined possible. 'I quite agree,' he began, mildly. 'But it would be if it's Moscow time, three hours ahead of London. Which it will be because it's customary – and I'm sure that custom hasn't changed, even though our role has – to use local times on messages. So eleven Moscow time is only eight in the morning, here in London.' He shook his head, verging on the theatrical. 'But that creates more questions than answers. You see, I didn't get back to the embassy until twelve-thirty Moscow time. The ambassador wasn't even there. He was still being briefed at the Foreign Ministry . . .' Charlie looked around the group, imposing the silence. '. . . So how could the Head of Chancellery complain about my insubordination in communicating direct to London instead of speaking to the ambassador first a full hour and a half *before* I got back to the embassy with anything to talk *about*?' Gotcha! thought Charlie, although he wasn't sure who it was in London he'd caught out, just that he'd hung Bowyer and Saxon out to dry.

Williams' face was sunset red. None of the others looked comfortable, apart from Rupert Dean who didn't appear discomfited at all.

'Was the ambassador told *everything* when you eventually did see him?' pressed Johnson.

Charlie did not immediately reply, uncaring if his new silence was inferred as guilt. 'I gave the ambassador everything I transmitted to London. Bowyer was with me when I did it.'

'Withholding nothing?' persisted the deputy.

Again Charlie paused. This could be the moment the sky fell in on him but there was no turning back now: this was, after all, why he'd sat for half an hour after yesterday's confrontation in the ambassador's study, totally fabricating five folios of apparent intelligence about the Pizhma robbery before finally marking it 'Withheld from ambassador' and putting it into his desk drawer. Looking steadily at the deputy Director, spacing his words, Charlie said, 'I don't think I need remind anyone in this room of the reaction when the robbery became public knowledge: of the near hysteria that's still going on. Throughout the Western embassies in Moscow there was a great deal of speculation, which tended to get out of hand, exaggeration piling upon hyperbole. I do not see my function to be that of spreading rumours and *false* intelligence. The opposite, in fact. That is why I separated information I considered unreliable. I did not want to mislead anyone here or the ambassador in Moscow . . .' All the time

Charlie held Johnson's attention in the totally hushed room. 'I kept that separated, unreliable information in my embassy office to prevent rumour and gossip wrongly influencing anything the ambassador or his Head of Chancellery might communicate to London . . .' His pauses were becoming practically cliché, as well as the words. '. . . Strangely – obviously one of those odd coincidences – ''withheld'' was the very word I wrote on the rumour analysis, to remind myself that it shouldn't be used in any assessment . . .' The final pause. 'So no, I did not withhold anything from the ambassador that he should have seen. Only what he *shouldn't* have been confused by.'

For the men whose lives had been refrigerated throughout the Cold War the atmosphere inside the conference room became glacial. Again there was a long-held look between Rupert Dean and his deputy, beside whom Williams remained puce-faced. Pacey look confused and Simpson appeared irritated.

'I think there's been a misunderstanding,' suggested Dean, easily, still looking directly at Johnson. 'A mistake, even. You were quite right, sifting the wheat from the chaff. And you were responding as instructed, by me. Which I shall tell Moscow.'

And which the man could just as easily have told him during their earlier lunch, instead of making the nebulous remark about embassy difficulties, Charlie realized, abruptly. Not even that! If Dean knew what the complaint had been – which he clearly did – there had been no need for it to be discussed at all. The man could simply have resolved it with Moscow, like he'd just undertaken to do. Charlie, too often the shuttlecock in too many bureaucratic games, accepted he'd been used again. For some reason Dean had wanted an audience, which presumably he would have manipulated if Gerald Williams and Peter Johnson hadn't tripped over their own tongues. Charlie conceded there was a lot of speculation in that analysis but it fitted to Charlie's satisfaction. Certainly it explained Dean's inexplicable refusal to discuss anything in detail at lunch.

'Perhaps we could go back to discussing . . . ?' started Charlie but stopped at the entry into the room of Henry Bates.

The man leaned too closely to the Director-General for Charlie to hear the exchange, offering a single sheet of paper at the same time. Dean scanned it, then looked at Charlie. 'Agayans was arrested at a Moscow road block this morning. Shelapin has also been arrested. Another three of the plutonium canisters stolen from Pizhma were found with him.' The man paused and then said, 'I think we'd best adjourn to see if you can learn anything further.'

'It's all coming together!' said Popov. He was at his favourite window spot at Natalia's office but looking at her. As well as repeated praise for her interrogation of Lev Yatisyna, there had also been a commendation relayed to Popov by Dmitri Fomin at the meeting they'd just left.

'Personal acknowledgment for both of us from the White House!' smiled Natalia.

'Well deserved, in your case,' said Popov.

'And yours,' said Natalia, enjoying his admiration. He'd called her questioning brilliant at the meeting, when the tape had been played in front of everybody.

'Well over ten kilos recovered now,' said Popov.

'I'll interrogate both Agayans and Shelapin, of course,' Natalia decided. She didn't expect either to be as easy as it had so far been with Yatisyna, but now they had both Family leaders she could bounce one against the other, with Yatisyna in between.

'You're going to have to handle it very carefully.'

'I can do it.' The confidence was quickly balanced by the recollection of Charlie's criticism. 'There's been a proper forensic examination, particularly on the canisters?'

'They were marked, as having come from Kirs. The numbering tallied with that listed on the train manifest.'

'What about fingerprints?'

Popov shrugged. 'Ask Gusev. He's in charge of the ground operation.'

'I want to hit them both hard, with as much evidence as I can.' Natalia wanted the interrogation of the two Moscow gang leaders to be as quickly productive as it had been with Yatisyna.

'The Englishman will be proven wrong, if we get it all back in Moscow,' said Popov.

'According to Yatisyna there was at least one Arab buyer for what they expected to get out of the plant,' reminded Natalia.

'But we're blocking it!'

It was a debatable point but Natalia didn't intend presenting the argument. 'We can do that if I break Shelapin.'

'I expected Muffin to try to contact me. He'll obviously know from the American he's been excluded.'

'How much longer will the American be allowed in?' It wasn't ignoring Charlie's advice. She wanted to be prepared in advance for any committee debate that included a minister or the presidential aide.

Popov shook his head. 'I personally don't think there's any usefulness in continuing the arrangement. He just sat and listened today.'

'It might be better to go on with it until everything is recovered.'

The man smiled, shaking his head at her. 'Think about it!' he demanded. 'Spy satellites miles high sounded impressive, but apart from making the identification of the lorries and the car easier and quicker it did virtually nothing to help the investigation.'

Natalia held back from reminding the man how much was still missing.

chapter 27

Some things were not strange or unfamiliar. Indeed, as he settled into the secure communications room in the headquarters basement Charlie had the very real sensation of never having been away. He liked it. He even recognized some of the technicians who recognized him, in return, but the duty officer tempered Charlie's comforting nostalgia by complaining that things weren't like they used to be and Charlie commiserated that they never were.

He was immediately linked to Kestler, who said he'd chosen a bad time to be away, although it all seemed pretty straightforward from the briefing to which Popov had summoned him, four hours earlier.

Both Agayans and Shelapin, recounted the American, had been picked up around Bykovo airport, where it had been pretty damned stupid of either of them to have been because it was the known turf both disputed and the most obvious place to look. His guess was that neither had wanted to give the other any edge, by going to the mattress. Agayans had been stopped at a road block. There'd been three cars in the cavalcade and six men picked up, in addition to Agayans himself. There'd been some shooting but no one had been killed, although a Militia man had been badly wounded. They'd got Shelapin in a house raid. The canisters had been found in a car, parked outside, belonging to Shelapin himself. The two seizures had occurred within four or five hours of each other and the Russians were cock-a-hoop. There was another ambassadorial briefing scheduled later at the Foreign Ministry and that evening Radomir Badim was giving a televised news conference to which all the major Western networks and news media had been invited.

'It's celebration time in the old town tonight,' said Kestler.

'It might well be,' accepted Charlie, a remark to himself rather than a response to what Kestler had said. 'Who was at the announcement briefing?'

'Usual crowd,' said the American.

Charlie stifled his irritation. 'No new faces?'

'No.'

'None?'

The insistence registered with Kestler. 'New faces like who?'

'I don't know,' avoided Charlie. 'No one missing from the usual crowd?'

'No.'

'None?'

'You pursuing anything particular here, Charlie? If you are, it might help if you told me what it was.'

'I'm just filling in all the details.' One, or maybe then again more than one, in particular, he thought. 'General Fedova there?'

'I already told you!' said the American, exasperated. 'There were all the usual people.'

'Who did the talking?'

'Popov, mostly.'

'About the arrests?'

'Yes.'

'Anyone else, about the arrests?'

'The Moscow Militia commander: they kind of shared it, like before.'

'General Fedova contribute at all?'

'Not about the seizure of Agayans and Shelapin. She appears to be heading the interrogations. Which also seem to be going well.'

Charlie listened intently to the account of the Yatisyna interview, although he'd already heard it from Natalia. 'The actual tape was played?'

'She's good. Treated him like shit. The old demeaning trick. Worked like a dream.'

'What about the ministry people? Badim?'

'Lots of back-slapping. Personal commendations, from the presidential guy.'

'To whom, specifically?' demanded Charlie.

'Popov and the woman.'

'What was said, exactly?'

'That it was an excellently conducted investigation and that it was an official commendation, to both of them.'

'Both of them?' persisted Charlie.

'Charlie!' protested the other man again. 'We together on this or has something come up I don't know about? If there is I'd sure as hell like to know.'

'I wasn't there. I want to get a feel of everything that went on.' It was the sort of protection, maybe insurance was a better description, that Natalia needed. He still hadn't guided the younger man to the significance of the Warsaw references on the satellite tape, which he'd half thought about during his meeting with Jurgen Balg. He could always avoid criticism from the American by pleading the analysis had been done in London and communicated direct, which he now knew it had been.

'OK,' said the younger man, doubtfully.

'What about the crooked cop accusation?'

'A little foot shuffling, but not much. It was kind of passed over. It's hardly the revelation of the decade, after all.'

'What about your contribution? You get any praise?'

'I didn't have anything to offer today.'

It was coming, thought Charlie: like pulling alligator teeth but it was coming. 'Nothing more from Washington?'

'They're still working on the audio tape.'

The younger man's reply told him that nothing significant had yet emerged from the eavesdropped conversation but Charlie's hair-tuned antenna to nuance twitched. 'What else from Washington?' he chanced.

'Some pretty confusing signals,' admitted Kestler. 'Which makes me think something is going on that I don't know about. Like I don't know what it really is you and I are talking about.'

Here was a ball that had to be juggled carefully, Charlie recognized. 'What sort of confusing signals?'

'It takes a year to open the door you pushed and the moment we get inside we get priority instructions to back off and not get compromised. It doesn't make any sense!'

It didn't, accepted Charlie. It merely added to the FBI uncertainty. But there again it might give him a route to follow. 'What are you doing about it?'

'Obeying orders. I just sat and listened today, like a fucking dummy. And we didn't make any request for Hillary to examine the car in which the containers were found. She protested that direct and was told to lay off.'

That made least sense of anything: removed the very reason for her being in Moscow. Which worried Charlie and for professional, not personal reasons: in everything she'd done so far Hillary had always found something of forensic value. 'Hasn't Lyneham asked for guidance?'

'The reply was that it was a policy decision. You got any idea what that might mean?'

There was an irony in the American distrusting him for the wrong reasons. 'How could I possibly know about a policy decision taken in Washington?'

'I thought it might be a *joint* policy decision, between Washington and London. And that you might have been recalled to be told what it was.'

'I was brought back to discuss the exclusion, nothing more.'

'Your people planning to protest it?'

'It hasn't been decided yet.' Kestler had reason enough to be suspicious, Charlie acknowledged: everything he said appeared either an avoidance or a refusal to give a complete answer. Which, he supposed, it had been.

'I'm being straight with you now, Charlie.'

The antenna twitched again. *Now*? When hadn't he been in the past? And about what? 'If I get any guidance I'll tell you. Trust me.'

'When are you coming back?'

'Soon.'

'I look forward to hearing from you.'

'You will.'

Charlie had left one direct question unasked because it was unlikely Kestler would have known anyway, so to have introduced it would merely have made the American even more suspicious. Natalia would know. And there was an arrangement of sorts for him to call her. But Charlie didn't, reminded by the presence of the technicians outside his soundproofed booth that all communication with Moscow was automatically recorded. Which meant, he supposed, that there was a voice record of the back-stabbing from Moscow unless Bowyer had communicated through the diplomatic bag. From the meeting that had just been interrupted, Charlie didn't think that it was going to be a problem any more. And there was no immediate urgency to settle the other query: it could wait until he got back to Moscow to ask Natalia. Far more intriguing was the rest of the conversation he'd had with the younger man. It *didn't* make any sense for the Americans to back off, no sense at all. And why now, when he'd been withdrawn to London? Coincidence or connection? Into Charlie's mind came the stored away conversation with the cynical Lyneham about Kestler's family connections. Was the policy decision a very limited one, affecting Kestler personally rather than the Moscow Bureau station as a whole? Not if the edict had been extended to Hillary. The Bureau – and America – generally then. So what could . . . ? Charlie positively halted the mental spiral, reminding himself the only effect of revolving in ever-tightening circles was to disappear up your own ass. He now had an easy way to introduce the Bureau into the discussion with Rupert Dean far above. It really was turning out to be a remarkably lucky day.

At first things did not go to Charlie's satisfaction. He'd guessed they wouldn't, but obviously he had to begin with the new arrests and the nuclear recovery. He tried to make what he'd learned from Kestler appear additional to the brief message Bates had delivered but there was very little and it showed. He finished actually looking towards Williams for the expected ridicule, but the budgetary controller said nothing, remaining hunched over the papers upon which he'd doodled while Charlie talked. It was the cadaverous deputy who pointed out that the further Moscow seizure didn't support Charlie's insistence that the material was moving westwards and even less the fear that it might actually have reached a middleman. Charlie repeated that more remained missing than had been found.

'Which, I suppose, we'll have to rely upon the Americans to tell us about?' sneered Williams.

'That might be difficult,' seized Charlie, deflating the accountant. Yet again the room was silent as he summarized the conversation he had just had with Moscow. And yet again there were several long-held looks between the Director-General and Peter Johnson.

'Ordered *not* to!' queried the Director, although without quite the surprise Charlie expected.

'Specifically,' confirmed Charlie. 'It's a policy decision to pull back from the cooperation they've achieved. The physicist they've put in was categorically told not to make any approach to examine what was found in the car.'

'That's ridiculous!' said Pacey.

'Fenby does move in mysterious ways,' remarked Dean, still more mildly than Charlie expected.

'Which surely has to be the explanation,' said Simpson. 'They're doing something, or know something, they're not sharing with us.'

'Then it's happening in Washington,' insisted Charlie. 'I was asked whether it was a joint resolve, involving us: whether, in fact, I'd be going back. I probably wouldn't have been told anything if the Bureau in Moscow hadn't thought there was some connection and that I could tell them what it was.' Kestler *had* been indiscreet about what was essentially an internal FBI decision although it did impinge upon their officially agreed cooperation. But there was the family connection to protect him from censure if it was queried from London, which it obviously would be.

'This was supposed to be a joint operation,' said Williams, addressing the Director-General. 'Wasn't there any warning they were going to do this?'

'Not to me,' said Dean, looking once more to his deputy. 'Were you told?'

'No,' said Johnson, shortly.

'We've obviously got to find out what it's all about,' said Pacey.

'Obviously,' agreed Dean.

Choosing his moment – and the exaggeration – Charlie said, 'In practical terms my expulsion was more inconvenient than a serious setback, as long as we had the American conduit. If they're going to abandon that then the idea of setting up a sting operation becomes even more valid, doesn't it?'

'Yes,' agreed Dean. 'I think it probably does.'

Petr Tukhonovich Gusev was a sparse-bodied, fixed-faced man who wore well the ribboned uniform of the Militia controller of the central Moscow region and whose reserve, Natalia decided, had nothing to do with the apprehension that both Oskin and Lvov had shown towards her and her rank. It was, instead, the natural demeanour of a totally professional policeman unwilling to venture an opinion ahead of all the evidence: the voice, when he did speak after considered pause, was as slowly pedantic as it had been at their first encounter on the day the Arbat vehicles had been found.

He accepted without hesitation the chair Natalia offered, formally straightened the uniform and sat without any discomfort waiting for her to tell him what she wanted. A witness.

'You're very much part of the efficiency and speed of this investigation that's been acknowledged. I have asked Colonel Popov officially to commend you. Which will, of course, be noted in your records.' Natalia wasn't as sure now that the complimentary approach, which she'd decided upon because the man had been present when she and Aleksai had been publicly praised, was the right one.

'Thank you,' said Gusev, automatically, flat-voiced.

'I am personally going to question Yevgennie Agayans and Vasili Shelapin.'

He nodded.

'I want to be as fully prepared as possible.'

'Of course.'

'So I want to know everything.'

'I understand.'

'Where were the canisters found?'

'In Shelapin's car. And another. It was outside the house in which we arrested him.'

'There was no resistance?'

'We hit it at dawn. They were all sleeping. Shelapin is homosexual. He was with his lover, a boy of twenty. It was in the boy's car that two of the canisters were found.'

'How old is Shelapin?'

'Fifty-five, sixty maybe.

'There was one in Shelapin's car?'

'That is correct.' He could have been giving evidence in a court.

'What cars were they?'

'Both Mercedes. They have large boots.'

'That's where the canisters were, in the boots?'

'Yes.'

Natalia hesitated, as the unprepared question came into her mind. 'Are you telling me what you've learned from those at the scene? Or were you there?'

'I was there, in charge. Bykovo is their area: it was the obvious place to concentrate. I led the Shelapin raid and was still there when we got a report about Agayans. So I organized the road block.'

'How did you hear about Agayans?'

'We had a report, from a radio car we'd put in the area.'

She'd moved away from the core questioning: time to get back.

'What happened to the Shelapin cars?'

For the first time Gusev's expressionless face showed a frown. 'I don't understand?'
'Were they seized?'
'Of course. Brought to the central Militia garage. So were the Agayans vehicles.'
'I'm only interested in those belonging to Shelapin at the moment. Were they brought to Militia headquarters at once? Or were they scientifically examined at the site, first?' Natalia took particular care posing the question.
'Scientifically examined. We had to establish the canisters were safe.'
'Quite,' agreed Natalia. 'So *who* carried out the examination? Nuclear experts? Forensic scientists? Or both?'
Gusev hesitated longer than usual. 'The nuclear people. It was only the canisters that were important.'
Natalia felt a dip of uncertainty. 'After they were found to be safe what happened to the canisters?'
'They took them away to be properly stored.'
'So they weren't *forensically* examined? For fingerprints, for instance?'
'No.'
Again! thought Natalia, anguished. She should have corrected the first omission with Aleksai. Too late now.
Gusev took the silence to be criticism. 'We have no facilities, for this stuff! We couldn't have stored it!'
'Storage wouldn't have been a factor if a forensic team had been brought to the scene, would it?'
'There was!'
'At the same time?' She was exceeding her remit – although not her authority – straying into an operational wilderness about which she knew nothing, full of unseen quicksands and sucking whirlpools. She'd have to tell Aleksai.
'No,' conceded the man. 'But I don't understand the significance.'
'Fingerprints could have guided us, literally, to who'd handled it.'
'It was in their cars!'

'You questioned Shelapin?'

'I tried to.'

'Explain that.'

'It was just abuse: obscene abuse.'

Natalia had interrogated too many people to accept that generalization. 'There was something,' she insisted.

'He denied any knowledge of the canisters: said they'd been planted.'

'How were they, in the cars? In boxes? Secured? Loose? What?'

'Loose.'

'Wouldn't they have rolled about, with the movement of the car?'

Gusev regarded her even more blankly than normal. 'There would have been some movement, I suppose.'

'You're a very senior Militia officer: have you ever had any dealings with Agayans before?'

'No. But I know of him. It's a major Family.'

'Tell me about his arrest.'

'We set up a road block. The moment they drove up to it I had other cars come in behind, so they were trapped. They began shooting at once. Uzi machine guns: Israeli. One of my officers will lose a leg.'

'How long did it last?'

'It was very brief. I had twenty-five men: they were outnumbered.'

'You heard the Yatisyna tape, about an Arab buyer?'

'Yes.'

'Is the Agayans Family big enough for an operation like they tried at Kirs: with contacts outside Russia?'

'They tried the robbery at Kirs!'

It hadn't been a considered question: she couldn't afford to be that casual with either of the gang leaders. 'What's your reaction to Yatisyna's claim, against the Militia? Were you surprised?'

'No.' There was no hesitation.

'Why not?' prompted Natalia.

'Every law enforcement organization in Russia is infected.

Are you surprised that virtually every former KGB officer is now involved in organized crime?'

'I would be, if it were true.'

'It is.'

'You're the head of the largest Militia division in Russia!' repeated Natalia. 'If you know it's true haven't you tried to do something about it?' She was going way beyond the original intention of the interview.

The face broke again, into a patronizing smile. Gusev's teeth were very bad, overcrowded and displaced: one in the front was practically covering another behind. 'Since 1992 I have initiated disciplinary proceedings against a total of two hundred and thirty officers, up to the rank of inspector, in the central Moscow division alone. The accusations against ten were unproven but I still dismissed them. The remaining two hundred and twenty are serving prison sentences.' Gusev paused. 'I knew Nikolai Ivanovich Oskin. I was looking forward to his being transferred under my jurisdiction. He was an honest man.'

'I was not making any criticism,' said Natalia. 'I was asking your opinion.'

'In my opinion there is no such thing as law and order in Russia,' declared Gusev. 'The country is collapsing into total chaos. And no one could care less.'

'A few care.'

'A few is not enough.'

'If I get what I expect from Agayans, we can provide cellmates for a lot of those you've already put into jail,' suggested Natalia.

'I'd like very much to see it.'

chapter 28

Natalia decided against repeating the dirty uniform ploy with Vasili Shelapin. She believed she had more upon which to work an interrogation than with Yatisyna. And the examination of the house in which Shelapin had been arrested with his lover, while fastidiously kept, was insufficiently effeminate to justify demeaning psychology. It might even have had the reverse effect. As she had with all the other arrests, however, she'd isolated Shelapin from the moment of his seizure, particularly from the boy, whose name was Yuri Maksimovich Toom and who was in the chorus of a transvestite stage show in a club close to the Arbat.

Natalia still insisted upon Shelapin wearing prison uniform and watched again through the mirror glass for signs of discomfort. There weren't any, from Shelapin, but Natalia was caught by the attitude of the two guards. She hadn't selected or briefed them this time. Both were men and Natalia's impression was of respect for the gang leader. Shelapin didn't bother with any chair-lounging performance. He surveyed the room, only once but completely, before propping himself against the table edge to look directly at his escorts. Who were unnerved. Shelapin was, she accepted, very much in control of the room. The attitude was not overtly homosexual: his sexual orientation was neither his boast nor his difficulty, simply his proclivity. She'd been sensible, not attempting the debasing approach: it *would* have been counter-productive. She had the recording volume turned up and heard perfectly the peremptory demand of someone accustomed always to being obediently answered when he asked who he would be seeing and what their rank would be. There was an irritated frown when the escorts said, apologetically, they didn't know. Natalia was curious that his interrogator's rank was important to Shelapin. When he asked how much longer he would have to wait – to which the uneasy men replied they didn't know that, either – Natalia delayed her entry, to fuel his impatience. He searched the walls for a clock and when he failed to find one glanced briefly behind him, assessing the interview set-up and said he needed a chair. The escorts looked at one another, each for the other to reply: the younger finally said they weren't responsible for the arrangement. Shelapin told them to find out who was, to get him something to sit upon. The younger one half turned towards the door before stopping to say they didn't have the authority and would have to wait. Natalia actually leaned forward against the glass for Shelapin's response, but he said nothing. Instead he leaned forward himself, intently studying the features of both men, each of whom wilted under the memorizing scrutiny. Enough, determined Natalia.

As she entered the room she looked hard at both guards herself before examining the gangster, which she did with the same head-to-toe distaste with which she'd regarded Yatisyna but to noticeably less effect. Shelapin remained propped against the table, examining her just as closely. Facially he was a fleshy man, heavy-jowled and with pouched eyes, and she guessed the ageing body would be sagged beneath the shapeless prison issue. The obviously dyed hair was deeply black and very full, in waves.

Natalia's file this time was thin, just the genuine arrest report. She opened it as she sat and for the benefit of the tape said, 'You are Vasili Fedorovich Shelapin?'

'I want a chair.'

'You will stand.'

'Am I supposed to be intimidated? Or impressed?'

'You're supposed to answer my questions.' He hadn't expected to be interrogated by a woman. It was an advantage.

He made a snorting, derisive sound. 'Who are you?'

'You are Vasili Fedorovich Shelapin?'

'I asked who you were.'

'My identity is no concern of yours.'

'Frightened?'

Now it was Natalia who made the derisive sound. 'Frightened! Of you! Why should anyone be frightened of you, Vasili Fedorovich?'

'A lot of people are.'

'I'm not one of them.'

'Yet.'

Natalia thought her ridicule had scored. 'A number of people were killed in the Pizhma robbery. The principal charge upon which you will be tried is murder, obviously. The nuclear theft also carries the death penalty . . .'

'. . . What are you talking about?' he broke in, impatiently.

'You know very well what I am talking about.'

'I don't know anything about murders or any nuclear robbery at Pizhma.'

'In the boot of your car – and that of Yuri Maksimovich Toom, who was with you at the time of your arrest – were found canisters of plutonium 239 stolen on the 9th of this month from a transportation train at Pizhma,' recounted Natalia, again for the benefit of the recording.

He gave a more genuine, sneering laugh and actually directed it towards the machine. 'Don't be absurd! It was planted: maybe you even know by whom.'

Behind him both guards shifted uneasily. So far this recording wasn't going to earn her any commendations, Natalia accepted. But it might do, from now on. 'There *is* evidence, in addition to the canisters,' she declared. 'Quite separate and even more incriminating.'

'What?'

'Photographs.'

'What the hell are you talking about *now*? What photographs?'

'Photographs of Pizhma,' insisted Natalia, anticipating his collapse. 'High-definition pictures taken from a specially directed satellite showing every stage of the robbery. And showing, too, the people involved: people that can be positively identified by using developing and enlargement techniques.' Kestler had talked of height, weight and dress identification, although not of facial recognition which she was trying to suggest without actually claiming it. If they *did* try to use the satellite pictures in a court hearing, which it was extremely likely they would, they couldn't logically exclude the Americans from any future progress meetings. That hadn't been touched upon at any ministerial or operational session she'd so far attended. She'd have to mention it. She pushed aside the digression, looking up expectantly at the man.

Who laughed at her again, quite genuinely, without any sneer. 'You've got *photographs* of the people carrying out the robbery?'

His reaction wasn't right, not right at all! Where was the collapse, at his believing he was trapped? 'Yes.'

'Good. Then you can release me right now. And everyone arrested with me. And all the people you picked up at Ulitza Volkhonka. You've tried to be too clever and fallen flat on your ass.'

Natalia had experienced a lot of bluff and a lot of bravado, more desperate last-throw attempts than she could remember. What she could very definitely remember, because she was proud of it, was that she'd never made a mistake separating genuine details from bluster. And her gnawing impression here, wrong though it *had* to be, was that Shelapin wasn't at all desperate and wasn't trying to bluff. Working to match his condenscension, she said, 'Why should I do that?'

'Because those photographs *prove* I wasn't involved. Nor any of my friends.'

'What about the canisters?'

'Is it likely, even if I'd organized the robbery, which I didn't, that I'd leave that stuff lying around in the trunk of my *own* car? Come on! I know it's difficult for everyone connected with the Militia to be honest but try, just for once!'

'They were found on your property, and on the property of

people connected with you. Those, and others, will be identified from the satellite pictures. And they'll talk: they always do in the end. And that will be sufficient to put you in front of a firing squad.'

'No, it won't!' he said. 'It might have been, by itself, fit-up though it was. But now I know about the photographs. *You've* given *me* the perfect way to prove your bullshit lies are just that, bullshit and lies. I'll insist they're produced! And you won't be able to identify me on anything they show. Nor anyone linked to me. You stupid, silly bitch. You've really fucked up, haven't you?'

'Of course you wouldn't have been at Pizhma yourself. That would have been too dangerous, particularly with what was done to the canisters. I guess you stayed home in bed, with Yuri. Is he your alibi for the 9th?'

He laughed at her yet again. 'Weak! Very weak! You think you're going to get under my skin, because I prefer to fuck boys rather than girls! I don't know if it was Yuri that night. I like variety. It might have even been a party, so I would have had more than one. Whoever it was, they'll tell you where I was: even what we did, if you're that interested. Are you interested?'

Toom might have been a weakness if there'd been any genuine affection but it looked as if she'd lost there, too. 'Your *not* being in any photograph isn't going to save you.'

Still he out-manoeuvred her. 'You've got to find someone, just one person, you can link with me, though, haven't you? If you can't do that, the photographs are in my favour.'

Abruptly, seeking firmer ground, Natalia changed direction. 'You're at war, with the Agayans Family, aren't you?'

'Am I? About what?'

'Crime control at Bykovo. The airport particularly.'

'You're talking nonsense. I'm a businessman. Freight: transhipment in and out of the country. That sort of thing. I've heard of someone called Agayans. He tries to extort money from genuine businessmen like myself, claims he can give me protection, against criminal gangs. I won't have anything to do with him.'

'You knew he'd set up a robbery attempt, at a nuclear installation at Kirs, didn't you?'

'I've got to get this straight!' mocked Shelapin. 'We've had a robbery at Pizhma, which was photographed. Now we've got another at Kirs. This is exciting! What were the pictures like there?'

Natalia felt the perspiration finding its way down her back and guessed her face would be shining. 'It didn't work but it was quite a sophisticated attempt at Kirs: Agayans and a local Family. It was from someone in the Agayans clan that you heard about it, wasn't it? And about the decommissioning that you used much more cleverly than they did, with the interception at Pizhma: where you got all the canisters that were found. Where are the others you and your people took?'

'Don't you have photographs?' he spluttered. Behind him the escorts came close to laughing.

'We've enough for a death sentence. Which we'll get.' Why hadn't the damned canisters been forensically examined?

'How much did you think you were going to get? Five thousand? Ten?'

Natalia stared at him, bewildered by what he said but not wanting to admit it. 'What I want is to know where the rest of the canisters are.'

Shelapin shook his head. 'You think I can't recognize a shake-down when I see one? I've been hit on by experts and you're no expert. You're very far from expert. In fact I've never known anything so pitiful! You know what you're going to get from me? Fuck all! I already told you, I don't give in to extortion.'

She had to conclude this, stop it degenerating any further. 'Vasili Fedorovich Shelapin, I am formally charging you with complicity in murder and with complicity in the theft of two hundred and fifty kilos of plutonium 239 at Pizhma on the 9th of this month. Whatever you say will be noted and may, upon the discretion of the Federal Prosecutor, form part of the case against you. Have you anything to say?'

'Yes,' said Shelapin. 'Go fuck yourself.'

Natalia had never had such a disastrous interrogation and she was demoralized. It had been her fault. She'd been over-confident, not properly thinking ahead or anticipating how touchy he might be. So he'd been right. She'd been stupid and she deserved the taped humiliation. What worried her most was that there was no obvious way to recover, not with Shelapin at least. She'd only break Shelapin with incontrovertible evidence – maybe not even then – and the Pizhma photographs certainly weren't it, not by themselves. It had been an appalling mistake even to mention them, certainly until they'd got more from some of the other arrested Shelapin Family members. The canisters themselves *were* incontrovertible, despite his contemptuous denial, so a successful prosecution was assured. But recovering the missing material was more important than a trial. And she hadn't done anything to achieve that.

As she entered the second observation room, on the opposite side of the Lubyanka, Natalia called upon all her training to put aside the Shelapin disaster, forcing herself to think only of Yevgennie Agayans. With whom she couldn't risk the slightest mistake. It had to be an unqualified success, to balance the débâcle she'd just suffered.

Through her unseen window Natalia saw a short, fat man, owlish in round-framed spectacles, dark hair greased directly back from his forehead. He didn't appear as controlled as Shelapin – walking back and forth in front of the table with what could have been apprehension more than impatience – although the how-much-longer demands, in a surprisingly deep voice, were as peremptory as the other gang leader's. The escorts, two men again, didn't appear as uncomfortable.

Natalia's file was thicker for this interview and she'd had a second although smaller tape machine installed, the prepared tape already set. The escorts came to vague attention when she entered the room and Agayans started to straighten before abruptly stopping, which Natalia saw as an encouraging if quickly corrected deference to authority. Moving to capitalize upon it, she immediately charged the man with complicity in murder and attempted nuclear theft with the failed Kirs robbery. In both charges she named Yatisyna.

By the time Natalia finished Agayans was smirking. 'Rubbish!'

Surer of her pressure with this accusation, Natalia started the intentionally over-tuned tape. Into the room echoed the selected and edited sections of her interview with the Kirov gangster naming Agayans as the mastermind at Kirs.

'More rubbish,' shrugged Agayans. He held his hands loosely in front of him and began picking at his left sleeve cuff.

'We've got six of your people, every one of them arrested at the scene, singing louder than larks.'

'I don't have any "people".'

'They say they work for you.'

'What as?'

'You tell me.'

'No. You tell me.'

'Enforcers. Thieves. Killers.'

'They described themselves as that?'

'They're prepared to, to save themselves. Testifying that they were always obeying your orders.'

Agayans stopped picking at his cuff to flick a dismissive hand towards the second tape. 'Play me their statements.'

'You'll hear what they say, in court.'

'Why not now?' demanded the man.

'Because I don't intend sitting here all day, swapping tapes for your amusement. Yatisyna has signed a statement that you're the ringleader: the planner of everything. Everyone else is fighting for clemency, to stay alive. They'll get their deals. But you'll die.'

For the first time there was the flicker of doubt. 'You've got nothing to bring me into court.'

Natalia knew he'd break, if she irritated the proper nerve; it just needed the right prod in the right place to push him over the edge. There was a way but it was a gamble and she'd already lost one, badly. 'There's enough, on the statements of Yatisyna and the six members of your own

Family. There's even the attempted murder of the Militia man when you were arrested.'

'It was self-defence. We were suddenly trapped in a road block. My bodyguards thought we were being attacked by gangsters.'

The deepness of the bass voice reminded Natalia of the incanting priests at the Kirov cathedral, which was an ill-fitting recollection. 'You'd recognize gangsters, wouldn't you?'

'What's that mean?'

'That you're one yourself. Head of a clan.'

'I'm a businessman.'

'Import–export? Joint venture development?' sneered Natalia.

He smirked at her again. 'Exactly right!'

Natalia decided to take the risk. She couldn't be caught out, not like before. 'That's not what Shelapin says.'

'What?' The change was dramatic. The complacency slipped and Agayans stopped fiddling with his sleeve cuff.

'Shelapin,' repeated Natalia. 'We've pulled him in, too, as part of the enquiry. He says you're an extortionist. He says he's a businessman, too, and that you've tried to terrorize him.'

'That motherfucker!' There was a laugh but it was uncertain. 'He's head of a Family! You know that!'

'We don't have any evidence to prosecute him for anything. Not like we've got against you.'

'You're setting me up!'

'I'm just telling you the strength of the case against you.' There was an irony in that Shelapin probably *would* give evidence against Agayans: tell any lie they asked him to. Agayans was shaky, so she had to keep up the pressure. From the file Natalia took the sketches of the Arab and the Frenchman described by Yatisyna, sliding them across the table towards the man. 'Recognize them?'

Agayans glanced briefly at the drawings. 'No.'

Natalia decided Agayans was still off-balanced by the threat of a rival gang leader testifying against him, which was how she wanted him to be, trying to think of several things at the same time. She'd personally supervised the positioning of the tape segments and restarted the playback at the moment of Yatisyna's account of his nightclub encounter with both, when he was with Agayans.

The plump man shook his head. 'I don't know anyone called Yatisyna. Or a French middleman acting on behalf of an Arab buyer for nuclear components. That's an illegal trade and I don't deal in illegal trade. I am a respectable businessman . . .'

'. . . Who travels with men carrying Uzi machine guns . . .' Natalia broke in.

'. . . Who travels with men carrying Uzi machine guns because there is no such thing as law and order in Moscow and respectable businessmen have to protect themselves,' he took over from her.

'That's not what Shelapin is going to tell the court.'

'Who's going to believe that lying bastard?'

'It's all part of a convincing case against you. The Federal Prosecutor has done a deal with Yatisyna: no request for the death penalty in return for his testimony against you.'

The man's head came up, sharply, as if he were physically confronting a challenge. He said, 'I don't believe you,' but he didn't sound sure.

'You've heard the tape!' said Natalia. 'That's enough for you to get an idea of what's being put against you.'

'I'm not going down, not dying, to save others! Or on Shelapin's lies.'

It wasn't the collapse she'd wanted but the concession was there. 'You don't really have a choice. It's already been made. Yetisyna is provincial: small time. You're head of a major Moscow group, part of one of the leading clans. It's much better for public opinion, here and outside, if the case is brought against you.'

The man smiled, which surprised her. 'You completely sure about that?'

Natalia didn't know how to reply. 'That's what the prosecutor thinks.'

'Does he know it was me?'

The question further confused her. 'Of course he knows.' Please God don't let that be the wrong reply!

The smile flicked on and off again. 'Tell him I shall be extremely annoyed if any charges are brought against me. Tell the Militia people, too: them most of all.'

'What are you saying?' demanded Natalia, remembering Yatisyna's insistence of Agayans' protective knowledge of corruption. Into her mind, as well, came the Moscow Militia commander's fatalistic resignation: *There is no such thing as law and order in Russia.*

'I'm not saying anything. Not yet. But I will, if this nonsense goes on. You tell people that.'

'Which people.'

Agayans shook his head. 'Just people. Those who need to will hear.'

'I don't understand.'

'*You* don't need to. I don't know you.'

It was becoming practically a replay of her interview with Yatisyna. There was certainly nothing to be gained trying to continue the interview. 'We'll speak tomorrow.'

'Maybe,' said Agayans, as if he were the person in charge, not Natalia.

Natalia nodded for the escorts to take Agayans away, remaining where she was at the table for the tape to rewind. She wanted to listen to it again, like she intended listening to the Shelapin encounter again. Neither had been good, although this had been better than the first, and she needed to be absolutely prepared for the criticism that was inevitable at the later ministerial grouping.

The scream was inhuman, animal-like and very short. For a moment Natalia remained frozen at the desk. Then she burst from the room, going immediately to her right, where she knew the detention cells to be. Several minor corridors led off a main junction. She hesitated, uncertainly, and then saw people running and ran with them, towards an already huddled group, shouting for people to get out of her way.

Yevgennie Arkentevich Agayans lay spreadeagled on his

back, one leg tucked beneath the other, gazing sightlessly at the ceiling through the owlish glasses that absurdly had remained perfectly in place. The top must have been broken from the bottle, although she couldn't see it because the jagged edge that had almost decapitated him was still buried deep in the man's neck: the bottom half of the bottle was intact and already almost filled with blood from the way it had torn into his carotid artery. As she watched, the pressure became such that the bottle was forced out of Agayans' throat, splattering them all with blood.

'You're making things untenable for me,' complained Peter Johnson.

'You're making things untenable for yourself.'

'You knew I was going to monitor him,' insisted Peter Johnson.

'It went beyond monitoring,' insisted Dean.

'I didn't know the situation at the embassy.'

The Director-General sat for several moments, silently regarding his deputy over his cluttered desk. 'You knew, even to the wording, of something you thought had been withheld from the ambassador. Bowyer came direct to you, like Fenby came direct to you.'

'We would have had to mount a defence, if something *had* been withheld.'

'You're saying it was to *protect* Muffin!'

'To protect the department.'

There was another accusing silence. 'You were undermining an operative specifically put into Moscow to *justify* this department!'

'Bowyer allowed himself to get caught up in internal embassy politics that I knew nothing about.'

'I shall formally protest, to the Foreign Office here and to Wilkes, in Moscow, at the blatant deceit of the Head of Chancellery.'

'That could lead to his dismissal: his withdrawal almost certainly.'

'What was he trying to achieve, against Muffin?'

'Bowyer grossly misinterpreted my instructions. But I did order the monitoring.'

'I know where the responsibility lies. He'll be disciplined but not withdrawn.'

'You're asking for my resignation, aren't you?' said Johnson.

'No,' said Dean, who an hour earlier had chaired the deferred meeting at which it had been agreed to propose the sting operation to Moscow. 'I want you personally to go to Washington. And I want Fenby's full support for this new idea. Just as I want your full support. In future I expect both of you to work with me, not against me.'

'I'm to give him an ultimatum?' frowned Johnson.

'Phrase it how you want,' said the Director-General. 'But tell him I don't want the embarrassment of what his well-connected protégé did becoming public. And I'm sure he doesn't.'

'I see,' said Johnson, slowly.

'That's what I want both of you to do. See things properly in the future.'

Bastard, thought Johnson and Dean knew it. That's how he wanted the other man to think of him.

'The Foreign Office hasn't raised any objection, so we're going to propose it,' the Director-General told Charlie, who hadn't been invited to that morning's meeting. 'There's absolutely no guarantee that Moscow will even contemplate it, of course. In fact I think it extremely unlikely.'

He'd got away with it! Charlie thought he'd made a reasonable case – but only reasonable – and the postponement the previous evening obviously for a private discussion had worried him. 'But I can go back right away?' Charlie had spent a depressing night in London. He'd actually gone back to The Pheasant, which had completely changed in three months: there was a bank of light-cascading fruit machines that had made his eyes ache and a constantly blaring juke box that had made his head ache. Excusing himself to ease past him, a shaven-headed youth with an earring had called him 'Pops'. And they'd stopped stocking Islay whisky.

'If the idea is accepted, you're going to have to be careful going to the embassy.'

'I always was,' said Charlie.

'There won't be any more misunderstandings,' assured Dean.

He might as well try to win everything. 'Was there some misunderstanding with Washington, too?'

The spectacles moved smoothly through the man's fingers and Charlie wondered if Dean ever used them for their proper purpose. 'Not any longer.'

'Do I need to know what they were?'

'No,' refused Dean, shortly.

He *had* been right about the man being like Sir Archibald Willoughby! 'I'm to continue dealing with you, personally?'

Dean nodded. 'We'll only give it a limited run, if they do agree.'

'I understand that.'

'How are you finding Moscow, apart from the job?'

'Pleasant enough,' said Charlie, non-committal.

At that moment, in Moscow, the final tape of Natalia's interviews clicked off. For several moments no one in the ministerial or presidential group spoke. Then to Natalia the expressionless Dmitri Fomin said 'Thank you,' and led everyone from the room and Natalia knew the recent commendation had become meaningless.

chapter 29

Natalia contacted Charlie within an hour of his getting back to Lesnaya and admitted calling several times before, the relief obvious in her voice that he was finally there. It was Natalia who wanted an immediate meeting and suggested the botanical gardens at Glavnyy Botanincheyskiy Sad, one of their favourite places when they'd been together. Charlie began to attach a significance until Natasha said it was conveniently close to the crèche from which she had to collect Sasha later that afternoon.

She was already there when he arrived, on the arranged seat near one of the tropical hothouses. She'd come close, but not quite, to covering the dark half-circles under her eyes, her mouth was pinched and for once the usually kept-in-place hair was disarrayed.

'It's all gone terribly wrong,' she declared, even before he lowered himself on to the bench beside her. 'And I'm the one identified with it, no one else.'

'How?'

Natalia had a debriefer's cohesive recall and recounted in detail and in sequence the contemptuous interview with Shelapin and what had happened immediately afterwards with Agayans. The escorts had been suspended but were still denying any collusion: one had left Agayans to collect the key to the central prison area, which regulations insisted be held at all times in the main control room and there were two other warders supporting the story of the second of his being called to a corridor telephone to a supposed summons from her, leaving Agayans momentarily unguarded. 'A minute, no more.' There hadn't yet been a public announcement of the killing but she'd told Shelapin, trying to shake him. And hadn't. He'd actually laughed at the murder and at her and continued accusing her of attempted extortion. All the other arrested Shelapin gang members denied any knowledge of the Pizhma robbery and of the canisters either in the Mercedes or in the garage at Ulitza Volkhonka. Shelapin's lover had named six people from the transvestite chorus line who'd been at a homosexual orgy at the time of the Pizhma theft and every one had testified Shelapin had been there. Although the Federal Prosecutor had ruled the satellite photographs inadmissible in a Russian court she'd asked the Americans for every positively identifying factor from the pictures. None of the men in custody, and certainly not Shelapin himself, matched any of the height, weight or physical details obtained by high-focus analysis. Because of the public concern the intended prosecution, based solely upon the evidence of the canisters, was to be open to the world media. Shelapin had warned his defence lawyers would publicly strip the skin off her, layer by layer 'until I bleed to death, as Agayans did'.

'And like it's been stripped off at every ministerial meeting,' Natalia added.

Charlie listened with his mind ahead of what she was saying, isolating points he considered important but not setting them out to her: he always had to keep in mind that in her permanent anxiety about the baby, Natalia might inadvertently say something to snag the fragile net he still hadn't properly woven. Gently, consciously taking advantage of Natalia's distraction, Charlie probed for more. There was a stir of satisfaction when Natalia identified the Up and Down club as the meeting place claimed by Yatisyna for the witnessed encounter between Agayans and the Arab and French nuclear purchasers. Natalia said they'd decided against publishing the artist's sketches until they were surer Yatisyna wasn't concocting the whole story: the club owners and staff denied ever having seen either man on the premises, which could have been more through fear than lack of recognition. Charlie had her go into much more detail of her interview with the Moscow Militia commander, confirming Gusev's presence at the very earliest planning meetings and at every major arrest and qualified several points in Natalia's account of the man's close-to-despairing resignation at the extent of Militia corruption.

'Which I'm now dragged into,' reminded Natalia. 'It was my name that was used to get the second guard away from Agayans. How's that going to look in an open court, alongside Shelapin's accusation that I wanted a bribe?'

Bad, in the way a clever lawyer could manipulate it, he thought. 'What's Popov say?'

'That it's not as bad as I'm making it.'

'I don't think it is,' lied Charlie, trying to lift her depression. 'These are professional Mafia. It's ridiculous to expect them all to roll over and play dead at their first interrogation.'

The weak autumn sun was abruptly swallowed by cloud and Natalia shivered. 'Neither he nor you are at the ministerial meetings. That's what they *do* expect. I don't want assurances, Charlie. I want advice on what to do. How to break them.'

Which Popov obviously hadn't offered. 'Any public trial is a long way off. That's not an immediate problem. Does Yatisyna know Agayans has been killed?'

'I haven't told him. The guards may have done.'

'Tell him. And tell him you might have to move him out of the security of solitary confinement, into a more open regime. Trade his continued protection against everything else he can tell you. Make sure he's properly frightened.'

'What about Shelapin?'

'Let him stew. He knows the canisters are enough.'

It sounded more constructive than it really was but Natalia nodded, her face softening very slightly. She looked at her watch, shivering again. 'I have to collect Sasha.'

'I've got something to talk to you about, first. Let's walk in the hothouse.' That had been another favourite.

She got up at once and they went side by side into the artificial heat and humidity. The giant-leafed plants and technicolour flowers seemed larger and more vivid than he remembered. 'I've only got a few minutes.'

'How is she?'

He *did* want to see his daughter! It was ridiculous living in the same city and not being able to be with his own child! Careful, he cautioned himself, for yet another time: he'd made Natalia a promise, which he had to keep. He had no rights: no demands.

'Perfect,' replied Natalia. 'She's changed the doll's name to Olga.'

He'd been at the airport before he'd thought of buying another present and the choice there seemed limited to more dolls, so he'd left it: he was very much an amateur father. He'd decided against buying anything for Natalia, too. 'You believe me now about Sasha, don't you?'

'I suppose so.' There was neither doubt nor acceptance in her voice.

'It would be nice to see her again.' She'd asked him for a meeting. And needed him. He was taking advantage of her vulnerability but not in any way to harm her. The opposite. He was doing it to protect and safeguard her and Sasha and knew he could do it better than anybody else.

Natalia sighed. 'Not now, Charlie. I don't want to talk about Sasha at the same time as everything else. She's part of it all, I know, but I don't want to think of it like that. Let me fool myself, just a little.'

If Sasha's safety and future were part of their thinking – which they were, not part but paramount – then the child had to be part of every discussion. But it was all right for Natalia to close her mind off to it. He'd think for both of them, *was* thinking for both of them. Doing now, in fact, what he should have done for both of them years ago. He wanted to tell her but didn't: she'd see it as more of a threat than a reassurance. Charlie was lifted by the thought of having someone to care for. It was a feeling with which he was unfamiliar and he liked it.

'What is it you want to tell me?' she asked, breaking into his thoughts.

They rounded a huge arbour to join a pathway deserted except for themselves. In contrast to the outside chill Charlie was now sweating. He spoke not looking at her but with his head bent, choosing his words. Long before he finished she reached out, bringing him around to face her. He liked the pressure of her hand on him. There was a slight sheen of perspiration on her upper lip, too.

'You're not seriously asking me to believe this?'

'I suggested letting a robbery run at the very beginning, remember?' It wasn't an answer but it would do. 'We might not recover any more of what was stolen at Pizhma. We can't wait for the next robbery to happen before we do something to get inside the business.'

'The bottle jammed in Agayans' throat filled up like the blood was coming from a tap!' she said, disbelievingly. 'These people are monsters!'

'I've thought about protection. Agayans wouldn't have been killed outside, with his people around him.'

Natalia sniggered nervously, shaking her head. 'No one will agree! They'll laugh at you, which is what they should do. I can't believe London even considered putting it forward!'

Neither could Charlie. He'd dismissed the easily anticipated financial objections of Gerald Williams before they even came but was astonished there hadn't been ridicule from everyone else, led by Rupert Dean. He wouldn't have had such an easy ride if there hadn't been all the other diversions – with the additional bonus of another seizure right in the middle – but now it *was* being officially suggested, which was all he wanted. He had to play by ear everything that followed now and hope to Christ he didn't lose both ears in the process. 'If you get involved in any discussion about it, particularly at ministerial level, I want you to support it.'

'No!' Natalia refused at once. 'It won't be discussed because it's too ludicrous. But if it is, I'll oppose it.'

Surely there was still some feeling, buried deep down! Or was it nothing more than simple, objective professionalism?

Not the time to think about that now. Or how she might have reacted if he'd suggested what he suspected he might find out. 'Please support it, if it comes up!'

'No!' she repeated.

'Then don't oppose it, either. Just stay out of it. But do something else.'

'What?'

'I want to know who goes for it and who doesn't.'

Natalia put her head to one side. 'Why's that important?'

'It is.'

'Why?' she insisted.

'I want to know how genuine the supposed determination is to block this business,' lied Charlie, smoothly.

Natalia remained frowning. 'I don't see the connection.'

'I might, if there is one.' And if there wasn't he was going to waste an awful lot of time and an awful lot of money to load Gerald Williams' siege guns to overflowing.

'It'll never arise.'

'If it does.'

'Aleksai found out, about your coming to Leninskaya,' she announced, abruptly.

Charlie set off along the lonely walkway and Natalia moved with him. 'How did you explain it?'

'That you were trying for some sort of advantage, from the first time.'

'You surely didn't . . . !'

'Of course I didn't,' she stopped him. 'I told him I threw you out.'

'He believed that?'

'He was very angry at first: wanted me to complain, officially. I told him that would be giving it more importance than it deserved.'

Charlie wished it hadn't been so easy for her to dismiss it like that. 'Has he mentioned it since?'

'No.'

'Never?' They rounded another giant display. The exit was at the far end of the corridor.

'Never. But that's why it's difficult for you to see her again. She said something.'

So that was the reason for Natalia's objection, not that she personally didn't want him to be with the child! Or here. 'I understand.'

'I don't see how it's possible.'

He'd find a way, determined Charlie, believing a door was being unlocked if not nudged open. 'Let's leave it for the moment.'

Charlie re-established contact with Kestler on his first full day back, saying he had things to sort out before he could come personally to Ulitza Chaykovskovo but he guessed there was a lot to talk about. The American said he didn't know about that. The ministerial press conference after the Shelapin and Agayans arrests had been a back-slapping affair but there hadn't been anything since and he wondered if the shutters had been put up against him as well now. Popov wasn't available and wasn't returning calls. None of which mattered much in view of the edict from Washington, which none of them had yet worked out. Charlie waited for the other man to talk about the satellite voice tape but he didn't.

Charile decided that re-entering the British embassy was like being the first of an invading force arriving at a village nervously unsure if he was going to shoot all the men and rape all the women. Those who believed, from his earlier efforts, that he was someone with special London influence were now totally convinced and either sought him out or worked hard to avoid him. It was from Thomas Bowyer, so quick to get to him the man must have had the gatehouse advise of his arrival, that Charlie learned of Nigel Saxon's recall to London. The Chancellery head wasn't expected to return and it was the only topic of conversation around the embassy. Bowyer talked of possible misunderstandings between them in the past and hoped there wouldn't be any in the future. Charlie, disinterested in continuing attrition, allowed the man his escape and said he hoped so, too. He warned Bowyer of his possibly spending much less time in the embassy which the newly briefed and disciplined Scotsman accepted without question, anxiously agreeing to maintain the telephone link that Charlie said might be necessary. Bowyer said that judging from the second recovery it looked as if the remaining Pizhma material could still be somewhere in Moscow after all, instantly turning a complete and instant backward somersault when Charlie said he didn't think that was so. Finally, unable to hold himself back, Bowyer suggested a lot seemed to have emerged from his London recall and Charlie, less generous than he had been at the beginning, said a lot had but that it was unfortunate it had happened in the first place.

Paul Smythe was one of the people who thought Charlie had God's private telephone number and went with him to the embassy commissary and logged without comment the largest single alcohol order ever recorded against a legation staff member, which Charlie judged necessary to stock Lesnaya if he was permitted to set himself up as a crime-serving entrepreneur and more than sufficient to keep out Moscow's winter cold if he weren't. Charlie also withdrew from the equally eager-to-please Peter Potter £10,000 in US dollars against an inadequate receipt listing it as a Special Contingency Fund, just to keep Gerald Williams' blood pressure bubbling.

He allowed Jurgen Balg to take him to lunch in gratitude for being told first of the Warsaw link to the Pizhma robbery and used it openly to urge that he be allowed in on the questioning if a German arrest came from it. The impudence briefly confused the German, whose halting protests that such unprecedented access was impossible abruptly stopped when Charlie announced as if it had already been agreed by the Russians his setting up as a phoney trader in Moscow. Balg changed direction entirely, agreeing that even if the Pizhma nuclear material had already been smuggled out of Russia the closest liaison was absolutely essential in the future and promising to press Bonn as strongly as he could.

Charlie hadn't expected Hillary to be in the FBI office at the American embassy, although it was the logical place for her to be: she simply hadn't attended any of the previous gatherings since her arrival. She winked at him as he walked in. With the Americans Charlie didn't try to infer Russian agreement, although he insisted he was confident it would come. Each reacted differently. Kestler said holy shit; Hillary said he couldn't possibly consider doing it; and Lyneham said forget it, it didn't stand a hope in a hot hell of Russian acceptance. Lyneham's remark gave Charlie the perfect lead to argue they might, in view of what was on the audio tape, and finally explained the significance of Warsaw which he claimed to have been deciphered in London. Lyneham thought the analysts in Washington were going to be pissed off at being beaten by the Brits and Charlie offered it as a bargaining reason for Kestler's continued admission to the Russian meetings.

'It goes against their argument that it's still somehow in Russia,' the man pointed out. 'They're not going to like the thought of losing it.'

'It's a fact they've got to know about. And you're the person to tell them,' said Charlie.

'What do you think the chances are of stopping it if it's still here?' demanded Kestler.

'God knows!' admitted Charlie. 'All the Russian borders are supposedly closed. And those of the intervening countries. There'd be a logic to cache it somewhere to let the heat die down. The Moscow recovery would help that; maybe even be designed to achieve it.'

'So your people told the Poles?' queried Lyneham.

'And the Germans,' said Charlie.

'That stuff's been adrift long enough to get it to the Middle East by slow mule train!' said Hillary. 'My money is on it already being there. You know what I think? I think we could be looking at another Gulf War fought very differently than the last.'

'No,' warned Charlie. 'Germany and Poland were warned days ago.'

'I don't hear any police sirens,' said the girl.

'Just strange noises from Washington,' said Lyneham.

Lyneham said he'd make a book on the sting idea being pissed on from a great height, offering odds of fifty to one against. Kestler wagered $5 and Charlie matched it with the first expense against his special contingency fund. Hillary said, contemptuously, she didn't think it was something to bet on. It was a long way into lunch together at the embassy canteen before she relaxed. After lunch Hillary walked him back on to Ulitza Chaykovskovo.

'You didn't call, you didn't write, you didn't send flowers!' she chided.

'I had a lot to sort out.'

'And now you have.'

Charlie gestured further along the multi-lane highway. 'The Peking's the best Chinese restaurant in the city.'

'Seven-thirty?'

'Fine.' Which it was. Hillary might have a very necessary place in his scheme of things, as well as being gorgeous.

Charlie thought the rice wine was tasteless but drank it anyway and they had duck in pancakes because that was the thing to do. Hillary insisted on doing most of the ordering and there was a sweet and sour course and chicken in cashews and steamed dumplings.

She dismissed FBI sting operations against the American Mafia as totally different – always controllable – from what he wanted to do and asked if he'd seen the torture photographs and what about that business in the club, that had frightened her shitless! She was unimpressed by his *spetznaz* argument.

'I'd need your help,' Charlie announced.

'My help!'

'Technically, if it ever comes to anything. To check out what I was offered to make sure it wasn't a con.'

Hillary regarded him warily. 'Charlie, I like the way I look! These guys don't fuck about: I don't want any facial remodelling.'

'Just a check to ensure I don't get caught out along the way with a load of crap.'

She smiled, nervously. 'I'm with Lyneham. It isn't going to work so it's a waste of time talking about it.'

'*If* it works,' he pressed.

'If it works we'll talk about it again.'

When he asked if she wanted to go on to a club Hillary said he had to be joking, after last time. There was no question of her not going back to Lesnaya. Charlie was worried that this time he didn't have the aphrodisiac of fear but he needn't have been. Afterwards she lay wetly over him, her head on his shoulder.

'Can I ask you a question?' she said, her voice muffled.

'Of course.'

'You take house guests?'

He pulled away, better to look down at her. 'You serious?'

'Sure.'

'Are we talking serious relationships or escape from embassy compounds?'

'Escape from embassy compounds. I don't go for serious relationships.'

'My turn for a question. What's the score between you and Kestler? You two didn't seem the best of friends at lunch.' And he was still curious at her earlier dismissal.

Now it was Hillary who moved away. 'There isn't a score. I don't go for guys who wave their dicks around their heads like a lariat. I like to make my own choice. Which I did. Which is why I'm here. OK?'

'OK.'

'You did it brilliantly, Charlie.'

'What?' he said, not understanding.

'Changed the house guest subject.'

'What would the embassy say?'

'Who gives a damn? It's personal, not professional.'

And professionally he would need her if the sting operation came even halfway near to being set up. 'You want your own bedroom?'

'Let's keep it for friends.'

They made love once more during the night, slowly, starting when they were still half asleep and stayed entwined afterwards so the telephone rang several times before Charlie could disentangle himself. As he picked up the receiver he saw it was just before seven, although it was still dark outside.

'We picked up five Russians at a place called Cottbus, just over the Polish border,' announced Balg. 'They had six canisters with them. And Bonn's agreed to your sitting in on the interrogation.'

It was the last of several meetings, a review of everything they had discussed while Peter Johnson had been in Washington, and they ate in Fenby's private dining room at Pennsylvania Avenue. There was no public benefit parading an unknown Briton at the Four Seasons.

'You've no doubt he'd make public what a stupid son-of-a-bitch Kestler was: and me with it?' It had been Fenby's recurring question, at every session.

'None,' insisted Johnson, who blamed Fenby for a lot of his own entrapment.

'So the bastard's got us by the balls?' He'd never lost control like this before, never had to be the one obeying the shots instead of calling them, and Fenby didn't like it.

'And can use what he's got like you tried to do,' agreed the deputy British Director. 'If anything goes wrong we're package-wrapped for sacrifice.'

'I guess we should cool things for a while.'

'I don't have any alternative,' said Johnson, anxious to separate himself from the American.

'I'm going to find one.'

'I don't want to know about it.' The southern fried chicken had been cold and Fenby hadn't served any wine, either.

chapter 30

Gunther Schumann, the intended Russian-speaking interrogator who met Charlie at Tegel airport, was a superintendent in the special nuclear smuggling division of the Bundeskriminalamt. An appropriate piratical black patch covered a missing left eye, although not the scar from it that ran down his cheek, and he'd developed the habit of winking the good right one conspiratorially when he talked, which he did a lot in excellent English during their preparatory lunch at the Kempinski, where Charlie had made a nostalgic reservation.

The arrests had been a coordinated German and Polish operation made entirely possible from the identification of the Warsaw hotel. The five Russians had arrived at the *Zajazd Karczma*, which Polish intelligence was staking out, eight days earlier. The initial reason for checking them had only been that they *were* Russian. On the first night the boot of one of their two cars was picked and three canisters discovered. It had obviously been a contact point because they'd stayed there two days; because he'd occupied the Napoleon room they'd decided a Russian carrying a passport in the name of Fedor Alekseevich Mitrov was the leader. There had been no calls made from the hotel. Mitrov used outside street kiosks five times, never the same one twice. He was the only one to telephone, a further indication of his being in charge. He'd been seen to make notes every time but they hadn't been found after his arrest. The surveillance had been constant, night and day, but there had been no meeting with anyone else in Warsaw or during the interrupted drive to the border. The accelerator cable of one car, a

Volkswagen, had snapped near Lodz and they'd lost half a day getting it replaced. They'd been allowed to cross the border because the German nuclear smuggling legislation was stronger and more wide ranging than in Poland. The Bundeskriminalamt had tapped the Cottbus hotel switchboard but again there had been no calls, either in or out. Mitrov had used a kiosk once, within an hour of their Cottbus arrival, but made no notes.

On their third day at Cottbus the group became very agitated. Two watching Bundeskriminalamt officers, a man and a woman, had been too far away at a pavement café to hear an obvious argument between two of the men, with Mitrov visibly gesturing around him to warn of their being overheard. The group had split, leaving separately: one man had gone direct to the railway station and noted train departures for Berlin. Frightened of losing some of the group – but more importantly what they were carrying – the decision had been made to arrest them. It had been done at four in the morning. They had all been asleep and there had been no resistance, although each had been armed either with Walther or Markarov handguns. Three Uzi machine guns had been found in the two cars, a Mercedes saloon in addition to the repaired Volkswagen. So had a total of six nuclear canisters, equally split between both vehicles. The cars had been legitimately bought, both for cash, from separate Berlin salesrooms, and each was registered at separate Berlin addresses, although the identities of the named owners on both the purchase and registration documents were false. The Bundeskriminalamt were totally satisfied the people living at the addresses – an accountant and his girlfriend and the widow of a railway inspector – were uninvolved and that their homes had been chosen at random, possibly from a telephone book. None of the arrested Russians had made any statement or admission. The canisters alone, marked with the fingerprints of each of the five, guaranteed a case that could be traced backwards to Russia but not forwards, to the plutonium's destination.

'And working from your count of twenty-two, there's still

ten containers missing, seven if we use the Russian figure,' concluded Schumann. 'Like always, nothing's ever complete: it's a bastard.'

'Maybe not quite as incomplete as usual,' said Charlie, tapping the bulging briefcase firmly wedged between his feet.

It took Charlie longer than it had the German to set out what he'd brought from Moscow and which had taken him a full day after Balg's early morning call to collect and collate, from the frantic-for-participation US embassy Bureau and from Rupert Dean in London. Long before Charlie finished Schumann was smiling and nodding, his good eye stuttering up and down.

'I couldn't assimilate all that properly to break them and they'd realize it: Mitrov quicker than the others. Is your Russian good enough?'

'Yes,' assured Charlie, quickly.

'We'll need to build a stage set!' announced Schumann.

'And give an Oscar performance,' agreed Charlie.

Late that evening Charlie surveyed the efforts of nearly seven hours' work and decided it was indeed very much like a stage set. There were pinboards stretching the entire length of one wall to display every one of the 150 satellite photographs enlarged to their highest definition. Each was accompanied by a separate enhancement of the individuals featured on the general prints, the physical analysis annotated alongside the images. The pictures showing the killing of the train guards were repeated in another display section. Along a second wall was installed a relay of specialized recording and replay equipment and halfway along the third were five full-length criminal line-up boards, calibrated to a giant-sized three metres. Alongside each were scales upon which a person had to sit for their weight to be accurately calculated by counters moved along a minutely marked pendulum bar. Each place was fronted by cameras, Polaroid as well as tripod-mounted. The centre of the room was empty except for five chairs side by side against a table. Official stenographers had their places directly behind and after them, on an elevated platform, were video cameras to record everything.

Schumann said, 'There should be music and someone yelling ''Lights! Action!'' '

'I want to hear much more than that,' said Charlie.

He and the German spent another hour that night and two the following morning finalizing their confrontation, Schumann eventually but without offence conceding the orchestration to Charlie.

The German still, however, initially played the lead. At Schumann's order the Russians were quick-marched, militarily, to the weighing and measuring section of the room. To their total, half-resisting bewilderment their height and weight were established and after that the medical teams carefully recorded chest, waist, stomach, biceps and leg dimensions. Finally they were photographed against the scaled height charts, both by the sophisticated cameras and on the instant Polaroid equipment.

Charlie and Schumann positioned themselves so that at all times they could gauge the reaction of the men when, one at a time but led by Mitrov, they were paraded with enforced slowness in front of the Pizhma photographic collage, finishing at the repeated section showing the guard murders at their moment of being committed. From each the reaction was total astonishment: in two cases it was brief, gap-mouthed astonishment. The procession concluded at the electronic equipment, where each warily uneasy man was questioned once more about his involvement in the Pizhma robbery – by Russian speakers other than Charlie and Schumann – to get voice recordings against legally established identities from the repeated although hesitant denials.

Mitrov was a blond-haired, pale-faced man whose thinness was accentuated by his height. None of the others was as tall, although Charlie estimated two to be just short of two metres. The third was middle height, the fourth much shorter. All were thick set, the particularly small man positively fat. In the chaired line to which they were led Mitrov maintained the best control. The small man feasted off his fingernails and another man, blond like Mitrov, kept palming back hair that didn't need putting into place.

It was a full half an hour before the leader of the physiological analyzing team invited Schumann and Charlie to go through the identification with him, putting the height, weight and body dimensions calculated by the Washington photographic examiners against the just-recorded detailed measurements of the arrested five.

'No doubt about any of them,' declared the man, matching the Polaroid prints to the satellite images. 'Three positive identifications with the shootings . . .' His finger jabbed out at three different prints on the separated murder-proving pinboard. '. . . Here, here and here . . . Each showing someone at the moment of their being shot . . .' He referred to the identity sheets to which the Polaroids were attached. '. . . Yuri Dedov, here . . .' he said, picking out the small fat man actually standing over his victim as he fired. The analyst attached a photograph of the averagely tall blond-haired man to another satellite print. 'This is Valeri Federov firing an Uzi at two guards emerging from the train. And this . . .' He pinned a picture of the man of middle height to another satellite print '. . . is Vladimir Okulov shooting in the back a guard who appears to be running away.' There were six positive identifications of Fedor Mitrov, in two of which the man was seen to be breaking open storage canisters, and four of the fifth man, Ivan Raina, helping him do it.

Schumann carried the matched photographs across to the five, all of whom were fidgeting and foot-shuffling with the exception of Mitrov, although a nerve had begun to pull at the corner of the man's mouth. The German dealt out his selection in front of each man and said; 'Everything witnessed, in provable detail, from a satellite . . .' He looked to the three killers, in turn, 'And there you are, caught in the actual act of murder. That's going to make your trial unique.'

On cue Charlie crossed to the bank of tape machines, still held by the excitement that had swept through him minutes before. The audio tapes had been synched by both Washington and London to the millisecond to the times of the satellite images and the German analyst had just identified Fedor Mitrov as the man who had joked about *akrashena* as he'd smashed open the plutonium containers. Which was the first segment Charlie had chosen to replay, never believing it would have the significance it now did. The transmission had been cleaned of static and the voice echoed clearly into the room, the sound so good they could even hear Raina's laugh, after the remark. Schumann and Charlie had decided against the actual interrogations being communal and Charlie snapped the machine off after a short while.

'Voice prints can be proven as accurately as fingerprints,' he said. 'That's why you were questioned earlier: to get your voices positively recorded against your names. In a few days we'll have every word each of you spoke, all the time you were at Pizhma: a complete transcript.'

The finger-gnawing Dedov said, 'What do you want to know?'

'Everything,' said Schumann.

The fast-winking German was so euphoric by the second day that he commuted overnight to the Wiesbaden headquarters to brief the alerted Bundeskriminalamt hierarchy that they were getting sufficient for a sensational international trial as well as the chance to target a major Russian Mafia Family domiciled in Berlin.

They carried out their questioning in the stage-set conference room, one man at a time after that first resistance-breaking group encounter, each Russian constantly reminded of the evidence of his guilt. An early conclusion was that apart from Mitrov, the other four were foot soldiers, fetch-and-carry gofers who pointed guns and pressed triggers at people at whom they were told to point guns and press triggers, without asking why.

They questioned the anxious-to-confess Dedov first and the subsequent cross-examination of the other three provided little more than elaboration of what the diminutive fat man told them. They *were* the Dolgoprudnaya, the leading Moscow Family. Stanislav Georgevich Silin was the boss of bosses of six subsidiary clans which he ruled American Mafia style, through a controlling Commission with himself as chairman. The organization was a pyramid structure run military fashion, even to military designations and titles. They never saw or dealt with Silin direct, always through corps commanders or clan bosses. Mitrov had been their corps commander for the Pizhma robbery. They'd not been involved in any planning: they'd taken their instructions from Mitrov, who had told them where the nuclear train was to be stopped and that the guards and the escorting soldiers all had to be killed, to leave no witnesses. Mitrov hadn't told them why some containers had to be broken open. After the robbery they'd driven further south, to Uren, where the majority of the twenty-two canisters had been transferred: only six were left in the original trucks. None of them knew where those trucks or the six canisters had been taken. They didn't know, either, where the other ten canisters had gone. They'd been loaded into three Mercedes and one BMW and they'd all travelled in convoy for the remainder of that day. They'd split northeast of Moscow, at Kalinin. Of course they'd heard of the Agayans and Shelapin Families, even of the territory dispute at Bykovo, but knew nothing about either being involved in a nuclear robbery. They were small time: punks. They certainly hadn't been at Pizhma: that had been entirely Dolgoprudnaya. None of them knew a Yatisyna organization. They'd stayed at the *Zajazd Karczma* longer than they'd intended because Mitrov had difficulty making contact from a public kiosk. And then been further delayed by the Volkswagen breakdown in getting to Cottbus, where they'd been told to go, and their buyers hadn't been waiting, as arranged. Okulov had caused the witnessed pavement argument by accusing Mitrov of screwing up and stranding them with a load of nuclear stuff they couldn't get rid of. It was Raina who had enquired about Berlin trains, intending to go the following day to make contact with the Dolgoprudnaya group permanently established there. Their middle-of-the-night arrest had come before Mitrov had given him the Dolgoprudnaya's Berlin address but Raina thought it was somewhere in the Marzahn district, in the old communist-controlled east of the city.

Charlie and Schumann began early on the fifth day with Fedor Alekseevich Mitrov but it was still well into the afternoon before they began a proper interrogation because the morning was occupied playing back the most incriminating parts of the other Russians' testimonies. Because Charlie had explained what he wanted – and because Schumann had already obtained so much to German satisfaction from the earlier interrogations – Charlie led the questioning. Mitrov started well, fervently denying any position of authority and even more fervently giving any murder orders. But the rejection was eggshell thin and Charlie moved quickly to shatter it.

'*Akrashena*,' he declared, simply.

Schumann looked incomprehensibly at Charlie and the Russian appeared confused too, although Charlie knew it wasn't from lack of understanding.

'*Akrashena*,' repeated Charlie. 'Explain that to me.'

The tall Russian sniggered in what was supposed to be ridicule. 'Wet paint.'

'I know what it means,' said Charlie. 'Like I know it was the code name for the militarily planned prevention of a nuclear robbery at Kirs.'

'I don't know anything about that,' said Mitrov.

'You do!' insisted Charlie, starting the satellite tape at its prepared section. 'That's your voice. We've had it scientifically and provably matched. That's you speaking at the scene of a *successful* robbery about one that was being militarily stopped elsewhere by an operation named *Akrashena*. So you tell us how you knew that. And how the Shelapin Family – Shelapin himself – came to be in possession of nuclear material from a robbery he wasn't connected with. And what's happened to the ten containers still missing. And who your customers were, for the six canisters you smuggled into Germany. And when you've told us all that you can tell us a lot more. Like how well-established the Dolgoprudnaya are here in Berlin and exactly where they are in the Marzahn district.'

Blatant cunning registered on the Russian's face. 'Tell me why I should.'

'Germany doesn't have capital punishment. Russia does,' said Charlie, simply. 'Murder, which you're guilty of by having given the orders, is a capital crime. So is nuclear theft. The crimes you committed in Russia take precedence over that of smuggling nuclear components into Germany. So you could be transferred back to Moscow to face trial on the greater charges. In Russia, you die. In Germany, you get a custodial sentence. Which, on past history, won't be very long.'

'Germany wants the glory of a trial! They wouldn't miss it by sending me back!'

'You sure about that?'

Mitrov wasn't and it showed: the nerve was tugging at his mouth. 'What guarantees would there be?'

'Cooperate and the trial, and the sentencing, will be here in Germany,' promised the German.

'Let's see how we go,' accepted Mitrov, doubtfully.

'Tell me about the Shelapin involvement,' Charlie demanded.

'They're a Chechen group,' dismissed Mitrov.

Charlie recognized the first crack in the dam. 'We know that. Were they part of the Pizhma distribution?' It wasn't a naive question.

'Of course they weren't! I told you, they're Chechen!'

'So how did some of the Pizhma containers end up with Vasili Shelapin? And more with another member of the Family.'

'I don't know.'

'But you knew six containers had to be left in the original trucks, after you unloaded?' pressed Schumann.

'Yes.'

'Why?'

'I don't know.'

'Yes you do,' challenged Charlie.
'I was just told they had to be left.'
'By whom?'
'At a planning meeting.'
'By whom?' repeated Charlie, refusing the avoidance.
'Silin.' The man mumbled the name, as if he hoped they wouldn't hear it.
'To be taken into Moscow?'
'Yes,' said the Russian, unthinking.
'So you knew the trucks were going on into Moscow!'
Mitrov hesitated, realizing the mistake. 'Yes.'
'Why? Why weren't they abandoned at Uren?'
'Silin said they were needed in Moscow.'
'Why?'
'He didn't tell me. Just that he wanted them there.'
'You're lying,' accused Schumann.
'Confusion,' blurted Mitrov.
'Decoy, you mean?'
'I suppose.'
'Was it your decision to break open the containers: risk a township?' demanded Schumann.
'No!'
'Silin again?' probed Charlie.
'Yes.'
'Why?'
'Confusion,' the man repeated. 'Delay.'
'*Akrashena*?' said Charlie.
'Silin.'
'So he knew about the Kirs attempt?'
'Yes.'
'When did the planning for Pizhma start?'
'I don't remember.'
'When?'
'Towards the end of the month.'
It wasn't the answer Charlie expected. 'Date?'
'I can't remember.'
'The day?'
'I'm not sure. Tuesday I think.'

'The thirtieth?'

'Earlier.'

'The twenty-third?'

'That sounds better.'

That was before the first Interior Ministry meeting to plan against the Kirs robbery, calculated Charlie. 'That was when Silin told you *akrashena* was the task force code name?'

Mitrov shook his head. 'Later. More than a week later.'

That fitted better. 'Did Silin tell you, personally? Or was it part of a discussion involving several people.'

'Several people.'

'All Family?'

The wary pause was too obvious. 'Yes.'

'That's a lie.'

'It was all Family when I was involved.'

'Explain that,' demanded Schumann.

'There'd been another meeting, before. Just Silin.'

'Who with?'

'The people he knows.'

There was a sharp spurt of pain in Charlie's feet at the first-time thought that Kirs had been even more of a decoy that he'd imagined, up until now. 'Who are these people?'

Mitrov grimaced. 'Who do you think?'

'I don't want to think. I want you to tell me.'

'Militia.'

'Who?'

'I don't know. No one knows. Only Silin. That's how it works. Just him and them.'

'*Them*!' seized Charlie. 'One person? Or several?'

'Several. I don't know how many. All Militia are crooked.'

'The Dolgoprudnaya are established here, in Berlin?'

There was another wary hesitation. 'Yes.'

Although he knew the answer, Charlie said, 'Where else, in Russia?'

'St Petersburg.'

'So where are these special Militia people? In Moscow? Or outside?'

'Moscow, definitely.'
'Why definitely?'
'The meetings are so easy. Any uncertainties can be resolved at once, which they couldn't be if the dealings were with people outside Moscow.'
'What rank?'
'I don't know.'
'Names?' came in Schumann.
There was a snort of derision from the Russian. 'There are never names.'
'You're a corps commander?'
Mitrov paused. 'Yes.'
'Who was the other corps commander, at Pizhma?'
'Malin.'
'Full name,' demanded Schumann.
'Petr Gavrilovich.'
'He's got ten men with him?' established Charlie, calculating from the satellite photographs.
'I suppose so.'
'And ten canisters?'
'Yes.'
'Where are they? What route are they taking?'
The man shook his head. 'You're too late.'
'Why are we too late?' asked the German.
'They went full south, through the Ukraine.'
'*Full* south?' questioned Charlie, curious at the phrase.
'The Black Sea,' said Mitrov.
'For simple, quick land access to anywhere in the Middle East after a short voyage,' accepted Schumann, more to himself than to the other two. 'When?'
'Five days ago. Out of Odessa.'
There was no way of knowing whether each canister was full, calculated Charlie, sickened. If they were, as much as a hundred kilos had been lost: twenty bombs, eighty thousand dead. 'Who were your buyers to be?'
'I don't know. I wasn't part of that. It was arranged here, in Berlin. By our people here.'
'In Marzahn?'

'KulmseeStrasse. Number 15,' smiled Mitrov. 'You'll be wasting your time. They'll have cleared out days ago. They were due at Cottbus the day we were picked up: you missed them by being four or five hours too early!'

'Who do you think the buyers were?' pressed Schumann.

Mitrov shrugged. 'Middle East. Who else?'

'How did the Pizhma planning come about?' demanded Charlie.

'I don't understand.'

'What happened first? Did Silin suddenly announce you were going to rob a nuclear train? Or did he say there was going to be a robbery at a nuclear plant that he'd decided to take advantage of?'

Mitrov thought for several moments. 'He said we were going to rob a train. Then he talked of the Kirs robbery.'

'He specifically mentioned Kirs!' pounced Charlie.

'Yes.'

'And talked about both robberies at the same meeting?'

Mitrov shook his head. 'Different times. Pizhma, at first. Then Kirs later.'

All this time! thought Charlie, anguished. All this time they'd not just been going around in circles but revolving in the opposite direction from that in which they should have been going even to half-understand what was happening. How much did he have to change his privately formulated opinion of how it had all been organized? Not much. He was sure now he was looking in the right direction.

Satisfied with what he'd learned, Charlie let Schumann conclude that day's session and shared the ritual celebration drink with the German before relaying the day's events to Rupert Dean through the quasi-embassy facilities being set up in preparation for the full diplomatic transfer from Bonn. The Director-General asked hopefully if there could be any doubt about the ten containers getting to some unknown destination and Charlie said he didn't think so and agreed with Dean they had the sort of disaster they'd feared. London was providing Moscow with a daily transcript to support their sting operation approach as well as advising Washington, but Charlie kept in daily personal touch with Kestler.

Before he could start that night the younger American said, 'The big gangs are at war here! Name who just got whacked!'

'Stanislav Georgevich Silin, the head of the Dolgoprudnaya Family,' said Charlie.

It was a long time before Kestler spoke. 'How the fuck did you guess?'

'I'm psychic,' said Charlie. After he replaced the receiver he said to himself, 'I hope you're not in over your head this time, Charlie my son.'

Natalia made Aleksai a drink and didn't invite him to share in Sasha's bath-time, which he usually did automatically, instead leaving him alone while she settled the child for the night. The assessment of the German investigation had taken a full day and been subdued throughout. There had been no open criticism of anyone because none was justified, but Natalia suspected Aleksai felt crushed by the German success. And not just German success: Charlie's success. Which wasn't confined to Berlin. The final decision of the day, greatly influenced by Germany, had been to accept, although with stringent Moscow-governing restrictions, the British proposal to attempt an entrapment operation in the hope of blocking such a robbery in the future.

Natalia waited until Sasha was dozing before returning to the main room. Unasked, she made Popov another drink and poured wine for herself.

'Do you want anything to eat?'

'No.'

'What then?'

'Nothing.'

'It wasn't a disaster!' she declared. 'There was nothing more you could have done.'

'I could have listened more to the Englishman.'

The admission surprised Natalia. 'The only obvious failures were my examination of Shelapin.'

'At least you'll be spared his court accusations of attempted extortion.' There had been brief but serious consideration of proceeding against Shelapin anyway, to smash a known Mafia ring; it had only ended when Natalia pointed out a fabricated prosecution was impossible – apart from being illegal – because of the evidence that would emerge at the German hearings.

'His release – and Agayans' murder – still reflect on me.' In any detailed examination of personal failure she had far more to be depressed about than Aleksai.

'It's over!' said Popov. 'Everyone is now busy making their excuses for what they did or didn't do to prevent enough plutonium getting out of Russia to start a full-scale war. And we're at the bottom of the pile, getting all their dirt dumped on us.'

'Me more than you,' accepted Natalia, her mind still held by the Shelapin débâcle.

Popov came forward on his chair, to face her more directly. 'Isn't it about time you made your decision? I've given you all the time you asked for. It's time you told me whether you want to marry me or not.'

'I know,' said Natalia. 'I . . .' She physically jumped at the telephone's ring, hurrying to it: it was more than likely Charlie was back.

The shock was so great and so complete that speech went from her: she gave a half whimper, half scream, holding the receiver away in horror. Popov leaped up, snatching it from her, shouting 'Hello! hello!' and then remaining with it limply in his hand.

'Dead,' he said. 'There's nobody there.'

'A man,' groped Natalia, the words croaking out in disbelief. 'He said to keep my face out. He said if I didn't Sasha wouldn't have a face. She wouldn't die but when they'd finished she wouldn't have a face.'

And then Natalia screamed, hysterically.

A *barbuska*, making her way home close to the Arbat, also screamed hysterically when she looked into the oddly parked

Mercedes in the hope of finding something to steal and discovered instead the bodies of Stanislav Silin and his wife. Both had been roped into their seats, as if setting out for a Sunday drive in the country.

chapter 31

The threat against Sasha changed everything. Charlie's personal feelings became professional now, in a seething mix. Throughout a lifetime of utter disregard of morality, populated by coldly unemotional killers and entrapment experts and out-and-out bastards who wallowed in the pleasure of being out-and-out bastards, the cardinal, self-preserving rule of Charles Edward Muffin, a man who acknowledged no religion, had been that of the Old Testament. Charlie had, however, refined the life for a life, eye for an eye, wound for a wound precept to a very personal, far less verbose creed. Charlie's lesson was that anyone who tried to fuck him got double-fucked in return: worse, if it were possible. He'd wrecked the careers of the British and American intelligence directors who tried to sacrifice him. And – as emotionlessly as the professional killers he always managed to run away from – he'd personally booby-trapped the escape aircraft of the CIA assassins who'd killed Edith. And felt unrepentant satisfaction as the plane disintegrated into a red and yellow fireball.

Now it was happening again. But not a physical attack upon him. The threat of one upon Sasha. Whoever it was had made a terrible mistake involving a baby – his baby – who shouldn't have been part of anything. The panic it indicated didn't matter. They'd done it. So they'd suffer. They didn't know that yet. But they would, because their knowing was part of the retribution. From the moment of Natalia's babbled story, at the botanical gardens again, Charlie's planned entrapment became a totally dedicated, totally personal, totally private exercise to go beyond discovering fresh smuggling attempts to find out who'd threatened his child. And then to make them regret the very day they'd come screaming into the world, which was the way Charlie intended them to leave it.

Even more than before the botanical gardens were obvious because of their closeness to Sasha's crèche. It was the day after his return to Moscow and at Natalia's summons, and he'd never known her so distraught, not even when he'd told her he was returning to London after his phoney defection, because then they'd made their reconciliation plans he hadn't fulfilled. Natalia was dishevelled and physically shaking, ague-like, unable at the beginning to hold a consecutive thought or a cohesive conversation. Although the shaking wasn't because of the cold he led her into the hothouse and sat her down there and tried to calm her and in the end let the account come when and how she wanted to tell it.

The words were staccato, stopping and starting, broken sometimes by near sobs. It took Charlie a long time to get the actual telephone warning and in the end he wasn't sure he had because Natalia was close to blanking it from her memory. And even longer for him fully to understand the precautions. Sasha was protected at all times at the crèche by a woman officer from the Interior Ministry's security section, in constant radio contact with a central control room. Natalia no longer delivered or collected her personally: they were driven by an armed chauffeur, always accompanied by an armed escort vehicle. A security check had been run on all the parents of the other children, particularly new arrivals, and upon all staff. There were two Militia cars permanently stationed at the front and rear of the building. There was also twenty-four-hour Militia protection and surveillance at Leninskaya and a respond-at-once telephone monitor had been imposed, which was why she'd called him from the ministry and why there couldn't be any more direct contact between them from her apartment.

'Why now?' she demanded, anguished. 'It's over!'

'And why you?' echoed Charlie, reflectively.

'I've been through that. With Aleksai. And the security

people. I was named, during the enquiry. *Moscow News* and *Izvestia* identified me as the division director and the person in charge of interrogation. And it was said Agayans died *under* interrogation. And everyone from the President down is still listed in the telephone book – if you can obtain a telephone book – like it was in the old days.'

'What about Shelapin? He's the most likely.'

'Aleksai had him rearrested. He denied knowing anything about it. Said he didn't fight kids. He and his people are being kept under surveillance. And know it.'

'The Agayans group then? Their man died.'

'The same. Total denials. Surveillance there, too.' Natalia was regaining control although she was wringing her hands in her lap. 'Whoever it was knew you had a daughter.'

'No one can explain that.'

Charlie wasn't prepared to try, not yet, although he thought he could: the threat against Sasha had hardened a lot of the beliefs with which he'd returned from Berlin. 'They'd rung off, when Popov took the phone?'

'Yes.'

'What about the voice?'

'A man.'

'You can guess ages from voices.'

Natalia shook her head. 'I wasn't rational, Charlie! He said Sasha was going to lose her *face*!'

Charlie was aloof, icily calm, all emotions suspended. 'Accent?'

'Russian.'

'Not a republic? Or a region?'

'I don't think so.'

'I don't want what you think! I want what you know!' he said, brutally.

'Russian.' She wasn't sure.

'Disguised?'

'I think so. It was distant, as if he were standing away from the mouthpiece. Or had something over it.'

'A private phone? Or did coins drop?'

'No coins dropped. I've been through all this!'

'Go through it again, for me. Did he refer to you by name?'

'I don't think so.'

'You can't remember?'

'Not really.'

'What can you remember?'

'Only about her face!'

She was tilting back towards hysteria. 'How were the words said?'

'I don't understand.'

'All at once, without a pause: as if they were written down or rehearsed? Or with pauses, as if he was waiting for you to say something?'

'All at once.'

Getting there, thought Charlie. 'How?' he repeated. 'Quickly: hurried? Or slowly? Measured?'

She nodded at his choice of definitions. 'Measured.'

'As if he was reading from something written down?'

Natalia frowned at the question. 'He could have been reading it, I suppose. No one asked me that before. Is it important?'

'I don't know. Maybe. What about background, from his end? Any noises?'

'No.'

'Sure?'

'No, I'm not sure! I thought it might be you. I wasn't listening for noises in the background. Then when he started to talk I wasn't thinking about anything!'

'A lot of people were upset – destroyed even – by the investigation,' he tried, uncomfortable with the effort as he made it. 'It could be empty harassment.'

'I'm going to quit, Charlie!' she announced. 'I thought the job was the way to protect Sasha, but it's not, not any more. It's made her a target. I certainly don't need the money and Aleksai's asked me again to marry him. He'll look after us: protect Sasha.'

'I don't think Sasha will actually be attacked.'

She frowned along the bench at him. 'You can't say that!'

'It was obvious that protection would be put into place. At once. If they'd seriously intended to hurt her they'd have attacked her first. You wouldn't have been *given* a warning. Sasha's disfigurement would have *been* the warning.'

'You really believe that?' she demanded again.

No, he thought. 'Yes,' he said.

'It's over now, with the German arrests. We know what was lost.' She was recovering, the words slow and considered.

'Yes.' Charlie said, doubtfully.

'There's no need for our arrangement, not any more.'

'She's my daughter!'

Natalia bit her lip. 'I meant about work.'

'What *do* you mean?' he demanded.

'I'm frightened, Charlie. Terribly frightened. I can't afford to make a single mistake. About anything. It would be a mistake for us to go on like this, behind Aleksai's back. Even though there's nothing in it. It's still cheating him. Which isn't fair. He's a good man. He loves me.'

He wasn't totally sure she'd lost all feeling for him, although perhaps love was hoping too much, but he definitely couldn't lose the special contact: it was more important now than ever. How far could he go to convince her? Hardly any way at all. Too much was still conjecture, sufficient for him but not enough to convince anyone else. 'There still might be more to learn about Pizhma and Kirs . . .' Charlie hesitated as the thought came to him, despising himself for considering it but knowing he was going to use it just the same. 'That's why the threat came against Sasha. I don't think she'll be attacked but I can't be sure. How long do you want Sasha going to school in an armoured convoy? One year? Two? Until she goes to high school? It doesn't matter if you quit. Aleksai will still be where he is: maybe he'll even be promoted, into your job. He'd be their danger then, not you. And Sasha will be his weakness: his pressure.'

Natalia regarded him blankly, wide-eyed. 'What can I do?'

'Go on helping me!'

'. . . But you're moving on from Pizhma? This entrapment idea . . .'

'It's through the entrapment that I might be able to understand what happened at Pizhma. And at Kirs.'

'How? I don't follow . . . '

'Fedor Mitrov, the Dolgoprudnaya man,' half-lied Charlie. 'The Germans have agreed a deal, in return for his guiding me to the right people here in Moscow.'

'The Militia are adamant Silin died in a gang battle. Died grotesquely . . . and his wife.' She shuddered.

'He was killed because he knew who the Kirs and Pizhma organizers were. And who the customers were, for what was stolen.'

Natalia held his eyes for several moments. 'Are you being completely honest with me? Completely honest about Sasha's life?'

'Yes,' said Charlie, meeting her gaze.

'Dear God, it must end soon!' said Natalia, despairingly.

'Yes,' agreed Charlie. 'Very soon. Will you go on helping?'

'What choice do I have?'

Hillary moved into Lesnaya the same week with three suitcases, a poster of Robert Frost ('the best American poet ever') and a long-lashed rabbit doll whose name – Lysistrata – she insisted was only a joke. Charlie said he was glad because he had a lot of fighting still to do, which prompted Hillary to doubt she had any function left: the German business seemed to have wrapped everything up and Washington had barred her from seeking participation before that. She was expecting a recall any day and was surprised it hadn't already come: it was over a week since she'd sent her complete analysis of how much plutonium 239 there would have been in the lost ten containers and what its bomb-making capability would have been. She'd guessed at twenty-five bombs, possibly twenty-seven of warhead size. Another guess, based largely on previous German interceptions, was that the material could have fetched as much as

$25,000,000. Hillary's withdrawal remark reminded Charlie to ask Rupert Dean to press Washington to let her remain in Moscow. The Director-General guaranteed at once that it wouldn't be a problem, which it didn't turn out to be. And that despite Hillary's warning that the US Head of Chancellery had protested it was unthinkable she move in with him at Lesnaya, which she hadn't made any secret of doing because she hadn't seen why she should. They both agreed that Heads of Chancellery were universal pains in the ass.

Charlie didn't expect the casual reaction from Lyneham and Kestler to Hillary's change of address. Lyneham begrudgingly handed over the money he'd lost betting against the sting acceptance and said he would have moved in with Charlie rather than live in the compound shithole if he'd known rooms were available. Kestler said Charlie was a lucky son-of-a-bitch. Lyneham also said it was the biggest scandal inside the embassy for years and Hillary had balls. He'd had to tell Washington, because she was attached to his Bureau office, but there hadn't been a headquarters protest, which was something else Charlie hadn't expected.

Charlie personally received formal Russian approval two days later from Dmitri Fomin. The presidential aide used the officially presented London proposal as their discussion paper. Apart from Fomin Charlie faced a familiar five; Badim and Panin from their respective ministries, Popov and Gusev and the taller of the two *spetznaz* commanders, whose rank and name finally emerged to be General Nikolai Bykov and whose antipathy to the entire project remained as hostile as it had been to everything else involving Westerners. Fomin did virtually all of the talking and Charlie was curious how many preparatory discussions there had been. Several, he guessed, from Fomin's monologue. He was to attempt nothing without consultation. He would be allowed plain-clothed *spetznaz* protectors and chauffeurs, despite which Russia would not be held responsible for his personal safety in any circumstances whatsoever. Office staff would be supplied by the Militia. Colonel Popov, his already established liaison, would be the conduit through whom he had to work, assisted by Colonel Gusev. No information was to be disseminated in advance of his fully advising either Colonels Popov or Gusev. The entire cost had fully to be borne by London. The experiment would be under permanent review and liable to cancellation, without consultation with him or London, whenever and however Moscow deemed fit. He could not personally be armed.

Charlie had expected constraints every bit as restrictive and would even have been unsure if they hadn't been. The function of every Russian assigned to him would be to spy upon him first and protect him second. The great uncertainty would be if any would be on a Mafia payroll: being appointed from this level made it unlikely, but he'd have to be careful. There was no reference at all to the Pizhma robbery or the Berlin debriefings, which Charlie thought petulant but hardly surprising, even though they had to accept there was little chance now of getting anything more back. And with Fomin clearly in charge, the failure to review the German information with the very person who'd obtained a major proportion of it had to be his decision. Popov remained blank-faced, like everyone else, but at the formal end of the meeting said he was looking forward to resuming their cooperation – the most immediate and important of which was fully to dicuss Germany – and hoped it would be productive. And on a better footing than in the recent past. He considered their disagreements a clash of professionalism and hoped Charlie thought of them that way too. Charlie said he felt exactly the same way and wondered if Popov would relay the conversation to Natalia. Both Popov and the Mililtia commander readily supplied out-of-office contact numbers.

Charlie's first move, the following day, was to ask the now readily available Popov for a foreign car outlet the Militia suspected to be controlled by a major Mafia Family. The two-day delay in Popov's reply gave Charlie time to draw $150,000, in cash, from a bulging-eyed Peter Potter. The dark blue BMW 700 it later took Balg and the Bundeskriminalamt a fortnight to identify, from the engine and chassis number, as having been stolen from the car park at Frankfurt airport, cost Charlie $70,000 from a salesroom on Ugreshskaya that Popov told him was run by the Dolgoprudnaya. The car purchase was his first use of Special Forces bodyguards, both of whom clearly regarded it as an assignment of a lifetime. They insisted on army security, identifying themselves only by their given names and patronymic. Boris Denisovich, the driver, was a dark-haired native-born Georgian with a tattoo on the lobes of both ears and Viktor Ivanovich was blond and raw-boned and smiled a lot, as if he couldn't believe his luck, which he probably couldn't. Remembering his first-thought requirement, Charlie acknowledged that each could have knocked shit out of him, but more importantly out of anyone else. Hillary came with him to buy the car and both Russians openly – although not offensively – appraised her and Hillary played up to it. The Russians, in their turn, performed their part perfectly in the salesroom. Boris expertly examined the car and insisted upon giving everyone a test drive, at one stage at 120 kilometres an hour along the inner ring road with a fitting Mafia disregard to speed limits or the law. Viktor remained tight to Charlie's shoulder when Charlie opened the attaché case in which the dollars were set out in elastic-banded bricks and carelessly tossed the purchase price, without haggling, to the gap-mouthed sales director. Charlie left the case open, with the rest of the money displayed, while he talked of setting himself up in business and possibly needing more cars and took both their cards with the promise to be in touch.

Charlie took an expansive office suite on the third floor of a block on Dubrovskaya – because he was assured by the Moscow Militia's Colonel Gusev the street was in the very heart of Dolgoprudnaya territory – again paying the deposit and six months' rental from his dollar-packed briefcase. He furnished it expensively in Finnish pine and large-leaf potted plants and pre-revolutionary Russian prints and transferred a lot of the embassy booze from Lesnaya to create a bar. He also installed an extensive range of closed-circuit television with freeze-frame and record capacity. The secretary Popov supplied was a dark-haired, doe-eyed girl named Ludmilla Ustenkov. Hillary was at Dubrovskaya when Ludmilla arrived and said if Charlie touched the girl's ass she'd have his and when Charlie looked surprised said she was only playing her part, which she thought she had to do.

That night, more seriously, she said, 'This isn't a game, is it Charlie?'

'No,' he said, matching her solemnity.

'Should I be frightened?'

'Aren't you?'

'Not yet. But I was that night at the club. So I guess I am going to be.'

'I'll keep you out of it. I'll need your help if we get close to anything nuclear, but I won't let you get into any danger.' It was, Charlie knew, a promise he couldn't keep, but he was determined to try as hard as he could.

'You seem to be in an awful hurry.'

'I am,' he admitted. He was ready. It had taken just two weeks.

On the day Charlie moved in to Dubrovskaya the Russian Foreign Ministry issued a formal statement regretting that at least one hundred kilos of weapons-graded nuclear material appeared to have been smuggled out of the country. It was hardly more than confirmation of the speculation that had continued since the German seizure, but it was the first official response and led to fresh media frenzy.

Things went on happening quickly, although not at the level or pace that Charlie really wanted. It began within two days of his advertising himself as an import–export specialist across a range of leading Moscow newspapers and magazines and proved the need for the three additional *spetznaz* the increasingly amicable Popov drafted into the Dubrovskaya office.

The ground-floor surveillance camera caught the three men entering, so Charlie was half prepared when they thrust into the outer office, told Ludmilla they didn't need an appointment and swaggered into where Charlie sat, now waiting. Their spokesman was a small, wiry man with sleeked-back, jet black hair and the swarthy complexion of a southerner, Georgian and Azeri perhaps. The heavies were just that, both hard Slavic-featured, each over two metres tall and thick-bodied and Charlie felt a jump of apprehension even though his three minders who would have already been alerted by Ludmilla were only the press of an alarm button away.

The approach was unadulterated Hollywood, which would have been amusing had Charlie not been sure each of the three would quite happily maim him at least or kill him at worst or do either if they simply felt like it. The small man said he represented an association that welcomed new enterprise to the district and actually used the word 'insurance' when he talked about the essentials of assured business success. With a message of his own to convey, Charlie offered drinks, which they accepted, and had a Macallan himself because he needed it. He personally arranged the chairs in the best position for the cameras and for the added advantage that sitting they would be at an initial disadvantage for what was to follow. Even so he wished the desk was broader when he retreated behind it. He was glad his hand wasn't shaking when he sipped the whisky.

The terms, the wiry man explained, were reasonable and fair. They wanted ten per cent of his turnover – not profit – and would expect regularly to examine all books to make sure there was a sound and proper understanding between them. When Charlie protested that sounded like a takeover the spokesman said the benefits included a guarantee against airport pilfering, loss of consignments and interference by any of the gangs he was sure Charlie had heard about and which made business so difficult in Russia. The smiles faltered when Charlie said he had indeed heard about such gangs and asked, with smiling politeness of his own, which Family they were from. The no-longer-relaxed spokesman hoped there wasn't going to be a difficulty and Charlie hoped so, too: he didn't intend paying protection to anyone for anything and he wanted them not just to understand it themselves but for the people who'd sent them to understand it, as well. He pressed the summons button as he made the announcement, which was fortunate because both the heavies were rising to the smaller man's gesture when the *spetznaz* came into the room.

They did it so quietly and so calmly that they were actually there – led by Viktor Ivanovich – before the extortionists fully realized it. One was trying to draw a handgun from his rear waistband at the same time as coming to his feet when he was kicked fully in the groin and went down retching. His companion made the mistake of going for a weapon, too, so that his arm was inside his jacket when it was seized and expertly yanked sideways and then down over an extended knee. It broke with a snap loud enough to hear. The small man's gun exploded harmlessly into the floor when it was deflected downwards and then heel-handed from his grasp in a chopping blow that broke his wrist and Charlie, dry-throated, managed; 'I want him to take the message back.' The man was howling in pain, holding his shattered wrist, and the soldier who disarmed him slapped open-handed across the man's face until his nose poured blood and his lips split and visibly began to swell before Charlie realized the misunderstanding and stopped the pummelling. The broken-armed man groped again for a gun and at Charlie's nod had his second arm broken, and the commando who'd brought the retching man down stomped on his clenched, outstretched right hand, crushing all the fingers and the hand itself. More kicks broke ribs. Charlie said, 'Enough!' and motioned for all three to be hauled back into the chairs in which he'd originally sat them. He had them searched and all the money they carried displayed in front of them, which he explained was to repair the mess they'd made. Charlie confiscated a knife as well as the handguns. He told the man whose lips were too swollen to respond to tell – when he could – whoever had sent them that any deal was on his terms, not theirs. This had been a lesson; another extortion attempt – any pressure at all – would end in their being hurt far worse. Charlie managed it – just – without his voice cracking, which he was frightened it would. He was still shit scared – literally – his stomach in turmoil. He walked tight-assed ahead of their escort down to the ground level and out into Dubrovskaya and their waiting Mercedes. While two of the *spetznaz* manhandled them into the vehicle – the broken-handed man only just the most able to drive – Viktor Ivanovich used one of the confiscated Markarovs to smash in the light clusters, front and rear, and all the side windows.

Charlie didn't tell Hillary, that night or two nights later when a Jaguar and another Mercedes tried to pincer his BMW into the major traffic island where Gorkiy Street reaches Red Square and which Boris Denisovitch prevented by grinding the BMW even harder into the Jaguar, forcing it on to the pavement near the Lenin library and bringing the Mercedes with them so that it was the Mercedes that smashed into the traffic island. Viktor Ivanovich, beside Charlie in the rear, put three shots from his Walther into the body of the Mercedes, but failed to explode the petrol tank, which was what he tried to do.

They didn't stop, despite the buckled and punctured rear wheel which very quickly stripped its rubber to the bare rim metal and screeched sparks all the way back to the Ugreshskaya salesroom. Charlie bought the replacement BMW, with cash again, the following day, after drawing another $100,000 from the speechless embassy finance officer. Charlie told Hillary the first car had been wrecked in a hit-and-run crash while it was parked off Dubrovskaya. She said she preferred the white colour of the new one, which again from the chassis and engine number the Bundeskriminalamt traced, with some irony, to having been stolen in Berlin from the small car park opposite the Kempinski where Charlie had stayed five weeks earlier.

From the freeze frames from the video, the small, dark-skinned man was identified as an Azeri named Pavel Suntsov, whom Moscow Central Militia listed as a small-time pimp working prostitution and pornography for the Dolgoprudnaya. The two thugs weren't on record.

The identification was provided by Petr Gusev at a progress meeting convened by Popov at the Interior Ministry, which Charlie took an hour to reach using all the surveillance-avoiding tradecraft he'd never imagined having to employ again but which he did, with nostalgia, to arrive convinced he'd lost the two men clumsily obvious outside the Dubrovskaya office. Gusev suggested posting protective Militia close to the building, even though Charlie's office was on the third floor and difficult to reach when the block was closed for the night. Three nights later a Militia street patrol disturbed an attempt to torch the whole building. None of the would-be arsonists was caught. As a further precaution Charlie took a ground-floor apartment at Lesnaya and moved Boris Denisovich and Viktor Ivanovich in permanently. There was no attempt to get into the building but the second BMW, which had to be parked in the street, was burned out. Charlie bought a third, stolen like the other two, at what he considered a bargain at $50,000. He referred Gerald Williams' appalled protest to the Director-General.

A week later a uniformed man who identified himself as the lieutenant in charge of the Militia post responsible for keeping law and order in the area arrived at Dubrovskaya with two street patrolmen and said he hoped Charlie was satisfied with the service he was receiving. They drank Macallan again and after half an hour Charlie agreed to a weekly $400 which the lieutenant said he would collect personally, every Friday, which he did. A tight-lipped and flushed Petr Gusev named the officer from the freeze frame as Nikolai Ranov, whom he'd considered honest and whom he'd considered promoting.

Charlie sent a short list of questions with the freeze-frame copies to Berlin, through Balg, and within days got back more than he'd bargained for from Gunther Schumann. Four of the six seized plutonium containers had been empty when checked by German scientists and the markings weren't consecutive with the stolen Pizhma batch numbers. Fedor Mitrov couldn't – or wouldn't – explain it. It did nothing to diminish the case against the arrested Russians, whose trial was being fixed for November. The formal witnesses list hadn't been prepared yet but it was a foregone conclusion he would be called, which Charlie accepted as his deadline: he wouldn't be able to run his phoney set-up after his court identification.

Mitrov named all the men in Charlie's photographs. Suntsov had graduated from pimp to corps leader and the Dolgoprudnaya regarded Lieutenant Ranov as one of the best and most reliable Militia officers on their payroll. The Dolgoprudnaya owned the Ugreshnaya garage. Schumann's message ended with the assurance that he'd kept Silin's assassination from the Russians, as Charlie had suggested before leaving Berlin, but asking again what the point was. Charlie said he hoped it might fit in with something he was investigating in Moscow, although he didn't tell the German what he'd learned from what he'd got from Natalia after his return from interrogating the arrested Russians, because he still didn't understand the significance himself.

By coincidence, the same day, several Moscow newspapers reported the shotgun murder by the river of a known Moscow gangster named Petr Gavrilovich Malin. Every account said the Militia considered him the victim of a gangland feud. Gusev provided what he said was the full file on the killing of the man whom Mitrov had identified as the successful courier of the lost ten containers. Gusev did so with the warning that upon Dmitri Fomin's orders, the dead man was not going to be connected with the Pizhma robbery in any public statement. As far as they were concerned the killing *was* a gangland dispute and would not be solved, like such disputes never were: they wanted nothing official to reignite the publicity over the Pizhma theft. Through Balg again, Charlie relayed it all to Berlin, but again suggested Schumann keep it from the nuclear smugglers and was glad he did after his next conversation with Natalia.

The advertisements produced more than sufficient business to occupy the now permanently guarded Ludmilla Ustenkov. Charlie accepted what he hoped was questionable and rejected those that were clearly honest, which only amounted to about six enquiries. With London the supplier and buyer, he traded cut-price IBM computers, German refrigerators, five Jaguar and Rover cars and Russian icons, triptychs and a case of semi-precious stones which, upon analysis, weren't even semi-precious: to fuel the legend he wanted to create Charlie told Viktor Ivanovich to rough the con man up if he tried to repeat the scam, which the man did. Charlie hadn't intended the man's nose to be broken. Or that he be forced to eat some of the worthless glass, either, which ripped his bowel when he passed it. Charlie actually made a profit – his only one – importing supposedly stolen computer chips to update American and German hardware, but a second consignment of computers was intercepted at Sheremet'yevo and all their screens smashed before Charlie got to the airport to collect them. That Friday Charlie served a second whisky to Ranov when the Militia officer arrived for his $400 and complained that no one benefited from the sort of skirmishes that had ruined his computer shipment. A lot of money – money that could improve the sort of retainers that Ranov was getting, for instance – could be made if instead of resenting his independence, people traded with him. He only wished he could get the message through to them. Ranov thought it was wastefully counter-productive, too, and wished there was something he could do to help.

Charlie strictly limited his visits to the British embassy and took even more avoidance care moving through Moscow's metro system, sure he detected special interest around the Dubrovskaya office and once close to Lesnaya. Always awaiting him at Marisa Toreza were fresh demands for expenditure explanations from Gerald Williams, which settled into little more than the man placing on record against any future enquiry his efforts to impose the financial control always overruled by the Director-General. Towards the end of the second month, Charlie was showing an operating loss of $500,000.

Hillary was frightened by the destruction of the second BMW and at first titillated by the need always to have bodyguards, but a lot of the time she was bored.

She kept Lesnaya immaculate and by the end of their second week together had started turning it into a home, with flowers and prints and books and a music selection rather than the sort of rain-sheltering resting place to which Charlie was accustomed. He liked it. She was a superb cook and Charlie complained of putting on weight, which she promised to get off by her own particular exercise, which she practised every night with even more exciting improvisation than she showed in the kitchen. Charlie liked that, too. After specific warnings of how careful they had to be arriving and leaving, Charlie risked inviting to dinner Lyneham and his wife and Kestler with one of his embassy harem, which turned out very successfully, so they repeated it over succeeding weeks. On the first occasion, while the women gossiped and helped in the kitchen, Lyneham said the way things were going Charlie stood a real chance of being blown away and asked how much longer he intended standing with the target on his chest.

The vicarious novelty of always having bodyguards palled for both of them, although Hillary accepted the need, particularly when they flashily toured the clubs, which Charlie felt necessary every week. On their first visit under protection to the Up and Down they saw the group who had demanded Hillary join them and Charlie reversed the invitation, which was accepted. They sat for an hour with the respective guards posturing Rambo body language while Charlie ordered Roederer Crystal and exaggerated his business success to the hirsute bear of a man, pressing cards upon the Russian with the assurance that there was nothing in which he couldn't, or wouldn't, trade. Hillary complained on the way back to Lesnaya that her face ached from keeping an idiot, non-comprehending smile in place. And that the hairy man gave her the creeps.

During one of Lyneham's visits, almost into the second month, Hillary abruptly asked the Bureau chief to find out from Washington how much longer she was expected to stay in Moscow, apologizing afterwards to Charlie for not mentioning it to him first, but saying it was a spur of the moment question. When the reply came that there were no withdrawal plans, Charlie said he'd understand if she wanted to move back to the protection of the embassy. Hillary kissed him and said that wasn't the reason at all and if she had to stay in Moscow, Lesnaya was where she wanted to be and Charlie was surprised how pleased it made him feel.

Charlie had anticipated most of what had happened after the advertisements, although not perhaps the degree of violence. What he hadn't anticipated was the open cooperation shown by Popov and Gusev. Over the course of several meetings at the Ministry, Charlie took both of them through the Berlin examination and at the end of the first month Popov announced both he and Gusev were going to the trial as observers if they weren't called as witnesses. At Popov's invitation they lunched in a private room in a discreet tavern up in the Lenin Hills and Gusev spent a lot of time discussing the Militia shake-down, producing personnel files not just of Nikolai Ranov but of the patrolmen involved, each of whom he promised to jail when the Dubrovskaya operation wound up. The bloody internal war among its six Families for supreme control of the Dolgoprudnaya was a constant subject of conversation: the death toll, after two months, was ten. It was at the lunch when Gusev produced that total that Popov made the obvious reference to the Lesnaya apartment, which Charlie let pass, imagining he'd misunderstood. He knew he hadn't when Popov repeated even more pointedly his admiration of pre-revolutionary architecture, not enough of which remained to be enjoyed. He would, responded Charlie, very much like to host a dinner party. Popov, at once, said he would be very happy to accept.

Natalia's contacts were intermittent, although always prearranged from the call that preceded it so Charlie could guarantee to be at Lesnaya. Apart from the Dolgoprudnaya request he had little professional to talk about so the conversation mostly revolved around Sasha. The continued protection was unsettling her; she'd started to wet the bed and was often sullen and rude. There hadn't been any more threats and Aleksai was convinced – like the official security division – that it had been nothing more than a nuisance call from someone connected with Shelapin: there'd been a decision to harass the Family to the point of bringing Shelapin in for questioning on several occasions. She'd discussed resigning with Aleksai, who'd said it had to be her decision. She'd finally agreed to marry him, although no date had been fixed. Aleksai had agreed to it being in a church. Charlie lied that he hoped they would be happy.

Hillary prepared for the Russian dinner party with her usual enthusiasm, deciding upon all-American pot-roast with pumpkin pie for dessert as a meal that would be different for them, relieved when Charlie told her that Gusev spoke English almost as well as Popov. She said, coquettishly, that she was looking forward to seeing Popov again: that day at the Arbat she'd thought he was as sexy as hell.

Charlie hadn't installed closed-circuit television at Lesnaya but the apartment bell was duplicated on the ground floor for Viktor Ivanovich to vet arrivals and Charlie had learned to time to the second how long it took people to climb the ornate and gilded stairway. Popov had just reached the outside landing when Charlie expectantly opened the door.

Petr Gusev wasn't with him. Natalia was.

It took John Fenby a long time to acknowledge he wouldn't quickly be able to keep the personal promise to even the score with the British Director-General. He didn't know how or when and accepted it probably wouldn't now involve Moscow – in fact Moscow was still so uncertain it was probably best if his retribution wasn't connected with Russia at all – but sometime in the future he'd get his chance to screw Rupert Dean and the British service and when he did the Limey bastard was really going to know he'd been screwed. All it needed was patience. Much better, in fact, than hurrying it. This way he could savour it.

It didn't mean, of course, that he was going to sit back and be dictated to. He was readily prepared to go along with the

British insistence that the woman stay in Moscow, although there seemed little point now that they were sure half of the plutonium had been lost. Fenby was quite happy for Hillary Jamieson to be as far away from Pennsylvania Avenue as possible and had already asked his scientific director to headhunt for someone to replace her, even if the qualifications had to drop. Shacking up with the Englishman like the slut had done gave him cast-iron grounds for her dismissal.

Fenby's preoccupation, as always, was with Kestler and Milton Fitzjohn and Fenby knew he had that all neatly wrapped up.

With his customary attention to detail, Fenby flew personally to Wiesbaden and then to Bonn after several fax and telephone exchanges preparing the way, to promise every FBI assistance at the trial of the nuclear smugglers, delighted how well it all fitted in when he learned how internationally high-profile the Germans intended to make it. Fenby's strongest guarantee was that James Kestler would publicly appear to present all the American satellite evidence, which he was confident would provide one of the sensational highlights of the hearing.

After which he planned to bring Kestler home in the glory the publicity would achieve and in which the grateful Milton Fitzjohn would be delighted. He hadn't decided whether to keep the kid at headquarters or to offer him one of the top-drawer embassy postings like London or Paris.

chapter 32

Charlie was as disoriented as Natalia had been realizing where she was when she had arrived downstairs, but she'd recovered by the time she reached the outside landing. Charlie was glad of its half light but wasn't concerned at some visible surprise that Popov wasn't accompanied by Petr Gusev. To reinforce the point he said so as he greeted them and used the word surprise at the same time as saying he was delighted to see her, which he was, although he needed to think a lot more about the circumstances before he was sure about that.

Natalia's second uncertainty was to be welcomed directly inside the apartment by Hillary Jamieson. The American girl had also expected another man and there was momentary, first-meeting hesitancy which Charlie thought easily overcame any outward difficulty.

Inwardly there were a lot of conflicting feelings trying to get to the forefront of Charlie's mind. Anger was chief among them, which he refused, because at that stage he wasn't sure he had anything to be angry about and in any case anger never helped rational thinking. So what was it rational to think? Viewed in an objectively straight line, Aleksai Semenovich Popov had accepted a social invitation for himself and the woman he was shortly to marry, not on behalf of himself and a Militia colonel. Which was perfectly reasonable – the only misconception his – and even maintained a perhaps necessary element of business because until very recently Natalia had been part of the nuclear investigation and still headed the specific anti-smuggling division. But was it as simplistic as that? Popov knew he'd gone to Leninskaya soon after he'd arrived. And that he'd been to Moscow before and that Natalia had debriefed him. But to have been as adamant as Natalia was that the man was unaware of their personal relationship meant what old KGB records survived were sterilized of any such suggestions. Which he already knew anyway, for Natalia to hold the rank and position she did. What was left then? A professional episode in the long-distant past which could conceivably explain his going to Leninskaya like he had? As wrong to cloud his reasoning by over-interpretation as it would have been to allow obscuring anger. For the moment he had to follow the straight line. Which didn't mean, of course, he shouldn't be on the lookout for unexpected curves. But then he always was.

Unwittingly Hillary, the perfect hostess, smoothly covered the immediate arrival, seating Popov and Natalia together on the high-backed, siderope-tethered couch and offering canapés while Charlie poured champagne for everyone except himself, remaining with his preferred whisky. The apartment was the obvious and immediate subject of conversation, which Hillary responded to as openly as she did with everything else and invited them to look around: her and Charlie's evidently shared bedroom was the last on the escorted tour. There was no cause for Charlie to feel uncomfortable, but he did. Natalia was quite controlled by then, smilingly attentively to the other woman although paying little attention to him, which wasn't Charlie's immediate disappointment. Hillary had the advantage of youth by maybe ten years – for the first time Charlie realized he didn't know how old she was – and although she hadn't dressed as exuberantly as she sometimes did for their club visits the silk moulded to her Greek goddess figure and stopped short enough to exhibit the forever legs and Charlie thought Natalia suffered by the side-by-side proximity and suspected Natalia thought so too. Natalia's dress was silk as well, although a subdued black against Hillary's crimson, but cut more comfortably and longer. The blackness drained what little colour there was from her face and she hadn't hidden the worry lines around her eyes and lips, and she'd pinned the chignon carelessly and stray hair was already escaping.

And Natalia wasn't just suffering from the physical contrast. In an austere but superbly tailored and waistcoated black suit and muted tie, Popov was more than ever a Romanov look-alike and was flirting extravagantly with the receptively flattered Hillary. It actually created a brief divide, separating Popov with Hillary and Charlie with Natalia, and provided a further comparison between the laughing banter against artificially subdued conversation. Natalia looked directly at him when she said he seemed to be settling in very comfortably after he agreed he had been extremely lucky to get the Lesnaya apartment. Charlie presumed Sasha would be at the crèche, under Militia protection, but Popov was too close for him openly to ask, even though the Russian appeared totally engrossed in some hand-waving anecdote of Hillary's. Remembering Natalia's concern during every conversation, particularly about the bed-wetting, Charlie was still surprised Natalia had left her.

Dinner began on the same facile social level, with Popov taking Hillary through the first-time-in-Moscow, how-do-you-like-it routine and smiling quizzically at Hillary's reply that it was interesting. Then, abruptly and still smiling, he turned to Charlie and said, 'But you, of course, were here before?'

'A long time ago,' replied Charlie, easily and at once. A curve in the line or something else he should try to consider rationally? Popov knew what he'd been, like everyone else. There hadn't been occasion to talk of it before – even at their now relaxed lunches – and it wasn't indiscreet now, because Hillary was officially FBI.

'What's your feeling, having known it then?'

'It's trying to develop too fast, without enough control.'

'Crime, you mean?'

'Not entirely. But mostly, yes.'

'There was as much crime in the old days. It just wasn't

obvious. And the government were involved up to their necks.'

'Like they are now?' demanded Charlie. If Popov wanted an open discussion, it was all right by him. He even welcomed it.

'Like too many of them are now, yes. Which is our problem. But we'll win. Not at once and not easily, but in the end we'll get control. Which is all any law enforcement organization in the West has ever tried to do, get some sort of control. No one's ever going to eradicate crime.'

Charlie didn't try to extend it and Popov didn't go on, instead trying to lighten the conversation by telling Hillary that the lack of fashion was an even greater problem in Moscow than crime, which Charlie thought was unfortunate in view of the difference between how Natalia and Hillary were dressed. It was only when the American tried to match the lightness with a comment about her protective suit that Natalia appeared to realize Popov had already met Hillary and knew who she was and Charlie, setting out on another objective straight line, encouraged Hillary to talk about it. Charlie was glad he hadn't told her about four of the canisters recovered in Germany being empty. He hadn't told Lyneham or Kestler, either. Or Natalia.

'You make the carelessness – and the experimentation – sound criminal?' suggested Natalia.

'I believe it was. And is,' agreed the American.

'But you're not solely accusing Russia?' clarified Popov.

'I'm accusing every nuclear nation.'

Charlie began to relax, content to let the discussion go on without him. He really wished he knew about Sasha.

'But we're the careless nation of the moment,' Popov was saying.

'That's not an accusation,' Hillary pointed out. 'It's a fact. Why we're all here.' She smiled. 'Although quite frankly I don't understand why I'm still here: what I came for is all wrapped up now, isn't it?'

'It will be, with the trial in Germany.'

'Which Aleksai will have to attend to give evidence,' said Natalia, proudly Charlie thought.

He would have preferred to wait longer but the cue was too good. 'London is beginning to question the cost of the entrapment idea.'

'So soon!' frowned Popov.

'They've become accustomed to things happening quickly,' said Charlie.

'That's no criteria,' dismissed Natalia. 'Although I don't think the risks justify the outside chance of your learning anything worthwhile.'

Charlie wondered if Popov had told Natalia of the attempted intimidation and got his answer when Hillary said, 'There's a lot of big guys on our side but it's costing a lot in cars.'

Natalia looked to each of them, finally to Charlie and said, 'What happened?'

'A car got burned out, that's all. It was inevitable.'

Popov said, 'There's a lot of protection in place now.'

The remark obviously connected with Sasha in Natalia's mind. 'For how long?'

'As long as is necessary,' said Popov. 'Or until London – or indeed Fomin or someone at his level – decides it's a waste of time.'

'Is that how you regard it?' demanded Charlie.

'What you've got so far is pretty low-level,' said Popov. There had been positive criminal identification from the surveillance camera pictures of the men who had imported the computer chips and the cars: a Jaguar had actually gone to the Ugreshskaya salesroom from which Charlie had bought the BMWs.

'This is becoming a serious party and parties aren't supposed to be serious!' protested Hillary, with sudden brightness.

'And we do have something to celebrate,' announced Popov.

'What?' demanded Hillary.

'Natalia and I are getting married.'

The ebullient Hillary whooped and clapped and actually kissed Natalia on the cheek and demanded Charlie open more champagne, which he did and forced a token sip despite his dislike of the acidity. Hillary insisted upon a toast, which Charlie gave, and he congratulated Popov. Natalia looked at him fully again when he congratulated her and smiled and thanked him. Hillary occupied the remainder of the meal and during coffee afterwards, peppering Natalia with preparation questions, to which Popov smiled indulgently and Charlie half listened. He heard Natalia say she hoped to retire after the wedding and Popov said his ambition now was to get an apartment like Charlie's. Just before they left Popov said perhaps Charlie and Hillary would come to the wedding when the plans were finalized and Hillary said they had their first acceptance if she was still in Moscow.

'Isn't that terrific!' Hillary enthused, after Popov and Natalia left.

'Terrific.'

'You didn't mind me accepting for us, did you?'

'No,' he lied.

'You know something odd?'

'What?'

'Natalia reminded me of the photograph that was here that first night I came back, after that business at the club.'

'My sister,' reminded Charlie, repeating the lie he'd made up at the time. 'I suppose there's a resemblance.'

'I haven't seen it around, incidentally. Or the one of the baby. There only seems to be the one of Edith now.'

'They must be here somewhere,' said Charlie, who'd put both in his embassy safe the day before Hillary had moved in, confident after his return from London that Bowyer wouldn't intrude. He'd told Hillary that Edith had died, but not how or why.

'Popov *is* as sexy as hell! I think Natalia's a lucky girl, don't you?'

'Very,' agreed Charlie.

'Hey!' said Hillary, misunderstanding his shortness. 'I didn't say he was my type! No need to get jealous!'

'I'm not,' denied Charlie.

Natalia was furious. They'd hardly spoken during the ride home and now she lay stiffly in the darkness, her body not touching his. She was glad of her cycle because she didn't want to make love.

'With Sasha at the crèche we could have gone back to my place: it's nearer,' Popov said.

'This is the number they've got.'

There was a long silence. Finally he said, 'What's the matter?'

'Why didn't you tell me where we were going! And why announce the wedding like that? And then invite them!'

'I wanted it to be a surprise. And why shouldn't I have told them we were getting married? I want everyone to know!'

'It was of no interest to them.'

'Hillary seemed excited.'

'She's that sort of girl.'

There was another silence, which Popov broke again. 'Odd, how this business has brought them together.'

'What's odd about it? She's a beautiful girl. He's amusing.'

'He wasn't particularly amusing tonight.'

'It would have been difficult, the way you took the evening over.'

'One of us had to.'

'What else has happened, apart from firing his car?'

'There was an extortion attempt. And another car was rammed.'

'Why didn't you tell me?'

She felt him shrug in the darkness. 'It was nothing we didn't expect. He's got *spetznaz* people looking after him: that's who checked us tonight when we arrived.'

'But he's under threat.'

'I suppose so.'

'Then I don't want him at the wedding. Sasha will be there. There could be a risk.'

'We've invited them now.'

'*You* invited them, I didn't. I don't want them!'

'Tonight wasn't a good idea, was it?'

'No.'

'I'm sorry. I'd apologized to him for the problems in the operation and we've seen a lot of each other and I thought it was an idea to get things on a friendly footing. I was wrong in not telling you where we were going and I'm sorry about that, too.'

'How long will you be in Germany?'

'I've no idea. Quite a while maybe.'

'I don't want the protection taken away from Sasha until you get back.'

'It was a nuisance threat, nothing more.'

'Not until you get back,' she insisted. 'And maybe not even then.'

Two days later, which wasn't a Friday, Lieutenant Ranov came smiling into Charlie's Dubrovskaya office and their conversation occupied most of the afternoon and settled some of Charlie's outstanding questions as well as raising more. It also made him angry at things he'd missed. It meant he was late getting back to Lesnaya. Hillary said, 'You've just missed Natalia. She called to thank us for the other night. Aleksai sent his regards.'

It wasn't arranged for Natalia to call him until the following day, so it had to have been social politeness. He wondered what it would be like when they did talk.

chapter 33

From the beginning Charlie had accepted the primary function of his two *spetznaz* minders was to ensure he worked within the operational strait-jacket imposed by Dmitri Fomin rather than to provide him with physical protection, just as Ludmilla Ustenkov doubtless monitored everything he did at Dubrovskaya even more effectively than Thomas Bowyer had watched over him at the British embassy. The only time Charlie couldn't be constantly accompanied was when he went either to the British or American legations, which he used as the excuse to move unobserved the day after Nikolai Ranov's surprise approach at Dubrovskaya. Charlie did so acknowledging he was taking the biggest chance yet in a situation already too dangerous and that if he'd miscalulated by a single jot – like he'd for too long miscalculated by a lot more – then he was dead. Maybe literally. He'd taken every precaution he could during the previous day's conversation with Ranov to ensure he wasn't shuffling blindly into a lesson-teaching reprisal for refusing the extortion, putting everything he'd learned from Gusev about the internal upheaval in the Dolgoprudnaya Family against what the crooked Militia lieutenant told him. And still felt like he was crossing a splintering plank stretched over a snake-pit.

He actually did go to the British embassy, ducking and diving from the metro to trolley and back to the metro again, and there was a message waiting for him from London. To the confirmation of his being officially called as a witness at the Berlin trial, Rupert Dean added that it would obviously mark the formal ending of Charlie's entrapment attempt.

Dean questioned whether it was necessary for Charlie to go to Berlin so early to review his participation in the debriefing of the Russians and Charlie said the request was all part of the German fanaticism for detail: the attempted sting didn't seem to be working anyway. The trial date gave Charlie just over a month. Everything depended on the chance he was taking and the man he was supposedly meeting and of his not making just one mistake. His talisman feet had every justification for throbbing like they did, quite apart from all the scurrying to avoid anyone discovering where he was going.

He gave himself a full hour and worked even harder at the evasion when he left Morisa Toreza. As he finally went up towards the Bolshoi square he saw that the traffic island flattened by the attacking Mercedes still hadn't been repaired, twisted metal and glass and bollards just roped off and lying where they'd fallen. He was still early at the Metropole, so he allowed himself a steadying drink before taking the elevator to the third floor and the room stipulated the previous day by Nikolai Ranov.

It was the smiling Militia lieutenant, sports-jacketed and open-collared, who answered the door and gestured for Charlie to enter, and as he did Charlie thought these room arrival shocks really had to stop. Relaxed in an armchair in a room furnished in Odeon-cinema style was the man who'd demanded Hillary's company at the Up and Down and whom Charlie had taunted there with a reciprocal invitation a month earlier. Charlie was reassured that the man was smiling, too, although it could, he supposed, have been in triumph.

'Sobelov. Sergei Petrovich,' introduced the man. He flicked between his fingers the card Charlie had forced upon him and said; 'I know who you are. And you came without your people.'

Which might just have been that miscalculation of his life, accepted Charlie, because Sobelov's usual companions were both at a window seat, hunched like Dobermans waiting for the attack signal. Nodding to the lieutenant, Charlie said, 'I was asked to come alone.'

'I wanted a gesture of trust.' The Russian swept an inviting hand towards a chair arranged to face him and said, 'Please.' There was a selection of bottles and glasses on the table between them.

'But you're not alone.'

'I wanted my proof first.' The man leaned forward to pour unasked and said, 'Macallan's, isn't it? Or would you prefer Roederer?'

'Whisky's fine.' It wasn't a lesson-teaching, Charlie decided: not a violent one, at least. That would have been in a back alley, at night, after getting him alone, not in the grandest hotel in Moscow in broad daylight. He started to relax. Again indicating Ranov – who had gone to sit respectfully with the two protectors – Charlie said, 'I was also told there was a special business proposition?'

The condescension went from Sobelov, with the smile. 'Eight canisters. Something in the region of eighty kilos.'

Charlie cupped his glass in both hands and sipped his drink, not hurrying to reply, his mind in total confusion. Part of the Pizhma haul? Or another robbery, to learn of which was why he'd set himself up in business. The volume of plutonium was about right, but the rest of the equation didn't make sense. But then neither did the four empty containers in Berlin. Different batch numbers, he remembered. That didn't make sense, either. 'Is this from the robbery there's been all the publicity about?'

'Yes.'

Excitement surged through Charlie. He didn't understand why the figures didn't add up or anything about empty containers in Berlin. Only that about eighty kilos they thought had gone – enough to make God knows how many bombs – was after all still in Russia, not in the hands of some madman or fanatical regime. He'd never been so glad in his life to be as wrong as he had been about it already having been smuggled out of the country. Cautiously, seeking time, Charlie said, 'Eight canisters – eighty kilos – is a lot.'

'And worth a lot of money.'

'What would you expect?'

'You're the broker.'

'Twenty million. Maybe as high as twenty-two,' said Charlie, relying on Hillary's valuation of ten containers.

'I want $25,000,000,' demanded the Russian.

'I could try.' The recovery was the essential, not the money. Which would never be paid anyway, although a proportion might have to be put up, for bait. Lost even.

'You can guarantee a purchaser?'

'It will need some negotiation. But yes, I can.' This was wrong, Charlie told himself: against all his own arguments that a robbery as brilliant as Pizhma came *after*, not *before* a buyer had been established and a price fixed. As wrong as figures that didn't add up when they knew exactly how much had been taken at Pizhma and empty containers and wrong batch numbers and . . . No it wasn't, Charlie abruptly corrected himself. It wasn't wrong at all. What had been wrong was his myopically believing the internal battle for ultimate control of the six-clan Dolgoprudnaya Family had begun after the murder of Stanislav Silin. He'd virtually had it spelled out for him by Gusev and not put it in context. And then he remembered a laugh and a word – *akrashena* – which he'd always known was important without properly realizing just how important. Charlie smiled and said, 'I think I should have offered congratulations before now.'

Sobelov regarded him warily. 'For what?'

'It's been a bloody battle. At least ten people killed if I've correctly interpreted newspaper stories.'

The Russian's wariness remained. 'That would show a most unusual business interest on your part.'

'Isn't the reason I'm sitting here, having this conversation, that I've already shown how seriously I regard business?' said Charlie, easily.

The smile returned. 'Which is how I expect you to conduct this business transaction: very seriously indeed. In the hope that it may be the first of many.'

'I hope there aren't any hard feelings about the confrontation with people asking me to take out operating insurance?'

Sobelov flicked an impatient hand, still holding Charlie's

business card. 'None. And thank you, for your congratulations. I'm pleased at the outcome.'

Not as pleased as he was, Charlie thought, as he left the Metropole an hour later with the arrangement to use Ranov as his conduit to the new Dolgroprudnaya boss of bosses. It took a lot to suppress the euphoria but he managed it, zigzagging a circuitous route to Ulitza Chaykovskovo. At the American embassy he was greeted by an equally excited James Kestler with the news that he was going to be the major prosecution witness at the Berlin trial and after that return to Washington for reassignment. Charlie offered congratulations for the second time that day and said he was going to Berlin as well and at once the enthusiastic Kestler began planning celebrations in Germany. They contented themselves that day with a single drink in the embassy mess, because Charlie was anxious to be back in Lesnaya for Natalia's arranged call. She flustered immediately into apologies for the dinner party. It had been something else Popov hadn't told her, until the very moment of their arrival. They'd argued about it, particularly about the wedding invitation. She didn't want him to come and Charlie said he didn't want to, either. It wouldn't be a problem. She said she thought Hillary was a very pretty girl: vivacious was the word she used. Charlie said she was a free spirit and that it wasn't serious and Natalia said she was sorry. When he told her, in Russian because Hillary was with him in the room, that he was going to Berlin but before that to be briefed in London – which was the explanation he'd given the Americans for his intended absence – Natalia said Popov had received an official summons, too. Charlie wasn't surprised when Hillary received her Berlin summons the following day because he'd pressed Balg for it to be issued, to give her the freedom of movement he wanted.

Charlie did fly to London but only to satisfy any Moscow exit check and only long enough to cross from the arrival to the departure section of Terminal 2, pausing on the way to telephone Gunther Schumann who was again at Tegel airport to meet him. The German conceded at once that he'd promised his superiors too much predicting they could break up the Dolgoprudnaya cell in Berlin – as Mitrov had sneered, the Marzahn address had been empty when they'd raided it – but that the forthcoming trial would more than compensate. And then he listened without interruption to what Charlie recounted before saying, 'We *have* got the prints! Of all of them. But we didn't make the comparison! So we just can't lose!'

'Providing they match,' cautioned Charlie.

They did.

Again Charlie had come with a lot of confidence-shattering evidence – although he'd only just got the most shattering of all – and although he knew he could direct it more accurately than before there was no stage-set theatricals this time, just the bare and windowless interview room with its sparse essential furniture. The only addition was an extra tape recorder.

There was an eyebrow lift at Charlie's presence when Ivan Mikhailovich Raina was escorted in but no other reaction. Charlie said, 'You did very well: almost beat us. The others supported you well, too. I thought they'd totally collapsed but they hadn't, had they? You must frighten them a lot.'

Raina frowned. 'I don't know what the hell you're talking about.'

'Your faction lost,' declared Charlie. 'There's been a lot of killing but Sobelov won.'

There was a brief narrowing of the eyes but that was all. 'You're still not making sense.'

'Let's look at some more photographs,' invited Charlie, opening the prepared package. 'This is the one that will interest you most . . .' He set out first the autopsy prints of the naked Stanislav Silin. 'He was obscenely tortured for a very long time: I'd guess the testicle crushing was the worst but you can see they pulled his teeth out, with pliers I'd guess. And the pathologist says he was blinded long before he died, probably with whatever the heated rod was that inflicted all those burns . . . And look what they did to his wife.' The pictures of Malin were also from the autopsy. 'See what they did to Petr Gavrilovich? They blinded him, too, but I don't suppose he had the name they wanted. To almost separate the two parts of his body like that the pathologist thinks they actually held the shotgun against his stomach and fired both barrels simultaneously: the skin is burned all around the wound . . .'

Raina had gone putty grey and his throat was moving where he kept swallowing and Charlie hoped he'd be able to get out of the way if the man actually vomited.

'. . . This one really affects you,' Charlie went on, sliding across the table the German photographs of the empty nuclear cylinders: in several, scientists were actually shown to be groping inside. 'Those are the ones you brought out. Which were completely empty and clean, otherwise those unprotected physicists wouldn't be feeling around inside like that. I don't know how the switch was made, any more than you do, but it was. I guess we'll establish Sobelov was at Pizhma from the physical comparison against the satellite prints: that's where it would have been done, at Pizhma.'

'None of this means anything to me,' rasped Raina, dry-throated.

'Yes it does,' insisted Charlie. 'It means that Sobelov had you carry into Germany canisters that would have been empty when they eventually got to the Middle East or wherever else you were selling them. Which would have been your death warrant . . .' He flicked across another photograph, of the emasculated con man found months before on the Wannsee Lake. '. . . They always kill people who try to con them, like they killed and mutilated him.'

Raina sat shaking his head but not talking and Charlie wondered if he should have been more direct. Still better to frighten the man, he decided. 'Listen!' Charlie ordered, pressing the play button on the second pre-set recorder. Mitrov's reference to *akrashena* echoed into the room. At once Charlie stopped and rewound it but before repeating it he said, 'This time don't listen to the word: listen to the laugh. Your laugh, Ivan Mikhailovich. Your laugh because you thought the joke was funny and you wouldn't have thought that unless you were part of the inner planning group and knew *akrashena* didn't mean wet paint. And you were very much part of the inner planning group weren't you . . . ?' Charlie groped unnecessarily for the Dolgoprudnaya list Natalia had supplied and which, until the tests that had been completed an hour earlier, Raina could have rebutted. Exaggerating, Charlie went on, '. . . But not in Moscow: you're not on this list and it names every member of the Dolgoprudnaya ruling Commission . . .' Break, you bastard, thought Charlie: he was dry-throated himself now from talking so long but he ignored the water carafe, not wanting the Russian to infer desperation when there wasn't any. '. . . There's no record of Mitrov, either. And he's a corps leader. Or of Dedov or Federov or Okulov. I know they're just street people but there are a lot of street people here, as well. And you know why?'

'Because there's no such thing as a Militia Records system and that list is a load of crap, probably something you made up yourself,' answered Raina, proving his knowledge of Militia inefficiency and lack of criminal intelligence.

Better, thought Charlie. He wanted Raina defiant. That way he'd drop further and more quickly when the trapdoor was sprung. 'No,' he said, positively. 'It's because none of you are part of Dolgoprudnaya in Moscow. You're the group here, arranging all the deals. One of the most important links in the nuclear trade: *the* most important, as the Dolgroprudnaya are the biggest Russian Family. But which you didn't want to come out because that'll greatly influence the trial judges here, won't it? And you and Mitrov aren't shown to have killed anyone on the satellite film, are you?'

The putty look had gone and Raina had recovered from the shock of the murder photographs, the defiance growing. 'You're talking crap and you know it. I don't know what you're trying to achieve – I hardly understand a word you're saying – but I can't help you any more than I have.'

Charlie sniggered a self-deprecatory laugh. 'There are so many wrong turns and outright mistakes in an investigation, until finally things slot into place. Like us spending all the first morning of his questioning playing the interrogation of you and the other three back to Mitrov, imagining it would bring an early confession – and then imagining that it *did*! – when what we were really doing was rehearsing him for what he had to say . . .' Charlie poured himself some water at last, staging the interruption now. 'And he was good: bloody good. But he made just one mistake and it's turned out worse than ours. But then it wasn't his fault entirely because he'd heard you name Marzahn as a district where the Dolgoprudnaya lived, so all he really did was pick up your bluff by naming KulmseeStrasse and the number and jeering that there wouldn't be anyone there, which he knew like you knew that there wouldn't be . . .' Charlie extended his hand towards the Russian, his forefinger narrowed against his thumb. 'And you came *that* close to getting away with it. The Germans took the place apart, did every forensic test there is, and collected enough fingerprints to fill a book. But no one thought of comparing them to yours or the others they already had in custody.' He shook his head. 'Like I said, there are so many mistakes that get made. We've corrected it, of course. Today. We've matched so many prints, of each of you to KulmseeStrasse – which Mitrov's on record as identifying as the Dolgoprudnaya house – that the forensic technicians are complaining of overwork!'

'Can I have some water, please,' said Raina.

Once it started the confession flowed freely, like confessions usually do, and Charlie sat back for Schumann to take over, needing the respite and because it was a very necessary part of what would now become an even more extended and sensational trial and it would be necessary for the court evidence to be presented by a German investigator. He listened and dissected every word, though. Raina confirmed that he headed the Berlin cell and that he had been the link between the purchasers and the Dolgoprudnaya supply, not just on this failed occasion but five times before. Pizhma had been by far the greatest – he doubted the total amount of all the five previous shipments came anywhere close to two hundred and fifty kilos – and had been by far the most complicated. He didn't know the details or the identities – a strict division was always maintained between Stanislav Silin organizing the supplies and his responsibility for their sale – but there'd been a lot of official help with the understanding of it continuing in the future. The dispute between Silin and Sergei Sobelov for supreme control of the Family had been going on for months, which was why Pizhma had been so important. Silin saw it as the way of proving to the six clans his right to be boss of bosses and fight off Sobelov's challenge. Raina had thought it would confirm Silin's position, too, which was why he'd remained loyal. It took a lot of pressure from the German to learn who the previous five purchasers had been, because Raina protested the names would obviously be false, although the government-issued passports would have been genuine because only governments could afford the money involved – a total, for the five earlier transactions, of $45,000,000. Schumann switched his demands and got the countries – two consignments to Iran, two to Iraq and one to Algeria – before eventually getting the names of the men with whom Raina had negotiated. Charlie re-entered the interrogation at that point.

'So Silin didn't *know* who your Pizhma customer was, here?'

'No. He used to meet them, but only once and then there were never any names.'

'I don't understand.'

'They usually want to see what they're buying. There's a lot of cheating.'

'So he didn't know the identity of who bought the ten canisters that Malin took to Odessa?'

'No.'

'Did Malin know?'

The Russian shook his head. 'He had to deliver them to an Iranian customs boat. I did the deal here, with the same man whose name I've already given you. It wasn't possible this time to go to Moscow because we were shipping direct from Pizhma. This time he dealt with me on trust.'

'What about payment?'

'Eight million paid up front. It's already in an account in Zurich. The remainder was to be paid upon successful delivery.'

'You have signatory authority on the Zurich account?' intruded Schumann.

'Jointly, with Silin. It's all lost now. And what we made before.'

'We'll get it,' promised the eye-patched Schumann, more to himself than to the other two men in the room.

'Sobelov should never have sacrificed you, should he?' lured Charlie.

'No,' said Raina, viciously.

'But then he didn't know your full role?'

The Russian shook his head again. 'It was just between Silin and me. We were related: proper family.'

'Sobelov's wrecked the Dolgoprudnaya, wouldn't you say?'

'Caused it a lot of damage,' conceded Raina.

'And put you in jail for the rest of your life?'

Raina did not reply.

'Wouldn't you like to bring him down? Destroy him, like he's destroyed you and Silin and all the others?'

Something approaching a smile came to Raina's face. 'How?'

'Tell me who your buyer was going to be here, for what you brought from Pizhma: who it was Mitrov phoned from Warsaw and who you were going from Cottbus to assure everything was all right, that you'd just been delayed. And tell me how to get to him: a way to introduce myself so he'll think I've come from the Dolgoprudnaya.'

chapter 34

The name – Ari Turkel – fitted Raina's belief that his buyer was Turkish, which followed logically from Germany's huge Turkish population, but everyone agreed with Charlie that Baghdad would not use a foreigner for something so sensitive: the better logic was that the convenience of the Turkish community provided the cover, not the conduit. That argument was backed by the care-taking complexity of the meeting arrangements, which were more convoluted than most Charlie had followed during his previous intelligence career. They were so labyrinthine, in fact, that after a day-long Bundeskriminalamt conference for which he and Schumann were summoned to Wiesbaden it was agreed, despite protracted opposition from German antiterrorist and counter-intelligence divisions, that Charlie had to work without any surveillance, no matter how expert or unlikely to be detected. And that he couldn't, either, be fitted with any recording or transmitting device. This wasn't just the opportunity to recover most of the biggest nuclear robbery ever: it was the unprecedented chance to arraign in a German court an Iraqi as proof of Baghdad's complicity in the nuclear trade. Nothing could be allowed to endanger either.

Dean met with disbelieving silence but no open challenge Charlie's insistence that his re-examination of Ivan Raina was not upon information he'd withheld from Moscow but because the Marzahn fingerprint had emerged during the evidence review.

'I'll not have tricks,' the Director-General warned.

'This is what we agreed I should do. Infiltrate,' reminded

Charlie. 'The incredible bonus is getting most of the stuff back.'

'Let's make sure it *is* what's been agreed: followed by you to the letter!'

Which is what Charlie did, although not to the alphabet the Director-General meant. The instructions Charlie had meticulously to obey hinged upon a telephone number – 5124843 – traced within an hour of Raina providing it to a street kiosk near the Spree bridge on GertrudeStrasse, in what had been East Berlin. He had to call at exactly 11 a.m. and to ask – using the precise words – if the red Volkswagen advertised in the *Berliner Zeitung* was still for sale. The reply had to be that it was not, but there was a white model available. If he was told it was the wrong number the attempt had to be repeated at the same time on succeeding days until the white model offer was made. The day after the right reply Charlie was to go, again precisely at eleven, for coffee at the Grand Hotel, on the FriedrichStrasse, once again in old East Berlin. He was to carry a copy of the *Berliner Zeitung* around which should be folded a tourist map of the city. After coffee he was to make his way to the Ganymed restaurant on the Schiffbauerdamm for lunch and afterwards return down the FriedrichStrasse to the U-bahn and take the train for two stops, going westwards. There was no other way to establish contact, which had created the problem from Warsaw and again after the breakdown delay reaching Cottbus. And why Raina was going to Berlin to start the routine later in the day he and his group had been picked up.

'It could take for ever,' warned Schumann, after their first unsuccessful telephone attempt the day they returned from Wiesbaden.

'That's what worries me,' said Charlie, working to a timetable no one else was following.

But it didn't take for ever.

He got the white car offer the following day and spent a further three wandering, on protesting feet, around the once-familiar streets of East Berlin and lunching at the restaurant he'd always enjoyed in the past and did again. Charlie detected his pursuers each day because they weren't very good, but for once he wanted to be followed. On the fourth day he was stopped entering the U-bahn by an olive-skinned man who ordered Charlie, in bad Russian, into a clattering, bone-jarring Trabant for what Charlie recognized to be a surveillance-checking tour around the eastern part of Berlin – actually going as far as Marzahn – before rejoining the FriedrichStrasse as far as Unter den Linden, where they turned in and stopped.

'What now?' demanded Charlie.

'Wait,' said the man, responding for the first time to Charlie's several efforts at conversation.

The man could, Charlie judged, have been from one of half a dozen Middle East countries. Or from anywhere else along or around the Mediterranean. The driver was already getting from the vehicle before Charlie was aware of the Mercedes drawing up behind. The man opened the rear door for Charlie to get out but then blocked his exit, patting him down so thoroughly that any wired device would have been detected, as well as a weapon.

There were three men in the Mercedes, all dark skinned. The man in the rear, into which Charlie was gestured, was diminutive, almost child-like in stature, apart from the features of a grown man. The size of the two in front accentuated the physical comparison. The Mercedes drove off at once, skirting the Brandenburg Gate, and Charlie realized they were going in the direction of the Wannsee forest and the lake on which another con man had been found with his testicles in his mouth.

In keeping with Charlie's thoughts, the man beside him said, 'Tell me why I shouldn't have you killed.' The voice was small, like the rest of him.

'Tell me why you should.' If he had such power, it had to be Turkel.

'To prevent being trapped.'

'What you'd prevent is yourself getting at least eighty kilos of plutonium 239. And if you'd thought it was a trap you wouldn't have kept the meeting.'

'Where were you told how to arrange things like this?'
'Moscow.'
'Who by?'
'The boss of bosses of the Dolgoprudnaya.'
'Stanislav Silin?'
Trick question or ignorance? He should have checked with Schumann if Silin's killing had been widely reported in German newspapers. But it had been in Moscow and people as careful as these would monitor the Russian media: there was even an embassy to do it. Trick question then. 'Silin's dead.'
The man at the front turned and Charlie fully realized how big he was, bull-necked and bull-shouldered and with a ham-like hand clenched along the seat back as if in readiness. What would life be like without bodyguards, wondered Charlie: at that moment he would have very much liked the reassurance of his *spetznaz* protection.
The man beside him nodded. 'So there have been changes?'
'Yes.'
'Was the arrest of Raina and the others part of that?'
Charlie hesitated, unsure how to reply. 'Yes.'
'Who has replaced Silin?
'Sergei Sobelov.' Charlie saw they were beginning to enter the forest. The red cabbage he'd eaten with the pork at the Ganymed began to repeat from a knotted-up stomach.
'You are not Russian.'
Another uncertainty. Russia was so large, with so many dialect and even language variations that he could easily lie, although it would be more convenient not to: of everything so far this challenge surprised him most because the other man's delivery was obviously accented. 'English. But I operate in Moscow.' Charlie tried a smile. 'Import–export.'
'Why should the Dolgoprudnaya risk trusting a foreigner?'
His Wiesbaden argument thrown back at him, Charlie recognized. Returning it a third way, he said, 'To avoid risking one of their own people. I'm disposable, if anything goes wrong. And where's their risk? I was given the system

– and a name – to reach you and a quantity to offer if the system worked. If you're interested I have to go back to Moscow and tell them. All I'm doing at the moment is carrying messages.'

'What name?'

'Ari Turkel.'

The man in the front seat shifted again as Turkel gave a brief but humourless smile of acknowledgment. 'You are well informed. As you would be if Raina has talked under interrogation.'

Dangerous ground, Charlie recognized. But Turkel didn't know the completeness of their evidence. 'To make things worse for himself? What have the Germans got? Some Russians with some nuclear material. That's all. There've been arrests like that before. What do the sentences average? Five years. Eight at the most. If Raina or any of them talked of networks and previous shipments and who the customers have been, they'd be talking themselves into twenty years. It wouldn't make sense.'

'Unless they were offered a deal.'

All he had was bluff, Charlie decided. He'd make a mistake – probably a fatal one – trying to improvise any more. Through the trees he saw the dull greyness of the lake. 'What risk are *you* running now? Today?'

'None. I made sure of that.'

Charlie gave a shrug, of finality. 'So we've driven into the countryside: wasted half a day. I delivered my message and you're not interested. I'm sorry. I could probably get transport back into the city if you dropped me near some of the public buildings by the lake, although I'd appreciate being taken back . . .' He offered his hand across the car. 'We don't want to deal with anyone who's uncertain, any more than you do. But there's no hard feelings. I'm sure you'll find other suppliers in the future.'

The attentive front seat passenger frowned at the dismissal and Turkel's face stiffened. 'I didn't say I wasn't interested.'

'No,' agreed Charlie. '*I* said *I* wasn't interested any

longer . . .' He pointed to a group of buildings at the lakeside. 'There! I'll be able to get a car there.'

Turkel snapped something in a language Charlie didn't recognize. The driver continued on. 'What's your offer?'

'Eight sealed containers – eighty kilos – for $30,000,000.'

'Too much.'

'That's the price.'

'Twenty.'

'Twenty-five.'

'Twenty-two.'

'I can offer it,' agreed Charlie. There wasn't any satisfaction, not yet.

'You're in touch with other people?' demanded Turkel.

'You don't expect me to answer that, any more than you would expect me to talk about you to anyone else.'

There was another approving nod. 'There will be no payment, of any money, until everything has been checked and guaranteed genuine.'

'Where?'

'Here, in Berlin.'

Turkel was inventing new rules for a new situation, imagining he was protecting himself from any entrapment in Moscow. Which couldn't be better! 'Where in Berlin?' pressed Charlie.

'You'll be told.'

'There'll be no examination of anything until we're sure of the money,' stipulated Charlie, making the demand that would be expected.

'The money will be available. Your commission comes from the purchase price, not from us.'

'Agreed,' accepted Charlie.

'What *is* your commission?'

Hopefully more than you could ever guess, thought Charlie. 'You're not paying it. So it's my business.'

Turkel permitted a thin smile. 'We'll use the same contact procedure.'

'It's time-consuming,' protested Charlie.

There was another mouth-stretching smile. 'But safe.'

Not the next time, thought Charlie.

Charlie and Schumann continued playing safe, too, not attempting any contact after Charlie's one alerting telephone call from the Kempinski's public booth until they were seated by Bundeskriminalamt connivance beside each other on the returning Moscow aircraft. It took Charlie practically the entire journey to recount the Wannsee episode. As the seat belt signs came on for the Sheremet'yevo landing Schumann said, 'We can do more next time but we still won't be able to cover you properly!'

'I know,' accepted Charlie.

'What's London say?'

'I haven't told them all of it yet.'

He still didn't from the soundproofed booth in the British embassy communications basement to which he went direct from the airport, although he did set out the Militia complicity he could prove as the reason for not officially informing the Russians.

'That's directly contrary to what was agreed,' insisted Rupert Dean.

'When those arrangements were made we didn't *know* the extent or the level of Militia corruption!'

'I'm not sure we do now.'

'There's no danger of losing the cylinders,' repeated Charlie.

'There's an enormous danger of losing Moscow's agreement to our being there. Which is vitally important for the future of this department.'

'Which would be cemented in concrete if I am right.'

'And buried in concrete if you aren't.'

'We can make it into a Militia success in the end.' That was ultimately essential, for what Charlie wanted to achieve.

'I agree it looks convincing,' wavered Dean.

'And we'll lose it if I tell them now. I'll never get another chance. So my being here will become pointless, a department disadvantage not a department justification.'

'You sure you need the American woman?'

Charlie felt the blanket-like warmth of satisfaction at the growing concession. 'She's necessary to ensure nothing goes technically wrong.' He could explain the lie away later.

'You'll never know how important it is for you to be right!' said Dean.

'I think I will,' said Charlie.

The weakest link in the ensnaring chain Charlie was trying to forge was the awareness of the unquestionably spying Ludmilla Ustenkov of the extorting Militia lieutenant. The gamble was that's all she and Popov and Gusev believed the man to be, a bribe-accepting opportunist he himself had reported to Gusev and not the channel to the new Dolgoprudnaya boss of bosses. Charlie took what precautions he could, refusing Nikolai Ranov any details of the Berlin visit and insisting that, having shown his good faith at their first meeting, his second with Sobelov had to be just between the two of them. Charlie, the arch-deceiver with the unshakeable belief he could divine it in others through a thick fog on a dark night, was encouraged by Ranov's easy, unarguing acceptance. And even more relieved when Ranov relayed Sobelov's agreement the next day.

It was the same room at the Metropole, which Charlie guessed the pretentious Russian kept permanently. Charlie approached the hotel with the same meandering caution as before, which he acknowledged would be a waste of time if he was wrong about Ranov. The man was in the lobby bar, with Sobelov's customary bodyguards. They let Charlie pass without any recognition.

The drinks were set out on the separating table and again the beetle-browed Sobelov poured but there was none of the earlier condescension. He predictably disputed the price to which Charlie argued he was lucky even to have got that with everyone in the business either having gone underground or quit the city altogether after the arrest of the Raina group. It was a take-it-or-leave-it situation: there was no guarantee of improving the offer even if he could locate another client, which he doubted. As soon as Sobelov accepted, Charlie negotiated his own commission, which Sobelov would have expected, comfortably haggling his way through the first scotch to get three per cent. On the second drink Sobelov announced he would go personally to Berlin to be paid, which Charlie mentally ticked off as another part of the entrapment slotted into place, with the reflection that Sobelov wasn't good enough to be a boss of bosses.

'Except for me, the person who has to bring you both together.'

'That's what you're getting paid for.'

'It'll have to be a simultaneous exchange, their handing over the money when they're satisfied what they're buying is genuine. Which I want to be satisfied about, too. I don't deal in fakes.'

'You know where it came from.'

'I'm the man in the middle. Literally. I'm not being *caught* in the middle. I want to see it and have it tested.'

Sobelov shrugged. 'I don't see a problem.'

'And I'm not transporting it. I'm not a delivery boy. I'll need to know all the details to coordinate everything but you fix it being taken into Germany. I need to be there way ahead of you.'

'I don't see a problem with that, either.'

But you will, Charlie promised himself: you and a lot of others. Continuing to cut Ranov out, Charlie set up during the hotel meeting the inspection of the plutonium canisters, allowing himself three days for Dean's assured Washington agreement about Hillary.

Charlie used one of the intervening days for a final, pre-Berlin session at the Interior Ministry with Popov and Gusev, alert for the slightest hint they regarded Ranov as anything more important than a bribe-grabbing policeman. Charlie let the Russians do most of the talking, which they were happy to do, Popov more eagerly than Gusev going through what became a review of the evidence each would present. They pressed him on his most recent German visit, which Charlie described as the sort of evidence rehearsal they were having now. He was reasonably sure the Germans had shared everything with him, although he couldn't be positive: certainly he didn't think they had withheld any major evidence. Charlie added that a number of foreign observers were attending to introduce his question about Dmitri Fomin. Popov said at once that the presidential aide would be there. Yuri Panin was going too, officially to represent the Russian Foreign Ministry.

'There'll be a lot to celebrate when it's all over,' predicted Popov.

'I hope you're right,' said Charlie.

Charlie had planned the container inspection during the day to provide the embassy visit excuse to dispense with their *spetznaz* guard. But the evasion – more important that day than any since the attempted entrapment began – was more difficult because it was alien to Hillary, who additionally was nervous and hampered by even the limited equipment they had to carry and didn't react or move as quickly as Charlie wanted. It took a long time before he considered they were by themselves and even then he wasn't completely satisfied. His feet ached like hell by the time they entered the warehouse between what had been built as the Komsomol theatre and the outer ring road.

Sobelov made no attempt to hide his astonishment. 'I thought she'd only be expert in one thing.'

'You'd be surprised.'

'I'd like to be,' leered the Russian.

'We here to work or talk dirty?' demanded Hillary, not needing a translation.

Apart from Sobelov there were six men, two of whom were his normal escorts, and a further three were visible in a raised office area at the head of a metal stairway. The Dubrovskaya extortionists weren't among them. The warehouse was divided into numerous storage sections beyond the open space directly inside the main door. There was a lorry and four cars neatly parked to one side. At Sobelov's gesture Charlie and Hillary followed to the first, part-walled sector to the right. The eight green-painted containers were laid out side by side, their markings uppermost, each held in place on either side with wooden wedges. They reminded Charlie of heavy gun shells, 155mm or heavier. The tops tapered slightly and on either side were gauges, their needles still. Also at the top were unusual half-handles which Charlie first imagined to be for lifting but then realized were the fixtures Hillary had already described to him to unscrew the containers.

Low voiced Hillary said, 'They're the Kirs consignment markings from the Pizhma train.' She ran her Geiger counter over each cylinder, double-checking on three, and hunched for several minutes over each of the unmoving gauge dials and their attached valves. The specialized thermometer looked like a stethoscope, although it had more leads, to each of which manually adjustable dials were attached. Hillary carefully adhered the suction pads in several places – particularly around the tops of each canister – and finger twisted the dial controls, before smiling up at Charlie. 'As clean and as cold as a Polar bear's ass.'

'Which they would be if there was nothing in them,' reminded Charlie. He told her of the four empty cylinders in Germany.

'The gauges registered but if you want to be sure, we know the unladen weight.'

'I want to be sure.'

It took less than five minutes from Charlie's translation for a cumbersome set of industrial scales to be wheeled in by two men whom Charlie told to wait, to lift each cylinder into place. As they gently replaced the eighth canister on to its wooden supports Hillary said, 'I'd have preferred my own equipment but this is good enough. They're full.'

Charlie stayed for several minutes imprinting the details of the containers on his mind before finally turning back to Sobelov. 'OK,' he said.

'Come,' ordered Sobelov, mounting the metal stairway to the mezzanine office. Inside he said, 'These are the men who will be driving . . .' He waved his hands over the balcony to the vehicles parked below. '... those cars.' He looked between Charlie and the three Russians. 'No names. Learn to recognize each other. There won't be another chance.' Directly to Charlie he said, 'Where do you want them in Germany? And when?'

'Frankfurt an der Oder,' said Charlie at once, prepared. 'On the fifteenth. The hotel Adrian ...' To the three, ignoring Sobelov, he said; 'If there's a problem, I'll be there to stop you. If I am not there by 10 a.m., start driving to Berlin. I'll be at the Kempinski ...' He handed over a card. 'That's the number. Contact me there for final directions ...'

'No!' stopped Sobelov. 'Contact *me* for final directions. That way I'll control everything until the last minute.'

That's what you think, thought Charlie. 'There must be the opportunity to stop them crossing the border, if a problem arises.' He went back to the couriers. 'Take a Polish route. It doesn't matter which, but I want you in Kalisz on the twelfth. Use the Atilia Hotel. I will come there personally to stop you, if I have to. On the thirteenth spend the night at the Kashubska, in Poznan. Again, I'll know where to stop you.'

The three nodded but Charlie said, 'Write the names down! I don't want any mistakes.'

'All very professional,' said Sobelov.

'You want it to be amateur? You must be at the Kempinski by the 15th.'

'Guaranteed,' assured Sobelov. 'You'll have everything in place by then?'

'Guaranteed,' echoed Charlie.

They went back down the stairs and on the ground floor Charlie listed the registration numbers of the BMWs and at Hillary's suggestion called down the three couriers to whom, with Charlie translating, she gave detailed instructions how the containers should be protectively wedged in the cars.

Hillary waited until they were some way from the warehouse before she said, 'That really wasn't as bad as I thought it was going to be.'

'That was the easy part,' warned Charlie.

To maintain the timetable Charlie imposed upon himself

they flew to Berlin the following day, Charlie with misgivings because there had been no contact from Natalia and he'd wanted to speak to her, although there was nothing practical to say. Gunther Schumann was waiting dutifully at Tegel with the announcement that the Bundeskriminalamt had taken over virtually an entire floor at the Kempinski and were installing visual and audio monitors in every room to be allocated to the Russian Mafia group. Schumann himself was occupying a suite on the floor above Charlie as a liaison centre. A conference was scheduled in Wiesbaden the following day of every German agency coordinating the operation. The German waited until he got them into the car and had recovered from his initial impression of Hillary before saying to Charlie, 'The Swiss cooperated over Silin's Zurich account: they always do when a provable crime is involved.' The German didn't attempt to start the car. Instead he handed a single sheet of paper across to Charlie. 'It wasn't the only account created by Silin. And this one required very different joint signatures. What do you think about that!'

Charlie didn't respond for several minutes. Then he said, 'Too many things to give you an answer you'd understand.'

'And we don't have the jurisdiction to do anything about it,' protested the man.

That bloody word hung like a banner in his mind, Charlie decided. 'Maybe it could come within your jurisdiction.'

'I'd like to think it could.'

'Why don't we work *very* closely together?' suggested Charlie.

'Delighted,' agreed Schumann.

chapter 35

Hillary Jamieson's presence initially created the sort of can-this-be-true reaction to which Charlie was by now accustomed, but that instantly changed at the sheer professionalism and obvious ability with which she recounted her Moscow examination of the stolen plutonium containers. There wasn't the most arcane question from the three German physicists present she was not able immediately to answer and there weren't many anyway, so comprehensive was her account. The cylinders were of a type she had only read about and seen in illustrations, an old design even by Russian standards, with an inbuilt refrigeration system. All the coolant meters had registered a stable temperature. The Curie reading on the gauges showed the plutonium to be highly enriched but each cylinder was well sealed and the meters and gauge had a secondary cut-off system to prevent leakage if any valve failed. The cylinders had no sign of corrosion or damage and she'd told the intended smugglers how to wedge and pack them: providing they did what she'd said there was no risk of leakage. Despite which it obviously made good sense to have the protectively equipped and suit-stocked removal vehicles available in Berlin.

In addition to their preparations at the Kempinski, the Bundeskriminalamt antiterrorist division had installed photographic surveillance as well as listening devices on the GertrudeStrasse telephone kiosk and in advance of the Wiesbaden meeting Charlie worked his way through the mountain of prints, insisting he couldn't recognize the olive-skinned Trabant driver featured upon them as a frequent user. Charlie insisted so again at Wiesbaden and repeated the danger of losing an Iraqi connection by unnecessary observation, which was the objection he made even more strenuously arguing against including the Polish authorities in a tracking operation between Russia and Germany. He'd already established contact points along the route and advised them through Balg before leaving Moscow that Sergei Sobelov intended to use the Kempinski. And because he was the only possible link between the two he would know where the containers and the money were to be exchanged between a Russian Mafia boss and the Iraqi emissary. That, Charlie maintained, was where the surveillance should be massively concentrated, not anywhere else, where a chance discovery or simple mistake could destroy everything.

Charlie's argument – and the sometimes shouted opposition to it – occupied a lot of the morning and continued into the afternoon and appeared to end with his winning it, although it was decided to maintain the GertrudeStrasse monitor. Charlie was sure one of the German agencies at the conference – counter-intelligence if not antiterrorism but most likely both – would try a lot more, because any service in the world would have done. But his main concern was to avoid Polish interference, which was why he stirred up the resentment he did, deflecting them from the en route hotels. They still hadn't been demanded by the end of the day – proving the point of which he didn't remind them that too many people involved in too much organization overlook basic essentials – which Charlie accepted to be only a temporary oversight. To be sure, as he needed to be, he'd have to make his move at Kalisz. Poznan had only ever been a failsafe insurance.

On the flight back to Berlin, conveniently separated from Schumann, Hillary said, 'There wasn't anyone back there who didn't think you were the most arrogant son-of-a-bitch they'd ever met: I even thought so and I know different. When are you going to tell me what you're up to?'

'Soon,' lied Charlie. Knowing Hillary as well as he now did, he knew it would be impossible to get her active participation: unfair – wrong even to consider it. This was his personal fight – his revenge for the threat against Sasha – no one else's.

She grinned, beside him. 'You think they'll have our room at the Kempinski wired for sound and pictures?'

'More than likely,' accepted Charlie.

'I'll ask for the film when everything's all over.'

This time there was only one day's delay between Charlie's successful connection to GertrudeStrasse and his interception at the U-bahn station. It was the same olive-skinned driver who detoured for even longer around the eastern part of the city, with Charlie braced more against an outburst of rear-view realization than the springless jarring of the Trabant. The exchange was on the Karl-Liebknecht-Strasse, directly outside the cathedral, the body-search as efficient as before. It was a different Mercedes. Turkel said immediately Charlie entered the vehicle, 'So we have a deal?'

'They've accepted your offer.'

'The same thing.'

'Not until they're satisfied how the payment is to be made and the handover achieved.' Charlie saw the car had gone completely around the square to drive past the cathedral a second time. The huge guard sat as before, arm at the ready along the seat back.

'I presume they want cash? The Russians usually do.'

'Yes.'

'And in dollars? They usually want dollars, as well.'

'Yes.'

'Peasants!'

'Peasants only trust gold.'

'It's still a lot of paper.'

They'd picked up FriedrichStrasse, although going east, and Charlie wondered how close the surveillance was. 'The Americans print $1,000 notes. Twenty-two thousand $1,000 notes takes up far less room in the boot of a car than eight plutonium cylinders. Three large-size suitcases should hold it quite adequately.'

Turkel shrugged, seemingly disinterested. 'You will guide the delivery vehicles to Wannsee, to the lay-by near the lake buildings: that's why we went there, for you to be familiar with it. The man who picks you up at the U-bahn will be there, to identify you to the people who are going to examine the containers and guarantee everything is genuine. Before you do that, you will have introduced me to the Dolgoprudnaya people. While the canisters are being checked, I will show them the sights of Berlin, from the comfort of a car . . .' Turkel held up a mobile telephone of which Charlie had until that moment been unaware. '. . . The line will be kept open, throughout the cylinder check. The moment I hear everything is satisfactory, I will hand over the money and at Wannsee my people will take delivery of your cargo. Does that sound satisfactory to you?'

Charlie could think of so many objections – chief among them his own personal intention – that he had difficulty deciding where to begin. So he said, 'No! It is completely *unsatisfactory*.'

The rejection brought the stir Charlie expected from the heavy man in front.

Turkel said, 'Why not?'

'You'd have no guarantee the Dolgoprudnaya wouldn't try to steal the money before handing over the plutonium. They'd have no guarantee you wouldn't try to steal the plutonium before handing over the money.'

'*Would* they try?'

'Of course they would! Just as you'd try to get the plutonium without paying for it.'

'Enough!' barked the man in front. The interjection – and the way the man leaned over the seat towards him – so startled Charlie that he physically jumped.

'No!' stopped Turkel, extending a stopping hand towards the man. 'It's all right.' He turned, smiling, to Charlie. 'What's your alternative?'

The bastard *had* intended trying to hijack it! He was paying too much attention to his own plots and not enough to anticipating those of everyone else, Charlie told himself.

'Sobelov is coming personally,' Charlie disclosed for the first time. 'He hopes this will be the first of several transactions . . .'

'. . . That would be interesting . . .' interrupted Turkel.

'. . . Then this must go perfectly,' resumed Charlie. 'After proving to Sobelov the money is in the cases it will be taken by you both to a safe deposit vault or a left-luggage facility. Sobelov gets the key . . .'

'But . . .' tried Turkel, but now Charlie held up the halting hand. 'But Sobelov doesn't get the money until you're satisfied: your money is safe. So you can personally ensure the plutonium cargo is genuine . . .' He looked quizzically at the small man. 'But not in the open, at Wannsee. That really wasn't practical, was it?'

Turkel shrugged, unembarrassed.

'Rent a warehouse. Or use a facility you already own or trust. We won't go there until after the money is deposited. Be there, with your experts – take us there yourself even – and personally see it approved.' They were so far at the eastern edge of the city that signposts were actually indicating Frankfurt am der Oder. There were still four days before Sobelov's delivery drivers were due at Kalisz.

'That seems to ensure safety on both sides,' agreed the man.

'We must foreshorten the meeting procedure,' insisted Charlie. 'Sobelov won't wait around for days, like you've made me do.'

'When's Sobelov arriving?'

'The fifteenth.'

'Do you enjoy the Ganymed?'

'I've become very familiar with the menu.'

'The Ermeler Haus then. My guests. One o'clock.'

'Sobelov will have people with him,' warned Charlie.

Turkel smiled. 'I'll have people with me. Some to make sure I'm not being tricked and others to show how unhappy I'll be if it's attempted.'

They dropped Charlie at the FriedrichStrasse U-bahn and on his way westwards Charlie tried to isolate the suspected

German observation but couldn't. Hillary was sorting through shopping packages when he got to their room. At once she announced that Schumann expected them upstairs. The German said 'thieving bastard' when Charlie related Turkel's virtually admitted hijack intention and nodded to the warehouse alternative.

'You still think he'll try to cheat?'

'Probably.'

'I guess you'll get the handover location at the lunch. It won't give us any time to get into position.'

'Which will make both of them feel safe,' Charlie pointed out.

They were interrupted by the arrival of Walter Roh, the head of the Bundeskriminalamt antiterrorist division and the most vocal opponent of Charlie's solo operation. Instead of the normal fixed-faced hostility there was an immediate smile from the man at being able to show – particularly in front of Hillary – that he'd either ignored or had countermanded Charlie's surveillance argument. In smirking triumph the thin-faced, flaxen-haired man announced that Turkel's Mercedes had been a Hertz hire, on a genuine Turkish passport and credit card with a billing address in Istanbul. After dropping Charlie at the station it had gone direct to Schonefeld airport, from which Turkel and his two companions had flown on the last direct flight that day to Cologne. From the airport they'd been followed – undetected, as they'd been throughout, stressed Roh – to the Bonn offices of the Iraqi Information Service, already suspected to be the operating front for Baghdad intelligence. Charlie was ready for the accusation when it came, the presentation to him, without anything being said, of that day's photograph of the olive-skinned man he'd earlier refused to identify. From Roh's new pile Charlie picked out a print of the threatening front-seat passenger whom he insisted had always collected him until today. He didn't think Roh – maybe not even Schumann – believed him but he was happy at the later excuse, weak though it was, that Roh's boasting would give him. And which he realized he'd need when the counter-terrorist chief tried to correct the Wiesbaden oversight by demanding the hotels at which the couriers would stop. Charlie risked the briefest of warning looks to Hillary and named those in Poznan and Frankfurt am der Oder. She said nothing. He gestured her to silence back in their room when he thought she might be about to say something, because he would have bugged their room if he'd been in the German position, so it was not until that night at dinner at a chosen-by-chance restaurant that she was finally able to ask why he hadn't said anything about the couriers' first stop at Kalisz.

'There's an army of people stumbling about, endangering it all. I want to check them through Kalisz by myself.'

'What about me?'

He still needed more technical guidance and he didn't think he had time to get it without possibly arousing her suspicion. 'I don't intend making any contact: that wasn't the arrangement. And I don't want you anywhere near the hotel. I want to check them out myself.'

She shrugged. 'I can't see why, but OK.'

Charlie genuinely liked Schumann and regretted the embarrassment he might cause the man, so before he left the Kempinski early the next morning Charlie left a note that he didn't want any help on a specific London enquiry, hoping Roh would be the one most upset by the exclusion. He would, promised Charlie, be back in Berlin at least two days before the arrival of Sergei Sobelov.

Having grown accustomed to Mercedes travel, Charlie hired one himself and drove hard to the Polish border, to avoid being traced by Walter Roh's service while he was still in Germany. Now he wasn't part of it any more, Charlie decided intelligence organizations were a bloody nuisance.

'I brought the equipment I can conveniently carry, just in case,' said Hillary, as they crossed, unimpeded, the easy Gubin checkpoint.

'It might be a good idea,' agreed Charlie. He wasn't at all sure about what might happen in the next few days.

The interior of an Orthodox church was not new to her but

Sasha still tightly clutched her mother's hand, nervously awed by the ornate gold filigree of the overwhelmingly intricate decoration and the smell of the incense smouldering in its burners and even more uncertain than usual of the black-gowned priests with huge beards and rumbling voices, because today they were much closer than normal, in a small office, and talking about things she didn't understand. She wondered if giants lived here. Before they left, her mother leaned forward with her head bowed for what seemed to be a long time from one of those wooden seats that Sasha always found so uncomfortable but she didn't wriggle because she knew she shouldn't whenever her mother knelt like that.

Outside, where the car and the lady in uniform who always took her to school these days were waiting, Sasha said, 'What were you talking to the man about?'

'Ley is coming to live with us: we might even get a new apartment together.'

'Why?'

'Because he loves you and he loves me and we all want to be together.'

'Does the man in the church have to say he can?'

'Yes.'

'Does that mean Ley's my daddy?'

'Yes.'

'Why hasn't he been before?'

'The man in the church had to say he could be.'

'I'll be like the others at school then?'

'Do you want Ley to be your daddy?'

'Will he still buy me presents?'

'I expect so. There'll be a party, after the church.'

'Do you want Ley to be my daddy.'

'Yes.'

Even though she'd been given the instructions, the damned woman shouldn't have taken off to Berlin without advising Washington, so there was another disciplinary reason for getting rid of Hillary Jamieson, although Fenby didn't feel he needed any more. But he didn't like the idea of her being where he couldn't know what she was doing. Which was easily resolved. Kestler had to be moved to Berlin at once, to keep a handle on everything.

He smiled up at Milton Fitzjohn's approach across the restaurant. 'Thought you'd like to know in advance that you're going to have a very famous nephew in the next few weeks,' Fenby greeted the House Speaker. 'So it's a good time to talk about the future.'

chapter 36

Quite sure he could judge her moral reaction from twice having heard Hillary's denunciation of nuclear cynicism and hypocrisy, it was unthinkable for Charlie to tell her in advance what he was going to do, even though he could have omitted the secondary intention and just argued his need to survive. Wrong, even, to have brought Hillary with him. But he still needed her. He'd hoped to have seen enough in the Moscow warehouse and thought he had, but Hillary's Wiesbaden account of the cylinder examination had convinced Charlie he needed to know much more, more probably than it was possible to assimilate.

Once safely across the border, Charlie drove more leisurely, satisfied they were undetected, and with time to spare stopped at a roadside shrine for Hillary to take photographs and again at an ornate church, where she crossed herself and genuflected and lit two candles and he realized she was a Catholic. Unasked, she said the candles were a prayer to keep everyone safe, them most of all.

He let Hillary lead them into it, when they started driving once more, waiting for her to ask again about Kalisz, feeling her eyes upon him when he repeated the danger of too many people.

'You sure that's all it is?' she challenged, openly.

'What more could there be?'

'You tell me.'

'It makes sense to see they're on schedule. The last time everything was thrown out by the Volkswagen breakdown.' Intent on keeping the conversation where he wanted it, he said, 'You seemed very confident there was no danger of the cylinders leaking?'

'No reason why they should, providing they aren't thrown around.'

'And then there's the secondary protection system,' he prompted. Which worked, as he'd expected it would, because with him at first and certainly at dinner with Popov and Natalia, he'd discerned the expert's pleasure Hillary got explaining her esoteric science.

Although enriched plutonium could act as an atomic trigger, by itself it was latent as an explosive but lethal in content. It could expand if there was an abrupt or sustained temperature change, which was why there was an inbuilt cooling system: America and Britain had once used the same sort of storage but didn't any longer. There was actually an additional protection in the Russian canisters, an expansion provision that was always allowed. Abrupt expansion could spring both the meters and the gauges, the primary function of which was measuring. The moment the pressure went beyond their tolerance, stronger seals were released completely to close off the cylinder neck.

It was more complicated than Charlie had imagined. 'The secondary system only operates under heat pressure?'

'That's all it needs to.'

'What would have happened at Pizhma? We know the canisters leaked there.'

'The tops were simply smashed off. It would have been easier just to unscrew them but I guess they didn't know that.'

'Using those half-handles on the same level as the gauges and meters?'

'And a lot of strength: they're filled at below zero temperature and the metal expands afterwards: it's a further way of ensuring a protective seal.'

Charlie thought there seemed far too many. 'You need a special tool?'

'Not necessarily, on those we saw. They're pretty basic,

like most of the Russian technology. But a wrench might help.'

'What if the meter or gauge controls came unscrewed?'

He knew Hillary was still looking directly at him. 'Charlie, you considering a Masters in nuclear packaging?'

'I'm trying to understand what could go wrong.'

'The ones I examined were split-pinned.'

Charlie hadn't noticed that. 'Split-pins can shake loose.'

'The ones we saw were spring-ended, splayed after being inserted to prevent that happening.'

'What's highly enriched mean?'

'That's it's highly irradiated.'

'I don't understand the danger of a leak.'

Hillary turned to look outside the car and Charlie was relieved. 'OK, you know what a laser is, an amplification of a monochromatic light beam? Seen all the movies of it cutting through metal on its way up to James Bond's crotch, stuff like that?'

Charlie nodded.

'Same thing here. Except that it's an X-ray and it's invisible. You don't feel it or hear it but it penetrates most things except substances like lead, and as I told you before, it melts bones like butter and you can take your pick of the cancers.'

'Why hasn't it affected Mitrov and Raina? We've pictures of them breaking canisters open.'

'We don't know it hasn't. But I'd guess they're OK. Our time frames give us just that: the times. They weren't exposed for longer than a few minutes, at any one time. Say half an hour, in total: maybe even less.'

'How long does it take to be fatal?'

'After two hours, closely exposed to something as hot as we're talking about, you're wasting your money buying a new suit for Christmas.'

'I wasn't planning to.'

'Don't plan anything else,' said Hillary, with a prescience Charlie found unnerving.

They got into Kalisz late in the afternoon, with the town already shrouded in winter half-light. It was almost completely dark by the time Charlie located the Atilia. There were no BMWs in the small parking area visible to the side of the hotel. Charlie drove by without stopping.

Having established his marker Charlie separated them from it by four streets before he actively began looking for where they could stay. He explored a further two roads before he found a pre-Solidarity relic boxed between a uniform row of shops and apartment buildings. It was an ugly, falling-apart example of the central planning hotel design once imposed from Moscow, a concrete and formica and factory-wood mausoleum. Off a cavernous vestibule there was an even more cavernous bar, already filled with noise and smoke. The carpet of their room was scarred by cigarette burns and ran the spectrum of stains. The wardrobe door was so thin it rippled as it opened and the bedstead achieved the same shimmer at the slightest touch. The sheets were grey and transparent and matched some of the carpet stains, and through the net of their curtains, which was all that covered the window, they could see through the net of the facing room a man scratching his groin beneath his underpants, which was all he wore. He saw them looking and went on scratching. There was no connected bathroom, which Charlie was glad about for the later excuse, if he needed one. The mirror over the handbasin was verdigrised in every corner and the basin grimy from the dirt of previous occupants. There was no plug. There was no heating, although the pipes groaned with the constipated effort to provide it.

Hillary said, 'You sure know how to give a girl a good time.'

'It'll do,' said Charlie. He would have sought out such a place if he hadn't found it the first time because its overwhelming benefit was that such hotels never closed and no interest was ever given to comings and goings. There was no restaurant and bills were settled at the moment of booking in. Charlie thought it was perfect.

'What happens if they got picked up crossing the Russian border *into* Poland?' demanded Hillary.

'We'd already know of an interception at the Russian border.'

'I'm not sure that's the point,' argued Hillary. 'You really being straight with me, Charlie?'

'I said I'd keep you safe.'

'That wasn't the question.'

'I'm being straight with you.' Charlie mentally chanted the mantra that the end justified the means, whatever those means were. 'I'm going to check out the Atilia. Alone.'

'I'm not sitting here watching that guy across the yard jerk off.'

From experience, Charlie went to the town square. The war legacy restoration had been done well enough for the wine restaurant to look original. They chose a table against the balcony rail, overlooking the ground-floor dining room and the spits upon which the meat slowly revolved, over two separate open fires. Hillary agreed the view was much better.

As he negotiated the sidestreets in the most direct line to the Atilia, Charlie tried to reassure himself with all the other reasons for the Russians being delayed, apart from that suggested by Hillary. The rendezvous with Sergei Sobelov and the man who called himself Turkel was still more than a week away. So there was more than sufficient failsafe time. And although it might spook them, which he wanted to avoid above all else, he could always postpone the transaction. Eighty kilos of nuclear material on the one hand balanced by $22,000,000 on the other was a powerful argument for a little patience.

But the BMWs were there.

Not at the side, which was now much fuller, but in a corner tight to the rear of the hotel and shadowed by some trees so that at first he didn't see them and momentarily felt the first dip of real alarm. There were enough other cars, as well as the tree canopy, for Charlie to get right alongside. The bonnet of each car was cold and Charlie guessed they'd already been parked when he'd passed the first time. He checked the dashboards of each for the warning flicker of an alarm system. There was none.

'They're there,' he announced as he sat down with Hillary thirty minutes later.

'Crisis over then?'

'There never was one.'

'You know I've got to check them, don't you?' she said.

'Do you need to go inside the trunks?'

She shook her head. 'If anything's gone wrong I'll pick it up from the outside.'

Charlie hurried the meal, wanting the advantage of the crowded car park and insisted on getting Hillary's equipment satchel from the boot of their Mercedes for the opportunity to check the tool kit. There were some pliers, although they didn't look particularly substantial, and a tyre lever but no other tool he could utilize. The tiny pen torch worked perfectly.

The going home exodus had begun by the time they got to the Atilia, which they intruded into as if making for their own car, needing only minutes for Hillary to check the readings virtually as she passed the BMWs. Back on the road, clear of the hotel, she said, 'There was no reading at all. Everything's fine.'

It was almost one-thirty before Charlie was sure Hillary was asleep. The bed creaked and groaned with his every movement to get out and he kept stopping, the excuse ready, but she slept on. He'd laid out his clothes when he'd undressed, finding them easily. The floor creaked, although not as loudly as the bed, on his way to the door and he waited for several minutes on the inside, listening for a change in her breathing. It continued on, undisturbed. There was scarcely a second's flash of light, as he went out into the corridor.

The lobby was still as busy as Charlie had known it would be and the side bar smokier, although the noise had dropped. No one paid him the slightest attention. The pliers and the torch from the Mercedes fitted easily into his jacket pocket but the tyre lever was awkward. His feet hurt like they always did at moments like this, as well as from all the walking he'd done that day.

He spent a lot of time watching the Atilia before approaching it. Most of the cars had gone, although there were still a lot of lights in the building and through the windows he could see people moving around inside. When he did move, he kept close to the building, to play the hopeful late-night drinker if there was a sudden challenge. It was coal-black beneath the trees and he didn't have to move cautiously any more. The standard method of springing boot locks was with a sharp downward blow momentarily to free the catch hook simultaneously with driving in the outer lock so the hook failed to engaged when the lid lifted again. Unable to risk the noise of the thump, Charlie tested with several pressing movements to ensure there wasn't a hidden vibration alarm, and then actually sat upon it, levering himself sharply up and down from the bumper at the same time as forcing the tyre lever between his legs against the lock, close to sniggering at how ridiculous it would look. But it worked. The boot lid came open with only a vague click, although he thought he heard the cylinders inside shift. Momentarily Charlie remained gazing into the dark interior, trying to make out the shapes, suppressing another snigger. Enough atomic material to destroy a city – certainly this city – kept in a car boot that could be opened by bouncing up and down on his ass. But where else could it be kept? The canisters could hardly have been carried up to the reservation desk or put in a bureau drawer, along with the spare shirts. And a guardian preferring to sleep in the back seat instead of a hotel bed would have made a lot of people far too curious.

He limited the torch, using it only to find the split-pins in the gauge nuts and get the pliers in place. Without being able to see what he was doing when he applied the pressure the pliers kept slipping off, sometimes with a sharp click when the plier teeth snapped together. The handles were slippery, too, where he was sweating, which was nerves, like the sniggering. Twice he had to stop, ducking behind the vehicle and pulling the boot lid down at the shouted departure of people with vehicles nearby. Once a man came out and urinated steamily against the wall and on another occasion he had to stop altogether for several minutes while a woman in a see-through nightdress stood at a window, appearing to look directly at him. She had very hairy armpits.

It must have taken him almost an hour finally to loosen two of the split-pins. There was almost another snigger at the ease with which each notched valve unscrewed. Charlie abandoned the remaining two cylinders, shifting to the second car. It was much more difficult bum-bouncing the lid open. The woman came back to the window and another group departed, halting him. He'd virtually decided to abandon it when the catch finally sprung. Here he tried jamming the tyre iron across the releasing handles and wrenching sharply and again they gave almost immediately. It took Charlie fifteen minutes to release three. Satisfied, he softly pressed the lid shut. Momentarily he paused against the car, forcing the breath into his body to recover until he realized what he was actually leaning against and jerked hurriedly away. There was a shout from the hotel as he went through the side parking area but Charlie kept walking and it didn't come again.

No one noticed his arrival back. On his own floor Charlie did use the bathroom, needing it, and rinsed his face and hands clean.

He listened carefully outside the bedroom door and then again directly inside. Hillary's breathing was undisturbed. Charlie creaked across the room, let his clothes lie where they dropped, and edged into bed. The bed sounded his arrival but it wasn't important any more. He knew he would be cold so he didn't let himself touch her, lying on his back in the darkness.

'Where have you been?'

Hillary's voice, unfogged by sleep, so surprised him that Charlie physically jumped. 'Toilet.'

'Bad bowel problem?'

'What do you mean?'

'I heard you leave. Three hours ago.'

'I couldn't sleep. Went downstairs for a drink. Thought I might as well go and check their cars again.'

'Something I don't think I mentioned about those gauges. From what I've read, the design was updated on the later cylinder models for the secondary protection system to operate if the valves are disturbed. It was only the prototype that was entirely controlled by temperature.'

'What were the ones we saw in Moscow?'

'The updated version.'

'Good.' He had to tell her: partially at least. She'd learn in the end but by then it would all have worked. 'I'm trying to protect myself.'

'Protect yourself!'

'I've got to link Sobelov and Turkel. And then get them with the cylinders. I need a way to get out. Otherwise I'm trapped with them, when the shooting starts.'

'You didn't know the secondary protection came in automatically?'

'No,' he admitted.

'So you were happy to kill people, to give you an escape?'

'I'm not asking you to approve. Just understand.'

'It's difficult.'

'They know what they're carrying. And that it could kill hundreds.'

'I've never gone for the God-like judgment argument.'

'It's done.'

'I guess I knew you were a bastard. But not this much of one.'

Charlie didn't speak.

'You just damaged the meters? You didn't do anything else?'

'No,' lied Charlie.

'You going to stop at Poznan?'

'No.'

'I'd like to get back to Berlin and forget about this.'

They left early and reached Berlin by late afternoon. Hillary didn't speak for a lot of the journey and said she wasn't hungry and wanted an early night.

Gunther Schumann was furious and insisted Roh and other agency chiefs were even angrier. 'We bent rules for you, particularly over that damned Zurich bank account.'

'The Zurich thing is quite separate: you want it as much as I do,' reminded Charlie, rejecting anger with apparent anger. 'This is different. We had an agreement. Roh broke it, not me. The other agencies too, probably. You wouldn't have got this far without doing things my way and this might be as far as you do get. The Russians are on their way: I've checked them. And should be at Poznan on time. Anything that goes wrong there or from now on is down to you, OK?' Arrogant son-of-a-bitch, he thought, remembering Hillary's accusation.

Charlie hadn't expected the glad-handing appearance of James Kestler, whose interruption ended the dispute. As annoyed as he still was, Charlie wasn't sure Schumann would go along with their previously arranged, all-working-together explanation that it was a German operation against the Iraqi and Sergei Sobelov, but the German did. Kestler said Jesus H. Christ and it was as lucky as hell Washington had sent him in early and that he wanted to be included, which Charlie and Schumann had also discussed and which had been agreed at Wiesbaden.

'The Russians, too,' added Charlie.

The Moscow party, headed by Dmitri Fomin, got to Berlin the following day. The Germans had monitored their accommodation, although not intruded, anxious to prevent any disastrous chance recognition with the arriving Mafia group. Because of its location, Charlie had half-expected the Russians to choose the Grand but they didn't: it was still in the former East, a virtual same-mould reproduction on the WaisenStrasse of the Kalisz emporium.

Charlie went there, with Kestler as well as Schumann, in advance of the Russians being officially received by the German Federal Prosecutor, but it was Schumann who disclosed, in as much detail as they knew and for the first time, how they intended ensnaring the Iraqi and the Dolgoprudnaya boss of bosses.

It was only at the very end that Charlie entered the discussion. 'Having debriefed Raina – and got Turkel's identity through him – I'm convinced Turkel knows the names of the Moscow government officials who set Pizhma up with the old Dolgoprudnaya leadership. Just as I'm convinced Turkel will break, after he's arrested, to try to save himself.'

'To tell us the Moscow names?' demanded Fomin.

'Each and every one,' agreed Charlie.

As the meeting broke up Aleksai Popov approached smiling and asked Charlie how Hillary was. Charlie said she was fine and asked after Natalia.

'Fine,' echoed Popov. 'The wedding's fixed. We haven't got an apartment like yours, though.'

chapter 37

The hostile resentment was general, although focused through Walter Roh, and Charlie thought it time-wasting because they had to use him whether they liked it or not – which they made abundantly clear they didn't – and he refused to be shat on, privately or publicly like Roh was attempting to shit on him. He threw back Roh's attack with the same argument with which he'd rejected Schumann, who seemed to have accepted it. The piratical Schumann was the only one remaining even half-friendly. Charlie impatiently ended the argument by insisting there were more important things than a pointless inquest, which made the resentment even worse. Charlie felt a nudge of support from Hillary, beside him. Throughout the squabble Kestler sat quietly, head following each speaker tennis-fashion. Although the connecting double doors of Schumann's suite had been opened to the next apartment it was still overcrowded, despite which the places for Popov and Gusev were slightly apart from the rest, like his and Kestler's had always been at all the Moscow meetings, which Charlie thought appropriate. The two Russians said nothing either, going from speaker to speaker as intently as Kestler, latecomers anxious to catch up on everything.

Denied any apology by Charlie, the disgruntled Walter Roh had no alternative but to do as Charlie said and go through the agreed planning for the benefit of Kestler and the Russians. He did so never once looking at Charlie, which Charlie dismissed as childish. Instead he began by formally welcoming Kestler, Popov and Gusev and announced Bonn's agreement to all three being present at the arrests.

Roh went on that both Tegel and Schonefeld airports were already totally under the control of civilian and military intelligence, in advance of the arrival of Sobelov and the Iraqi. He identified Turkel from surveillance pictures and said the man had already boarded an incoming flight from Cologne, accompanied by at least ten others, all men. The moment Sobelov and Turkel left their respective arrival terminals an inescapable net would be sealed behind them: both airports would be closed and all major roads and possible waterways out of the city blocked by one centralized telephone call if either man was lost from surveillance for longer than five minutes. At all times at least three out of the total of twenty commando-carrying helicopters would be airborne, at instant readiness for any eventuality, and as soon as Sobelov and Turkel were wherever they expected the plutonium handover to take place, every road in a square half-kilometre area around it would be cut against both vehicles and pedestrians entering or leaving. No cars or pedestrians would be allowed back into the area, to clear it as much as possible because of the content of the cylinders, despite their belief there was no danger of leakage. At that Hillary nodded and said, 'There's always the possibility of damage, during transit.'

At last Roh looked at Charlie. Equally as important – more important, in fact – as arresting the traffickers was the total recovery of the nuclear components. To minimize to the utmost any risk to innocent people, no seizure would be attempted until the Russians and the Iraqis were with the cylinders. The assault teams would be led to the exchange location in two ways. The BMW cars, still as of 8 a.m. that morning at Frankfurt am der Oder, would be followed by road and air when they moved. Roh made an elaborate gesture towards Charlie: also under intense surveillance would be the intermediary who had to bring Sobelov and Turkel together to complete the deal. Roh added, dismissively, that Charlie would be unprotected, exposed with two separate criminal groups and the nuclear consignment, in the first minutes of the attack: the German assault teams would be warned of his presence but there would inevitably be indiscriminate shooting.

Abruptly all attention was upon Charlie. Popov went sideways to Gusev and muttered something. Kestler said, 'Surely there's got to be some back-up?'

'There's never been a bigger or more comprehensive back-up in a criminal investigation in this city,' assured Roh. 'But nothing can be done *before*, only after.'

'So what protection does he have?' persisted the American.

'None,' intruded Charlie, disliking being talked about as if he wasn't there. 'I'm totally reliant on the quickness and efficiency of the antiterrorist units.' He'd intended it to be sarcastic but it sounded admiring and he wished it hadn't.

'What about a wire? A weapon at least!' said Kestler.

'The Iraqis are too cautious,' said Charlie. 'I can't risk being searched. They've always searched me so far.'

'These guys will post lookouts!' protested Kestler. 'We won't be able to hit them without warning!'

'It's a risk Mr Muffin has taken upon himself,' said Roh. 'Of course we are prepared for lookouts. They'll be neutralized as quickly as possible. We will still have some element of surprise: and hopefully the advantage of confusion. The exposure shouldn't be more than minutes.'

'I'll be the one prepared for it. They won't,' said Charlie. 'There's no cause – and there won't be any time – for them to realize I've led them into a trap.'

'What if they *do* make the connection?' said Kestler.

'It's too late to change everything now,' said Charlie.

There was a moment of silence in the room, everyone thinking there should be more to say but no one knowing what it was. The squawk of an army telephone broke the impasse. The operator whispered to Roh who said, 'Turkel has just landed at Schonefeld. At least three men who disembarked from the Moscow flight at Tegel matched the physical description of Sobelov but we're not sure. And the cars left Frankfurt am der Oder fifteen minutes ago.'

'I'd better get ready to meet them,' said Charlie.

Popov intercepted him at the door. 'There's a lot we should have been told. But haven't.'

'You'll know everything by the end of the day,' promised Charlie.

'I think it is something we should discuss later with our government representatives,' said Popov, stiffly formal.

'I think you're right,' agreed Charlie, at once. To the hovering Gusev he said, 'You'll both be present at the arrests: Russian presence – your presence – will be publicly made known.'

Popov's frown went at Hillary's approach. He smiled and said he hoped to see more of her during their time in Berlin and Hillary said she'd like that. She walked with Charlie to the elevators. While they waited she said, 'I do understand. No one's being harmed, so it's all right. It just took me a while. I'm sorry.'

'Thanks,' said Charlie, hating himself.

'Suddenly it doesn't seem as straightforward as it did at Kalisz, though.'

'It'll go like clockwork,' said Charlie, sounding more confident than he was. He looked directly at her. 'Stay out of things. Wait here until I get back, when it's all over.'

'Make that soon, Charlie, OK?'

There were three other men Charlie didn't recognize with Sergei Sobelov's two regular protectors when the Dolgoprudnaya boss flounced self-importantly into the Kempinski. Charlie moved at once to intercept them because the identification was necessary for the room allocation: two of the supposed reception clerks, both women, were Bundeskriminalamt officers. Sobelov offered an effusive handshake, gesturing the others to complete the registration and demanded the bar. Charlie chose a table in the centre of the room, for further identification. The net was sealed, he thought: with him inside it. Sobelov's escorts came in and settled themselves at adjacent tables, virtually encircling them: tight inside it, Charlie added to the reflection.

Sobelov nodded agreement to the money exchange and

said he was being as careful with his part of the bargain. The nuclear couriers using the hotel as a liaison point as Charlie had suggested would only follow the delivery instructions he gave when he used a phrase understood just to himself and them, to prove he wasn't under any duress or arrest.

'No evidence, no crime,' he smiled.

'Very wise,' agreed Charlie.

Sobelov examined the large bar. 'Where are your people?'

'Time off. I don't need protection here. Only in Moscow.'

Sobelov shook his head. 'You shouldn't take chances.'

'I'll share yours.'

Sobelov laughed, looked around him again, apparently searching. 'What about your clever and gorgeous girlfriend?'

'Shopping, like they always are. She'll be around later.'

'If we're going to work together we'll be seeing a lot of each other.'

'That's what I'm hoping,' played along Charlie.

Sobelov leered. 'You mind sharing your toys?'

'Not at all.' He was going to get a lot of pleasure putting this bastard away for life.

'She fuck well? Looks as if she does.'

'Wonderful,' said Charlie, with no alternative. The Russian was working hard at the tough-guy role, enjoying the smiling approval of those around him, and Charlie abruptly guessed it was Sobelov's first time out of Russia and away from his own territory and that the act covered an uncertainty. Charlie hoped he was right: it would be in his favour in the first few moments of the assault.

Turkel wasn't uncertain. He was already at the Ermeler Haus when they arrived, occupying one of the private upstairs rooms, and Charlie supposed the four men in the adjoining salon were from the ten-strong escort. Charlie thought he'd spotted three in a car outside on Markisch Ufer – where Sobelov's group had remained – and wondered where the other three were. He'd warned Sobelov during the drive to the restaurant but there was still the briefest blink of surprise at Turkel's smallness, even more noticeable against Sobelov's towering bulk when they came close to shake hands. The comparison was only slightly less when they sat at separate sides of the round table, with Charlie between them.

The encounter became a series of acts, each performing their chosen parts. Sobelov increased the macho charade, dismissing the importance of the previous smuggling group's arrest ('they were going to be replaced anyway') and of grandiose intentions for the future of the Dolgoprudnaya ('international links, with Latin America and with Italy'). Turkel played the see-all, hear-all, say-nothing entrepreneur diplomat ('my function is a special one, defying description') with access to limitless resources for required items ('there's always a need and always the money'). Charlie adopted the mantle of the fawning broker eager to impress important new clients, encouraging further promises and exaggerations from both. Charlie wondered how it all sounded on the recordings that were being made.

Because Turkel's appointment at the Dresdener Bank was for two-thirty it was a hurried although excellent meal and they managed two bottles of Moselle. Their cavalcade – Charlie, Turkel and Sobelov together in a car escorted in front by five of the Iraqi group and behind by five Russians – arrived exactly on time. Sobelov completed the deposit vault documentation, which Charlie savoured witnessing, after which they were taken to the basement security area where, after explaining the shared key locking system – Sobelov retaining one key, the bank official the second – the official left them alone with the three suitcases carried by Turkel's driver and the glowering giant who'd been present at every encounter. There was nowhere to sit and it took Sobelov two hours to satisfy himself the money was right and at the end Charlie's feet burned.

In the Mercedes on their way back the Russian handed his bank vault key to Turkel, for return when the plutonium cylinders were declared genuine, a change to the arrangements Turkel had insisted upon during lunch. The Iraqi also insisted on accompanying Sobelov – for whom four contact attempts were already logged – to his room, and upon

Charlie being with them, before identifying the delivery location.

Which was an Iraqi diplomatic warehouse in the freight storage section of Schonefeld airport.

That officially made it Iraqi territory, inviolate from German intrusion, Charlie supposed. Certainly it would be impossible to clear and seal a square half-kilometre around it because quite apart from the volume of people affected, flights couldn't be suspended without it being obvious, from the simple absence of sound. So there was virtually nothing left of the carefully constructed seizure plan which made Charlie very grateful indeed that he had made one of his own. For his further satisfaction he tried to pick out Sobelov's protective phrase when the contact call came, half an hour later: it was something about both their journeys being uneventful. How uneventful would it continue to be?

There were uncertainties, although Charlie thought they were manageable. There was no way he could be personally suspected of tampering with the cylinders, although there would be an accusation of sorts because he had taken Hillary to authenticate them. But he could rebut that easily enough by arguing they had been damaged in transit. One doubt was who was going to carry out the examination for Turkel. If it was a qualified physicist the man would know the two-hour fatality danger. But if it was a layman – Turkel himself maybe – told only what the meters should show or how heavy the containers should be if they were full, he'd have to intercede. Which shouldn't be a problem. Sobelov knew his relationship with Hillary: knew she was an expert and would accept he'd learned enough from her to warn of the danger created by misreading meters. So all he had to do was yell fire – or whatever the atomic equivalent was – and lead them out to handcuffs and a lifetime in jail. It wouldn't achieve the arrest the Germans wanted but that wasn't possible now anyway if they respected the protocol of diplomatic territory. Which was not Charlie's problem:

Charlie's problem was staying alive and he felt very strongly about that.

Perhaps the biggest unknown now was what the Germans would do. They'd surround the warehouse, even if they couldn't clear the area. And in minutes. But could he get everyone outside before the Germans tried to take out the guards? If he didn't and the shooting started, he was buggered. No one was going to believe they would die from something they couldn't see or feel by following him out into a gun battle they knew damned well could kill them.

Charlie saw the airport indicators first and then the buildings themselves and watched as one plane landed and another took off, so synchronized they could have been at either end of a pendulum.

'We'll be first,' predicted Turkel. 'They'll have to find the place once they get to the airport itself.'

They were. There was no sign of the BMWs when their driver pulled up outside a white-painted, unmarked building after negotiating a criss-cross of storage hangers, outbuildings and warehouses, most of which were identified with company names. There was no sign, either, of any special attention around a building the Bundeskriminalamt had known about for more than two hours, which Charlie found both unsettling and reassuring and told himself he was a bloody fool who couldn't have it both ways. All around there was the rumbling of arriving and departing planes at a still-operating airport.

Turkel's driver and the customary bodyguard entered the building through the small pedestrian door but in minutes swung open just one of the two main doors sufficient for their three vehicles to drive in. Apart from their cars the warehouse was totally empty. It also, strangely, appeared to have no separate side or back entrances. They were driven to the far end and each car turned to face the only exit. Everyone got out. Charlie walked the length of the building, as if anxious for the first sight of the Russian arrival. The doors were reinforced with an inner lining of what looked like steel. Running from top to bottom of the divided halves like the trunk of a straight tree was a central metal pole attached to which at intervals, tree-like again, were cross-branches. With one door open the cross-branches lay straight down and parallel with the trunk. When they were closed, he realized, they could be swivelled by handles from the bottom to knit into a series of rigid cross-bars. There was a single cross-bar already in place across the small pedestrian entry. He turned to see something resembling a marching platoon, four Iraqis and four Russians, approaching the open door to form an outer guard. Sobelov and Turkel remained standing at the far end. The rest lolled around the cars. Two Iraqis had remained inside the middle car. Charlie had still counted only seven in Turkel's party: perhaps the other three in the German count were the examining experts. Something Sobelov called was lost beneath a louder shout from outside and from outside the huge door was pushed open just enough for the BMWs to drive in. They swept past him but stopped short of the other vehicles, roughly in the middle. Sobelov and Turkel got there before Charlie, who wasn't hurrying. He checked the time, stopping as far away as he felt he sensibly could to watch the newly arrived Russians get out. Only one man looked unwell, grey-faced and sweating. He said something to Sobelov who shrugged, disinterested. Turkel was on his mobile telephone, gesturing with his free hand for the door to remain open. Almost at once the missing three entered, one behind the other. The one leading was bespectacled and elderly. The following man carried a satchel larger than Hillary had taken to Kalisz. Charlie decided he wouldn't have to play amateur physicist. He took a step towards the more easily opened pedestrian door, letting the technicians get between him and the BMWs. In the language Charlie recognized from the Wannsee visit the elderly man spoke to Turkel, who replied in the same tongue. No one was paying the slightest attention to Charlie, who edged a little further from the now surrounded cars. It put him ten metres away, maybe a little further. It had been six minutes since the cars came in. The elderly man was accepting from the satchel carrier a hand-held counter similar to the one Hillary used. Any minute now, thought Charlie.

And then there was a shot.

There was a lot of noise from overhead aircraft and no one noticed it but then there was shouting and several more shots and a thump against the door from the outside, as if someone was banging to get in. Inside there was brief but absolute panic. All the Russians except Sobelov had guns, mostly Markarovs, and began to move towards the door but then stopped, looking back to be told what to do. The elderly man, still holding the Geiger counter but no longer bent over the cars, said something shrilly to Turkel who babbled back, just as hysterically. Sobelov looked at Charlie and said, confused, 'What is it?' not accusingly but as a question to be answered.

'I don't know,' said Charlie but the words were lost beneath a sound much louder than any aircraft, even far away but it didn't stay far away but grew ever louder, the whining, low-geared roar of a huge engine and then there was an echoing, ear-pounding crash against the door, which shivered and dented inwards but held. The roar went on, the tone fluctuating between gears and there was a second and a third and then a fourth crash against the door. It began to buckle, not from its central tree but from the side hinges, to the left. One of the Russians fired at it and the bullet ricocheted bee-like off the steel lining.

Sobelov had recovered but Charlie couldn't hear what he was shouting and doubted anyone else could, either. The Russian had a gun now and gestured with it for one of his men to bring a car from the back. The rest were actually crouched around the rear of one of the BMWs. Charlie didn't know if it was the one in which he'd unscrewed the cylinder tops. Turkel was going back towards the cars, too, herding the cowering nuclear experts ahead of him.

Charlie couldn't decide what to do. He wanted to be down by the door when it collapsed, quickly to get out, but that would put him literally in the crossfire when the shooting began. And if he fled back to the neatly parked cars he'd set himself up like a funfair target in a shooting gallery to the people who'd within minutes be pouring through the now sagging door. Still safer at the back, he determined, remembering his thought as he'd come into the warehouse: not *in* a car but behind it. To hide until the shooting stopped. As he got to the rear of the building, two of the cars surged forward, isolating him with the remaining vehicle. Turkel was driving one and Charlie wondered how his feet reached the pedals.

With a groaning crash the doors finally gave way, lopsidedly, under the battering from what looked like a tank equipped not with a gun and turret but with a bulldozer scoop. Black-suited commandos surged in. They all wore helmets and Charlie realized why when the first stun grenade reverberated. It made his ears sing, deafening him, but it didn't knock anyone unconscious and neither did the second because to be effective the space had to be enclosed and the building was too large. To think of escaping by car had been panicked and stupid. Both Mercedes had slewed to form a barrier with the BMWs and the windscreens and windows of every vehicle shattered under the concentrated automatic fire. Glass burst all over Charlie from the car he was sheltering behind. Four commandos dropped, despite their protectively metal-padded suits, and four men – Charlie couldn't tell if they were Russian or Iraqi – went down as well, one screaming. He saw the tiny Turkel crawl from his bullet-pocked car and, still on his hands and knees, scurry to the back. There he sat on the floor with his back to the vehicle and the invading soldiers with his eyes closed, as if everything would stop and go away if he didn't look at it. A man Charlie did recognize to be Russian suddenly threw his hands up and tried to run towards the assault group and Sobelov shot him, twice, in the back and then brought down a commando who'd stopped firing to accept the surrender. But then Sobelov was hit, in the shoulder but not badly, spinning him also to the back of a car where he slumped, shocked, in a sitting position close to Turkel. There seemed to be a lot of bodies around the cars and without either Sobelov or Turkel the resistance became sporadic. Although his ears were still blocked by the grenades, Charlie heard the amplified loud-hailer demands in Russian that they give up and guessed it was the same message in Arabic. The firing did stop, although the men remained crouched behind the cars and Sobelov began scrabbling, crab-like, to get up.

And then others came in, too quickly, behind the assault group. Charlie saw Roh and Schumann first, then Popov ahead of Gusev. And then Kestler. They all had guns – Roh a machine pistol – but only the Germans had flak jackets. Sobelov was on his knees now, levering himself up, hidden from them like three other Russians to whom Sobelov spoke were hidden.

Charlie came from behind the car, waving his arms high for identification and yelling for them to stop, pointing to the hidden Russians, too deaf properly to hear his own voice. The warned Roh saw one of the ambushing Russians as the man rose to shoot and the burst from the German's machine pistol sprawled the man, chest blown open, over a BMW bonnet. Sobelov turned at Charlie's warning and levelled his gun and Charlie realized he was going to be shot and there was nowhere to hide and that he was too close for Sobelov to miss. There was an explosion but no pain and Sobelov's head disintegrated. Charlie saw Schumann on the far side of the car, hunched in a marksman's crouch, gun still outstretched after the shot.

And he saw Popov behind Schumann. The Russian was edging along the car, but snatching looks inside, and appeared to see the slumped Turkel and Charlie at the same time. For a moment the gun wavered and then he brought it back to the Iraqi and Charlie screamed 'No!' and heard himself well enough that time. Kestler reacted first, seeing what was happening and yelling 'No!' as well and throwing himself forward, so that he was directly between Popov and the tiny man when Popov fired, at point-blank range, directly into the American's chest.

It was one of the concealed Russians who killed Popov. That was also virtually at point-blank range, from the other side of the car. The shot hit Popov full in the face, hurling him into Gusev, who stumbled backwards but still managed to hit Popov's killer, high in the shoulder to knock him sideways and down. And Gusev's gun kept moving, less undecided than Popov, but as it swung towards the cowering Turkel, Schumann put his pistol directly against the side of the Russian's head and said, 'Don't,' and Gusev didn't.

To Charlie, Schumann said, 'I had to stop Sobelov killing you. I was too slow here.'

'You were quick enough,' said Charlie, gratefully.

'We lost Popov, so it wasn't a good idea.'

'One's enough,' said Charlie.

chapter 38

Charlie had known for a long time that for personal reasons it was going to be the worst resolution to anything in which he'd ever been professionally involved, except obviously what had happened to Edith, which was more personal than professional. There'd been vindictive satisfaction destroying the killers who'd shot Edith. There wasn't satisfaction now, at Aleksai Popov's killing, although neither was there the slightest regret at the man, who'd used Sasha like he had and Natalia like he had and who'd clearly intended killing him, being blasted faceless. That perfectly fitted Charlie Muffin's eye for an eye, tooth for a tooth interpretation. Charlie's compassion was for Natalia.

Like it was for James Kestler's death. The young American had been brash and gauche and unthinking and at the very beginning a total pain in the ass who'd caused a lot of inconvenience and even been a professional encumbrance, but it had all been forgivable – even the encumbrance – and Charlie *had* long ago forgiven the man. He'd liked him. Kestler would never have been a brilliant agent, perhaps not even a good one, because at the bottom line he'd been too genuinely decent and nice and honest. Charlie still didn't have a clear idea of what his FBI problem had been – just that he'd been the shuttlecock and that Rupert Dean had somehow taken the racquets away – but Kestler would have been a coerced player. He guessed Kestler would have considered his silver-spoon Washington connections an embarrassing disadvantage, not a benefit.

All of which were personal feelings. Charlie knew that

publicly everything would all be massaged into an overwhelming success. The Germans would have their sensational trial – maybe more than one – after throwing diplomatic niceties out the window, and Iraq would be the pariah and the whole Middle East trade would be further disrupted by the trial evidence of Ivan Raina. Russia's foremost Mafia Family was wrecked, although it would rebuild over time, like all established organized crime groups. They still didn't know precisely how much nuclear material had been lost – although they might after the interrogation of Petr Gusev that was shortly to start – but it was nothing like the original estimate of two hundred and fifty kilos. And according to the telephone conversation Charlie had insisted upon with Rupert Dean in London, before agreeing to be medically checked by a doctor for the unfelt lacerations from shattered glass, the department's FBI-functioning future – and his in it, in Moscow – was irrevocably established.

Charlie winced through the administration of antiseptic and refused the offered tranquillizer although shock was still shaking through him, because he needed to remain clear-headed.

'It's a mistake not to take them,' insisted the doctor.

'This one I can avoid,' said Charlie. There were a lot he hadn't, but then there usually were. One day, perhaps, he'd get everything right the first time.

He was certainly determined to get everything right – answer the outstanding questions – with Petr Tukhonovich Gusev. He'd been surprised the Germans had agreed to his leading this virtually instant interrogation, although after Dmitri Fomin's official intercession they needed an immediate admission to keep the Militia colonel in custody. It had been Schumann who'd been Charlie's advocate – like he'd pressed Charlie's idea of supposedly involving the two Russians at Schonefeld, expecting them to make incriminating errors – arguing Charlie was the best person to achieve the necessarily quick confession, because of his complete knowledge of the investigation, in every country.

Dmitri Fomin had insisted on attending the interrogation as an observer, just as he had insisted upon talking to Gusev in his cell upon arriving thirty minutes earlier. Charlie had hoped the presidential aide would have watched through one of the mirrored screens but the tall, aloof man followed Gusev into the same interrogation cell in which Ivan Raina had been questioned, where the recording equipment was still installed. Because they hadn't expected a fourth person there was a delay while another chair was brought in.

Even before he sat, the head of the Moscow Militia said, 'I would like the recording equipment started,' and when Charlie obliged, went on, 'I want officially to protest my arrest and detention. It is totally without justification and I demand my immediate release.'

There'd been a lot of holding cell rehearsal between the two Russians, Charlie realized. He looked at Fomin and wondered if the investigation was going to be completely solved. Charlie said, 'Working with Stanislav Georgevich Silin, the former boss of bosses of the Dolgoprudnaya Mafia Family, and with Aleksai Semenovich Popov, operational commander of the antinuclear smuggling division of the Russian Interior Ministry, you organized the robbery of a nuclear transport train at Pizhma and were responsible for the theft of approximately two hundred and fifty kilos of highly enriched, weapons-graded plutonium 239. You are also responsible for or involved in a number of murders. Just as you were prepared at Schonefeld today to kill a man known as Ari Turkel, believing he could identify you in connection with the Pizhma theft.'

Gusev spluttered an incredulous laugh. 'That is total and absurd fabrication.'

Fomin shook his head. 'I demand proof of these ridiculous accusations. Unless it's produced immediately I demand the release of Colonel Petr Gusev.'

Unspeaking, Charlie offered the single sheet of paper to Gusev.

Fomin said, 'What is that?'

'The record of a deposit account at the main office of

Credit Suisse, in Zurich, in the sum of $8,000,000,' identified Schumann. 'It's a joint signatory account, in the names of Petr Tukhonovich Gusev and Aleksai Semenovich Popov. We have bank-guaranteed examples of the signatures of both. It was opened three weeks before the Pizhma robbery by Stanislav Silin, who held another account there, jointly in the names of himself and Ivan Raina, whom as you know we have in custody on charges of smuggling plutonium from that robbery. In accordance with Swiss banking practice for accounts held by overseas clients, the Popov–Gusev records also list passport numbers. We have already compared Popov's passport, which we took two hours ago from his body at Schonefeld.'

Fomin stared sideways at Gusev, switching his outrage. 'Explain this!'

'I did not . . .' began Gusev, spiritedly, but then he coughed, as if something abruptly jammed his throat, and then he sagged for a brief moment, no more than seconds, but Charlie thought the man had ingested a poison and that they were going to witness a suicide but Gusev coughed again, clearing the obstruction, but the false protest drained from him. 'It was so good, so perfect,' he said. 'But we misjudged too much: we believed Silin could stay in control of the Dolgoprudnaya, which he thought he could if the robbery was a success. And then there was the satellite . . .' He looked bitterly at Charlie. '. . . the satellite and how you used it. Realizing *akrashena* meant there had to be official involvement . . . That frightened us most of all.'

'Is that why you never challenged me on it, to avoid drawing attention to yourself? Hoping I'd think it came from the military.'

'Aleksai Semenovich said it would never be traced to us: that too many other people knew so we should just ignore it.'

If they were going to get a confession it might as well be a full one, Charlie decided. 'What was more important, carrying out the robbery? Or using it to discredit myself and the American . . . ?' Charlie paused. '. . . And General Fedova?'

Gusev looked at Charlie warily. 'The robbery, for me. Both, for Aleksai Semenovich. He had it all worked out.'

Charlie thought he had now, too. He'd been guessing, making assumptions, but it was clearing in his mind. He still needed more guidance, to avoid making a mistake. 'Tell us the sequence. Starting with you and Silin.'

'We'd known each other for years. Worked together: his territory was my area. It was a good arrangement. I knew Silin had traded nuclear: he had a contact at Gorkiy. We didn't interfere: we got our share. Then Aleksai Semenovich started to talk of getting into the business ourselves: becoming millionaires. That's how it began, just a nuclear robbery but a big one . . .'

'Which is why Oskin was posted to Kirs?' interrupted Charlie, wanting to get it all.

Gusev nodded. 'Aleksai Semenovich was in charge of nuclear operations: he knew all the plants that were being decommissioned and chose Kirs. So he sent Oskin to Kirov, to do the groundwork . . .'

'. . . And Oskin put Lvov into the plant?' anticipated Charlie, confidently.

There was a further nod from the Russian. 'It was they who decided it would be easier to stop the train at Pizhma rather than attack Plant 69. Which it was. But then you were appointed. Popov didn't like that. He didn't think much of the American but he said he knew all about you . . .' There was a contemptuous snicker. 'And he did. He said everyone would start setting up if you had any success. So you had to be made to look stupid.'

What was there for Popov to know all about him? It would be wrong to break the flow now, but he wouldn't forget it. 'So the phantom robbery was set-up?'

There was another snicker. 'Actually by Popov, the man supposed to be stopping it. That's what he went to Kirov for and then took the woman up there and made her think she was part of something important, like you all thought you were part of something important and it was all bullshit, absolute bullshit.'

The woman, picked out Charlie, offended. 'Like the interrogations were all bullshit, people knowing nothing, so whatever General Fedova did would fail?'

'Absolutely,' agreed Gusev. 'Like we thought we could make your ridiculous sting idea fail, putting people around you to tell us all you were doing.'

'And he did ensure that people knew she'd failed,' intruded the presidential aide, suddenly.

'What?' queried Charlie.

'He criticized General Fedova from the very beginning,' disclosed Fomin. 'Complaining reports, sent over her head. Particularly about the Shelapin and Agayans debriefings. That they were pointless: got nowhere. That she should be removed from the investigation entirely.'

'Like you would have got nowhere if you'd concentrated on Moscow, which is what we'd planned . . .' picked up Gusev, shaking his head. 'The fucking satellite!'

'We're losing the sequence,' stopped Charlie. 'Kirs became a total decoy, like the finding of the lorries and some canisters were decoys, but what about the Agayans and Shelapin Families? Why them? Just convenience, because the stuff had to be planted on some group?'

'Part of the fighting within the Dolgoprudnaya that we didn't take enough notice of. Agayans and Shelapin were siding with Sobelov, although they're personally at war. So Silin, through whom we were going to traffic what we got, wanted to harass them: teach them who was the stronger. That's why we had Oskin approach them, for the Kirs raid. That was all a trick: we could orchestrate everything they did.'

'Who killed Agayans? And why?'

'I don't know. Nothing to do with us. The story is that he knew people, in the Prosecutor's office, who were afraid he might talk. He threatened to, apparently.'

'Was Lvov going to talk?'

'He was going . . .' started Gusev and stopped, just as abruptly.

The wrong approach would destroy the admission, letting

the man retreat. Which way? 'He'd already gone, hadn't he? Gone across to Sobelov? Like Ranov had gone across to Sobelov. But Lvov *was* important. Four of the containers seized in the first interception here were empty, but they had markings from the Kirs plant. The only person they could have come from to enable Sobelov to make the switch was from someone inside the plant. Which was Lvov. But Sobelov had *eight* containers, to set himself up in the nuclear business. So he switched another four of the consignment which went to Iran, via Odessa.'

'I don't know about that.'

'But you killed him, didn't you?' demanded Charlie, harsh-voiced. 'As a warning to Oskin and when you thought Oskin might defect you killed him, too. And his family, obscenely. Did you rape Lvov's girls yourself? Or just pass them around among the Militia from Kirov who helped you?'

'I didn't do any of that! And you can't prove it.'

'We can,' said Charlie, looking to Fomin. 'The bullets that killed them will have been recovered, during the autopsies. Like the bullet that killed the Shelapin man in whose garage you dumped the plutonium cylinders as part of your diversion. They'll match ballistically, won't they, Petr Tukhonovich?'

Gusev's throat worked but initially he couldn't speak. Then he said, 'Aleksai Semenovich! He organized it. Everything. Popov told me what to do, always . . .'

'Did he tell you to come in so closely after us today?' demanded Schumann. 'That wasn't how we planned it, was it? You had to wait until everything was secure, like the American had been told to wait but ran in after you . . .'

Gusev pointed a wavering finger at Charlie. 'He said he guessed from what you said when we arrived that Turkel knew who we were!'

'So Turkel had to die as well?' said Charlie. He'd quite recovered from the warehouse assault – forgotten any physical part of it – his mind icily sharp. He had to lead up to it and he'd been given the way. His voice as cold as his mind, Charlie said, 'Popov knew all about it? That's what you told me. "*He said he knew all about you.*" What did he know about me, Petr Tukhonovich? And how?'

The smirk came back, the expression of a lost man lashing out in desperation. 'Everything. Your phone's tapped, in that fancy apartment. The woman's, too, long before she thought it was done. He read your KGB record and got the baby's birth certificate and the record of the woman's divorce and her husband's death certificate. Everything! And he knew every time you met outside. Had photographs, in the botanical gardens. He was going to use them and the tape of your telephone conversations to show she was your spy, if the other ways to get rid of her didn't work. It was obvious he'd get her job.'

'General Fedova was told her phone was being monitored after the threat to her daughter. Was that a way of trying to get rid of her, to make her resign, through fear?'

'And it worked! She'd told him she was going quit.'

'It had to be you who made the threat. Popov was with her at the apartment and the only other person could have been you.'

'Popov told me what to say: wrote it down,' said Gusev, defensively.

'That was a panicked mistake, involving the child,' said Charlie. 'Narrowed down who it could be far too much, although it was clever of Popov to be with her when the call came.'

Schumann leaned forward, picking up the bank deposit. 'What's the benefit of having money in Switzerland when you live in Russia?'

'Run money,' admitted Gusev. 'That's why it was so important for us to get here, to find out what all the evidence was: be in court to listen to anything that might emerge. We were ready to run, if there was the slightest danger.'

'He was going to marry General Fedova,' said Charlie, quietly.

'Only if she'd quit and he got the job. But not, obviously, if we had to run.' The man moved his head. 'Imagine it, him the head of the entire nuclear anti-smuggling division and me the head of the Militia in Moscow. It would have been fantastic!'

Fomin grated his chair back and stood. 'I officially withdraw the Russian protest to this arrest. And waive any diplomatic rights and requests involving his trial.' The man hesitated. 'And apologies.'

'Bastard! Lying, fucking bastard! *Why*?'

'Too much could have gone wrong: too much *did* go wrong. The plutonium could have got through.'

'Poisoning – killing – people as it went. Which wouldn't have stopped a device being made because there were some that were still sealed!'

'The source wouldn't have been trusted again.' And somehow at the trial at which Popov and Gusev would have been fêted as honest Russians he would have made the suggestion in his own evidence that they were the two who had sabotaged the shipment to mark them out for the vengeance pursuit from Baghdad.

'It was murder!' said Hillary, disbelievingly.

'All three died in the shootout. And they were killers.'

'Their dying another way isn't any defence! And a court decides whether killers die, not some self-appointed vigilante.'

'It's over,' said Charlie.

'You're right,' said Hillary. 'There's an embassy plane coming in to take Kestler's body back to Washington. I'm going on it. And I'm going to quit, like Natalia.' Her anger suddenly went. 'Poor Natalia!'

'Goodbye then.'

'Don't say you'll keep in touch!'

'I wasn't going to,' assured Charlie. 'Safe trip.'

'It will be. You won't be on it.'

chapter 39

The priest with whom Natalia had discussed the wedding officiated at Popov's funeral. He'd been content enough in the warmth of the church but the first snows of winter were in the air and outside he hurried through the graveside ceremony. There were only the two of them, Natalia and Charlie, and both shook their heads to the offer of casting the earth.

'Thank you for coming with me,' she said, as they walked side by side from the cemetery.

'I wasn't sure you'd want me to.'

'I'm not sure that I did.'

The Berlin prosecutor had ruled the personal details in the taped confession weren't relevant to the trial and didn't intend offering them in evidence and Charlie hadn't told Natalia of the surveillance Popov had imposed upon them, although he had insisted it was safe for Sasha's protection to be lifted. He had told her everything he expected to become public but hadn't described the Zurich account as an escape fund. Fomin had handed over everything Popov had assembled on them and kept locked in his office safe. Charlie hadn't told her about that, either. Just destroyed it all. Natalia hadn't cried: shown any emotion. But then Natalia was not a crying person. 'My posting here has been confirmed. I'm going to be here permanently.'

'You want that?' she asked.

'Yes.'

'I still might resign.'

'Why?'

'My part was hardly an overwhelming success, was it?'

'It couldn't have been, with Popov manipulating everything. Has anyone asked for your resignation?'

'No.'

'Then don't offer it.'

'How long did you suspect Aleksai?'

Charlie shrugged. 'Not too long,' he lied.

'Why didn't you tell me?'

'You wouldn't have believed me. You would have thought it was jealousy. I didn't have any positive proof, until he got to Berlin.'

'Were you jealous?'

'You don't have to ask me that.'

'I did love him. I can't now, not after how he tried to use Sasha. But I did love him before.'

'It's over now.'

They reached Natalia's car. 'You going straight back to Berlin?'

He nodded. 'I'm being called tomorrow. They rearranged things so I could come here.'

'Hillary with you?'

He shook his head. 'She's gone back to Washington.'

'Sorry.'

'It wasn't serious. I told you, she was a free spirit.'

'Do you want me to run you to Sheremet'yevo.'

Charlie was surprised by the offer. 'It would make you tight for time getting back for Sasha. I'll take a cab.'

'She's very confused. Keeps asking me when Ley is coming to live with us. We're both confused, I suppose.'

'I'd like to see her sometime.'

'Not for a while.'

'There'll be a lot of time, now that I'm living here.'

'Yes,' said Natalia, distantly. 'There'll be a lot of time.'